PRAISE FOR JOHN VORNHOLT

"John Vornholt's Gemworld series sucked me right in from the start. . . . A *Trek* adventure where there's substantial character development . . . and the aliens are all fascinating. . . . An action-filled science fiction story."

—Michelle Erica Green, *Mania Magazine*

"[Gemworld is] a cracking good ride, as fun and fast as a bobsled dash. Vornholt infuses the book with a flavor of old-time sci-fi without losing his grip on what makes *Star Trek* a genre unto itself."

—Wigglefish.com

PRAISE FOR
THE GENESIS WAVE: BOOK ONE

"Fans of both the movies and *The Next Generation* should love *The Genesis Wave*. . . ."

—Trektoday

". . . [A] fast-paced story. . . . Lovely character work. . . ."

—Get Critical

PRAISE FOR
THE GENESIS WAVE: BOOK TWO

"I loved it. . . . Fantastic. . . ."

—Michelle Erica Green

Also by John Vornholt

The Troll King

STAR TREK
THE NEXT GENERATION®

THE GENESIS WAVE
BOOK THREE

John Vornholt

Based upon STAR TREK and
STAR TREK: THE NEXT GENERATION
created by Gene Roddenberry

POCKET BOOKS
New York   London   Toronto   Sydney   Singapore

POCKET BOOKS, a division of Simon & Schuster, Inc.
1230 Avenue of the Americas, New York, NY 10020

Originally published in hardcover in 2002 by Pocket Books

This book is published by Pocket Books, a division of Simon & Schuster, Inc., under exclusive license from Paramount Pictures.

ISBN: 0-7434-6383-8

First Pocket Books paperback printing February 2003

10 9 8 7 6 5 4 3 2 1

POCKET and colophon are registered trademarks of Simon & Schuster, Inc.

For information regarding special discounts for bulk purchases, please contact Simon & Schuster Special Sales at 1-800-456-6798 or business@simonandschuster.com

Printed in the U.S.A.

For Martha Lee and her Hospitality

STAR TREK
THE NEXT GENERATION®

THE GENESIS WAVE
BOOK THREE

one

She was the only one left of her species, and now they were trying to kill her. They wanted what she carried, and she knew she could save herself if she left it behind. Like her, it was the only one of its kind left.

The disruptor beam streaked past her crouching body, charring the corrugated tin wall and burning a hole in the vacant building. For an instant, the dusty alley was illuminated by blazing beams and molten metal. She clutched the bulky chrome box to her torso, knowing she could not disguise it from *them*. Her pursuers knew her true identity, and they were wearing environmental suits to protect themselves from her spores. No doubt, they were only firing to keep her pinned down. She counted three of them, and she assumed them to be Romulans, judging by their weapons and their knowledge.

A red fog drifted across the two slivered moons of Torga IV, giving the dingy alley a patina of exotic mystery. They could have rushed her, but they feared her. Feared what she could do with the box.

It was so strange being known, being exposed, when she had operated for years undercover. She and the other Seedlings had infiltrated every nook of the Federation, but it was never to cause disruption. It was always to gather information—to find out how the meat creatures could help them escape their dying world. Their roots had found nourishment in the garden of Starfleet. With the Genesis technology, they had discovered a way to prepare new homes and propagate their species at the same time.

All of that had ended three days ago, when their world was invaded and their base destroyed. After living among the meat creatures—impersonating them—the Seedling could appreciate the irony. The repository of all data on Genesis had once been a lone human being, and now it was the awkward silver box in her appendages.

If the Romulans had tracked her down, it meant they had ransacked the home base, deciphering the records. There was no other way for them to know about her— that she had been entrusted with a portable device for a new experiment. No matter what, she had to resist giving the emitter to the Romulans, who were ruthless and unscrupulous. She either had to destroy it or give it to someone who would do no harm. Genesis could no longer benefit her species, but perhaps it could benefit someone.

The Seedling gazed up into the sky of Torga IV, where the bloodred night clouds had parted to reveal a sliver of stars. Somewhere up there were worlds full of her kind, but she was sworn never to go to them. They were new worlds, unsullied by past corruptions. If the meat creatures would allow, her species could have a fresh start—without the temptation of humanoid hosts.

However, a rebirth was not to be for the Seedling, who knew too much and would corrupt them with her knowledge. She was doomed to perish no matter what else should happen.

A figure in a black environmental suit darted from an abandoned hovercraft to a Dumpster, coming a few meters closer to her position in the alley. They were careful with their disruptor fire, because they didn't want to hit the box; but they wouldn't hesitate to kill her if they had a clear shot. That's why they were getting into position.

If she could draw their fire, decided the fugitive, she had to make them hit her precious box. If she couldn't save it from them, she had to destroy it. The alley was open behind her, but it was a long run to the walkway. The Seedling did not move swiftly, especially carrying the bulky device, which was nearly a meter tall and half a meter wide on each side.

At that moment, her salvation arrived in the form of a loud and rowdy crew of Bajoran miners and their consorts. They came weaving down the dusty walkway, toasting, drinking, and singing. The Seedling instantly called out in her most helpless voice. When they didn't stop, she screamed again and again until the unruly party halted on the sidewalk and peered into the dark alley.

There was a chance the miners were all about to be slaughtered, but the Romulans were like her species, she reasoned. They preferred stealth and guile to brute force and messy scenes.

The Bajorans came stumbling down the alley, and it took them a while to locate her and focus their eyes upon the pleasing Bajoran shape she had become—at least to those within range of her spores. This subterfuge was second nature to the Seedling by now, and she instantly roused their concern and helpfulness.

"What's wrong with you?" asked one brawny male. His nose ridges rippled, and she sensed that he was attracted to her.

"Are you injured?" said another, kneeling beside her. *I remind him of an instructor he had in the orphanage. Such a broken, pathetic life he has endured.*

The miner took her arm and gingerly helped her sit up. The Seedling feigned dizziness for a moment as she absorbed more of their thoughts.

"Where did *she* come from?" sniffed one of the females to her female friend. Their antagonism was a side effect she could do nothing about, so she ignored them and concentrated on the males.

"They tried to rob me," she rasped.

"Who?" snapped several Bajorans at once.

She pointed behind her at the narrow alley, where dim light faded into mist, shadow, and abandoned machines. The brawny one instantly ran down the thoroughfare, stomping and making his presence known. Her pursuers had been lurking there, but they were certainly gone now.

"Don't see them!" he called.

"It's okay," said the gentle one. "Let us get you some brestanti ale—that will fix you up."

"Thank you," she replied with a smile. "Don't let me forget my luggage." She touched the shiny metal box, and he gallantly picked it up.

As they strode from the alley, the Seedling glanced

over her shoulder at the dark passage between the corrugated buildings. She hadn't brought herself more than a few minutes of respite, and her pursuers were probably already on the roofs, planning their next move.

"What's the matter?" asked the gentle one. "You afraid they're still out there?"

"Yes." With a pleasant smile, she enhanced her similarity to the teacher he had loved at the age of ten.

"My name is Wislow. And yours?"

"Arden," she answered, choosing the identity she had used the most here.

"Pretty name," said the Bajoran male with a simpering smile.

When they reached the sidewalk, Arden gripped his arm and another male's, trying to keep herself surrounded by their flesh. She looked around and saw cheap industrial buildings lit by garish neon and halogen—an instant city built on a dead planet. At least Torga IV had been dead until the discovery of cormaline deposits and the importation of thousands of impoverished Bajoran workers.

A string of small two-seater hovercraft swerved down the street, and pedestrians had to scatter. The majority of residents were Bajoran, but other races loitered on the dusty sidewalks. Down one alley, a contingent of Klingon miners were fighting *targs*, in contradiction to the law. From a low-slung balcony, females were soliciting males to enter a casino. Torga IV was a brutal, corrupt place, inhabited by the dregs of the quadrant. It had been a perfect place for Arden's canceled experiment, and now it would be a fitting place for her death.

"We're here!" said the gruff miner, grabbing her by

the shoulders and trying to push her into a dimly lit tavern. She willed him to remember a lecture his grandmother had given him about the treatment of females, and he instantly released her.

"No. Please, not here." She appealed to Wislow. "What I want is someplace spiritual—like a temple or a chapel."

"We've got them," answered the miner, "but you don't want to go there. They've been slammed with refugees from the Genesis Wave. Every morning they come to the commissary, looking for food we're throwing out."

"Even the bars are crowded," said one of the females with a wave of her hand, "and it's the middle of the night."

"We've got to celebrate surviving the wave!" said the brawny one, trying to hustle them through the door.

Arden remained steadfast as she concentrated on the sensitive Bajoran. "Wislow, I could use some help getting to the nearest temple."

"All of you go inside," he ordered confidently. "I'll escort the lady to the . . . which one?"

"The Shrine of the Prophets on Aurora Avenue is the closest," answered one of the females. "I've got friends working there, and I better hear from them that you showed up!"

The others laughed. *An odd reaction*, thought the Seedling, considering that billions of their fellow meat creatures had perished in the last few days, and billions more were homeless. But Torga IV had been spared, and the sleepy backwater had turned into a bustling city hosting an impromptu festival. Such were the recuperative powers of the meat creatures, who were to be envied. If she could find the right one to trust, she would give up her secret. But not to the Romulans, whom she had grown to detest.

Arden thought she saw someone in a black hood and suit moving among the convivial crowd. She tugged on Wislow's shoulder and said persuasively, "Let's go now."

The bawling and mewling of the children never stopped, and most of them weren't even Bajorans. Prylar Yorka recoiled from the noise and the stench and sunk back into the vestibule atop the staircase. His elegant, richly appointed temple had been turned into a glaring warehouse for humanoid suffering. They were hungry, disoriented, grief-stricken, and sick . . . some very sick. He had called in the auxiliary volunteers, and Starfleet had contributed food and medical supplies; but they were still overwhelmed.

Plus the wretched smell had returned. They were taxing the sewage system, which was never designed to support this many residents; nor was it built to last this long. Who knew that the haphazard mining colony would last a decade and have its population doubled in a matter of hours?

Yorka stroked the wispy gray hair atop his head and considered bolting back to his private chambers, but he couldn't hide. This was what he was trained to do—step in where needed and help the poor and afflicted. He pulled his maroon robes around his stout figure and tried to look officious and unruffled, when he felt out of his depth. He was nothing more than a prylar, a monk, but this sect respected him as a former vedek in the assembly. Yorka was their leader in all but name and rank.

He disdained titles now, feeling that ambition had caused the ills of mainstream Bajoran religion; and the Vedek Assembly disdained him, not recognizing his sect. For food, they had to depend upon local resources, but all of the replicators in town were churning out ale and appetizers for revelers and well-funded refugees. When he really needed help from the powers above him, none was forthcoming.

The aging Bajoran tried to put the worries out of his mind; he had to lead his acolytes and volunteers through this tragedy. The old lion had to muster the confidence needed to inspire them, even though he felt nothing but dread. *Starfleet will return to relieve us,* he told himself, *just as they promised.* Even so, they were disturbingly vague on when that might be.

I could pray to the Prophets, but they—and the leaders of my faith—have abandoned me here. I have tried to shine the light of the Orbs, but no one has shown me any grace.

"Prylar!" he heard someone yell.

Yorka broke out of his troubled reverie and glanced down the metal staircase, where Acolyte Bowmyk came charging toward him, his yellow robes dirty and blood-splattered. "Sir, you've got to come," said the young Bajoran, twisting his thin hands nervously. "We've had another one of those mysterious deaths—we can't figure out why."

"Call the coroner," said Yorka, stomping down the stairs and brushing past him.

"We have, but they can't be here until dawn. That won't be for hours." The acolyte chased after his master, a worried look on his pinched face.

"What does the doctor think?" grumbled Yorka.

"The doctor has left for the day."

"What?" The burly monk stopped in his tracks, surrounded by refugees, overflowing the pews, sitting in the threshold of the sanctuary. His young assistant stared at him, and he knew he had to be forceful yet calm. This madness could not go on for long.

"What did the doctor say before he left?" asked Yorka evenly.

"He couldn't figure out what had killed him, but he said it wasn't anything contagious. There were some unusual tricorder readings, but no clear cause of death."

Yorka nodded sagely and managed a smile. "You see, there's no reason for concern, if it's not contagious. Take the bodies to the storage room."

"Where the food is?" asked Bowmyk, aghast.

"There's precious little of that," muttered Yorka. He pointed to a blood spot on the acolyte's satin tunic. "And change your clothes. Put on something more practical, if you're going to assist the sick."

"Yes, Master." The acolyte bowed and hurried off.

Yorka was immediately besieged by Ferengi, and he gritted his teeth. No one was more difficult to mollify than a suddenly impoverished Ferengi. A middle-aged businessman with three wives, who were wearing blankets at Yorka's insistence, shook his fist with such anger that his earlobes wiggled.

"You've got to get us back to Ferenginar!" he demanded. "You don't know who I am—you don't understand! I've got to file reports—insurance forms—"

The words were just a babble in Yorka's ears, because he already knew his reply. "I have no transportation to furnish, and you're free to leave or to stay in our house of worship. If you want to remain in our care, you must behave yourselves and abide by our rules. We'll do our best to feed and shelter you."

"That's not what they promised us! That's not what they promised us on the ship!" insisted the Ferengi.

"This isn't the ship," answered Yorka calmly. "Normally we're not a refugee station—we're a temple offering outreach to the Bajoran community here. May I suggest that you pray to the Prophets? We're having services in half an hour."

"This is outrageous!" sputtered the Ferengi, stomping on the floor and wiping away real tears with his knuckles. "I lost my whole fortune—my factories, my latinum . . . I lost *everything*."

Yorka raised an eyebrow. "You still have your life. And your wives." Behind him, three females looked at one another as if that wasn't a certainty.

"All I need is a few strips of latinum to help us get home," begged the Ferengi. "Perhaps *you*—"

"Look around you, Sir," snapped Yorka. "Do we look like we are hoarding extra latinum? I recall two Rules of Acquisition, which I believe a Ferengi in your situation ought to consider deeply."

The distraught merchant blinked at him with surprise, and even his wives drew closer to hear the words of the Bajoran religious figure.

"Rule number two-hundred-thirty-six: You can't buy fate," began Yorka. "And rule number twenty-two: A wise man can hear profit in the wind. You call yourself a businessperson? Look out in the streets, and you will see merchants profiting from this disaster, while you sit here and whine. You're a disgrace to your people."

That stung the Ferengi, and he lowered his head in shame. Yorka went on, "So a strong wind has hit and destroyed your holdings. Do you ignore the opportunity? I can soothe your soul by quoting you prophecies—or Rules of Acquisition—but you must find a way to triumph over adversity. What are the services which *you* need and cannot find? Others must be seeking them, too, and would be willing to pay once they collect their insurance."

The stout Ferengi lifted his head, and his droopy face brightened into a smile. "These are times of confusion— a good time to make money!" he agreed.

In the human fashion, he took the Bajoran's hand and pumped it. "They told me to come to this temple, saying that you are a wise man. And they're right. My name is Chellac, and if you ever need anything, you just let me know. Whatever it is, you'll get it wholesale!"

"That will be welcome," muttered Yorka, pulling away from the beaming Ferengi. Other refugees bombarded him with questions, and the prylar was forced to raise his arms and plow through the crowd at an accelerated pace. His destination was the southwest corner of the temple, where they kept the sick.

"I'm sorry! We can't provide you with transportation, private rooms, things we don't have," he announced, more for the benefit of his workers than the refugees. "But we have more to offer than food and shelter. Our teachings are free to all who will listen. In the words of our enlightened Kai Opaka, we cannot control the forces around us—we can only control our reaction to them. Although grief and confusion are understandable, the Prophets tell us to search for true meaning within our lives."

He paused, hoping he had their attention, except for the bawling babies. "Remember Shabren's Fifth Prophecy—the Golden Age will not come until we defeat the Evil One. I believe that has happened! The terror which brought you here is over, and now we can rebuild. All of you are frightened, but you're still breathing. Yes, your lives have been changed forever, but you must ask yourselves *why*?

"Change is normal, and we believe these cycles have a purpose. This purging process has happened often in Bajoran history, and we are experts at interpreting the will of the Prophets. We have a service in about thirty minutes, and I will deliver a talk I gave on this subject at the Vedek Assembly. Find out what this disaster means for your—"

The front door slammed open, and someone screamed as a shrouded figure staggered into the temple. The withered, wraithlike visitor was carrying a shiny box that seemed half her size, and people shrunk away from her. Yorka peered over the top of heads, unsure what he was seeing—the figure was like a moving blur that became more distinct as she came closer to him.

"Yorka!" croaked the visitor, lurching toward the staircase. The former vedek felt compelled to follow, although he didn't know why. The crowd parted for him as he approached the insubstantial figure on the vestibule stairs. Everyone in the temple seemed to know this was a momentous occasion, but it was hard to tell why.

"Privacy," she insisted. He wasn't sure if she had spoken or merely thought it, but he understood.

He pointed up the stairs. "The vestibule."

"Take my luggage," she added, "and hurry. I'm dying."

He took her box as commanded and escorted her up the metal stairs to the richly appointed vestibule, where he met with worshipers privately or in small groups. Her arm felt brittle and bony, but there was something familiar and comforting about her presence. He felt as though he knew her, although he could not yet see her face because of her hood.

Passing through brocaded curtains, they reached the vestibule, and he motioned to an upholstered bench. A closed door at the end of the chamber led to his private office and sparse living quarters. If his visitor was ill, he wouldn't hesitate to let her lie down in his own bed. Yorka felt that much concern over her comfort.

She turned around and dropped the hood, and he gasped! It was Kai Opaka, alive and smiling beatifically at him. The kai was a short woman, but she seemed to expand in her garments, becoming more regal with each passing second. Despite her calm expression, she was clearly injured, because she clutched a scorch mark on her side which was seeping dark fluid.

"Let me fetch a doctor!" cried Yorka. "It is a profound honor, but we must treat you and—"

"No," murmured Kai Opaka. "My time is short, and you must listen to me."

When she said her time was short, Yorka suddenly remembered that Kai Opaka was dead—had been for over ten years. Yet here she stood before him, ebbing in and out of his consciousness. He thought that this was either the sign from the Prophets he had been waiting for, or proof positive that he was too insane to help anyone.

There came shouting and commotion from the front door of the temple, and Yorka was momentarily distracted. "What is that?"

"My pursuers. I have less time than I thought." The Kai affixed him with baleful dark eyes, and her ear jewelry seemed to vibrate with the force of her presence. "Listen to me, Vedek Yorka, for I bring your salvation. It's inside this box that you carried. But you must guard it from the Romulans—they cannot be trusted with such power. Guard it from all—I am entrusting you with the greatest force in the universe. May the Prophets guide you in its use."

With eagerness and fear in equal measure, the monk touched the gleaming box. Before he could even find the latch, more noise and shouts sounded from below, and he heard Acolyte Bowmyk's voice over the others. "Prylar Yorka! You must come! Please!"

He stuck his head out of the curtains of the vestibule and saw Bowmyk struggling up the stairs. "What is it? I'm very busy."

"Sir, strangers are looting the temple. They're in the sanctuary!" The acolyte pointed urgently to multiple disturbances among the refugees.

Yorka gazed grimly at the bedlam in what had once been his solemn and austere temple. Two figures in black environmental suits were overturning beds and pews as they ransacked the place, and a third was interrogating witnesses at the point of a weapon. Still the refugees pressed forward, venting their anger and frustration at these masked strangers, who dared to make their lives even more miserable. It was clear from their body language that the intruders feared for their safety in this volatile crowd, which was turning into a mob.

The monk fought the impulse to yell at the intruders, but he needed distractions at the moment. "Come inside," he whispered to the acolyte. "I want you to meet someone."

"But the refugees . . . they're in danger from—"

"Leave them." Yorka pulled the youth into the vestibule and motioned toward his special guest. But the kai was gone. Instead there was nothing but a pile of moss and dead leaves littering the floor. Clothing was piled atop the dried brush, but it was common street wear, not the elegant raiment the kai had been wearing.

"What is the meaning of this, sir?" asked the acolyte. The skittish look in his eyes told Yorka that he was about to bolt and never come back to the temple. With determination, the elder got a grip on his fear and turned to look at the metal box, which was intact and unchanged.

She is gone . . . perhaps in hiding. Maybe it was a changeling. At this moment, Yorka needed help, and he couldn't appear as befuddled as he felt. Although he couldn't explain what he had seen, he knew the mysterious box was real.

"I have a valuable object here," he began. "It was given to me by a servant of the Prophets. We must protect it with our lives."

Yorka stuck out his chin confidently and scanned the room, looking for anything which might help them. His eyes lit upon the circuit box which controlled the flow of power to the industrial building. Until the remodeling, the vestibule and monk's quarters had been the control room for an automated warehouse, and the regulating equipment was still located close at hand.

"I want you to make a dash out the front door and distract them," said the Prylar. "Don't worry—before you even get halfway there, I'm going to shut off all the lights in the building. Then I'll go out the back door. It should be mass confusion, and they'll be stuck in darkness for a while."

"Yes, sir," answered the young acolyte with a nervous gulp. He didn't look convinced.

"Be brave," said Yorka, gripping the youth's scrawny shoulder. "I know you think this is odd, but when you've been around as long as I have, you'll see that the Prophets act in strange ways. We can't stop to debate their choices or the cycles of life—we have to seize what is presented to us."

He gazed at the rectangular box, which was almost a meter long. "You'll never do anything more important in your life than this, Bowmyk. If you could have *seen* her—"

"Seen her?" asked the acolyte puzzledly. He glanced at the pile of moss and old clothes.

"Don't view this through the lens of the everyday," cautioned the stout monk. "This is the beginning of something grand . . . something which will change our dreary lives and this dreary place. You must do exactly as I tell you—for the will of the Prophets. Repeat it with me!"

He grabbed the lad's hands and said, "For the will of the Prophets, I will do this." The acolyte dutifully repeated it with him.

Moving like a man possessed, the former vedek grabbed a red velvet curtain from the wall and wrapped it around the chrome box. For a decoy, he grabbed a bra-zier from the altar and wrapped it in an identical curtain. "You take that, and act like it's priceless. Run now out the front door. Go!"

The youth hesitated. "How will . . . how will I find you, sir?"

"I'll find you and the others as surely as this wonder has found me. Go on!"

Inspired by the energized monk, the acolyte rushed from the vestibule and pounded down the stairs. Yorka grabbed the unknown object and ran to the circuit box on the wall. He waited until he heard the unfortunate screams, then he pressed the membrane keypad, where it read, "All Circuits Off."

At once, every cubic centimeter of the building was plunged into darkness, and frightened wails and screeches reverberated in the metal building. Yorka moved swiftly to the stairs, which he trod a hundred times a day. Even in darkness, he could navigate them without much trouble, letting his legs remember the spacing and distances. The dark wasn't constant, because there were disruptor blasts that illuminated enraged, panicked refugees swarming in every direction.

Yorka was remarkably calm as he ignored all of this. Clearly the kai's pursuers were in the service of evil—she had mentioned Romulans. His feet hit the carpet, and he was jostled by figures moving in every direction; it was all he could do to maintain his grip on the box. But Yorka envisioned his path in his mind, using the walls as touchstones. Familiar ramparts ran all the way from the stairs to the back door, and all he had to do was navigate them. For ten years, he had lived in this manufactured city, and he knew where to hide. He even knew where to get transportation.

As screams, shouts, and disruptor beams enlivened the darkness inside the temple, Prylar Yorka muscled his way past the mob choking the back door. He spilled into the street along with several others and staggered to his feet, still gripping his prize. A crowd was forming, attracted by the chaos inside, and Yorka heard sirens. Police hovercraft were headed down the narrow side street, and terrified refugees rushed out to meet them. This wasn't any time to be questioned, not until he understood what he possessed.

Pulling a hood over his head, the Bajoran monk slipped into the wall of onlookers and made his escape. *Thank you for remembering me,* he said silently to the Prophets. *I won't disappoint you.*

two

"Captain," said Data from the ops console on the *Enterprise*-E, "we are approaching the unidentified vessel in sector 734. Partial sensor readings are active again." The android's fingers were a blur as they worked the instrument panel. "Warp signature indicates it is a *Steamrunner*-class starship, and the only one of those still missing is the *Barcelona*. If it is the *Barcelona*, it is forty-two degrees and one point five light-years off course."

Beverly Crusher turned around in the command chair and glanced at the android. "Do we have a visual yet?"

"Only with interference." Data activated the large viewscreen at the front of the bridge, plus several smaller auxiliary screens. The image suffered from occasional static, but it was clear enough. In a desolate sector of space floated a sleek, slate-gray starship about half as large as the *Enterprise*. Her nacelles were below the hull, which made her look something like a Klingon ship. Her running lights were still blinking, but the bridge crew had seen that before during this search-and-rescue operation.

Beverly was afraid to ask the next question. "Any lifesigns?"

Data shook his head. "Sensor readings are inconclusive. I am attempting to compensate for the interference, which I believe is caused by the radiation. The radiation readings are still inaccurate and will take time to analyze."

"Keep our shields at maximum, and keep trying to hail them."

"Yes, sir," replied the Andorian officer on tactical.

The red-haired doctor rose to her feet and adjusted her tunic, as she had seen the regular captain do on more than one occasion. "Conn, take us to half impulse and get as close as we need to verify the lifesign readings. Then pull back to maximum tractor-beam range."

"Yes, sir," answered the Deltan male on the navigation console. After three earlier salvage operations, the crew was getting used to this routine, grim as it was.

They had many good reasons not to haphazardly enter one of these abandoned ships, and the best was the possibility of infestation by the moss creatures. Crusher knew firsthand the devastating effect *that* could have on a person . . . and a ship. Despite their precautions, all they had found so far were crew remains—no moss creatures, alive or dead. Under those circumstances, it was a simple decision to tow a ship to a starbase and do a thorough examination under ideal conditions. As yet, the doctor hadn't heard why some crews near the wave's path had died while most lived, and she was getting impatient for an answer.

The threat should be over, except for the cheering and the funerals, but the mop-up had taken on a gruesome life of its own. Maybe these new anomalies weren't related to the Genesis Wave, which made them an even greater mystery. It might take researchers decades to sort out what exactly that terrible emitter had done to this chunk of Federation space.

As they approached the *Barcelona*, the image on the viewscreen grew more distinct, and again Crusher was struck by how peaceful the starship looked. Maybe they weren't too late to help the crew. At that thought, a shiver seized Beverly's spine, and she realized that if the crew was still alive, moss creatures could be among them. She tried to tell herself that what had happened to her was an aberration . . . a desperate move by a foe who was cornered. Since the Genesis Wave was unleashed, there had been only a handful of reported cases of infestation in Starfleet, she reminded herself. But those odds didn't reassure her, not when she thought about the ease with which they had taken over her body, mind, and ship.

"Captain," said Data suddenly. "I am reading three distinct lifesigns aboard the *Barcelona*."

Crusher looked at him with surprise, then turned to the image of the ship on the viewscreen. "Can you isolate them?"

"Roughly, yes. They are not together." With incredible speed, the android flipped through pages of information. On the main viewscreen, three blips appeared overlaid on the starship—one toward the pointed bow, one midship to port, and another in the stern, perhaps a torpedo bay.

"Can we use transporters?" asked Crusher.

"Inadvisable," answered Data, "with these levels of radiation. It would also be inadvisable to lower our shields."

The acting captain looked at the Andorian on the tactical station. "Any answer to our hails?"

"None, sir," reported the dour, blue-skinned humanoid. "We have tried every known frequency."

The doctor nodded decisively. "Conn, take us back to a safe distance, say a million kilometers. We could take a shuttlecraft over there, or we could tow it out of the radiation field . . . maybe. Either way, we'll need a medical team. Data, alert sickbay."

"Yes, Doctor," answered the android, subtly hinting that she had just reverted back to the ship's medical officer.

Crusher took his hint and pressed her comm badge. "Crusher to Riker."

"Yes, Doctor," came the voice of the first officer.

"I'm sorry to interrupt the poker game, but a situation has come up. That bogey we're investigating is a *Steamrunner*-class cruiser, and we've got three life-forms on it. I want to take a medical team over there."

"We have to consider our orders," said Riker hesitantly. "I'll be there in a moment."

While she waited to be relieved, Beverly Crusher tapped the companel again and said, "Crusher to Ogawa."

"Ogawa here," came a voice with only a hint of sleepiness.

"Are you up for a little excursion outside the ship?"

asked Crusher. Alyssa's husband, Andrew, was still among the missing after the Genesis disaster, and Beverly was being careful how much work she gave her longtime colleague. She wanted to maintain a balance—give Alyssa enough to keep busy but not so much that she couldn't meet with Counselor Troi and deal with her emotions.

After a pause, the lieutenant answered, "I heard the call for a med team. I was about to respond."

"Then I read your mind," said the doctor. "I'll meet you in sickbay as soon as I get off the bridge."

"Yes, sir," answered Ogawa, sounding as efficient as ever. "I'll organize the rest of the team for you."

"Thank you. Crusher out." She moved behind the conn and discussed their positioning with the pilot, making sure they were well beyond the range of the radiation. The radiation field was difficult to assess because of fluctuations in the scanners, but there were a number of exotic types, all intermingled. From their new position, no lifesigns registered on the distressed ship.

Just when Crusher was beginning to think Riker would never arrive to relieve her, the turbolift door slid open. Riker was there all right, but it was Captain Picard who entered first. Will had decided to fetch the captain, although she would have preferred to let Jean-Luc sleep.

Picard nodded curtly to her. "Doctor, I hope you don't mind my coming along. The commander knew I would be interested in this. Please report."

In businesslike fashion, she informed him about their approach to what they thought was a derelict, the discovery of three lifesigns, their withdrawal to a distance away from the radiation, and her wish to take a shuttle-craft over to the stricken vessel.

The captain frowned sharply, his laugh lines crinkling to the point where only his brow remained smooth. "We're under orders not to crack open these ships unless we have to. From a shuttle, you would have to force an entrance."

"We have three lifesigns," pointed out the doctor, "out of a crew of eighty-nine, so time may be important. We can't use transporters because of the radiation, but I have a backup plan. We lock on with tractor beam and tow the ship out of the radiation field, if we can."

"Although the *Barcelona* may be the source of the radiation," cautioned Data.

"I like that plan," said Riker with a quick smile, "better than the first one. But I want to think carefully about who goes over there."

"They may be injured . . . dying," insisted Crusher.

"What we don't know is what else may be over there," said the captain with finality. "Data, you lead the away team. Take three security and three medics. Dr. Crusher and—"

"Ogawa, and the duty officer," she answered. "Dr. Pelagof. We all need radiation suits, even Data."

"We still have some of Dr. Brahms's phase-shifting radiation suits," said Riker. "They'll withstand anything, including the Genesis Wave."

"They may be needed," answered Data, "unless we can succeed in lowering the radiation levels on the *Barcelona*. It is difficult to understand how anyone could still be alive."

"Unless they have the suits, too," said the doctor. "Conn, take us to tractor-beam range."

"Yes, sir."

Crusher turned and looked apologetically at Captain Picard. "Excuse me, sir. Did you wish to assume command?"

He waved his hand and smiled. "I haven't relieved you yet, but I will now. Well done, Doctor."

She hadn't accomplished much, but words of praise from Jean-Luc were always welcome. The doctor nodded and said, "Computer, transfer command of the bridge to Captain Picard, effective immediately. Crusher reporting to sickbay."

"Command transfer acknowledged," replied the computer.

"We'll need signal amplifiers to beam you and the survivors out of there," said Riker, leaning over the transporter console. He lifted his recently clean-shaven face and surveyed Crusher, Data, Ogawa, and the other members of the away team gathered in transporter room two. "So you'll have to go aboard and find the life-forms. I know it's going to be hard to carry anything else, but you're going to have to take the amplifiers."

Beverly nodded, which wasn't easy in the bulky environmental suit. These were standard issue suits, not even the larger prototypes developed by Leah Brahms. Tricorder, medical kit, utility belt, phaser, air tanks, and other gear already hung from her, and she waited patiently while Riker hung a long cylinder with telescoping legs over her shoulder. If she got a chance, she would shorten the strap later.

The first officer returned to the transporter console, ready to do the honors himself. He studied the readouts for a moment, then nodded. "The radiation is down sixty percent since we moved the *Barcelona*, but that's as good as it's going to get. Prepare for boarding."

Crusher and the other six members of her party stepped upon the transporter platform. Data was in charge, so she assumed he would be taking the lead, which made sense, since he was unaffected by the moss creatures. The medical team would follow, each one of them guarded by a security officer. On this mission, she wouldn't mind having a bodyguard, thought Crusher, because she remembered all too well when she had beamed over to inspect the *Neptune*. She had been tricked by the moss creatures into thinking Wesley had returned, but it wasn't really her son. The doctor shivered in the hot, bulky suit.

Data checked his team, then nodded to Commander Riker. "Energize."

The first officer plied the controls, and Crusher felt the familiar tingle that told her that her molecules were about to be disassembled and reassembled. The flutter in her stomach was a bit stronger than usual, due to her nervousness. *It can't happen again,* she told herself. *I won't let it happen again.*

They beamed aboard the bridge of the disabled starship, where they found the red-hued emergency lights shining eerily. The three security officers instantly leveled their weapons and formed a protective triangle around the others. Crusher, Ogawa, and the chubby Tellarite doctor, Pelagof, opened their medical tricorders, while Data stepped to the ops console.

"Hmmm," said the android with a slight cock of his hooded head. His voice was amplified in Beverly's helmet. "They were on red alert with reports of a hull breach. I do not recall any sensor readings which indicated a hull breach."

"Me either," answered Crusher. "How long have they been like this?"

"Since the Genesis Wave struck seven-point-eight days ago," answered Data, working the board. "Their shields were destroyed immediately."

"By what?" asked the doctor.

"Unknown," answered the android. "All systems seem to have failed except for emergency life support."

"Yet they weren't in the path of the wave," said Crusher puzzledly. "According to our records, they were merely monitoring and charting its course."

"If this ship had been in the wave's path, it would no longer exist," replied Data, "in any recognizable form."

Pelagof snorted importantly. "Doctor, I've got a life-form reading on a level just below us. It's very weak, and I suggest we hurry."

Data motioned to the security officers to follow him to a rear corner of the bridge, where he bent over and, with a twist of his wrist, popped off the access panel for the Jefferies tube. The android singled out two security officers and motioned them down the hatch to the ladder which ran between decks. Perhaps Data could eventually get the turbolifts working, thought Crusher, but this was faster and more certain. Still it was disconcerting to think about crawling into a confined space on this nearly deserted vessel.

After a long minute, security reported back that the

way was clear, and the team descended one after another into the Jefferies tube. They emerged through a bulkhead hatch into the corridor a deck below, which was also illuminated by emergency lighting. Data consulted his tricorder, got a fix on their target, and led the way down the corridor. He was flanked by security guards, weapons leveled.

At an intersection, the android stopped and held up his hand, pointing out a row of phaser scorches on the bulkhead. Within one deep phaser hole, sparks shot intermittently from damaged circuits. Despite the signs of a battle, there were no bodies or blood in sight, although the life-form registering in Crusher's tricorder was close to death.

"We have to hurry," she said.

"Understood," answered Data. The android stepped out into the intersecting corridor and was instantly drilled by a phaser beam. Fortunately, his extraordinary reflexes allowed him to duck away from the blast, which struck his upper arm instead of his chest before he could dive behind the corner.

One of the security officers rolled into the corridor to return fire, and he was struck in the collarbone. He kept rolling into the next corridor as one of his comrades leaped out to fire. She managed to jump after her comrade before the foe's weapon could orient upon her, and the phaser beam went wide. Already two crew members were wounded, thought Crusher, and no contact had been made with the life-forms onboard. Data stepped forward, leveling his phaser.

"Wait!" yelled the female security officer named Kosavar. She panted to get her breath. "I saw something

on a tripod. I think it's a phaser rifle . . . automated."
After reporting that, she knelt down to inspect her
wounded comrade.

"Probably on motion sensor," said Data. He activated
the comm channel. "Away team to transporter room
two."

"Riker here," came the response.

"We have encountered phaser fire," said Data, calmly
touching the burn on his upper arm. "Two injured—
myself and Ensign Tyler. Ensign Tyler needs to report to
sickbay immediately. I can continue, but my environmental suit has been compromised."

"Set up Tyler's signal amplifier near him," ordered
Riker. "We'll direct-beam him to sickbay, and I'll send
down another suit for you. Who's firing at you?"

"We believe the phaser fire was automated, keying
upon motion sensors."

"Don't take any chances," ordered Riker. "Remember,
I can't beam you out unless you set up the amplifiers. I'll
send more security, too, if you need them."

"It would be advisable to keep them in reserve until
we investigate the nature of the threat. Data out."

Crusher glanced to the other side of the corridor and
saw Kosavar already setting up the signal amplifier. If the
wounded officer wasn't getting help soon, she would
have tossed her medkit over to his companion.

"Ready an electroplasm dispersal grenade," said Data,
nodding to the security officer on his side of the intersection, a Bolian named Wapot. He opened a pouch on
his belt and removed a small, round device.

"That won't hurt the survivor, will it?" asked Crusher.

"Not if he has survived the radiation levels on this

ship," answered Data. "But it should cause the phaser and controller devices to malfunction."

The security officer nodded that the grenade was ready, but Data waited until Ensign Tyler disappeared in a cloud of shimmering transporter particles. Where the wounded man had lain, there was now a neatly folded environmental suit. Data held out his hand to take the grenade, while he motioned the others to move back down the corridor.

As soon as they were about ten meters away, Data dashed into the intersection and threw the grenade. A phaser beam nearly chopped off his arm, but the android dove to the other side of the intersection, to join Kosavar. As they waited, he stripped off his damaged environmental suit.

The grenade exploded, bathing the scarlet hues of the corridor with a shimmering, pulsating glow. The readings on Beverly's medical tricorder went off the scale, and she feared it had been damaged. But the device soon returned to normal, showing that the nearby life-form was still alive, but barely.

After donning his new radiation suit, Data stepped bravely into the corridor. Nothing happened, and he and the two security officers charged ahead. The three medical workers cautiously followed, tricorders leveled and blinking.

They found the survivor at the end of the corridor in a weapons storeroom, surrounded by spent phasers and power packs. He'd had his choice of weaponry to defend his position in the doorway, and he had chosen well. After growing too weak to stay alert, he had mounted a type-3 phaser on a static sentry device. The survivor was wearing a radiation suit identical to theirs, and a comrade behind him also wore the same suit. But that crew member had been dead for days—it was the first corpse they had seen.

After Data removed the phaser rifle from its tripod, Ogawa slipped past him to reach the dying man. In the confines of the closet, there was room for only one of them to attend the man, so Crusher hung back and continued to take tricorder readings. Despite his suit, there was no doubt that the man was suffering from acute radiation poisoning and had only a short time to live.

"We have to get him to sickbay," declared Ogawa. "We can't do anything for him here."

"Are you satisfied that he is a member of this crew?" asked Data. It was a diplomatic way of asking whether he was a moss creature.

"Yes," said Ogawa, "I'd stake my life on it."

Data made a rapid decision. "Very well, set up a signal amplifier. But quarantine restrictions must be followed in sickbay."

"One of us had better return with him," said Dr. Crusher, glancing at her medical team. "Dr. Pelagof, will you go back with him?"

"Certainly," answered the Tellarite, not hiding his relief at the idea of leaving the derelict ship. He quickly set up a signal amplifier for both of them, while Data contacted the transporter room and arranged for two more to beam to sickbay.

The doctor and his patient had just vanished in a swirl of sparkling particles, when Riker's urgent voice broke in, "Data, we've got movement on that second lifesign. It's gone from midship, level six, to level two. In fact, it's moving rapidly toward your position. That is, unless we're getting false sensor readings."

"A distinct possibility," allowed Data. Nevertheless, he motioned to his remaining two security officers to flank the medical team. "We are on alert. Data out."

Those who weren't gripping weapons gripped their tricorders, and Crusher was getting a strong lifesign reading, which was only getting stronger by the second.

"That's convenient," said Ogawa nervously, peering at her own readouts. "We don't have to go searching for this one—he's coming to us."

"Deploy more signal amplifiers," ordered Data. "We may have to leave quickly."

They gladly busied themselves with that task, while Data tried to contact the approaching figure over several intra-ship frequencies. Without warning, a monstrous, churning whirlwind came whipping down the corridor. It caught the two security officers off guard and yanked them off their feet, spinning them around like marionettes caught on a ceiling fan. Their weapons flew out of their hands, and so did a stray phaser blast that whizzed by Crusher's ear.

She hit the deck, as anyone would do in a tornado or a phaser fight. Voices crackled over the headset in her helmet, but she couldn't understand a word. When none of them transported out of the corridor, she assumed they couldn't. There was nothing to do but keep her tricorder running and watch the destructive living force before them—a wild funnel of debris, crackling sparks, and living beings.

Then the tricorder was ripped out of her hands, and

she felt herself skidding across the deck toward the whirlwind. Crusher yelled just as a strong hand gripped her ankle, and she jerked to a stop. She saw flailing arms and looked over to see Ogawa, also in Data's grasp. The android's feet were locked around a conduit, which was bending under the stress of holding the two women.

Like a screaming child smashing his dolls, the dust devil hurled the two security officers against the bulkheads. Tired of them, or satisfied, it flew down the corridor leading to the bridge. Crusher dropped to the deck with a thud. Bits of shiny insulation fluttered down, covering the two female security officers with silvery snow.

Kosavar groaned and managed to turn over. The other officer lay as still as Crusher's smashed tricorder, the remains of which were embedded in the ceiling. She staggered to her feet, anxious to help the fallen security officers. In her helmet, the doctor could hear Data's voice and Riker's replies—but the babble was incomprehensible. Maybe her comlink had been damaged, or her head. She heard Riker say something about "The third lifesign."

In doctor mode but still woozy, Crusher crawled to the side of Wapot, who wasn't moving. She appeared to be dead. Ogawa stepped past her to reach Kosavar's side; then the lieutenant took a glance down the far corridor and recoiled in horror. With a lunge, Ogawa grabbed Ensign Kosavar and tried to pull the officer out of the way of something . . . approaching swiftly. Crusher could feel the deck vibrating.

The doctor's stomach twisted with fear, and she

looked up to see a misshapen beast with matted black fur, numerous circular mouths ringed with teeth, and short writhing appendages. It had so many legs it shouldn't be able to walk, let alone gallop like it did. With steam snorting from its orifices, the monster turned to regard her; she couldn't see any eyes, but maybe they were in the tentacles. Coldly it studied her, while exuding a fear which overwhelmed her mind. Death was going to be a relief.

three

Overwhelmed by waves of dread and nausea, trapped in a dead-end corridor, Beverly Crusher scrambled to escape from a hideous unfathomable creature. The beast reared up, turning into a wall of fur, gristle, and stubby tentacles. She realized she had left Ensign Wapot at the monster's feet, and she considered going back for the security officer. Then a voice crackled in the helmet of her radiation suit. "Stay low!" warned Data.

A phaser beam streaked over her head, and it drilled into the misshapen beast, setting a chunk of its fur on fire. Writhing in agony, the thing stomped all over Ensign Wapot's body, and repeated phaser blasts failed to drive it back. Just then, a maw of dancing prism lights appeared from nowhere, engulfing both the beast and the fallen officer. As Crusher gaped in amazement, this rippling rainbow passed right through the bulkheads, seemingly coming from all directions to converge on their position.

Abruptly, Data grabbed her from behind and hauled

her back to the weapons storage room. Then he helped Ogawa drag the unconscious Kosavar to cover. In front of them, the kaleidoscopic maw began to turn black as it consumed both the beast and Ensign Wapot. In a short time, the swirling cataclysm of colors had turned into a jagged black rift that split the corridor in two.

Crusher had to close her eyes. When she forced herself to look back, the apparition was gone, and so were Wapot and the hideous beast. Crusher's retinas felt burned, as if she had gazed at the sun or a strobe light without protection, and she felt drained of energy. A blurred hand hovered into view, and she blinked uncertainly at Data.

"Are you well enough to stand?"

"Yes," she answered. But she needed the android's help to rise unsteadily to her feet.

"I believe we have encountered all three life-forms," said Data. "Plus one which did not register on our initial scans. That is, if it *was* a life-form. Radiation levels have increased by twenty-eight percent. Would you like to leave the *Barcelona* now?"

"Yes," she rasped hoarsely. Crusher rubbed her eyes, hoping the side effects of gazing at the rainbow anomaly were only temporary. By concentrating, she found that her vision cleared a little. She managed to make out Ogawa, who was bent over the injured Kosavar, preparing to give her a hypospray as soon as possible.

"Four to beam up," reported Data to the transporter room.

With considerable relief, the doctor felt her molecules rearranging themselves, along with those of Ogawa, Data, and Kosavar. As the red-hued intersection in the corridor faded from view, she looked in vain for the Bolian, but Wapot was not returning with them. Beverly shivered. She hadn't thought she could see anything worse than a moss creature on this derelict ship, but she had seen something worse. Far worse.

In the mirror, she saw the same short, light-brown hair she always saw. By now, her hair had so much gray in it that it was mostly a drab sandy color, but she could live with that. Her eyes were still piercing blue and deep-set, her mouth thin and determined. But nobody would notice those features, not when half her face was weathered by decades of command and strife, and the other half was as smooth and pristine as a teenager's. On one side, the bags, wrinkled, jowls, and discoloration of her years were prominent; on the other side, they didn't exist. One half was spotted with age, and the other half was freckled with youth.

It was the most startling face she had ever seen, and Admiral Alynna Nechayev was rather proud of it. Her visage was so bizarre that one had to laugh, while shedding a few tears at the same time. *Yes, I'm a survivor of the Genesis Wave*, she thought, looking at her reflection in the mirror.

As the admiral gazed at herself, she couldn't help wondering what the Genesis effect could do for the rest of her body. It could make all of her as youthful as a teenager, which was both frightening and tempting. The Genesis technology had so much potential for good that it was tempting to try it again—to see whether it could be tamed.

Yet Nechayev knew her face was a cautionary tale, saying to anyone who looked that the Genesis Wave did not create life out of nothing—it altered what had existed there before. In her case, that was seventy years of worry, experience, laughter, and tears—all traces of which were gone from the left side of her face.

That's why she had elected to have the youthful half of her face aged, rather than have the older part sculpted to look young. Besides, the surgeons didn't think they could duplicate what the glob of still mutating Genesis material had done. Commander La Forge's desperate act had created a walking billboard for what was wrong with the Genesis technology.

Admiral Nechayev glanced at the clock in her hospital room and saw that she had only five minutes left to change her mind. She could have either side changed to look like the other, or she could leave her face as it was. That was tempting, if only for the shock value, but the admiral didn't need medals or external representations to show dedication. Her subordinates knew who she was; all of Starfleet knew who she was—she was the one who had slipped up and let Carol Marcus be abducted by an enemy bent on their destruction. Her split face was not a symbol of heroism, but of failure, and it mirrored the conflict in her life.

I need to change more than this face, decided Nechayev.

She adjusted her hair and the collar of her hospital gown before turning away from the mirror, then she crossed to her desk. Befitting her importance, this room had a computer terminal, comm link, library on isolinear chips, map screen, and other devices patched into Starfleet Headquarters. She was kept fully apprised of the cleanup effort, which was already behind schedule after only a week.

The admiral sat down at her desk, both sides of her face looking determined. "Computer," she said, "relay this message to Admiral Rendelez, Chief of Starfleet Command, standard routing." That would ensure he wouldn't get the message until she had entered surgery.

"Admiral, effective immediately, I am resigning from the admiralty and Starfleet Command. You have been very considerate in not busting me down to an ensign over my handling of the Carol Marcus affair, and my slow reaction to the Genesis threat. I can see I will have to do it for you. I don't want to command fleets anymore, or worry about security for the entire Federation. I just want to command one ship with a good crew. I want to get out there and do some good on a localized basis, like the captains I admire. We've talked about them."

She cleared her throat and went on, "Therefore, I am requesting to be demoted to captain and assigned to a ship in the fleet. It shouldn't be a flagship—just a regular ship that needs a captain. If you do not grant this request, I'll have no choice but to resign completely from Starfleet and seek a post in a civilian relief organization. I have several ideas how I might be useful there, too. Sincerely, Alynna Nechayev. Computer, send."

"Message sent."

The admiral sat back in her chair and breathed a sigh of relief, just as the chime sounded on her door. The chime was followed by the pleasant smile of a young female orderly. "Admiral, they've asked me to tell you there's going to be a half-hour delay. We've been swamped with victims of radiation poisoning."

Nechayev sat up with interest. "Radiation poisoning? What kind of radiation poisoning? From where?"

"I don't know," admitted the young woman. "I only know they were brought here from a starbase, where they couldn't help them."

"Couldn't help them—at a starbase?" Now the admiral jumped out of her chair and walked toward the orderly. "Get me a wheelchair. I'll sit in the hall if I have to, but I'm getting out of this room. Understood?"

"Yes, Admiral!" snapped the young woman.

At least for now I'm still an admiral, thought Nechayev. *I might as well use it while I can.*

A few minutes later, Nechayev was sitting in the corridor outside triage, with the wrinkled side of her face turned toward the wall. A young man came up to her, but upon seeing her entire face, he recoiled, mumbled something apologetic, and left. Nechayev smiled wistfully at this, thinking about what might have been were Genesis used as a Fountain of Youth. Now more than ever she realized why her predecessors had wanted to keep Genesis a secret. And why they had all failed.

When two more doctors walked past, the admiral went back to eavesdropping on the personnel who came and went in the corridor. She had learned a great deal during her time spent sitting in the hall. As she had suspected, the five recently admitted cases of radiation poisoning were very serious, because the radiation couldn't be identified and conventional treatments didn't work. The only ones left from twenty-some original cases were these five, all Deltans, who were known for being hardy. Still they were dying.

She had many questions she wanted to ask, but Nechayev admitted to herself that she was a patient here, not in charge. The staff had plenty to do without a nosy layperson butting in, asking dumb questions. She would eventually read a report, and soon she would be conducted into the inner sanctum herself. If she wanted information, she had to be patient and let the medical staff gather it.

They didn't conduct her into surgery until almost an hour later, and she could tell from the glum faces that something had gone wrong. "What is it?" she asked her lead surgeon, a Coridan named Heshreef.

"Nothing out of the ordinary," he lied. "We don't win them all, you know."

"The five Deltans," replied Nechayev knowingly. "I heard they're not going to make it."

"You're well informed as usual," said Dr. Heshreef with a forced smile. "One is already dead. Maybe some unconventional treatment will work on the others."

He motioned to the operating table, while he turned on a whirring piece of equipment with an overhead viewscreen. "Your turn, Admiral. Let's hope we have better luck with you. Nurse, prepare the anesthesia."

"Yes, Doctor."

"What are you doing for the Deltans?" asked Nechayev as she lay down on the table.

"We can't do much for them," admitted the doctor, studying the readouts on his equipment. "The cellular damage is just too extensive. They're all comatose. We've brought in a Vulcan mind-meld specialist to see if she can determine what they were doing when they were stricken. Without more data, we're helpless."

"I'd like to see that mind-meld," said Nechayev, rising from the table. Suddenly anything sounded better than surgery.

"And so you will . . . after your own procedure," answered Heshreef, pushing her back onto the table. "Nurse, anesthesia."

Suddenly, figures in white hooded suits were hovering over the admiral, and she felt a hypospray on her neck. Alynna Nechayev guessed that she had to relinquish control of her life for the next few hours, something she had never been good at doing. But if she was going to be a captain at the beck and call of the admiralty, she had to learn to do just that.

With so many beds filled, Captain Picard felt as if he were touring sickbay after a fierce battle in the Dominion war. Despite hearing Riker's report, he still wasn't sure what had happened on the *Barcelona*, except that one member of the boarding party was lost and the others were in sickbay with injuries. To top the bad news off, the ship's chief medical officer occupied one of the beds.

The first two beds were occupied by banged-up security officers, one of whom was wearing a cast from head to toe. The other had a phaser wound that had nearly taken off the top of his skull, by the looks of it.

Beverly was in the third bed, with Ogawa hovering over her. She gave the captain a wan smile as he approached, and he managed a similar anemic smile. "Hello, Beverly. I heard you injured your eyes. How do you feel?"

Beverly gave him as much of a shrug as her tired body could muster. "I'm okay, Jean-Luc. I'll be up in a minute . . . just having my final checkup."

"I expect you to use the eyedrops and get some rest,"

warned Ogawa, "or this won't be your final checkup."

"All right, I will," promised the doctor. As the two women continued to discuss her treatment, Picard's gaze drifted to the fourth bed, where an unknown Antosian lay in a stasis tent, unmoving. His sculpted hair, which was seldom out of place on any self-respecting Antosian, was a rat's nest, a far cry from the beautiful asymmetrical waves his race preferred. All this mayhem, plus the loss of Ensign Wapot, to bring a dying man back from a haunted ship.

On the fifth bed reclined a patient who was having his surgery performed by the chief engineer, Geordi La Forge. Picard slipped away from Beverly to check on Data's progress. "Will he live, Mr. La Forge?"

"Yes, sir," answered the engineer as he worked. "But this is only a temporary fix—when we have more time I want to replace that lateral servo amplifier. He was lucky."

Data frowned curiously at his friend. "A wound like this, and you would consider me *lucky?*"

"Lucky compared to what *could* have happened to you," answered La Forge. "It could have been worse."

"No, a type-3 phaser rifle on setting four would have produced an identical wound on any part of my anatomy," answered Data with certainty. "It could have been in a different place, but it could not have been worse." He cocked his head and added, "In fact, it could *not* have been in a different place, since my reaction speed is always identical, as is the aiming and firing ability of the static sentry device."

"Okay, Data, I give up," said Geordi with a laugh. "This wound could not be worse, and it was meant to be." With a cauterizing wand, he closed the incision in Data's upper arm.

"I'm not sure it was meant to be," said Picard with a scowl. "I'd like to know how it happened."

Data gave a concise report, filled with wonders even when told in the android's literal style. When he finished, Data glanced at the Antosian in the bed to his left. "Perhaps he could tell you why it happened, Captain, but I cannot. Although his efforts at self-defense endangered our party, they were certainly justified. To ascertain what happened to the *Barcelona* would require going over crew logs, computer records, and video logs without any guarantee of success. Unfortunately, the *Barcelona* is an unsafe place in which to work, as the anomalies we witnessed are swift-moving and lethal."

"Not to mention the radiation," said a voice. Picard turned to see Beverly Crusher standing beside him, apparently finished with her examination. She gazed thoughtfully at the injured Antosian in the stasis field and vowed, "I'm going to keep him alive until we get to a starbase."

"I'm sorry to say that may be a while, Doctor. I'm not going to tow the *Barcelona* anywhere near a population center," said Picard. "We'll keep it right here until we find out more about it. Data, can't we access the *Barcelona*'s records remotely?"

"Yes, sir, but breaking their security safeguards and accessing the computer will require approximately one hour of work on the *Barcelona*'s bridge. Longer if the computer is damaged. The final entity we encountered is able to pass through solid matter, and all of them moved with considerable speed. Standard shields and weaponry are ineffective against them."

"We can all testify to that," said Beverly, motioning to the beds filled with wounded. "Our injured will recover, given time." She gazed intently at the captain, her Irish green eyes looking more weary than usual. "I'm not so sure about the Antosian. He's not responding to treatment, and he's too weak for any experimental treatments."

"I'm sorry," said Picard gravely. "That ship is like a booby trap, and we have to guard it. I'm going to ask Starfleet to let us stay here until we answer some questions about the *Barcelona*. And your patient."

"I've got one answer," said a voice. They turned to see Dr. Pelagof, seated at a computer console in the corner. The Tellarite rose to his feet and strode toward the stasis tent, his large stomach leading the way. "I've identified him—Lieutenant Raynr Sleven. There were only two Antosians on board the *Barcelona*, and the other was female."

"Were they related?" asked Crusher.

"No, not according to records," answered the Tellarite. "As for his treatment, I've been thinking about something. The Antosians pioneered a drastic process called cellular metamorphosis, which we're unable to use on most species because of the side effects. But *he* might be able to withstand it. Offhand, I believe that's the only thing that will save him."

"I only know the theory," said Crusher uncertainly. "I've never done it."

"I have," said Lieutenant Ogawa, stepping into the conversational circle. "I assisted when I was fresh out of school, in the last clinical trial on humans. They were all terminal cases."

"And what were the results?" asked Beverly.

"Same as always. Great recovery rates, but unacceptable mental problems, among other things."

"Excuse me," asked Picard. "What are the full side effects of cellular metamorphosis?"

Everyone looked to Ogawa. "It cures anything," she answered, "probably even systemic failure from unidentified radiation poisoning. We didn't know anything about it until a hundred years ago, when the Antosians treated a certain Captain Garth."

"Garth of Izar," said Picard with awe in his voice. "He went mad—"

"And was able to shape-shift, impersonate other people," replied the nurse. "Spontaneous postmorphosis syndrome is unusual, but it occurs in around twenty percent of patients who undergo cellular metamorphosis, in all species. It's impossible for humans to have the power to shape-shift without having mental problems, and spontaneous postmorphosis really speeds up our metabolism, causing us to age rapidly. I wouldn't consider it for a human, but an Antosian—"

All eyes turned to the still figure in the stasis tent, who already looked like a body in a shroud.

Dr. Crusher gazed at the vital signs projected above the patient's bed and frowned. "We can keep him in stasis for now, but his cells will continue to slowly degenerate. We could try this procedure, but not if we're hit with any more injuries."

"I'll try not to send any more of the crew your way," said Picard with a thin smile. "I believe Data will be the only one going back to the *Barcelona*. We also need to have a service of some kind for Ensign Wapot. I assume that all of you who were there believe his disappearance to be permanent?"

Ogawa nodded quickly, and Beverly nodded more slowly. Data sat up in bed, with a quizzical look on his face. "We do not have enough information to answer that question. However, if you are looking for a 'gut' instinct based on our visual observation . . . no, he is not coming back."

"Okay," said Crusher, gazing wistfully at Captain Picard, "you'll schedule a funeral, and I'll schedule a procedure."

"It's ironic," said a voice behind them. The crowd in the middle of sickbay now all turned to look at Geordi La Forge.

"What is ironic?" asked Data.

Geordi's brow furrowed above his pale bionic eyes. "Cellular metamorphosis . . . it's one of the processes we identified in the Genesis matrix. The Genesis emitter couldn't work without it."

four

Prylar Yorka stood impatiently in the drizzling rain outside the rusted corrugated warehouse, waiting to get in. The Bajoran monk felt exposed in the blackness of the rainy night, even though two loyal acolytes stood at his side. That was mainly because of the object he clutched in his shivering arms—the box given him by the spirit of Kai Opaka. Although he still he no idea what it was—and was afraid to open it—he was certain it had great power. In his fantasies, he even imagined it was one of the missing Orbs of the Prophets—perhaps an Orb no one knew about.

Despite the empowering presence of the object, this was very discourteous treatment, forcing him to stand out here in the rain. Yorka understood the necessity of privacy—he was certain that the authorities of Torga IV were looking for him, as were the Romulan assassins. But why not let him stand where it was dry? This whole process of flight had been much more difficult than he anticipated. There was a restriction on travel, a shortage of ships, and a long, official waiting list for departures.

It had taken begging and outright blackmail for the former vedek to secure passage for the three of them and their luggage. Plus they had lost a whole day, most of it spent in hiding. That was another humbling aspect of this misadventure.

Still it will be worth it, Yorka told himself as he clutched the case to his ample torso. *Everything in my life has been leading up to this!* Yorka heard some scuffling on the sidewalk, and he and his small entourage whirled around with alarm. The Bajorans were ready to bolt into the darkness, until they saw an unprepossessing figure with big ears and a shiny skull cap come splashing through the puddles.

Yorka peered curiously at the approaching stranger, for it was not a stranger but someone he had met before. Yes, the night the kai had come to him with her gift, this little Ferengi had been in the temple, with his three wives. What was he doing here?

The Ferengi grinned, obviously recognizing him, too. "Ah, Prylar Yorka, I see that we have the same idea. I don't blame you for getting away—after that fracas at your temple."

"Chellac, isn't it?" asked the monk. "When I last saw you, you were in difficult circumstances."

"I took your advice, and I thought about the rules you quoted me." The Ferengi smiled blissfully, showing an array of jagged teeth. "You saved me, Prylar Yorka. In time, I'll recover my losses, and there's plenty of money to be made in a disaster of this scope. Opportunity is everywhere! Many people think I'm dead, which is always useful. I'm eternally grateful for your wisdom, Prylar."

"I'm glad I helped," said the Bajoran. "Where are your lovely wives?"

He shrugged. "Well, that's how I got out of my circumstances. I looked around to see what I had of value, and all I had were the clothes on my back and my wives. I hated to lose them, but sometimes you must divest in order to gain. Now let me ask you something: Why are you standing out here in the rain?"

Boldly, the Ferengi stepped up to the metal door and banged loudly, causing Yorka to cringe from the noise. A small window on the door slid open, and two beady eyes peered out. "It will be a few minutes!" growled a voice.

"No, it won't be!" snapped Chellac. "We are paying customers—paying exorbitant prices—and it is inexcusably stupid to keep people waiting when they are trying to give you money! A robber could come by and steal our money before *you* have a chance to steal it. Did you ever think of that?"

The little window slammed shut, but they could hear bolts being drawn and latches clacking open. Chellac folded his arms and looked disgustedly at the Bajorans. "In a tragedy, even the worst businessman can make money. Terrible."

Finally the door creaked open, and a beefy hand loomed out of the darkness to usher them inside. They stepped into a vast warehouse that featured four pools of light and handfuls of people in far-flung corners. The only light in their vicinity came from a single portable light stick. In one pool of illumination, a short line of people waited to step onto a single-person transporter platform, which was powered by numerous gel-packs strung behind it like the tentacles of some ocean creature.

"Be quiet," cautioned the doorman in a raspy voice. "The group ahead of you is still leaving." To emphasize his point, the beefy guard stepped into the dim pool of light and glowered at them with a pale, weathered face. From his dress and accent, Yorka deduced that he was Angosian.

"How much are you paying for all those gel-packs?" asked Chellac.

"What do you mean, how much am I paying?" The brutish Angosian frowned at him.

"Just what I said. You must use a ton of those power packs trying to get around the official waiting list. Moreover, you shouldn't be in this building, we both know that. So you're probably paying too much for power. Besides, those Starfleet packs are junk—they leak all over, or mutate into weird biomass. Now if you had Ferengi gel-packs—or better yet, Orion gel-packs—you could double your output for half the price."

Prylar Yorka tuned out the rest of their conversation. He had noticed that in one of the pools of light there was a replicator, and he wondered whether it was also for hire. "You stay here," he whispered to his two acolytes. "Stand in the shadows, so they won't see I'm missing."

While the doorman was occupied, Yorka slipped into the darkness and ambled across an expanse of dusty floor until he reached the next lit area, where two hulking Centaurians sat around a replicator. The kiosk-sized device looked as if it had been yanked from an office wall, with bits of plaster still clinging to it.

"Need something for your trip?" asked one of them. "This here's a tool replicator, but we've programmed more articles into it. No food, though."

Yorka held out his gleaming metal box. "Can you replicate this?"

"You want us to duplicate your luggage?" asked the Centaurian doubtfully.

"Yes," answered Yorka. "Contents and all, without opening it, without saving the pattern. Can you do that?"

"It will cost you," said the vendor. "Without knowing what's in there, we can't guarantee an exact duplicate."

"Would you guarantee it, if I opened it up?" asked Yorka.

"No, probably not." They quickly arrived at a price, because Yorka didn't want to negotiate. The meager savings he had amassed from the funds which floated through the temple were of no concern to him now. He didn't think he would need money, because he was going to be exalted by his people.

When Yorka received the replicate, he shoved a small piece of putty into one of its narrow hinges. It was a small thing, not likely to be noticed by anyone else, but the monk would know which was the fake. He still didn't know if the new device would function as well as the old one, because he didn't know what the original did. Until he was sure he was perfectly safe from his pursuers, he couldn't risk inspecting his prize.

There was a good chance that it would do something which drew attention, so he'd go someplace isolated, even more isolated than Torga IV.

Yorka returned to his traveling companions and handed the fake box to one of them before the Angosian guard noticed him. The big doorman scowled. "Where were you?"

"I took a moment of solitude to pray," answered Yorka.

The Angosian grunted under his breath. "Well, you're next. Time to pay up, but only half the price you were quoted."

"Only half?" asked Yorka puzzledly, reaching for his purse.

"Professional courtesy," said the Ferengi, nudging him in the ribs. "We're doing business with these folks now. I gave them our best discount, too . . . on the gel-packs."

"Of course," answered Yorka with a jovial laugh. "I forget that my partner here can never go anywhere without conducting business. Sometimes I'm content just to enjoy the trip."

"That's why I'm the salesman, and you're the engineer," replied Chellac with a snaggle-toothed grin.

After they had paid their fare and were walking toward the transporter platform, Chellac nudged the Bajoran again. "You know," he whispered, "I *will* be your partner."

Yorka blinked in surprise. "I . . . I don't need a partner."

"Oh, I think you do, because you have something of value." He pointed to the box. "You had *one* of those, and now you've got *two*. These thieves wouldn't replicate a dead vole for less than top price, so you must have something of value. Considering what happened in your temple, I'd say people are willing to kill for it."

"I appreciate the discount you got us," said Yorka, feeling possessive of his prize. "But this is none of your business."

The Ferengi shrugged. "It's a long flight to the

Meldrar System. You have time to get to know me better and realize that you *do* need me."

A statuesque, dark-haired Vulcan woman of indeterminate age turned and regarded Admiral Nechayev coldly. "Can I help you with something? Are you looking for another room?"

"No, I'm in the right room," answered the admiral, stepping cautiously into the semiprivate quarters of two comatose Deltans. There weren't very many people who intimidated Nechayev, but this Vulcan might be one of them. "You are Teska, the expert called by Dr. Heshreef?"

"Yes. And you are obviously a patient here."

"I am," answered the human, gingerly touching her face, which still tingled from the procedure. She didn't know or care how it looked. "I'm also an admiral, Alynna Nechayev, and this is a Starfleet hospital."

"I requested privacy," said Teska.

Nechayev sunk into a chair with a sigh. "You have a very interesting record. Ambassador Spock is your uncle, and you spent your younger years on Earth. From an early age, you showed an aptitude for the mind-meld, and you're a highly regarded priestess back home. Yet you still work with us. The number of commendations you have is extraordinary."

"You left out that I am married to a Romulan," she remarked dryly.

"But how long has it been since you've seen him? Six years?"

"I see him every seven years," answered the Vulcan matter-of-factly. "He knows when to come home."

"I'm sure," said Nechayev, her new face blushing slightly. "Has anyone told you? . . . . Our information shows that Hasmek may be dead."

Teska raised an eyebrow. "Then I will have to take a new mate when the time comes. Is this a job interview, Admiral? I hope not, because I already have a job, which is to communicate with these injured officers. Now, if you will excuse me, you have to leave."

Nechayev pointed around the room. "There are devices everywhere, making a video log of this. I could walk down the hallway and watch you, but I was hoping you would let me stay. I promise not to move from here or say a word. Please, it would mean a great deal to me."

The Vulcan nodded. "Very well, Admiral. But please do not interfere with me, even if I appear distressed."

"All right."

Teska stepped between the two beds containing the sick Deltans, and she pulled back the tents to look at them, one by one. "Since you are here, Admiral, what can you tell me about these two?"

"They were part of a work crew at the Talan Shipyard, which was near the path of the Genesis Wave. We evacuated the place and ordered all the ships pressed into service, but there was one running behind schedule. As the wave approached, we realized it would miss the shipyard, so the crew was allowed to stay behind to finish the work. When they were found, they were as you see them."

Teska nodded her regal head and knelt on the ground between the two beds. She slipped a hand under the protective covering of each patient and placed long fingers at precise spots on their faces, melding with both at once. The Vulcan's head jerked back as if she were slapped in the face, and she writhed in apparent agony. Nechayev was on the edge of her seat, ready to help, when she noticed that the Vulcan's hands never lost contact with the comatose patients. Teska was still in control.

Finally the Vulcan slumped forward, maintaining contact with both the Deltans. She looked drained but content, as if she had conquered whatever demons she had initially faced.

Teska remained in a kind of trance with her eyes closed as she cried, "The fear . . . the utter dread! *What* are they? *Where* are they! Here they come again, with that blinding beam. Shields . . . phasers . . . not working. Death, be merciful. Evacuate! Into the pods. Getting weaker . . . can't escape. They're gone for now. Another night . . . just hang on."

She swallowed hard and bowed her head. "We want to die. We can't see anything but horrors that shouldn't exist. They haunt even our death memories. Can't live . . . in this existence."

With a grunt, Teska pulled her hands away from the Deltans and slumped forward onto the floor. Nechayev was again tempted to help her, but she remembered the Vulcan's admonition not to intercede.

Finally Teska stood and composed herself, turning back into the regal Vulcan who must look splendid in her ceremonial robes. "That was difficult," she said hoarsely.

"Why?" asked the admiral, rising to her feet and stepping closer.

"Because the attack was very frightening and brutal."

"Attack?" asked Nechayev with concern. "I didn't hear about any signs of an attack."

"That was how *they* perceived it," replied Teska, looking back at the patients. "To them, it was an attack. At any rate, they were not performing any tasks or working with any material that might have caused the poisoning. It came from an external source—from a kind of shining rift—along with the monsters."

"Monsters?"

"Yes," said the Vulcan dispassionately. "Quite horrible monsters. They were bad enough to frighten one to death. Human mythos is full of such creatures, but these are not humans. In fact, Deltans are not overly given to fantasy and wild leaps of imagination. To scare these two as they have been scared—it is beyond my ability to describe how it happened. Still I will file a report. These are quite literal monsters, not figurative ones."

"Monsters did this to them?" asked the admiral, frowning at the comatose patients. "And fright?"

"Yes, and letting them die would be merciful," added the Vulcan.

The door chimed, and the admiral called, "Come!"

A young lieutenant walked in, brandishing a padd in his hand. "Excuse me, Admiral, but we've just received urgent orders for you."

"Teska, please don't leave yet," said Nechayev, motioning to the Vulcan to stay. She took the padd and nodded to the lieutenant. "But you can leave."

"Yes, Sir." He hurried off.

The admiral frowned as she read the missive from Starfleet Command. "Hmmm, they only busted me down one star, so I'm still an admiral. But I have a ship, the *Sequoia*, and a destination. Teska, would you consider shipping out with me as a mission specialist?"

"What is the mission?" asked the Vulcan.

"To help us clean up Lomar, the homeworld of the species who unleashed the Genesis Wave on us," answered Nechayev. "The enemy is gone, but they left behind extensive underground facilities. The Romulans ransacked the place before we got there, but we may still find clues to study. That's not what I need you for, though."

The admiral began to pace the hospital room, feeling the tension in her own jaw. "One of our tasks is to revive the humanoid slaves left in suspended animation—and question them, if possible. There are hundreds of them, and I hear that most are very weak. Many were destroyed during the fighting. It's been difficult just to keep them alive."

"Hence the need for mind-melds."

"Yes," said Nechayev with a sigh. "It's similar to what you've been doing here, only on a bigger scale. Other Vulcans are already on site, helping us."

She glanced back at the two Deltans, who were as quiet as corpses. "Death is still on duty, it seems. I'm not saying this will be pleasant work, but it's absolutely necessary."

"When do we leave?" asked Teska.

"You'll go, then?" replied the admiral, happily surprised. "That's excellent. I want to get settled in as the captain of the *Sequoia* and take her on a test flight. Shall we say thirty-two hours from now?"

"That will give me time to pack and prepare my report," answered the tall Vulcan. "Good day, Admiral."

Teska sauntered out of the room, apparently unaffected by the raw emotions and horrific images she had experienced during the mind-meld. Nechayev wondered whether anyone could really see what she had described without losing her sanity. If anyone could, it would be that icy Vulcan.

Teska will be invaluable, decided the admiral, *because we need to put panic behind us and think logically. Now there's just one more specialist I need to recruit.*

The Genesis Wave had passed, but in its wake lay destruction, danger, and secrets, now scattered to the winds like confetti. How much had gotten out about the Genesis technology? How much did the Romulans know? Nechayev could feel the peril as surely as she could feel her altered face still tingling from the surgery.

Lieutenant Alyssa Ogawa staggered wearily into her quarters, surprised that all the lights were on. Even though it was the equivalent of the middle of the night, little Suzi's voice rang out, "Mommy!"

The six-year-old came charging around the corner from the sitting area, and she plowed into Alyssa's legs, gripping her in a fierce and happy hug. She was followed by the ship's counselor, Deanna Troi, wiping sleepiness from her eyes.

Ogawa hugged her dark-haired, freckled daughter, the freckles reminding her of Andrew. "Are you all right? I thought you'd be asleep." She looked quizzically at Counselor Troi.

The Betazoid shrugged. "She contacted me a few hours ago, said she couldn't sleep, and that you were going to be gone for a long time. So I came down here."

"I'm sorry," said Ogawa, "I checked on her from sickbay, and she looked like she was asleep."

"I can pretend to be asleep," admitted Suzi, "but sometimes I'm not."

"Well, I got a good nap." Troi stretched her arms luxuriantly. "And I got some reading done before that."

"I owe you one," said Ogawa, standing and holding her daughter's hand. "The procedure went longer than expected."

"How did it go?" asked the Betazoid.

Alyssa opened her mouth to answer, but Suzi piped up, "My mom says that cellular metamufus is going to drive her patient crazy."

"I hope not," said the nurse, "but it's a possibility. On the other hand, we've given him a good chance to live, much better than he had before. Since we used a process perfected on Antosians, I'm hopeful he'll avoid the worst side effects. It shouldn't take long to find out."

The counselor moved toward the door. "I'll have to stop by sickbay to see him. Will you two make your appointment at seventeen hundred hours?"

"Yes, we'll be there," Ogawa assured her. "Thanks again."

After the door shut behind Deanna Troi, the mother turned to her daughter, who was beaming as if nothing had happened. "You told me you could sleep by yourself," she said softly.

"Well, when I'm asleep, I can sleep by myself," answered Suzi. "But when I'm awake, I don't like to be awake by myself. After Daddy comes home, you can work as long as you want."

"That's right," said Alyssa, kneeling down and hugging her daughter before she could see the tears welling in her eyes. "When Daddy comes home, it will be a lot easier." She wiped her eyes quickly before she pulled away from Suzi.

"Tell me again where Daddy is?" asked the six-year-old.

"I don't know exactly," said Alyssa, strolling to the food replicator. "Are you hungry?"

"You know where he went, right?"

"I know he went to help some people survive the Genesis Wave. It's only been a few days, and there are a lot of places for Starfleet to check."

"He is okay, isn't he?"

Ogawa froze in front of the replicator, her hunger for food dissipating. "As we discussed with Counselor Troi, your father is considered missing. That means we don't know where he is . . . or how he is."

"But *you* know, don't you, Mommy?" asked Suzi, coming close and taking her hand. "You would know if Daddy's all right."

She mustered a smile and knelt down to face her young daughter. "Yes, and I think he's still helping people. He's probably just as worried about us as we are about him."

"Yes, probably!" said Suzi with a giggle. "He's such a worrywart."

"I have an idea. After Daddy gets back, let's go visit Grandma and Grandpa."

"Yay!" exclaimed Suzi, clapping her hands together. "What a great idea—when can we go? When? When?"

"Soon," she answered, thinking that would be true either way. "I know you miss Grandma and Grandpa, but you don't mind that you're not living with them, do you?"

"No, not really." Suzi frowned in thought. "But it gets a little lonely here—this place needs more kids. More grandparents."

"I agree," answered Alyssa with a smile. "There used to be a time when the old *Enterprise* was full of families. But then we had wars and too many emergencies for all those families to stay. But they'll be coming back soon . . . more and more of them. You're just one of the first children to come home."

"I know," agreed the child. "I just want all of us to be together."

Sniffing back a tear, Ogawa turned to the replicator. "I think I'll have some miso soup. What about you?"

Suzi shook her head and rubbed her eyes wearily. "Can I sleep with you tonight? I won't be a bed hog, I promise."

Alyssa nodded. "Sure, Kiddo. Just get in bed and wait for me. I'll be right there."

"I'm glad you're home, Mommy." After another quick hug, Suzi padded off to bed.

"Me too, Sweetie, me too." Still she wondered how long it would be before she could admit that Andrew would not be coming home.

When Captain Picard strode onto the bridge of the *Enterprise*, he nodded to Commander Riker and looked at the viewscreen. The *Barcelona* continued to float in the glittering starscape, looking deceptively peaceful.

"Report," said the captain.

"Situation unchanged," answered Riker, folding his hands behind his back, "except for sensor readings, which change constantly. The last time we looked, there were *five* lifesign readings on the *Barcelona*, and combined radiation was up six percent."

The captain's lips thinned into a frown, and he paced behind Data at the ops console. "You've had some time to think about it, so does anyone have a recommendation on how to proceed? What about an excursion by yourself, Mr. Data?"

"I have considered the matter," answered the android, "and I have discussed it with Commander La Forge. He feels that my best chance of survival would be to use the Brahms radiation suit. It would somewhat hinder my movements, but I should have enough dexterity to operate the computer.

"My concern is that our sensors and tricorders do not recognize all the entities which inhabit that ship. Either our sensors are faulty, or the number of entities is in flux. Either way, I could be taken by surprise with no time to escape and no means of defense."

"If your suit fails," said Picard, "then we've lost you on a gamble."

Riker leaned into the conversation. "I don't think it's worth the risk to send anyone else over there. We could transport major components of the computer off the *Barcelona* and study them over here."

"Yes, and what else might we transport off?" asked the captain. "Plus we still have to send people over to set up the signal amplifiers. We were lucky to get that one survivor. I'm not comfortable with dismantling the *Barcelona* and bringing pieces on board until we have a better idea what caused this."

Data cocked his head. "If we reject both of these

options and similar plans, the only alternative is to make the entities depart. Then the *Barcelona* would be a safe place to conduct an investigation."

Both Riker and Picard looked expectantly at the android, as if he would tell them the magical solution in the next breath. But Data shook his head. "I do not have enough information on the entities to devise a plan to drive them away."

"Then let's prepare a probe," said Picard. "In fact, several probes. We can beam them over and let them collect information on the entities. Perhaps there are patterns to their movements, which we can use to our advantage. I'd rather lose probes than crew members."

"Yes, Sir," answered Data. He rose to his feet, and Riker signaled for a replacement at the ops console. "Four probes should be sufficient until we obtain initial data. I could transport the probes from a shuttlecraft, allowing the *Enterprise* to maintain—"

"Captain!" announced an urgent voice behind him. The bridge crew turned to see the Andorian peering wide-eyed at his tactical console. "Three starships are coming out of warp sixty degrees off the port bow."

"Are they Starfleet?" asked Riker.

The dour Andorian held up his hand for a moment, then he grimaced. "No, Sir. They're Romulan."

"On screen," ordered the captain.

Three mammoth *D'deridex*-class warbirds slowed to a stop in front of them, looking like emerald-green vultures with their beak-like bows and hunched wings. Picard already had shields up to protect against radiation, but he wasn't going to progress to an alert. He had to keep this contact on a friendly basis. After all, the

Romulans had aided them in evacuating planets and ending the Genesis threat.

"Hail them," ordered Picard.

"A recorded message is already coming through," said the Andorian, working his board.

At once, the viewscreen switched to the image of a striking female Romulan, standing erect on her bridge. She wore the inflated shoulders and self-inflated air of most Romulan officers. "*Enterprise*, I am Commander Kaylena of the *Javlek,* also commander of this task force. We have reason to believe that you possess phase-shifting technology which belongs to the Romulan Star Empire. You have one hour to turn over this technology, plus documents related to it. Comply, or you will be boarded. Depending on our scanner results, we may require permission to board your ship and search for said technology. End transmission."

The overhead image went back to a view of the three massive warbirds, which filled the screen impressively.

"They must mean the Brahms suit," said Riker. "I can't think of any other technology of theirs that we have. We have no cloaking devices."

The captain turned to Data. "Ready the probes for the *Barcelona.*"

"Yes, Sir." The android nodded and hurried toward the turbolift.

"Tactical, forward the message from the Romulans to Starfleet and report our situation. Request assistance."

"Yes, Sir," answered the Andorian as he plied his console.

"Captain, there are no Starfleet ships within a day's travel," noted Riker.

The captain tugged thoughtfully on his black tunic. "We chose this place because it's isolated. We can't outfight them, and we can't outrun them. I think you had better gather up the Brahms suits, plus the records."

As Riker headed for the turbolift door, he grumbled. "Do you suppose if they had any Genesis technology, they would turn it over to us?"

"It never hurts to ask," answered the captain thoughtfully. "Perhaps we should find out more about the *Javlek*."

five

"Listen, what do I have to do to make you realize that I'm completely sincere?" asked the Ferengi, eyeing the three Bajorans who sat across from him in the mess hall of the freighter. The *Bateret* was on its second day of slogging through space, but they were nearing their first port of call.

"I really only want to look after your interests and repay the kindness you have shown me," said Chellac, holding out his hands.

"How can we trust him?" asked the younger acolyte. "He just sold his wife!"

The elder Yorka shook his head forcefully. "That is indeed hard to understand much less forgive. But we all do terrible things in time of need. Look at how we abandoned our brethren in the shrine. I even turned off those lights, knowing there would be injuries. These are times of great change, and we have to maintain open minds."

"I don't believe him," muttered the other acolyte, a

sour-faced zealot. "He doesn't follow the will of the Prophets. What if he tries to steal it from us?"

Chellac opened his elegant vest. "Look, I'm unarmed, and I don't have any way to overpower you. I don't have a ship or any confederates. You know my circumstances— they are the same as your own. We may be able to travel expensively, bucking the restrictions for a few more days, but eventually we're going to run out of money."

That remark hit home, he could tell from their downcast faces. So the salesman pointed to the gleaming box and pressed his advantage. "You're going to need a way to promote this and raise some money with it. And you're going to have to do it fast but secretly, because you know people are trying to kill you for it."

"That's precisely why we don't want some loud-mouthed Ferengi—" began the young acolyte.

"Quiet!" snapped Yorka. Fortunately, there was nobody else in the mess hall with them. The religious leader gazed intently at Chellac, as if measuring him against a congress of saints. "I need more than your word. Can you give me one good reason why I should take you into our confidence?"

The Ferengi met the gaze of the big monk. "I know you don't have any idea what's in that precious box of yours, and neither do I. We're all operating on faith— faith in *you*, Prylar. I feel compelled to help you, and I don't really know why."

That must have struck the right note, because the Bajoran's face softened. "We need to open the gift," he whispered. "But someplace quiet . . . isolated . . . with no one knowing."

"Well, Meldrar I is a sleepy place," said Chellac. "The

biggest employer is the penal colony, and you wouldn't confuse that with Deep Space Nine. I have an idea what we can do."

When the Ferengi hunched forward conspiratorially, even the acolytes who had opposed him leaned closer to hear his plan. "Our crew says there are commercial tours of the colony by shuttlecraft. While this ship is off-loading their cargo, maybe we can get one of these shuttlecraft and head around to the other side of the moon. It's deserted. I'm sure there must be somebody we can bribe to do this. Let me handle it."

He gave Yorka a snaggle-toothed smile. "Partner."

"Commander Kaylena of the *Javlek* wishes to speak with you, Captain," reported the tactical officer on the bridge of the *Enterprise*.

Captain Picard awarded himself a brief smile, then turned serious as he strode to his command chair in the center of the bridge. Seated beside him was Counselor Troi, quietly concentrating on the viewscreen. "Put her on," ordered the captain.

The beautiful Romulan appeared overhead, and her dark eyes smoldered with anger under her impassive expression. She was surrounded by glowering officers in their brocaded finery, but Picard found himself watching only Commander Kaylena.

"What is the meaning of your message?" she demanded. "Are you mocking me? You wish *us* to turn over Genesis records and emitters before you'll return the technology you *stole* from us? What makes you think we have any such devices?"

Picard tried to muster some charm. "I assure you, it's

a legitimate request, and I would never mock you. According to our records, the *Javlek* was one of the first ships to arrive on the planet Lomar, where you wiped out the moss creatures and searched their underground facility. It's a good guess that you retrieved Genesis hardware and data. I believe this is an equitable exchange."

"You're wrong. We do not have any of this Genesis technology." Kaylena lifted her chin defiantly, and Picard could see a wisp of dark hair on her neck that was out of place. Otherwise, her elegant coif and demeanor were perfect. "I suggest you prepare to be boarded."

"I was going to suggest that we meet face-to-face," answered the captain, remaining cordial. "Wouldn't that be simpler than bringing your whole crew? I fully expect to hand over the radiation suits, but I've got to say that you've set yourself an impossible task. We distributed millions of these suits. They're all over the quadrant by now, and everybody has seen how well they work. You can't bully every ship you meet—or start a war—just to collect a few suits. Why exactly do you want to search our ship?"

"You have thirty more minutes to comply. End transmission." The viewscreen went dark for a moment, then switched to a split-screen view of the Romulans in one half and the derelict *Barcelona* in the other.

"I think she's lying," said Deanna Troi, folding her arms. "And I don't like her either."

"I have a feeling she's just following orders," said Picard with sympathy. He turned to tactical. "Go to yellow alert and contact Starfleet."

"Yes, Sir."

*   *   *

Dr. Beverly Crusher dozed in the chair beside her Antosian patient, Raynr Sleven, until her elbow abruptly slid off the armrest. She blinked awake and looked around; seeing the sleeping figure in the bed, Beverly remembered the radical procedure he had undergone. The cellular metamorphosis was presumably successful, thanks to Ogawa's experience. At any rate, he was still breathing ambient air without any difficulty.

Crusher craned her neck to check the vital signs on the display over his bed. They were normal, and apparently stable, which was amazing considering that he was in stasis only a few hours ago, much closer to death than life. Now if he would just regain consciousness and give them a glimpse into his mental state, the doctor could sleep easily. They had various means to revive him, especially in his improved condition, but she didn't want to risk any of them. The dire warnings of side effects had her worried, and she didn't want to mask these effects or aggravate them with other treatments. Cellular metamorphosis was risky enough without adding anything else to the mix.

Sleven was now assigned to a private room in sickbay, away from the other casualties, who were gradually recovering. Kosavar would be released in the morning. Crusher had isolated the Antosian in case he took a turn for the worse, or exhibited the behaviors they had been warned about. She had little idea how long recovery ought to take, or why she was still sitting here, except that she was overly curious.

"If only you'd wake up," she muttered, "I could go home and sleep in a real bed. Although it's not like there's anyone to go home to." Beverly rose to her feet and began to pace wearily in the small room.

The doctor stopped and considered the dark-haired male, who looked like an honest, forthright character with a strong jaw and good muscle tone. Of course, he might wake up stark raving mad with a tendency to shape-shift spontaneously. Even without the side effects, he might be suffering trauma from his ordeal on the *Barcelona*. The doctor had expected Deanna Troi to stop by, but she knew the counselor had been called to the bridge. So they would have to cope without the counselor. Sedatives in various strengths were close at hand, but Beverly hoped they wouldn't have to use any of the hyposprays.

"I was in your situation just eight days ago," she said to the sleeping Antosian. "I was lying in sickbay, unconscious, just like you. Something alien—unexpected—had taken over my ship. But the worst part was yet to come. Waking up healthy and happy was the worst, because I learned that my son, Wes, had not returned. I was still alone. His presence had been like a dream . . . a good dream from my perspective, even if it was fake.

"You haven't had a good dream, I know that. And waking up is going to be a pleasant surprise. Then you'll be alone—all your crewmates and friends gone—and you'll have to deal with it. Just remember, I can relate to you. Be thankful that when you awaken, you'll find things are better than in your nightmare."

"Water . . ." he rasped weakly, licking his lips. Crusher stopped and blinked at her patient in surprise, then went to the nearby replicator and ordered some ice chips. Raynr Sleven had received intravenous fluids, so he wasn't truly dehydrated, but she could understand why he felt thirsty.

When she returned to his bedside, she placed a few chips in his mouth with a spoon and studied his vital signs overhead. The Antosian looked strong and healthy, without any outward indication of the ordeal he had gone through.

"I'm Dr. Beverly Crusher," she said gently, "and you're in sickbay on the *Enterprise*. You've been rescued, and treated."

"The others . . . the others!" he rasped, trying to sit up.

She firmly pushed him back down, feeling brawny shoulder muscles under his shift. "We didn't find any others, just you and one dead. Don't try to tell me now what happened. We have a pretty good idea . . . having been over there. You'll get a chance to talk, but wait until you're stronger. You'll meet our command staff."

He nodded wearily. "The ice tasted good . . . thank you."

"You can drink more and eat solid food when you wake up. Right now, you should try to sleep." Beverly patted his hand and rose from the side of the bed.

"I . . . I don't remember much of it," he said with surprise. "Maybe that's good."

"Maybe it is," she agreed, moving toward the door. "Good-bye, Lieutenant Sleven."

"Raynr," he said softly. "Please call me Raynr. And thank you, Dr. Crusher. I don't know how you did it—I must have been nearly dead."

She gave him a thoughtful smile. "After you've rested, I want to discuss your treatment. I also want you to report to me any unusual symptoms you have. *Anything*. Is that understood?"

"Yes, Doctor," Raynr Sleven answered dutifully. He touched his unkempt rat's nest of ebony hair and his unshaven face. "My appearance—"

"I'll send our barber by," said Crusher. "He's Bolian, but the Antosians I know swear by him."

"Thank you, Dr. Crusher, for everything." The tousled lieutenant beamed at her with a look of adulation.

"It's been an hour and ten minutes," complained Deanna Troi, pacing across the command platform on the bridge. She stopped and threw a disgruntled gaze at the image of three Romulan warbirds on the viewscreen. "Our friends aren't very punctual."

"Counselor, may I speak with you in my ready room?" said Captain Picard, motioning her toward his private office. The door whooshed open, and he stepped inside with the Betazoid on his heels. She was still smoldering over some injustice or other, and he wasn't sure what it could be.

"You don't seem yourself," he remarked. "Is something troubling you?"

Troi stopped her pacing and rubbed her forehead. "I didn't think so, except for the usual lack of sleep. But there is something about the *Barcelona* . . . and whatever it harbors. It gives me a feeling of dread so overpowering that I respond in anger. And it seems to be getting worse. I've probably transferred some of this angst onto the Romulans, but I don't like the way they're treating us."

"Neither do I," admitted Picard, tight-lipped. "But we've got to stall for time as best we can until reinforcements arrive."

With a sigh, she let her tense shoulders slump. "I've been meaning to go to sickbay. Maybe this would be a good time to check on the survivor and our other casualties."

"Go ahead," said Picard with an encouraging smile. "I don't think your opinion of the Romulan commander is going to change any time soon."

The companel on his desk chirped, and the Andorian's urgent voice broke in. "Captain Picard, we have just gotten a message from the *Javlek*. Because they have received no answers to their hails from the *Barcelona*, they are boarding her."

"Tell them to stop!" insisted Picard, rushing toward the door. "It's too dangerous."

"They aren't answering hails," reported the Andorian.

Captain Picard strode back onto the bridge and addressed his tactical officer directly. "Have they actually started sending people over?"

"Yes," answered the Andorian as he studied his board. "Transports are in progress from the *Petrask*, which must be their troop ship. It's quite a contingent—three squads of eight each."

"Open a channel," said the captain, stepping in front of his command chair. Troi eased into the seat behind him and seemed as composed and confident as ever.

"Commander Kaylena of the *Javlek*," pleaded Picard, "you must stop sending troops over to the *Barcelona*. They're all in danger for their lives. Not from us, but from certain anomalies. Plus there are deadly levels of unidentified radiation on that ship. Please, Commander, listen to me and withdraw your boarding parties." The captain looked expectantly at his tactical officer.

The tall Andorian shook his head. "No response, no acknowledgment."

"It's their funeral," said Deanna Troi with unexpected harshness. She swiveled in her chair and regarded him icily. "This would be a good chance to escape."

He tapped his comm panel. "Bridge to Data."

"Yes, Captain."

"Delay the probes, and return to the bridge immediately."

"Yes, Sir."

Captain Picard stared grimly at the viewscreen, where four vessels lolled in the deceptive tranquillity of space. "Tactical, keep sending them my last message. And go to red alert."

Centurion Tarsek stood motionless in the unfamiliar corridor of the Starfleet ship, with red lights casting an eerie pall over his eight-man squad. He was glad of their black environmental suits, which no doubt hid the fear on their faces. The haughty gray-haired warrior didn't want to see fear. These fresh troops had tasted killing in the planet with the moss creatures, but that wasn't the same as a humanoid enemy, especially one as devious as Terrans.

They were in the rear, outside the aft torpedo room, where scanners had discovered two life-forms. Tarsek checked the portable scanner on his wrist to see which way the life-forms were headed, and he picked them up immediately. They were stationary in the torpedo launcher, a logical place to protect if a ship still wanted to maintain some offensive capability.

He gave the signal for the scouts to move out, and his

two bravest rushed down the corridor to confront danger. Without breaking communications silence, he used hand signals to move his squad forward, bringing up the rear himself. The old centurion had a war wound in his left knee joint, and he swore it got sore when there was danger around. Right now it was no worse than usual; he could have been taking his morning walk in the greenhouse on the ship.

Tarsek followed his squad down the red-hued corridor until they reached a locked hatchway that was guarded by a recognition system. His scouts were already rigging plasma explosive charges; but Centurion Tarsek felt magnanimous, so he called out, "Inside the torpedo room, listen to me! Open the door and give yourselves up. We only want to search the ship and question you briefly. You will not be harmed!"

The centurion waited for his men to finish rigging the charges. They nodded to him and moved back down the corridor, along with the rest of the squad. "Call out, bang on the door, or do something!" he ordered. "Or we will use force to gain access. Surrender now, or I cannot be responsible for your lives!"

Tarsek waited again, and there was no response. The old centurion shrugged. "Very well. Stand by to ignite." He jogged toward his scouts, who were stationed behind vertical beams at an intersection in the corridor. Dropping his hand, he gave the order to detonate, and everyone ducked. No one wanted to stare at a plasma charge going off in a confined area, because the light went beyond bright to searing. The brilliant explosion created a shock wave which nearly knocked the old Romulan off his feet, and smoke and dust filled the corridor.

"Attack!" he ordered, his voice booming over the comlink in his helmet. The need for silence was certainly over after that blast. His squad rushed toward the smoky gash in the hatch, which was just wide enough for one man at a time to enter. He heard no firing, which was good.

Meanwhile, the centurion checked the scanner on his wrist and noted with satisfaction that the number of life-forms inside the torpedo room had doubled.

Then he heard the scream—a mangled cry of horror. This was followed by bleats of alarm and half-a-dozen voices babbling at once. "Be valiant!" growled the centurion, rising from his position to lead his squad. "Press forward!"

Instead they were stampeding back, overrunning his rear position. Two of his men crashed right into Tarsek, spinning the centurion around. With the butt of his disruptor rifle, he smashed one soldier in the face and dropped him to his knees. "No one called retreat! Get up, you coward!"

The bleeding soldier could only babble and point toward the gash in the hatchway. With a scowl, the centurion turned to look, and the anger on his face froze into a fresco of pure terror. Slithering from the gash was some tentacled creature that was as black as space. Its body was almost opaque except for a dozen eel-like jaws, which snapped, writhed, or chewed on bits of bone and environmental suit. Behind the beast, there was nothing but darkness—a black void into which most of his squad had vanished.

He hauled the bleeding man to his feet and pushed him down the corridor after the other fleeing soldiers.

As the centurion plodded away from the nightmarish beast, he felt as if his legs were mired in quicksand. He activated his comm channel. "Squad one to *Petrask*. Situation urgent! Encountering unknown hostiles. Abandon the mission and evacuate!"

A voice crackled in his ear. "Losing your signal. Too much interference. All squads—" In a burst of static, the voice stopped completely, and Tarsek was forced to look back.

Like a giant slug with a dozen bristling antennae, the dark beast oozed down the corridor, closing upon the old warrior. Where it passed, it left a trail every bit as dark as itself, seeming to erase the deck, bulkheads, and ceiling behind it. Tarsek began blasting it with his disruptor, but the thing absorbed his blazing beams without slowing down. In desperation, he set his weapon to overload and threw it into the oozing maw. It disappeared with a crackle of lightning.

The centurion was no longer sure if he faced death, which he understood, or something worse. But he was certain he couldn't outrun this.

Suddenly, there was flash of light—like a transporter beam—and a figure in a white radiation suit appeared behind him. "Hold onto me!" he said, wrapping an arm around the startled Romulan. In his other hand was a cylindrical metal tube. Tarsek gripped his savior just as the blackness reared up like a hellish wave. He tried to stand erect to meet his death, but the bottomless jaws cowered him.

Then he felt the miracle of the transporter beam as it spirited his molecules away, along with those of the brave figure in white.

Tarsek was instantly gratified to find that he was standing with his fellow soldiers from the mission. Seven of them in all, counting their savior. But it was an unfamiliar, brightly lit transporter room not on any Romulan vessel. It was empty, except for a hulking human at the main transporter console.

"Please," said the man, holding up his hands to show they were empty. "We'd appreciate it if you put down your weapons. We have just saved your lives."

Tarsek ripped off his helmet and barked, "Put down your weapons!" In confusion and relief, the soldiers did as he ordered.

"Step off the transporter platform," ordered the human, "and we'll rescue more of you. Data?"

The hero in the white suit remained on the platform, a sling of cylinders hung over his shoulder and a tricorder in his hands. He looked as calm as if he were headed to dinner. After Tarsek ushered the others off the platform, he turned to give the brave officer a salute, hand to chest. The hero acknowledged it before transporting off in a sparkling column of light.

"I'm Commander William T. Riker," said the other human, working the transporter controls. "Welcome to the *Enterprise*. Just be patient. I'm busy right now."

"Thank you, Commander, and your brave assistant." Centurion Tarsek saluted him, too, and he glowered at his fellows until they all saluted the human.

six

"I didn't kidnap them," said Picard, addressing the angry visage of Commander Kaylena on the bridge viewscreen. "I saved thirteen of your crew members. You don't have any idea what they encountered on the *Barcelona*, and neither do we. When you didn't use some kind of signal amplifier to transport your people back, you condemned them to death."

The dark-haired Romulan bristled at that suggestion. "We would have retrieved them."

"What happened to the eleven we didn't retrieve?" asked Picard.

"That's what I would like to know." The Romulan's dark eyes drilled into him. "If you think holding them will save your ship—"

The turbolift door opened, distracting Picard from her arresting face. He turned to see Riker, accompanied by Data and a gray-haired Romulan with a weathered countenance. "One moment please," said the captain apologetically. "I'd like you to hear from someone who was there."

Picard motioned to the Romulan to approach the command center, and the grizzled veteran did so. He clicked his heels and respectfully saluted the image on the viewscreen. "Commander Kaylena, I am Centurion Tarsek of the Fourth Legion. I owe my life to the crew of the *Enterprise*, as does every survivor of our mission. Once I make a full report, you will see how their hero-ism and quick action saved us, especially the bravery of the one they call Data. It saddens me to report that not all were rescued." He lowered his head, as if he recog-nized his own failure to be more careful.

Commander Kaylena's expression softened into an irritated scowl. "Centurion, report to their transporter room. I expect you and the others to return to your posts as soon as possible."

"Yes, Commander." With a click of his heels, the gray-haired centurion hurried toward the turbolift, where an escort awaited him.

Once again, Captain Picard tried to muster some charm for his recalcitrant counterpart. "I feel it's more important than ever that we meet face-to-face and share what knowledge we have. Before you disrupt our mis-sion, you ought to know what we're doing."

"Very well," answered the Romulan commander. "When you return my personnel, you may come along for a brief meeting. But our requirements haven't changed. End transmission."

When the viewscreen reverted to a view of the ships arrayed against them, Captain Picard let out a sigh of relief. He had bought more time, plus a face-to-face meeting, during which he hoped to buy more time yet. He wouldn't hurry over to the *Javlek*—let her cool her heels waiting for him.

"Captain Picard," said a feminine voice. He turned to see Deanna Troi seated behind him; the counselor had been so quiet since the emergency started that he had almost forgotten she was there.

"Yes, Counselor?"

"She's afraid now. She doesn't know what to do. And she's hiding something."

Picard nodded in agreement, because he could sense it, too. The veneer was about to crack.

Chellac had been to some desolate, commerce-forsaken places in his long life, but he had never been anywhere more foreboding than the moon of Meldrar I. The developed side with the prison was not too lively either, but at least it had a spaceport and some shops. This bleak wilderness had nothing but gray sand, weather-beaten mountains, and a few scrubby plants growing in the thin atmosphere. A perpetual twilight hung over the place. Although the large moon had fairly normal gravity for humanoids, the Ferengi had to draw frequently on the oxygen mask hanging at his side. He was glad it was Yorka carrying the box and not him.

"Uh, where do you think you're going?" asked their nervous shuttlecraft pilot, a young human female who traipsed after them.

"I told you before," grumbled Yorka, "we need some solace in the wilderness. You don't have to come. Why don't you stay with the shuttlecraft?"

"But you're *my* responsibility," she insisted. "We're not even supposed to be *out* here!"

"You didn't have any qualms when we tipped you extra and asked if you would take us anywhere," said Chellac, trudging through the sand, trying to keep up with the three Bajorans.

"Well, I didn't know what you wanted to do," said the pilot anxiously. "I thought you just wanted to see the usual spots—the usual tour. Say, wouldn't you rather see the Xnar Treasure caves? They're right past the dunes!"

"This is where we want to be," answered the Ferengi, "and we don't have much time if we intend to get back to the freighter before she leaves. So either leave us alone, or tag along and keep your mouth shut. What's your name?"

"Cassie Jackson," she answered.

The Ferengi smiled sincerely. "Cassie, someday when you're a veteran pilot, you'll realize that the occasional suspicious fare like us is the spice of life. Who knows what opportunity this might present? You'll wish this happened more often, trust me, dear."

"I don't think I'll trust you," said the young woman, "but I'll keep my mouth shut."

With Yorka in the lead, clutching his box, the small party trudged across the lunar landscape. The Bajoran was followed by the two acolytes, the pilot, and the Ferengi, who huffed liberally from his oxygen tank. Their shadows were obscured by the dimness of perpetual dusk as reflected off the mammoth bronze planet which hovered in the sky.

*   *   *

Captain Picard materialized in the Romulan transporter room with the old centurion at his side, plus the last of the rescued Romulans. "I bid you farewell, Captain," said Tarsek with a bow. "My gratitude to Data and your crew."

"I'm glad we could help," answered Picard.

"All detainees report to the medical center!" announced a voice. "All detainees report to the medical center!"

As Tarsek and his fellows marched swiftly toward the exit, Picard stepped off the transporter platform in a more leisurely fashion, looking for an official welcoming party. He spotted the commander herself, standing in the corner, half-bathed in shadows. She was taller than he expected, with a regal bearing; since Romulan officers depended upon family influence to gain their commissions, she was probably of noble birth. When she stepped toward him, he admired her healthy physique before finding himself again looking at her fierce eyes, which were darker and more intense in person.

It was difficult to guess her age, but he assumed it was close to his own. Even a Romulan with excellent family connections would need to put in a lot of years before getting command of this ship and this task force.

"Commander," he said warmly.

"Captain Picard," she answered with a nod. "Welcome aboard the *Javlek*. Would you like a beverage in our officers' retreat?"

"Thank you, yes," he readily agreed.

Side by side, they left the transporter room and strolled down the elegant corridor, which was adorned with golden metallic trim and mosaic designs executed in jewels and tile. Passing crew members were respectful but kept their distance.

"You think we are treating you unfairly," said Kaylena, "that our demands are unreasonable. Don't you recall that the Federation agreed to return our technology to us when this emergency began? I can show you the correspondence and documents."

"That doesn't give you permission to board our ships and conduct searches," answered Picard firmly.

She held up her hand and motioned to a door emblazoned with golden symbols. It slid open, and she conducted him into a small, tasteful clubhouse with overstuffed chairs, a bar, and gaming tables. The walls were decorated with lifelike holographic renderings of Romulan ships attacking the enemy, including Starfleet. The room was suspiciously empty at this hour, although there was an attendant behind the bar.

Kaylena motioned to the servant. "What would you like to drink?"

"Synthehol," he answered.

She smiled gayly. "The only thing you're allowed to drink at official negotiations? Will you at least try it the way I like it—with a sprig of Talosian Sipping Plant?"

"Very well," answered Picard.

The drinks were served in tall glasses, befitting the lovely flowered stalk, and they sat in comfortable chairs at what appeared to be a card table. Commander Kaylena lifted her glass to him. "On behalf of my crew, thank you for your quick work in saving members of our boarding party. Although we detected the radiation, we never realized what dangers existed there. The *Petrask* has flown closer to the *Barcelona* to begin more extensive scanner readings."

Picard frowned and banged his glass on the table. "Once again, you've taken action without consulting us."

"As far as I can see, it's a derelict ship in neutral space," answered the commander with a haughty shrug. "You're not on board, you haven't taken any steps to salvage it. What action were you going to take next?"

He studied her carefully and decided to be truthful. "We were going to send probes over."

"Then we're of one mind," answered Kaylena with a brief smile and a soothing tone. "We withdraw the request to search your ship, although you will turn over the prototype radiation suits made from our technology."

"And the Genesis technology?" asked the captain, stirring his drink with the graceful, pink-petaled stalk. At once, the Talosian Sipping Plant produced a beautiful whistle which varied in pitch the faster he stirred it. His drink also grew cloudy with a pink pulp, and he grew oddly light-headed.

"I believe this plant is illegal in the Federation," remarked Picard.

"Ah, but you're not in the Federation now," she answered slyly. "It's the only thing which makes synthehol palatable."

He took a sip, and the heady aroma was almost enough to knock him out of his chair. Picard placed the exotic drink back on the table and regarded his adversary. "We were talking about Genesis technology you may have found on Lomar?"

" 'May have found' is the operative phrase," answered the Romulan. She tool a prolonged drink of her beverage. "You discovered the moss homeworld first, but you left it for us. And now you want to discuss technology which you always claimed didn't exist . . . until two weeks ago." She laughed heartily. "Even if we had it, you have no legal basis to demand we return such technology."

Picard touched the long sprig of Talosian Sipping Plant. "If we give you the radiation suits, you'll leave?"

"No," she answered with a troubled frown. "Now that we've lost personnel on that derelict, we have to investigate for our report. Unless you can tell us what caused those deaths—and I know you can't—we must pursue this."

"We're in the same position," said Picard. "We should cooperate and share information. If you'll show me what you're doing, I'll try not to duplicate it with our probes."

"To do that, we have to leave this lounge," said Kaylena wistfully, as she admired their richly appointed surroundings. "I haven't been to the officer's retreat in months—I've forgotten how restful it is. I thought it might be the right place to inspire conversation, and it has."

Picard looked around the empty room. "It appears that your officers could use more rest."

"Couldn't we all?" With a sigh, the elegant Romulan rose to her feet and resumed her military bearing. "Very well, I'll take you to our observation lounge and show you some of our scanner results. We may not even need your probes."

"Fine," answered Picard, taking a last look at the beautiful flower in the tall glass of pink liquid.

*   *   *

"This is far enough!" declared Yorka, breathing heavily and sweating in the thin air of the moon. Despite his bulk and his exhaustion, he set the metal box very carefully in the slate-gray dirt. The other two Bajorans and the young pilot stopped and sunk wearily to their knees. Wheezing, gasping, and limping, Chellac brought up the rear.

"If you thought someone was following us," rasped the Ferengi, "rest assured, we've lost them."

"I didn't think anyone was following us," said Yorka.

"Then why did we drag ourselves way out here?" demanded the Ferengi. Wheezing, he sunk to the dusty ground.

Prylar Yorka looked around at the lifeless mountains and sooty dirt of the enormous moon. The only thing noteworthy was the bronze-colored planet, Meldrar I, that dominated the night sky. Despite that gleaming beacon, this side of the moon was dismal, which was all to his liking, because it was far removed from prying eyes. He was a bit concerned about the two nonbelievers in his party, but the monk knew he couldn't do everything alone. He needed people like the Ferengi and the pilot if he were going to make a huge impact. People would have to be taken into his confidence, but he would have to be selective.

Before worrying about the next step, it was time to see what had brought them all this distance. Yorka knelt down in front of the metallic box and reached for the delicate recessed handle on the polished door. His hands were trembling.

"Easy there," said Chellac. "What are you going to do?"

"I'm just going to open it and take a look," replied the Bajoran, as if this were an everyday occurrence. But for the first time, he got a new fear—what if there was nothing in the box? What if it was all a cruel hoax . . . or something important to the Romulans that he couldn't use?

But no, every cell in his body told him that he was a tool of something grand—something much bigger than himself or his small entourage. "I'm going to open it," he declared.

Chellac and the pilot, Cassie Jackson, drew closer, as did one of the acolytes. The other acolyte had wandered up a craggy stone to take a look at something in the distance. Deciding not to wait for him, Yorka gripped the handle, and opened the box with a quick but sure motion.

Nothing happened, except that a gorgeous red and black display glimmered in a language and symbols which Yorka had never seen before, and he was well read. Around this brilliant screen were large jewel-like buttons, well-spaced as if for a child. The primary colors of the buttons attracted him—red, green, blue, plus yellow—and he again thought that a child was supposed to use this device. Was it a toy?

Once again, the prylar had a pang of doubt, and he wanted to press all the buttons at once and see if he had been fooled.

"You don't have a user's manual, do you?" asked the Ferengi with a nervous laugh.

"Yellow," whispered Yorka. "It's the color of the wormhole."

Before they could stop him or say anything, he

pressed the yellow button. The other buttons began to blink in an alternating pattern, the red screen displayed large but unknown script, and the box began to make a low, ominous hum. At a guess, it was powering up . . . for some purpose which was no doubt glorious. Yorka placed his hands on the wondrous object, wanting to communicate with it, wanting to know its secrets and powers.

Without even thinking, his thumb hit the green button, and the object began to vibrate under his hands. "Praise be to the Prophets!" he shouted with joy. A sudden but furious wind picked up on the barren plain, whipping the dust into the thickening atmosphere. Dark clouds began to gather, obscuring the bronze planet; the prylar could feel intense prickling all along his skin.

"Turn it off!" shouted Chellac, looking over his shoulder. "You don't know what you're doing."

"Oh, I think I do!" cried the prylar in triumph. In quick succession, he hit the red and blue buttons, and the very ground beneath their feet began to rumble. With a whirring sound, the back of the box opened, revealing a lens, and a glowing beam shot out. A shock wave knocked Yorka back on his haunches, but the excited monk scrambled to his knees in time to watch the beam fan across the gray dust. Wherever it played, the land burst into flames—with brilliant green waves that scorched everything in an expanding triangle from their position.

"Oh, my gosh!" exclaimed Cassie.

Yorka heard a scream and realized that the youngest acolyte was somewhere out there, in the midst of the searing green flames. The other acolyte started forward, but the prylar grabbed him and pulled him back before he could step into the beam—for he was certain it would mean death.

"Leave him," he told the lad. "You can't save him— he's gone!"

Sniffing back tears, the acolyte nodded, and soon their attention was riveted on the extraordinary metamorphosis taking place in front of them. As the green flames began to recede, shapes began to rise from the desolate moonscape; these dark forms twisted and writhed as if alive, and Yorka realized they were enormous plants, growing at an accelerated pace. A whole new ecosystem was being created out there in the wilderness—in thousands of square kilometers of nothing.

"I hope the shuttlecraft isn't out there, too," muttered Chellac worriedly.

"It isn't." The Bajoran pointed down at their tracks, which led away from the churning horizon. Wind and sleet swirled around them, dense growth rose from the dust, while the astounding relic blazed new life on this desolate moon. He heard the others mutter and gasp, and well they should—for this was a gift from the Prophets.

The beam suddenly stopped, and the small lens on the back of the box closed again. The red display returned to what looked like a waiting state, as if this miracle could be produced again at his will. It would have to be at his will, thought Yorka, if he hoped to swiftly rejoin the Vedek Assembly and then be declared kai—the first true kai since Opaka.

Prylar Yorka grinned with delight and threw his

hands into the air. "I have found it . . . the Orb of Life!"

The observation lounge of the *Javlek* was equivalent to the stellar cartography room on the *Enterprise*; it featured a brilliant three-dimensional display with multi-level platforms, where observers and astronomers could insert themselves into the action. Right now, the panoramic display had begun to shimmer and break apart, as if affected by interference. A moment later, the mammoth warbird shook as if it had been struck by a quantum torpedo. Captain Picard staggered to stay on his feet, as did Commander Kaylena.

A momentary panic ensued among the astronomers, but their commander calmed them down with a few curt orders. "Everyone, stay at your posts! Try to track the disturbance . . . get the source. The rest of you, check on the other ships!"

She squeezed her stiff collar, activating communications. "Commander Kaylena to the bridge—are we under attack? Are shields up?"

There was no answer, except for an ominous crackle, and Picard tapped his comm badge. "Picard to *Enterprise*." He waited for an answer, and none came. "Picard to bridge," he repeated with the same result.

"Commander!" called a nervous technician from his console. "The *Petrask* is no longer registering on scanners. Neither is the Starfleet ship."

"Which ship?" demanded Picard.

The Romulan checked his readouts. "The derelict . . . the *Barcelona*. They were right next to each other."

"Can you get anything on viewscreen?" asked the commander.

"No," answered the scientist. He looked at his colleagues in the observation lounge, and none of them were able to offer any enlightenment.

One finally said, "Commander, I'm monitoring our main systems from the bridge. There are shipwide failures . . . shields are down . . . and we're on emergency power reserve. Impulse power is out."

"The shuttlebay is not far from here," said Commander Kaylena, looking pointedly at Picard. "We could take a look for ourselves."

He nodded, and the commander dashed toward the door, shouting orders. "Stay at your posts! Take scanner readings, and try to reestablish communications!" As Kaylena flew down the corridor, Picard had to run to keep up with her.

The Ferengi gazed in awe at the incredible tangle of misshapen vines and sprawling trees; still moving, they covered the ground like maggots on a ripe piece of meat. A noxious mist was forming over this grotesque growth, making Chellac gag. He took a drag on his oxygen mask and said, "You know, I'm not really sure that's an Orb. I have a better guess as to what it is."

With a scowl, the big Bajoran stepped toward the Ferengi, towering over him. "*I* say it's an Orb."

"Okay, Orb of Life it is," agreed the Ferengi. "Catchy name, has a presold recognition, and it delivers . . . life!" He looked nervously at the popping, sprouting jungle in front of them, wondering how they could ever explain it without getting into heaps of trouble. Every instinct warned him to run away from this madness, but he was indebted to the prylar. Besides, this was a fascinating opportunity if ever there was one.

"How do you want to promote it?" asked Chellac.

"I want everyone to know, especially the Vedek Assembly," said the prylar with a triumphant smile. Then his jowled face grew somber. "But we have to be secretive . . . to keep it away from others. And protect it."

"That's for certain," answered the Ferengi, tugging thoughtfully on a dangling earlobe. "What we need is to show this to people with influence, important figures whom everyone will listen to and trust."

"Wait a minute," said the pilot, Cassie, holding up her hand and stepping into the conversation. "First of all, you need *me* more than anyone, because that mess is going to draw attention, even out here." She pointed at the grotesque mutation which was turning a chunk of the moon into an alien landscape.

"We can't even think about going back to the spaceport . . . or the prison." She looked into a dull green sky full of swirling gray clouds which hadn't been there a few seconds ago. "In fact, the guards will be here soon. So what am I bid for one shuttlecraft ride out of here?"

Yorka jumped to his feet, puffing out his barrel chest. "You'll get nothing! We paid you a fair price for your services, plus a generous tip. You're just being an opportunist—"

"Ignore him," said Chellac, putting his arm around the young woman and taking her aside. "You're absolutely right—at the moment, you *are* the most important member of our team. So we'll give you all we've got, as soon as we can. If you want me to empty my pockets and my purse right now, I will."

"Aren't you even going to bargain with her?" asked the acolyte, still rubbing away tears.

"No," answered Chellac. "You don't bargain with somebody who has all the supply when you only have demand. You throw yourself on their mercy, which is what I'm doing. But we should get moving now and negotiate later."

"We're within transporter range of my shuttlecraft," said Cassie matter-of-factly. "But we can only beam one at a time."

"Why didn't you tell us that before?" demanded the Ferengi.

"Well, you all seemed to want to walk so badly, so I let you walk," she answered with a shrug. "Besides, I needed the exercise."

She flipped over a lapel on her uniform to reveal a combadge. "Jackson to Shuttle 1347, acknowledge."

"Acknowledge transmission," answered the computer's efficient voice. "What is your order?"

"Can you lock onto my transporter signal?"

"Yes."

"Stand by, Computer." She motioned to Chellac, Yorka, and the acolyte. "All of you, gather together!"

They had to tear themselves away from the bizarre spectacle in order to obey her order, and Yorka grabbed the Orb of Life, clutching it protectively to his chest. "Does your shuttlecraft have warp drive?"

"Yes, it's the latest model," answered the pilot. "Computer, transport me first, then lock onto the other three humanoid life-forms in this vicinity. Energize when ready."

Chellac was very relieved when the young pilot disappeared in a shimmering pillar of swirling particles, and he patiently waited his turn. Much to his chagrin, Yorka went next, followed by the acolyte. While the Ferengi fidgeted nervously, he glanced over his shoulder at the hellish growth consuming this chunk of the moon. If there were any real profit to be had in this discovery, he reasoned, it would probably be in *preventing* the device from being used.

Finally Chellac felt the familiar tingle of the transporter beam, and he relaxed as the unreal scene in front of him gradually faded away.

With Commander Kaylena at the controls and Captain Picard in the copilot's seat, a small green shuttlecraft soared away from the space doors of the *Javlek*. They banked around the starboard nacelle of the warbird and set course for the most recent positions of the *Barcelona* and the *Petrask*. It hardly mattered that the scanners weren't effective, because a vast field of debris floated in space where the two ships had been. The extensive collection of scrap metal was silhouetted against a huge black curtain that blocked out half the stars in their viewport.

"What is *that?*" asked Kaylena in amazement. "That black field behind the ships. Did *it* destroy them?"

"I don't know, but I wouldn't get too close," warned Picard. He peered at the staggering wreckage and the equally strange darkness. "I think I see something moving in the debris. It might be survivors—"

"I see it," answered Kaylena, working her controls. "But I'll have to get closer to get a visual contact. Don't worry, Captain, our shields are at full strength."

Dropping to a speed that was little faster than their momentum, the small shuttlecraft slowly edged into the field of debris. Small clumps of dust spattered and sparkled against their shields, but still the Romulan commander piloted the craft deeper into the sea of destruction. The *Petrask* must have had a crew of several hundred, thought Picard, yet the stoic commander said nothing about the massive loss of life. Picard could see the concern etched into her face, but he could also see the clench-jawed determination to confront this mystery and solve it.

Without warning, a score of spinning, tentacled creatures came hurtling through the confetti of debris, striking their shields and splattering like paint balls. They looked like giant starfish to Picard, and they sizzled on the shields like fried eggs on volcanic rock.

"Shields failing!" exclaimed Kaylena.

"How can that be?" asked Picard in alarm.

"Something in the composition of those creatures," answered the Romulan. With sure motions and no hesitation, she brought the shuttlecraft to a spinning stop, then applied rear thrusters in an attempt to drive off the attackers. The tentacled beings seemed to be intent upon streaking toward their position and sacrificing themselves to weaken the shields.

"They appear to be coming from that black cloud," noted Picard, "if I can trust my vision."

The craft shuddered as it began to hit debris, and Kaylena fired forward thrusters to slow them down. "Shields are gone!" she exclaimed with frustration. "I can't escape without incurring too much damage."

The starfish creatures continued to perish on their aft

thrusters, but the thruster burns were causing them to move too fast through the dense field of rubble. Without shields, a moderate collision could be disastrous.

"I'm shutting down everything but life-support," declared Kaylena.

"Do you think they're attracted to our energy sources?"

"They seem to be, but without power, perhaps we can blend in with the debris." She gazed at the captain with wide, brown eyes. "I'm sorry to have gotten you into this situation."

"I came of my own free will," he answered.

seven

Captain Picard waited tensely but silently as the Romulan commander worked the controls of the shuttlecraft. Suddenly the instruments at every station went dark, all sound stopped, and the lighting in the cabin switched to a dim blue. Thrusters no longer fired, but Kaylena had done a good job of matching the approximate speed of the debris around them—so they could drift on their momentum among the glittering wreckage. More importantly, the starfish creatures were no longer attracted to the shuttlecraft, and there was just the occasional thud as they brushed against debris. It was almost peaceful drifting among the sparkling remains of the two starships, the *Barcelona* and the *Petrask*.

"Do you have environmental suits?" asked Picard. "Without shields, we're vulnerable to radiation. We can't tell if it's increased, but it probably has."

"Good point," answered the commander. She rose from her seat and stepped to the rear of the craft, where she opened a locker and removed two black, hooded suits.

As she approached Picard with the suits, Kaylena frowned apologetically. "Once again, Captain, I'm sorry to have put you in danger. As humans say, 'It seemed like a good idea at the time.'"

"It *was* a good idea," replied Picard. "We're the only ones out here . . . the only ones who know what's happening, even if we don't have any answers."

"My crew knows where we are, so I assume we'll be rescued." Kaylena handed him an environmental suit, keeping one for herself. "You'll have to remove your uniform to put this on. At least I will have to, because of the design of these shoulders."

"I understand," said Picard with a comforting smile. "The light's dim in here."

"Yes, it is," agreed Kaylena as she began to unbutton her tunic.

The captain managed to keep his eyes cast downward as the two of them stripped and put on the environmental suits, but contact was hard to avoid in the cramped confines of the shuttlecraft. Even with the dim light, he couldn't help noticing that Commander Kaylena had a fit, statuesque frame to go with her regal bearing. When they had finally donned the suits, they sat at the dark controls and gazed at the remains of the two great starships. At least one of them had been empty, or inhabited only by a handful of unidentified poltergeists. It was numbing to think how many Romulans had been lost aboard the *Petrask*.

"What do you suppose happened?" asked Kaylena, her whisper amplified in his hood. "What aggravated this anomaly and destroyed these two ships?"

Picard shook his head. "We knew very little about it

before, and now we know even less. I wonder if it would be possible to capture one of those flying creatures? I don't see them now, but there must be more coming from that rift, or whatever it is."

"We have to join forces." Kaylena turned to look at him, and her ebony eyes blazed into his, even through their faceplates. "I failed in my primary mission—to search your ship—and now I've lost a warbird . . . with all hands onboard. I will have to pursue this to the end."

"Why did you want to search our ship?" asked Picard.

She leaned back in her chair and tried to put her hands behind her head, but it was an awkward maneuver in the bulky suit. "To see what you discovered on the moss creatures' base, in that fake asteroid. We also have a legitimate complaint about our technology, which you used without our permission. Even if millions of those phase-shifting suits were handed out, you did promise to return the technology. A high-profile example of the *Enterprise* returning the suits would be useful to our campaign."

"Consider it done," said Picard.

The commander motioned out the window at the all-encompassing cloud of metallic dust and gleaming shrapnel, and her voice took on an edgy tone. "Of course, that mission pales beside this carnage. The immediate question is—how much help do we ask from our superiors?"

"I have help coming," admitted Picard.

She sighed. "I assumed as much. Well, you can send some of them back, because we're one ship less."

"They won't be here for about twenty hours, at best," said the captain, "and it would probably take longer for you to get reinforcements. So we're on our own."

"Literally," she answered, settling back in her seat. "If you hadn't been with me when the ships exploded, I probably would have blamed you."

"And I you."

"I'm glad you were persistent in your desire to see me." The Romulan turned to him, and her high cheekbones were softened by the dim blue light and the shadows from her hood. "I want to work closely with you on this . . . until I'm relieved."

He frowned back at her. "Do you think there will be such serious repercussions?"

"Oh, yes. At this moment, the underlings who covet my post are reporting the loss of the *Petrask*, and that we failed in our mission. But I'm in charge until then, even if I spend the time floating with a human who doesn't answer to me."

"If I can intercede on your behalf," he replied, "please don't hesitate to ask."

"I wish you could intercede to rescue me first," she muttered. "Although we might chance using our personal communicators."

She touched her neck and intoned, "Commander Kaylena to the *Javlek*. Attention: Kaylena to the bridge of the *Javlek*." The commander waited, then shook her head when there was no response.

Picard tried his communicator, too, but he got no answer. He gazed out the window at the closest objects, several of which seemed to be moving at new speeds and angles. He rubbed his faceplate, thinking that perhaps he wasn't seeing it correctly, then he realized that the gravitational fields must not be stable.

"The debris is bouncing around out there," reported Picard. He pointed out the window just as they were abruptly jolted and nearly knocked out of their seats. The shuttlecraft spun around, resulting in several serious thuds as they struck debris, sending it colliding with other rubble, creating a ricochet effect of crashing shrapnel.

"Where are we going?" asked the Romulan, leaning forward. "Toward that black cloud?"

"*Something* has got us," agreed Picard. "But it may be ours . . . yes, a tractor beam! Out there, you can see a ship coming closer, trying to get us within their shields." Both of them peered through the window into the swirling fog of metal bits, and they could see running lights, blinking rhythmically, although nothing else was clear.

"Your ship?" said Kaylena.

"I would think so, yes."

The star-shaped creatures had also seen the ship enter the debris field, and they massed into a steady stream, headed toward the intruder like a line of ants at a picnic. This created more chaos in the whirling mass of rubble.

"Can we do anything to help them?" asked Kaylena.

"Not that I can see, but perhaps we should move to the rear—in case there's a hull breach." He looked urgently at his companion and saw a flush of excitement in her cheeks.

"Good idea." She grabbed his gloved hand and bounded from her seat, leading him to the rear, where the cool blue light was even weaker. They crouched down in a tiny space and held each other, protected by the anonymity of the bulky suits they wore. This was a welcome distraction; because the craft started moving again, and the hull was pummeled by debris.

Despite the beating, the shuttlecraft held together, and they could see the amount of rubble lessening. Within a few minutes, which seemed longer, the pummeling stopped altogether, and Picard assumed they were finally inside the protective bubble of the *Enterprise*'s shields.

A familiar voice crackled over his combadge, "Bridge to Picard. Captain, are you all right?"

"Yes, Number One, I presume we're all right." Reluctantly, he moved away from the comforting body next to him and rose to his feet. He offered a hand to Kaylena and helped her to get up, but she stumbled and fell into his arms.

"Excuse me," she said, pulling away slowly.

Riker's voice continued, "We have you in our tractor beam, and we're pulling back to a safe distance to transport you. The *Javlek* vaporized some of the wreckage for us, and they were ready to back us up. They want to know if their commander is all right."

"She's fine," answered Picard. "We'll want to collect information and call a staff meeting as soon as possible."

"Yes, sir. You'll be aboard in just a few seconds," said Riker. "Stand by to transport."

He looked again at his Romulan cohort, and she was deep in thought. "We must have a memorial service for the crew of the *Petrask*," she declared, "and the others who have died."

"I have officers to honor, too," said the captain.

"Can you return to my ship in four hours?" asked the Romulan. "We can honor our dead and discuss a plan of attack."

"Yes," he agreed. Then the captain bent down and picked up their hastily discarded uniforms. "Don't forget your clothes."

With half a smile, she took the bundle from him. "The last time someone said that to me, we became very close friends."

"I hope that's the case," answered Picard, matching her uncertain smile. The moment ended when the transporter beam seized their molecules and whisked them back to reality.

"Captain on the bridge," intoned the tactical officer importantly. The captain strode from the turbolift onto the semicircular bridge and glanced with satisfaction at the fully staffed consoles. Backup staff waited attentively at auxiliary stations. They all looked younger than the captain remembered, and more sure of themselves than they ought to be.

"Report."

"We are cleared by station ops to depart," answered the ops officer, a Bynar who worked closely with his partner, the conn officer.

"Course laid in for Lomar," reported the other Bynar. Alynna Nechayev nodded. "Estimated arrival time?"

"Eighteen hours from now at maximum warp."

"Captain Nechayev," said the tactical officer, "there's a hail for you from Admiral Whitcleff."

The newly appointed captain pointed to her ready room. "I'll take it in private. Make ready for launch."

"Yes, Sir!" came a chorus of replies, all of them sounding a bit too eager to please. They seemed to be convinced that her assignment to the *Sequoia* was temporary, and if they were real nice to the slumming admiral, she would go away and make room for a real captain, perhaps their first mate, whose resentment was palpable.

Nechayev ducked into her private office, walked behind the desk, and activated her flat screen. Up came the welcome visage of an old friend; he was gray-haired and heavier but still handsome.

"Good morning, Alynna, getting squared away?" asked Admiral Whitcleff.

"Hello, Jeremy. Yes, we're ready. Here to give the *Sequoia* an official send-off?"

"Not exactly." The admiral's smile vanished, and his face turned downcast. "You've been out of the loop, but we've been dealing with some very strange anomalies since the Genesis Wave . . . disappearing ships and crews, strange creatures, unidentified radiation poisoning—"

"I saw *that* in the hospital," she cut in. "I can tell by your face that it's gotten worse, hasn't it?"

"All of a sudden," he answered, shaking his head puzzledly. "Within the last hour, it's gotten quantitatively worse, with reports coming in from all over. And we've got no explanations whatsoever."

"Have our orders changed?" asked Nechayev.

"No, not at the moment. They desperately need you on Lomar, where it's something of a mess. However, Lomar is not an emergency, and this other thing might turn into one. I just wanted to give you a heads-up that the *Sequoia* may be uprooted and sent elsewhere on short notice. Don't get too comfortable there, Alynna."

"I'm never too comfortable," she replied dryly. "Is Lomar one of the places where you're seeing these phenomena?"

"Oddly, no," answered Whitcleff. "We've seen it mostly in regions along the path of the Genesis Wave, but there's no direct correlation. Some of my advisors doubt whether the two are even connected."

"Look for patterns," said Nechayev. "Have you done a spectral neutrino analysis?"

Whitcleff smiled. "If you were still in the admiralty, Alynna, you'd be deeply involved in this. But now you're a ship's captain with a single mission. Concentrate on that, but be ready to make a change."

"Yes, Sir," answered Nechayev smartly, almost saluting.

Admiral Whitcleff cleared his throat and glanced at a padd on his desk. "I see that you've requested to keep your black-box account open . . . for covert operations. You know, it's not common for a ship's captain to have undercover operatives."

She managed a smile. "I just have a few longtime informers who I'd like to keep on the payroll. I don't want to lose them, that's all. You never know when they'll be useful."

"Then I'll approve it," answered Whitcleff, tapping his padd. "Just remember your new role, Alynna. You don't want to turn into one of those rogue captains you always criticize—the ones who run off on their own. Whitcleff out."

"Yes, Sir," she grumbled, tapping off the screen. Taking a deep, bracing breath of air, she walked to her door, waited for it to open, then strode back onto the bridge.

Her first officer, Commander Marbinz, was now present, and the blue-skinned Benzite gave her a fishy look as he rose from the command chair. Of course, it was hard for him not to look fishy with those pale eyes, scaly face, and blue tentacles around his mouth. It didn't help that Marbinz was the highest-ranking Benzite in Starfleet and expected to become the first of his race to captain a ship after the *Sequoia*'s skipper retired. He had not gotten his wish, as the post was usurped by Nechayev. The problem was that the entire crew was distracted by their ongoing drama, and Nechayev often caught them watching her and Marbinz whenever they were together on the bridge, anticipating fireworks.

She was going to disappoint them, if it killed her. For a long time, Nechayev had been used to getting her own way without playing politics; but she was the newcomer to this crew, so she was the one who would have to prove herself. She would have to deal more thoroughly with Marbinz—but at an opportune time, and this wasn't it.

"Ops," said Nechayev, crossing to the captain's chair, "has Mission Specialist Teska reported onboard?"

"Yes, Sir," answered the Bynar.

"Two and a half minutes ago," replied the other Bynar.

"All personnel are accounted for," added the first.

"Begin launch sequence," she ordered, "and take us out to warp distance at one-eighth impulse."

"Yes, Sir." Even if they thought one-eighth impulse was rather slow, no one said anything.

The stately *Galaxy*-class starship began to move away from Spacedock, leaving the repair facility in Earth's orbit for the twinkling vastness of space. The Bynars kept up a running commentary of reports while the *Sequoia* soared into the starscape, passing within hailing distance of an incoming ship.

At optimum distance, Nechayev gave the command to enter warp, and they began the longest leg of their journey. It felt oddly freeing to be the captain of a great starship, as if she were finally master of her fate. If only it weren't for the two hundred eighty lives directly under her guidance, this would almost be a vacation. Those lives—and the well-being of this ten-year-old ship—had just become her biggest responsibility. Nothing else seemed to matter.

She turned to Marbinz and tried to make amends. "Commander, I want to familiarize myself with the crew, so I'd like to look over your crew reports. So far, I've found them very complete and well-organized. Continue course for Lomar, and I'll be back at the end of your shift. At that time, Commander, I would like you to have lunch with me, if you're available."

"Yes, Sir," he answered with a startled expression. Recovering, the first officer bowed politely. "I'll be looking forward to it, Admiral."

Another dig, thought Nechayev as she strode toward the turbolift, *when he called me admiral instead of captain. I'll have to bite my tongue and live with it. Imagine having to mollify an underling just to keep the peace. I'm definitely not in Starfleet Command anymore.*

eight

Beverly Crusher sat near one side of the bed where Lieutenant Raynr Sleven rested, and Deanna Troi sat at the other side. The strapping Antosian seemed to appreciate their attention, especially since the ship's barber, Mot, had groomed him to be presentable. His vibrant good health and helpful attitude belied the terrible ordeal he had suffered, yet Crusher wondered how much longer she would be able to keep him in sickbay.

Deanna Troi had thought it best to hear his story while it was still fresh in his mind, and his mind was still lucid. But the captain and most of the crew were busy, so she had asked him to tell just herself and the doctor.

"Well," began the Antosian, "we were supposed to watch the Genesis Wave go past, and take sensor readings and live samples. The astrometrics department was charting the wave's outward boundary, according to patterns of destruction. But the only thing we witnessed was our own destruction."

Raynr Sleven shook his head and grimaced at the remembrance of it, and Troi touched his hand. "You don't need to relive it now, if it's too painful," said the Betazoid.

He bit his lip and took a deep breath. "There were just so many of us taken in the first moments . . . before we knew what it was. I couldn't do anything to help them, because those things were attracted to crowds of people. And I was alone."

"What do you mean, they were 'taken?'" asked Crusher.

He appealed to her with an earnest face, and she could see the confusion in his eyes. "We thought it was a hull breach—or several hull breaches at once—and that the casualties were being sucked into space. That's until we realized that these pockets of void were moving throughout the ship."

He covered his eyes with the palms of his hands and began to cry. "It was everyone for himself . . . I should have done more to help them, but the corridors were full of *monsters!*" Raynr looked pleadingly at Crusher. "You've seen them, Doctor. I know that other patients here in sickbay have seen them, because they talk about it. I was able to save Grenmoy before I hid in the weapons room, but he's not here—?"

"That was the dead man we found with you," said Crusher sympathetically. "He was dead long before we got there . . . from the radiation. Your choice of weapons kept you safe, I guess."

"Dumb luck," he insisted. "From the beginning, I was lucky, because I was repairing a plasma conduit on level two, where you found me. The weapons room was close by, and it had phasers, armor, radiation suits, emergency rations, medkits, everything I needed. The captain ordered the crew to abandon ship, but I had a feeling they wouldn't make it. So I stayed put. I don't think anyone made it, did they?"

"We didn't see any evidence that escape pods were launched," said Crusher.

"Well, you should double-check the pods when you go back over there," suggested the Antosian.

Crusher glanced at Troi, and the the counselor delivered the bad news. "The *Barcelona* was destroyed, and so was a Romulan ship that was too close to it. There's been a flare-up in the radiation . . . and whatever force attacked your crew."

"They were taken somewhere else . . . into the darkness!" The lieutenant sat up and gripped Crusher's forearm. "You saw it, didn't you? Sometimes it looks like a blazing light, and other times it's a black pit with no bottom. But it takes them away . . . and leaves those monsters behind."

Deanna Troi's brow furrowed with concern, and she looked away from Raynr to stare at the bulkhead, transfixed by something beyond Crusher's sight.

"I know I'm not making any sense," said the Antosian apologetically. He slumped back into his bed. "I wish I hadn't seen these things, but you saved me for a purpose. If our ship is gone, no other record exists—so I must tell my story."

"Excuse me," said Deanna Troi, rising unsteadily to her feet. "I have . . . I have some things to do before the staff meeting." She turned to Crusher and managed a weak smile. "You're doing very well with your patient—you should be pleased. And, Lieutenant Sleven, I'm sure you will make a complete recovery. I'll drop in again. Goodbye."

"It was a pleasure to meet you, Counselor!" called Raynr as Troi hurried out the door. After the door shut behind her, he confided to Crusher, "I have a feeling she's not well."

"We've all been under a lot of stress," replied the doctor, rising to the defense of her friend's privacy.

"No one more than you," said the Antosian. "When will *you* stop for a moment to rest . . . and recover?"

"Doctor, heal thyself? I'll take that under advisement," she said with a wry grin.

With a gentle hand, he lifted her chin and gazed into her green eyes with his black orbs. "I'm serious, Doctor. You look tired. Lovely, but tired."

Gently but firmly, Crusher pulled away from him. She had seen that look in patients' eyes before. It was natural to mistake gratitude for something more. "I appreciate your concern, Lieutenant, and I assure you I'll get some rest. When this is over."

"Of course," he said apologetically. "I didn't mean anything derogatory. It's just that it's hard to believe it ever will be over. I've cheated death. I shouldn't be here, but I am! And I feel better than I've ever felt in my life—rested and healthy. I want to jump out of this bed and run around the ship! If you have a theater, I want to perform."

He touched her shoulder and added, "I want to fall in love."

"I make it a rule not to fall in love with my patients," replied Crusher, removing his hand. But she felt vulnerable at the moment, and the brawny Antosian was attractive. If circumstances were different—but they weren't.

"I'm not going to be a patient much longer, am I?" he asked cheerfully. He pointed back at the vital signs on the overhead display. "I mean, I'm perfectly healthy, aren't I?"

"Yes, you are," she admitted. "But your treatment was experimental—we have to keep you under observation."

"I know, cellular metamorphosis," he answered with a smile. "When I was pretending to be asleep, I heard the attendants talking about it. But it's approved where I came from—we accept the risk of the side effects."

"It's approved on Antos IV, but it's still only used in dire cases," said Crusher, rising to her feet.

"Let me walk around at least," begged Raynr. "See something of the *Enterprise?*"

She frowned, although she was inwardly pleased by his his eagerness to be active. "*If* I have time after the staff meeting, I'll come back to check on you. I'm not promising anything. Until then, I'll see that you get a uniform and can take a brief walk with Nurse Ogawa."

"Thank you," said Raynr Sleven with a broad grin. His asymmetrical bun of black hair framed his robust face and made him look almost childlike, or maybe that was just his incredible joy at being unexpectedly alive. Whatever it was, Beverly Crusher wished she could bottle a little of it and take it with her, because she was feeling low.

"Keep up your good spirits," she said as she left the room. *I'll try to do the same*, she told herself.

*   *   *

At their staff meeting in the observation lounge, Captain Picard paced in front of the elegant conference table, which was occupied by the *Enterprise*'s senior officers. Through the observation window, both of the remaining Romulan warbirds glimmered in the velvety stillness of space, but the captain didn't notice this impressive sight. He was consumed with frustration, thought Crusher.

"So our probes have been destroyed," he concluded.

"Not destroyed, Captain," said Data, "absorbed. They have been absorbed into the dark anomaly, which is either the cause of this or the residue."

"If it can expand without notice," said the captain, "it's a ticking time bomb. Have we managed to capture any of the creatures?"

"We have not been able to find any of the creatures," replied Data. "Inexplicably, they have vanished."

"And time has become a crucial factor," added Will Riker. "Captain, can I relate our last message from Starfleet?"

"Go ahead."

The big man nodded. "After we reported that relations with the Romulans had improved, the ships coming to help us were recalled. Starfleet reassigned them, because apparently there are a lot of these events to investigate. Since we aren't near any population centers—and there's no ship left to salvage—our situation is not considered urgent anymore. In fact, there's a good chance we might be pulled away from here."

"We're supposed to minimize our risks," added the captain, his lips thinning, "while we station warning buoys to keep shipping away from the area. If the

Romulans want to do our job for us, we're supposed to step back and let them. Does anybody have anything to add?"

When no one else answered, Dr. Crusher spoke up, "My patient from the *Barcelona*, Lieutenant Sleven, is doing well and has given us a report on his experiences." She looked at Deanna Troi, but the counselor's attention seemed far away. So the doctor went on, "Despite having spent a week with the entities, Lieutenant Sleven couldn't tell us much that we don't already know. But he felt that his crewmates were somehow absorbed into the dark entity."

"There seems to be a theme here," said Geordi La Forge, "of things getting absorbed."

"It has an unusual gravitational pull," said Data, "very localized, not commensurate with its size. It does not obey the physical laws of black holes, quasars, wormholes, or any known phenomenon. We need time to devise the proper safety precautions to study it."

"Time we don't have," concluded Picard. "In two hours, we've got a memorial service to attend on the *Javlek*, and some of you have already volunteered to go with me. Right after that, we begin laying the buoys. Unless we make some headway here, we'll probably be leaving soon. Is there anything else?"

When no one spoke, the captain said, "Dismissed."

Alyssa Ogawa strolled down the corridor with Lieutenant Raynr Sleven at her side, and the big Antosian smiled and greeted everyone they passed. He was so full of good cheer that just being around him lifted her spirits. If he could be returned to his loved ones, she reasoned, then why couldn't Andrew be returned to her and Suzi? She tried not to think about what a miracle it had taken to rescue the sole survivor of the *Barcelona*, and that Andrew would probably need similar luck.

"Have you got any family?" she asked him.

He nodded. "I have my parents and lots of relatives on Antos IV, but no wife or children. We Antosians tend to marry late in life, and like most people in Starfleet, I always thought of my mates as my family. It doesn't seem possible that they're gone, even though I saw it happen. But now that the *Enterprise* is on the job, I suppose we'll get to the bottom of it."

"We can hope," said Alyssa.

"And what about *your* family?" asked Raynr.

She blinked at him. "My family?"

"Yes, you're wearing a wedding ring, and you have the worried look of a mother who wants to report home."

That drew a smile from her. "I guess it's obvious, isn't it?"

"In a good way," he assured her.

"Since we're just taking a stroll," said Ogawa, "would you mind if we stopped at home to see my daughter? She should just be getting back from her morning classes."

"Absolutely!" answered Raynr heartily, "I would love to meet your daughter. Lead on!"

Ogawa figured her patient would rather do anything than go back to his bed in sickbay, so she took him to her residence on deck seven.

When she opened the door, a familiar voice rang out. "Mommy!"

The dark-haired imp came tearing through the living

room and tackled her mother around the waist. Raynr Sleven looked on, his handsome face beaming at the sight of the reunion.

"Suzi, this is my friend, Lieutenant Sleven. He came from the other ship, the *Barcelona.*"

"Pleased to meet you," she said with a proper curtsey.

"Charmed," answered the strapping Antosian. "You have a very nice residence here. I bet you're a big help to your mother, keeping it neat and clean."

"I try," answered Suzi, "but Daddy is really the one who's neat."

Raynr laughed. "Good for him! Is this your father?" He crossed to a shelf by the dining table, where several family holographs were displayed. With an unerring instinct, he picked up the likeness of Andrew.

"Yes, that's my Daddy!" exclaimed Suzi proudly. "He'll be coming home soon."

Ogawa cringed at this topic of conversation, but she kept a polite smile plastered to her face.

"What department does he work in?" asked the Antosian.

"He's helping people get through the Genesis Wave," responded Suzi. "He's been gone a long time, but he's coming home soon."

With dawning realization, the lieutenant looked at Ogawa, who lowered her head. "Starfleet needs to find him like they found you," she said, hoping he would read between the lines.

"He's hiding from them," insisted Suzi with a smile. "He's good at playing hide-and seek."

Raynr looked awkwardly from the pained wife and mother to the unsuspecting six-year-old, and he realized he had stepped into something. "Your daddy's very handsome," he finally said, putting the picture back on the shelf.

"Are you going to stay for lunch?" asked Suzi.

The Antosian glanced at Ogawa and smiled. "Well, I haven't been asked yet."

"I'm asking you," said Suzi. "If it's okay with Mommy."

Ogawa nodded. "Sure, but we have to be fast. We're just supposed to be on a little walk."

Suzi stood on her tiptoes and asked importantly, "What would you like?"

"I'd better stick to bland food," answered Raynr, "because I've been sick. What about some oatmeal?"

"Oatmeal it is!" answered Suzi, rushing off to the food replicator.

When she was out of earshot, the Antosian turned to Ogawa and muttered, "I'm sorry about your husband. What are his chances? I mean, do they have any idea?"

Alyssa sighed and looked away. "He's missing, and that's all we know. We can't do anything but wait, and it hasn't been easy."

"All right, let's talk about something else," said the lieutenant with forced cheer. "There's a topic of conversation I've been dying to ask someone about."

"I'll help you if I can," said Ogawa.

"All right, tell me about Beverly Crusher. She's not married, is she?"

Ogawa fought the temptation to roll her eyes. "No, she's been widowed for a long time and has a grown son. He's also missing. There's somebody on the ship with whom she's been involved—on and off—but it's hard to figure out where that's going."

"I'm terribly smitten with her," admitted the Antosian. "It's not just because she saved my life . . . I just think she's terrific."

"She is that," acknowledged Ogawa. "But whether she has any brain space for romance, I don't know."

Just then, Suzi showed up with a steaming bowl of oatmeal and a big spoon. "Here you are, Lieutenant," she said proudly, handing over the bowl. "What do you want to eat, Mommy?"

"I'm not hungry, dear."

"But you've got to eat," insisted Suzi.

"She's right," said Raynr, his mouth full. "Mmmm, this is delicious!"

"All right, I'll have some too."

They ate lunch, making small talk about Raynr's homeworld and some of the more famous escapades of the *Enterprise*. The Antosian said he would ask Captain Picard for a permanent transfer to the *Enterprise*, since he was already on board and it was the flagship of the fleet. Ogawa said that he might have to spend time in a Starfleet hospital, undergoing evaluation for both his radiation poisoning and his radical treatment, but the Antosian insisted that he felt great.

As the trio dined, the nurse was reminded how pleasurable it was to have a man's presence. With the three of them seated at the table, it almost seemed as if Andrew was back. Almost. Raynr Sleven glanced often at Andrew's picture on the shelf, and she could tell that he was saddened by her husband's absence. He was a sensitive soul, and Ogawa found herself thinking that Beverly should loosen up a bit and go out with him. Guys like him didn't exactly fall out of trees.

"We've got to be getting back to sickbay," she said reluctantly. "They'll be looking for us."

"Let them look. We'll keep hiding," said Raynr with a conspiratorial glance at Suzi, who giggled in agreement.

"Don't make him go," she told her mom.

"He's got to, and you also have afternoon classes," insisted Mom. "But maybe we can do this again tomorrow."

"Please!" exclaimed Suzi excitedly. "I would like that."

The three of them left together, and they walked Suzi to her classroom. At the door, Raynr bent down and shook her hand. "It was a pleasure meeting you, Suzi. Keep up your faith, and you will soon see your father again."

"Do you really think so?" she asked, her brave veneer cracking for a moment.

"I do think so," he answered. "See you tomorrow, Suzi."

"I hope so. Bye, Mommy."

Skipping happily, Suzi headed into her classroom, but Ogawa frowned at Raynr, not quite so happy with him. "You shouldn't offer her false hope," she whispered.

"Have you told her that she'll never see her father again?"

"Well, no," answered Ogawa, turning and heading down the corridor. "I don't know that for certain."

"It's a good guess, though, isn't it?" said the lieutenant. "Until she has no hope, I don't think it's wrong to give her some."

Ogawa sighed heavily. "I'll admit, I'm not sure how to

handle this. She's at a difficult age—not old enough to hear the truth yet . . . but too old to be fooled."

Raynr Sleven smiled. "You're never too old to be fooled, if it can spare you heartache."

A party from the *Enterprise*, consisting of Captain Picard, Counselor Troi, Commander Riker, and Commander La Forge, arrived on the *Javlek* and were conducted to what looked like a grand ballroom, with a cathedral ceiling, numerous green crystal chandeliers, and intricate mosaic-tiled flooring. It was empty except for hundreds of piles of sand arranged in lengthy rows. Lying upon each pile of sand were a number of small personal items: medals, rank insignia, and holographic photos. Seeing these stark representations of so many dead was a sobering experience for Picard, and it brought home how many had been lost upon both the *Petrask* and the *Barcelona*.

"Wait here," said their escort. "Commander Kaylena and the rest of the funeral procession are on their way."

The captain nodded. "Thank you."

A moment later, the lights in the great hall dimmed, and they could hear a somber drumbeat and chanting voices from the open door. Picard and his party stepped aside to allow the procession of drummers and mourners to enter. The Romulans were dressed in scarlet robes emblazoned with gold trim, their traditional colors of mourning, and more than a few of them were weeping as they entered. It was always odd to see a race identical to Vulcans behaving emotionally, but Picard quite understood. He had buried too many comrades not to understand.

At the end of the procession came Commander Kaylena, bearing a golden scroll in her hand; she was dressed the same as the others, without any indication of her rank. Continuing their solemn chant, the mourners filed into the great hall, and each one took a position beside a pile of sand and mementos. Kaylena strode to the middle of the hall and halted beside a slightly larger funeral cairn. Picard suspected that it represented the captain of the *Petrask*.

When everyone was in place, the drummers beat a resounding conclusion to their dirge, then they stood perfectly still on the periphery, along with the visitors from the *Enterprise*. Commander Kaylena surveyed the assemblage, then she lifted her regal chin and began to speak:

"Loyal citizens of the Star Empire, and distinguished guests from the *Enterprise*, we are gathered here to honor our fallen comrades from the *Petrask* and the *Barcelona*. They have given their lives in the pursuit of science, attempting to save others from death and destruction. As yet, we do not know the names or motives of their assassins—or if there was any intelligence behind this cowardly act—but we will never rest until we have avenged these brutal killings."

For several moments, the mourners chanted and wailed, and the drummers beat a rapid tattoo. Then the great ballroom quieted again, and Kaylena went on, "We know one thing—that these heroes will be welcomed back to the *Vorta Vor*, where they will serve as honor guards as long as the stars shine in the firmament. The grief of their loved ones and comrades is shared by every citizen of the Empire, and of the Federation. We also honor the fallen heroes of Starfleet, whose spirits will accompany our companions to the world beyond this plane of existence."

She turned to the visitors. "Captain Picard, would you like to speak?"

"Yes, thank you," he answered, stepping forward. "So far, the *Enterprise* has lost only one comrade on this mission, Ensign Crago Wapot, and we cherish the memory of this brave officer. He gave his life so that others may live, and this is the highest calling of the security department, in which he was a squad leader. Eighty-eight beings perished aboard the *Barcelona*, and only one survivor lived to tell their story—but all of us will tell of their sacrifice many thousands of times. For every member of the *Barcelona*'s crew, we wish peace in the afterlife, in whatever form they believe, and we pray for comfort for their loved ones in their hour of grief." He nodded to Commander Kaylena to indicate he was through.

She continued, "Thank you, Captain Picard. With these witnesses present, we commit their ashes—in this case symbolic ashes—to the stars. As in the days of our ancestors' arrival on Romulus, when they sought refuge in the Cave of Winds, we use the power of the wind to ferry our dead to the World to come. As I read the Roll of Honor, will the attendants release the mortal remains of our fallen comrades, allowing their spirits to depart."

Kaylena unfurled her golden scroll and began to read names aloud. As each name was read, an attendant standing beside a heap of sand placed a small blinking device on the pile. At once, the sand and mementos began to swirl into a funnel cloud, like a dust devil.

Within seconds, each one of these swirling funeral pyres rose toward the cathedral ceiling, where they commingled into a great, roaring circle of sand. Picard realized that the green chandeliers produced not only light but the energy needed for this impressive undertaking.

"I think those devices negate the artificial gravity on this deck," whispered La Forge.

Some attendants had more than one comrade to honor, and they moved throughout the hall, taking new positions. As the amount of wind increased, it buffeted mourners and visitors alike, until it was as if they were standing in a storm. Finally, the last name was read, and Commander Kaylena raised her arms to the impressive cloud of dust whirling over their heads.

"May the void of space accept our legion of heroes!" intoned the commander. At once, the glittering chandeliers aimed white beams into the whirlpool, and the sandstorm began to glow with a billion burning embers, like fireflies caught in a tornado. It took almost a minute, but all the sand and relics were eventually dematerialized—outside the ship, the captain presumed. It was an intricate burial procedure, but strangely effective and efficient.

When the last speck of sand was gone, the wind stopped, and the drummers started a steady beat to accompany the mourners on their way out of the ballroom. There was no small talk among the Romulans—they were done with their service. Commander Kaylena remained behind to confer with her guests.

"Thank you for coming," she said. "It meant a great deal to us."

"And to us as well," answered the captain. "I believe

you've met my officers." There was a round of introductions, and the Romulan graciously welcomed each member of Picard's party.

"I'm also thankful that you returned the radiation suits in your possession," said Kaylena with the wisp of a smile. "Now, Captain, do you have a few minutes to discuss our next course of action?"

"I'm afraid we don't need a few minutes," answered Picard grimly. "Our new orders are to station warning buoys around the debris and the anomaly, then be prepared to leave here. The reinforcements we sent for are not coming either."

The Romulan looked shocked. "You would abandon this extraordinary—and dangerous—situation?"

"It's not my doing," answered the captain, "but a direct order from my superiors. Apparently, this problem is more widespread than we thought, and there are other places to investigate. It should only take us about a day to set the buoys, and we're going to start right now. Then we'll assist you until we're ordered to leave."

Kaylena scowled. "By that time, my replacement will be here to relieve me." The beautiful Romulan looked up at the glowing green chandeliers, and her eyes grew misty for a moment. "I will certainly lose command of this task force, but I had hoped to maintain command of my ship. Your presence to testify on my behalf, Captain Picard, would have been helpful."

"Commander, it certainly wasn't my intention—"

"Enough," she barked, cutting him off. "We must proceed with our investigation, and do so immediately. The centurion will conduct you back to the transporter room. Good day to you and your party, Captain."

Angrily, Kaylena stalked off, leaving the visitors in the hands of the escort who had brought them to the ballroom.

"This way, Captain Picard," said the stiff-necked centurion, leading the way into the corridor. The guests dutifully followed, with Riker and La Forge discussing details of the buoy assignment.

"You seem troubled," said Deanna Troi, falling into step beside the captain. "You didn't wish our collaboration with them to end like this."

"No," he said with a frown, "I didn't wish it to end like this, not when it was just getting started."

nine

Teska surveyed the humanoids hanging from the ceiling like the sides of beef she had once seen in San Francisco, where she had spent her childhood. She knew she would never forget that image, and she doubted if she would ever forget this one either. They were encased in transparent bags, which expanded and contracted at the rate of normal breathing. Shining a light into the morass, the Vulcan could see vines and clumps of moss snaking everywhere among the dark rafters. A thick green mucus dripped to the floor from many of the still forms. Here and there, the life-support system had been blasted away by disruptor fire, and there were scorch marks and burnt bodies among those in suspended animation. Even a perfunctory glance told her that many humanoid species were represented among the ranks of slaves in this underground chamber on Lomar.

Unfortunately, the Vulcan's tricorder informed her that the vast majority of the bags in this section of the complex held corpses. In their battle to eliminate the moss creatures, the Romulans had decimated much of the life-support system, dooming those hanging in suspension.

Although trained all her life to discount emotion, Teska almost wished she could muster some anger and indignation at what the moss creatures had done to so many innocent beings—not just the hundreds here but the billions who had perished during the Genesis Wave. Slaughter on such a grand scale was beyond intellectual comprehension—it demanded an emotional response, which she was unable to give. Her two escorts, who had come to Lomar days ago, looked benumbed by their experiences. To them, these now *were* slabs of beef, waiting to be catalogued and distributed.

"Staggering, isn't it?" said the human medical officer, Franklin Oswald, as he gazed upward at the disturbing sight.

"Yes," she admitted, "it is. They obviously did not consider humanoids to be their equals."

"No, they considered us to be food, tools, and transportation," said her other colleague, a female Tiburonian biologist by the name of Pokrifa.

"Not to mention raw material for their new planets," muttered Oswald. He studied his tricorder readings as he strolled beneath the grim shapes hanging from the rafters. "You know, some of these bodies are centuries old, and so are the ships that were recovered. They must have needed them all to build this facility; but after that, they stored them, just keeping a few active. We've found whole crews that were listed as missing during the Dominion war."

"Have you successfully revived many of them?" asked Teska.

"We've got eighty-seven of them on the hospital ship," answered Oswald, "and only a few are any better off than these poor souls. The rest are like vegetables—alive, but nothing left of their minds. We're still trying various techniques to revive them, but the Romulans made such a mess of things that it's hopeless, in most cases."

Teska nodded solemnly. "Have my predecessors retrieved any useful information?"

"No," answered the Tiburonian, Pokrifa. "They're too confused when we revive them, and they're dying. I've never seen a Vulcan look discouraged before, but I swear the last one did. Where do you want to begin?"

"Admiral Nechayev wants all of them liberated and interrogated as quickly as possible."

"Well, that's the problem," said Pokrifa. "Do we hurry and do this efficiently, or do we take our time and do it with at least a small probability of success? Remember, each one of these slaves was infested by the moss creatures, and that parasitic relationship is the only thing keeping them alive. It takes time to remove the vines and tentacles without hastening their death."

Oswald nodded his head in agreement. "I don't think your admiral knows what she's gotten herself into here."

"She knows," Teska assured her colleagues. "She warned me this would be an unpleasant experience."

The medical worker gave a humorless chuckle. "That's the understatement of the year."

"We could spend a year just trying to identify these people," said the Tiburonian. "And the autopsies are difficult with all the foreign bodies in them. We're glad to see you, but we need more help."

"More help is not forthcoming," answered Teska. She reached up and touched the dangling foot of the closest humanoid, who appeared to be a Vulcan like herself. Or perhaps it was a Romulan or a Rigelian, both of whom were physically indistinguishable from Vulcans.

"Have you tried to interrogate them without cutting them down?" she asked.

Oswald and Pokrifa looked queasily at one another as if nobody would consider such a selfish course of action. "That won't save their lives," replied the human.

"True," answered Teska. "But you have told me that saving their lives is virtually impossible, and that interrogating them in a confused and dying state is impractical. Therefore, the logical procedure would be to interrogate them first."

"A bit cold-blooded, isn't it?" asked Oswald.

The Vulcan cocked an eyebrow. "The Romulans have seized everything of value from this facility, and our only access to information is these impaired witnesses. Would you sacrifice their doubtful future in order to find out if the Genesis Wave is about to be unleashed again?"

"Well, yeah, if you put it that way," answered Oswald hesitantly.

"Get me a ladder," ordered Teska.

On the bridge of the *Sequoia*, Admiral Nechayev gazed squarely at her first officer, the Benzite named Marbinz, wondering if he would ever accept the fact that this was not his ship anymore. It never was. If he were the captain of this vessel, she would cut him down at the knees, stuff him into a shuttlecraft, and send him home. But he was her first officer—her liaison to the rest of the crew—and how she handled him would determine how well she related to all the others. So she held her tongue and let him make his point.

"I'm sorry, Captain," said the Benzite staunchly, "I can't in good conscience let you to send ninety percent of our crew down to Lomar without objection. This ship has just been refitted—we have ongoing diagnostics, testing, and training that requires our engineering staff and other crucial departments. We're here in support, not to take over this planet and leave ourselves short-handed."

"Objection noted," replied Nechayev calmly. "You have every right to put your objections in your log and send them to my superiors. But be smart when you pick your fights, Commander. They're not going to back you when they've charged *me* with bringing some order to this operation. I've just come back from Lomar, and believe me, we're in far better condition than the people down there. They're woefully shorthanded. Save your firepower until you really need it for a battle you can win. Now get those work crews together and get them down there."

The Benzite blinked at her, stunned by her candor and bluntness. "Yes, Sir." With a brusque nod, Commander Marbinz strode toward the turbolift and exited the bridge.

Nechayev gazed at the rest of her subordinates as they snapped their heads back to their consoles. That was all the lessons on the chain of command they were going to get today, decided the admiral.

The Coridan on the tactical station looked up with a quizzical expression. "Captain," he said, "an unsecured, anonymous, subspace message has arrived for you. It's very brief and doesn't make much sense. Shall I erase it?"

"No," she barked. "I don't wish anybody to screen my messages for me. Please remember that in the future. What does it say?"

"The eel-bird chases the *sehlat*," replied the officer puzzledly.

Nechayev let a slight smile escape from her lips. "Thank you. Now you may erase it."

Although there were quizzical expressions all around the bridge, Nechayev ignored them. The admiral was a wily poker player, and one thing she had learned long ago was never to show *anyone* her hole card.

The invitation, which was printed on reed parchment like the ancient Books of Prophecy, read:

"You have been chosen to receive the most important revelation to the Bajoran people since the discovery of the Wormhole. Through diligent research and years of archeological exploration, a former vedek has uncovered a previously unknown Orb. This is the most powerful Orb of them all—the Orb of Life. Our enemies are still active and still determined to prevent the Bajoran people from restoring spiritual health in the Alpha Quadrant. Therefore, secrecy must be maintained. We urge you not to reveal the contents of this message to anyone, not even your closest associates.

"If you wish to experience firsthand the incredible power of the Orb of Life, please report to shuttlebay 42 in the ancient city of Tempassa one hour before dawn on the first Day of Redemption. In the cause of maintaining secrecy, we urge you to come yourself or send *one* representative with this invitation in hand. Each invitation has been coded with latinum filaments embedded on the cellular level, and duplicates will not be accepted. You will not return to Tempassa for forty-eight hours, so bring provisions for a two-day trip. This will be the most incredible journey of your life."

The invitation was signed, "Protectors of the Orb of Life."

Chellac reacted to his reading with a toothy grin and folded up the extra invitation. "Not a bad job of writing, if I do say so myself."

"Do you really think they'll keep it a secret?" asked the young shuttlecraft pilot, Cassie Jackson.

"No, of course not," answered the Ferengi with a laugh. "If you want the word to get out, you tell people it's an incredible secret. That stands to reason. There aren't any latinum filaments in these things either, but nobody knows that but us. When our guests start arriving, we've got to make some sort of show of checking these invitations."

Cassie looked thoughtful and pointed under the instrument panel of her shuttlecraft. "I've got a trash receptacle down here. I could stick the invitation in, press a few buttons, and declare it valid."

"Sounds good to me," answered Chellac. "I'll keep them distracted while you do that." He smiled at his human accomplice. "Are you sure you don't have any Ferengi blood in you?"

"I was raised in an orphanage," she answered, "but I don't think so."

"Would you *like* some children with Ferengi blood?" Chellac sidled closer to the attractive human and batted his eyelashes under his thick brow.

"No, thank you," replied Cassie, pushing the amorous Ferengi away. "I just want lots of latinum."

"Ah, a woman after my own heart. I have no doubt that you will be a great success in life."

"I still don't see how we're going to make money from this," complained Cassie.

"You leave that to me, like I leave the flying to you." Chellac gazed out the viewport of the shuttlecraft. "Ah, I think our first passenger has arrived."

"Is he alone?" asked Cassie, "like he's supposed to be?"

"Yes." The Ferengi and the human peered out the window at the fog-shrouded gangplank and could see a lone figure striding briskly toward them. Golden-hued street lamps cut through the darkness, but it was still impossible to see the details of their passenger's clothing and rank. As he approached, Cassie opened the shuttle-craft hatch, and they waited expectantly for their guest to enter.

He stuck his head in first, and it was a noble head with a thicket of gray hair atop a deeply lined face that was creased into a smile. The notches on the Bajoran's nose looked as prominent as the ridges of a Klingon's forehead. He brandished his invitation. "Hello, is this shuttle to see the newest Orb?"

"It is indeed!" crowed Chellac, taking the invitation and motioning their visitor inside. The Ferengi glanced at the name on the back of the parchment and looked up with surprise. "Ocman Danriv?"

"Yes. You sound surprised." The friendly Bajoran

stepped into the craft and handed the Ferengi his luggage.

"Well, I didn't expect Bajor's greatest poet to arrive before anybody else," answered Chellac.

"And why not? Not all artists are habitually late, you know. I happen to pride myself on being very punctual." He strode to the back of the six-passenger craft and took a seat in the last row.

"Of course," answered Chellac, "no offense intended. My name is Chellac, and this is our pilot, Cassie Jackson."

"Just to point out the obvious," said the poet, "but neither one of you looks like a former vedek."

"We're not. We're—"

"Another one coming," said Cassie, pointing out the viewport.

Conversation ended, and they waited expectantly as their second passenger walked cautiously down the gangplank, carrying a small bag under her arm. This was an older female wearing the regal rust-colored robes of the Bajoran clergy. With a stern look on her round face, she stepped into the shuttlecraft and crossed her arms. "This had better not be a joke," she grumbled.

"I can assure you, Vedek Zain, it is no joke," Chellac assured her. "Your invitation?"

With a scowl, she handed over the slip of parchment and surveyed the interior of the shuttlecraft. "Oh, we have an entertainer onboard," she said dryly.

The poet smiled. "I'm not half as entertaining as the Vedek Assembly."

"Let me check those invitations," said Cassie, breaking the tension somewhat. Chellac handed them over, and the pilot made a careful show of inserting them into her trash receptacle. Vedek Zain pointedly took a seat in the first row, far removed from the poet in the rear. She stuffed her bag under her seat.

"What's this?" said Cassie. "Now there's a whole group out there."

The Ferengi peered out the window, and he could see the silhouettes of a large party on the gangplank. One of them broke away and ran toward the shuttlecraft, carrying a weapon in his hand. Chellac almost shut the door, but he decided it was best to maintain a brave front. A moment later, a young soldier stuck his head in the doorway and, without saying a word, scrutinized all of them. Then he shouldered his weapon and dashed back to the group.

"Well, so much for secrecy," observed Cassie. Chellac gave her a slight smile.

"That's got to be the military," said Ocman Danriv. "You don't expect them just to enter an unknown shuttle-craft, do you? They're not as brave as civilians like us."

"Or as foolish," muttered Vedek Zain.

Now two figures broke off from the clutch of soldiers and walked toward the shuttlecraft. One of them was a stiff-backed male in a gray uniform, and the other was a short female with a pronounced limp. With relief, Chellac noticed that the squad of soldiers retreated into the fog.

"General Mira," said Chellac, meeting them at the door. "And Minister Gatryk, it is a pleasure to welcome you to our craft. Your invitations, please."

The haughty general looked snidely at the Ferengi as he drew the parchment from his breast pocket. "You have a lot of gall summoning us here with this cryptic nonsense."

"Cryptic?" said the poet in the rear. "On the contrary,

General, that invitation is a model of suspenseful writing, promising a great deal but delivering precious few details. It's guaranteed to make one investigate further, as proven by your presence."

"Why, thank you," said Chellac proudly. "Minister Gatryk, your invitation?"

The short female fumbled in the pockets of her brown suit for several seconds, then she seemed to remember something. With a smile, she reached into her luggage, pulled out the invitation, and handed it over. "I must say that anyone who spares me two days of sitting in the Chamber of Ministers has my gratitude."

"Thank you, Minister." Chellac studied the invitations for a moment, then he handed them to Cassie for her bogus processing. "May I stow your luggage?"

"I'll keep mine," answered the general, who promptly sat in the front row beside Vedek Zain. "So they roped you into this, too?"

"I'm afraid so," replied the religious figure.

Minister Gatryk limped to the rear of the craft and sat beside the poet, and the two of them exchanged greetings and small talk, while Chellac stowed what luggage he was given.

"I have many questions," said the vedek.

The Ferengi smiled pleasantly. "And all will be answered in due time."

"I only have one question," said the general. "When do we leave?"

"We await one more passenger," answered Chellac, peering out the window. "But we won't wait long for him, because he may have difficulty getting here."

"And why is that?"

"Because he's a wanted criminal. His name is Bakus."

"Bakus, the Maquis leader?" asked General Mira in alarm. He jumped to his feet. "This becomes more ludicrous with every passing moment."

"Please look around you, General," begged Chellac. "Every segment of Bajoran society is represented on this craft. Except for one—the rebels, the criminals, the outcasts. And they're as big a part of Bajor as any of you. They always have been. Bakus is known and loved among those people, and we have to tell them about this discovery, too."

The general wagged his finger at the Ferengi. "All I've got to say is—this had better be good."

Chellac laughed nervously. "Well, you know how the Orbs are. Good or bad, they're never boring."

"Don't speak lightly of the Orbs of the Prophets," warned Vedek Zain, her dark eyes flashing with anger. "And I agree with the general, because if this is some kind of trick—"

"Someone's coming," said Cassie, leaning forward to peer into the fog. "One person, alone."

Conversation on the shuttlecraft mercifully stopped as all five of them waited for the lone figure to emerge from the fog and approach the open hatch. He was wearing a simple monk's robe and a hood which covered his face, making it impossible to identify him. Without a word, the new arrival stepped into the shuttlecraft, and Chellac quickly closed the hatch behind him. He couldn't give a definite reason, but there was something about this last passenger that made him nervous.

When the guest pushed back his hood to reveal his face, there were several gasps of surprise. It wasn't another Bajoran, but a distinguished-looking Vulcan with a smattering of gray in his straight black hair. Slung over his shoulder was a large knapsack, made from the same crude material as his robe. From a pocket on the knapsack, he pull the invitation and presented it to Chellac.

"I am here to represent Bakus," he announced. "He sends his regrets."

"Oh, I'm sorry he couldn't make it," said the Ferengi, taking the slip of parchment. He handed it to Cassie, who once again pretended to scan it. "But it's understandable."

"Quite understandable," answered the newest arrival.

"Do you have a name?" asked the vedek snidely.

"Yes, but you could not pronounce it." He motioned to the two empty seats in the middle row. "May I be seated?"

"Please do," answered Chellac. "Can I take your bag?"

"No." Without another word, the mysterious Vulcan sat in front of Ocman Danriv.

"You are a Vulcan, aren't you?" asked the poet.

"I am."

"So, you can't lie."

"That is correct. Instead of lying, I am more than likely to say nothing."

"Very commendable," said the poet with an amused smile.

"Listen, can we go now?" asked Cassie, starting the prelaunch sequence on her instrument panel.

"Sure." Chellac took a seat beside the Vulcan as Cassie asked permission from shuttlebay operations to take off. Five minutes later, the shuttlecraft lifted off the pad and streaked away into the night sky of Bajor.

Everything seemed fine to Chellac until his pilot blurted a colorful swearword in the Terran tongue. "We've got a military ship following us," she complained.

"General," said the Ferengi, "could you please tell your boys to back off?"

Huffily, General Mira crossed his arms. "I don't know what you're talking about."

"Okay, Cassie, let's transport the general back down to the planet," said Chellac. "The Bajoran military can learn about the Orb of Life from the news reports."

With a scowl, the general rose to his feet and went to the empty copilot's seat. "I'll send them the code to withdraw." He worked the board for a minute, then returned to his seat.

After a few more minutes, Cassie announced, "They're gone. All right, everybody, get ready to go to warp."

Chellac looked around at the somber, frightened faces. "Come on, cheer up. You're not going to be disappointed by this trip, I guarantee it."

"If you've really discovered a new Orb," said Minister Gatryk, "you're going to be more renowned than any of us."

"I'm not the boss here," answered the Ferengi. "Save your accolades for the one who deserves them."

In a brilliant flash, the six-passenger shuttlecraft shot into warp drive with the cream of Bajoran society on board, having no clue where they were headed. Such was the drawing power of the Orbs of the Prophets, thought Chellac; even a fake Orb was better than none.

ten

Teska almost lost count of how many mind-melds she attempted on the slaves hanging in suspended animation in the underground chambers of Lomar. Even restricting herself to those who seemed relatively healthy, according to tricorder readings, it was an exercise in futility. She found brain activity—subconscious functions such as breathing and heartbeat—plus a few basic emotions. Ironically, most of their emotions were an odd amalgam of contentment and happiness, although the subjects were one step away from death. The Vulcan attributed this to the aftereffects of the infestation, even if the moss creatures themselves were dead. What she encountered wasn't just a dulling of senses and memories but a decimation of them.

In three of her initial subjects, there were memory fragments, but they seemed false and removed from reality, like half-remembered dreams. She found memories of loved ones, often long dead but inexplicably alive again. There were fragments of familiar places—

hometowns, resorts, beloved starships, and favorite work environments. Since the slaves had been deluded for years, there was virtually nothing real for her to latch onto. Unlike normal mind-melds, everything she found seemed untrustworthy.

Of course, these weren't the ideal circumstances— performing a mind-meld while perched atop a ladder with one's hand inserted into a gooey stasis bag covered with vines and moss. But the Vulcan persevered with the knowledge that she had hundreds of potential subjects. With even the lowest probability rate of success, one from all these unfortunate victims was bound to have a functional mind.

Her breakthrough came on the twenty-second subject. It was a human female, which made sense because she had always felt strong identification with humans due to her early upbringing. As soon as Teska inserted her hand into the slimy innards of the bag and touched the face of the blond woman, she felt a slight shock. That was a good sign, yet she steeled herself for another failure.

"Begin recording," Teska told her colleagues, the human medical officer, Franklin Oswald, and the Tiburonian biologist, Pokrifa. She ignored the glances they gave one another, intimating that all of this was pointless.

Getting a good grip on the ladder with her free hand and steadying her legs on the rung, Teska closed her eyes and touched the woman's face. As soon as she made contact, the Vulcan felt a ripple of pain and longing, which was different from what she'd felt with any of the previous subjects. It showed critical thinking, and she instantly tried to capitalize on this by telling the young woman where she was. For the sake of her associates recording the conversation, she related their thoughts aloud:

"You are being held prisoner."

I am?

"Do not be alarmed. You are safe now."

I can't feel my body!

"You are in suspended animation, and our minds are melding."

I'm scared.

"That is understandable, but I am here to help you. We need information to help you. Where do you think you are?"

On my ship . . . the U.S.S. Tempest.

"In reality, you are in an underground facility where you have been tricked into working as a slave for enemies of the Federation. I am a Vulcan—I cannot lie to you. My name is Teska. Who are you?"

Linda . . . Linda Feeney. I feel you're telling the truth.

"Linda, this is crucial. What is your job here? What project were you most recently working on?"

Engineer, second class. I'm working on the emitter.

"What emitter?" With her eyes closed, Teska couldn't see her two colleagues move closer, but in her heightened state she could sense them.

The portable emitter . . . the small one.

"The Genesis emitter?"

The Life Giver . . . the Tree Maker. I'm scared—I can't feel my legs!

Teska sent her subject waves of unemotional tranquility, hoping it would calm her. After a few moments, Linda Feeney seemed to relax and reopen her mind.

"You say there is a small version of the Life Giver?"

Yes, for tests. Also for the backup plan.

"How many of these devices did you make?"

A few . . . I saw others working on them.

"And where are the portable devices?"

They're in the laboratory. One is in the field . . . Torga IV. Can you save me?

"We will try," answered Teska with a nod. "Did something recently happen to you that was unusual?"

Yes, I got sick. They took me to sickbay and treated me. I was lonely there.

"You are now among friends, and we will care for you."

Tony . . . he said he loved me! Is Tony all right?

"Unknown. You must rest now, Linda, because you need your strength to get well."

Thank you . . . Teska.

With a grunt, the Vulcan broke off the mind-meld, letting Linda Feeney drift back into her troubled slumber. In a swoon, Teska almost fell off the ladder, but Oswald caught her and held her in place until she could recover her balance and step down.

"I think you'd better take a break," suggested Oswald.

"The way you talked—you were like two different people," said Pokrifa with awe. "Can we believe her when she says there are portable Genesis devices?"

"The mind-meld does not lie," answered Teska, regaining her composure. "Also Dr. Carol Marcus was known to have a portable device, which she used to create the Genesis Cavern on the Regula asteroid. So we know it is possible."

The Vulcan glanced up at the human engineer, whose body was swinging slightly in the musty air. "Apparently, her illness caused the creatures to relinquish some of their control over her mind. I must inform Admiral Nechayev immediately. Make preparations to transport Linda Feeney to the hospital ship. Use appropriate caution, because she is invaluable."

"But we haven't found any portable devices like the one you described," said Pokrifa.

Teska fixed her colleague with a baleful gaze. "But we were not the first ones here."

After hearing the Vulcan's report, Admiral Nechayev frowned deeply and rose from the desk in her ready room. "This coincides with another report I received. The large moon of Meldrar I had sudden and inexplicable plant growth over twelve thousand square meters of land. And we're talking about an arid wasteland. Nobody knows anything about it, except that a shuttlecraft from the penal colony and a few passengers from a freighter are also missing."

"Starfleet should begin a massive investigation," said Teska.

The admiral scowled and swept a hand through her blond-gray hair. "Starfleet is strung out all over the quadrant, trying to find and rescue survivors of the Genesis Wave, plus investigating all these other strange occurrences—disappearances, radiation poisoning. Everyone considers this just one more bizarre event among hundreds."

"Can we investigate it?"

"We already have an assignment," answered Nechayev stiffly. "And it's starting to pay off. But if the Romulans have gotten hold of Genesis emitters—" She didn't need to finish the sentence.

Instead the admiral sat back at her desk and fired up her computer terminal. "Engineer Feeney said there was a device out in the field. Where did she say they put it?"

"A planet named Torga IV."

The admiral nodded and began working her board. Within a few seconds, she had brought up the earlier message. After rereading it, Nechayev sat back in her chair with a stricken look on her face.

"The freighter which went to Meldrar I . . . it came from Torga IV."

Teska cocked an eyebrow. "That is near Bajor, if memory serves me. We must cease operations here and go to investigate."

"You mean disobey our orders?" asked Nechayev with alarm. "We've got work to do here—lives to save."

Impassively, the Vulcan replied, "It is a logical assumption that unknown parties have a portable Genesis device and tested it on a moon. It is also a logical assumption that these unknown individuals obtained a shuttlecraft and have escaped, perhaps to go into hiding. They are not Romulans."

"Why do you say that?"

"Romulans would not test the device in Federation space, where the results could be so easily identified."

"No, I suppose not," agreed Nechayev. She groaned and rubbed her eyes. "Talk about the cat being out of the bag."

"We must leave here and investigate," insisted the Vulcan. "Any other information we would learn here is insignificant compared to this. The number of lives we could save pales in comparison to the number at risk. Even if we were to resuscitate every slave in suspended animation, none of them could confirm or deny that the Romulans have Genesis devices. We must assume they have them."

"They'll deny it," said the admiral.

"Of course. They are known for being untruthful."

"You're married to a Romulan," said Nechayev, "do you have any contacts there?"

Teska shook her head. "As you pointed out, the whereabouts of my mate are unknown, and I trust no other Romulans. We must investigate this ourselves, and do so immediately."

"I can't do that," muttered Nechayev, staring at her computer screen. "The best I can do is report all of this to Starfleet and ask for guidance. Until then, we proceed with our mission."

Teska replied, "You used a colorful human expression: 'the cat is out of the bag.' If I were to use a colorful human expression, it would be: 'Nero fiddled while Rome burned.' "

"You remind me a lot of your uncle," grumbled Nechayev. "You're dismissed."

With a nod, the beautiful Vulcan turned on her heel and marched out the door. Nechayev looked up from her desk, scowling, but she had to admit the truth: Teska was right. The trail might already be cold, but somebody had to get on it immediately. That couldn't be the *Sequoia* unless she disobeyed direct orders and became one of those captains she often denigrated.

It would shake the admiralty to their core when she told them that the Romulans had possession of Genesis, but there was little anyone could do about it, except to make urgent diplomatic inquiries. There was *nothing* she could do about it—not while she orbited this dead planet, struggling to keep scores of brain-dead patients alive. For the first time in her life, Alynna Nechayev felt helpless.

"What is this forsaken place?" asked Vedek Zain as she peered out the shuttlecraft window at a barren desert with various crumbling plateaus in the distance. Piloted by the young human, the small craft swooped downward into a landing approach.

"Does it matter?" asked Chellac with a contented shrug. The five passengers looked at him suspiciously, except for the Vulcan, whose expression hadn't changed in several hours of warp-speed flight. "Be thankful that we're here," added the Ferengi.

He rose to his feet and slipped into the copilot's seat beside Cassie Jackson. "Any sign of them?"

"Right down there." The pilot pointed at two specks and a glittering silver circle, which was a reflective tent pitched in the middle of the vast expanse of sand and shale.

Chellac felt Ocman Danriv hovering over his shoulder. "For the dwelling of the Orb of Life," said the poet, "this is an awfully lifeless place."

"All in good time," answered the Ferengi. "Please return to your seat—we'll be landing soon."

As they zoomed closer, the two specks on the ground turned into two Bajorans, a fat one and a thin one, who covered their eyes from the blowing sand as the shuttlecraft settled to the ground.

"Good flying, Pilot," said General Mira appreciatively as the engines whined down and the dust stopped blowing.

"Thank you, General," said Cassie with a smile. She popped the hatch, and the passengers rose to their feet, forming a line to exit.

As each one stepped out of the shuttlecraft, he was greeted by a beaming Prylar Yorka. "Vedek Zain, it's good to see you again!"

"Yorka!" she said with surprise. "I thought we sent you to one of the provinces after you refused to recognize Kai Winn."

"You did," he replied magnanimously, "but I rose above my circumstances. And didn't I turn out to be right about that fraud, Winn?"

The vedek winced but said nothing as she stepped aside to let the next passenger out.

"General Mira," said Yorka, gripping the hand of the stiff-backed soldier. "We've never met, but I am Prylar Yorka."

"If you've brought us here under false pretenses—"

"I haven't," Yorka assured him as he maneuvered the general aside. "Minister Gatryk, it's a pleasure to see you again."

The small Bajoran with the limp peered curiously at their host. "We've met before?"

"At the Vedek Assembly, when I was a member," replied Yorka. "That was a few years ago."

"So *you* are the former vedek we were promised in the invitation?" asked Ocman Danriv from the hatchway.

"None other." The monk rushed to greet the poet. "I've been a fan of yours for as long as I can remember. I especially loved 'Ode to the Prophets' and 'The Soul of Gratitude.'"

"Ah, those are old works," said the poet dismissively. "You ought to read my latest, 'Descent of the Pahwraiths.' "

"Where I've been, I'm afraid I haven't seen much recent literature," said Yorka apologetically. He turned his attention to the hooded Vulcan emerging from the shuttlecraft. "I don't know you, Sir."

"Nor should you," he answered. "I am the representative of Bakus, who sends his regrets."

Yorka looked slightly disappointed, but he managed a smile. "And your name?"

"Is that really necessary?"

"Well, no, I suppose not," answered the monk hesitantly.

Chellac and Cassie stepped out of the craft and leaned against it with their arms crossed. The Ferengi wanted to take over the presentation, but he knew this was Yorka's show. When it came down to asking for cash and support, he would perform that onerous task. To him, that was the important part of the ceremony.

"All right, Yorka," said General Mira, "you've got us here. Now what?"

The monk turned to his waiting acolyte and said, "Fetch the Orb."

The dour Bajoran nodded and hustled into the reflective tent. Now the five guests no longer looked so disdainful as they pressed forward to get their first look at a sacred relic. A moment later, the acolyte emerged, holding the familiar metal box in his hands. With reverence, he handed it to Prylar Yorka, who gripped the receptacle as if it contained gold-pressed latinum.

"That doesn't look like any Ark I've ever seen," muttered Vedek Zain, perusing the gleaming metal box. "Although it is about the right size."

"Do we look at it one at a time?" asked Minister Gatryk.

"In private, I hope," added the vedek.

Yorka shook his head. "No, this isn't the kind of Orb one gazes at in quiet contemplation. The Orb of Life is more of an *active* Orb, as you will see."

"May I inspect it?" asked General Mira.

"No, but you may gaze in wonder at what it does." Yorka walked several meters away from the shuttlecraft and the clutch of observers and set the box on the crusty sand. When he opened the door of the container, the general and the vedek pressed forward to see, and Yorka waved them back. "I wouldn't get too close. You will be able to see just fine where you are."

"Hmmph!" snorted Vedek Zain, crossing her arms. "I have a feeling we're about to see a parlor trick."

"I hope it's not disappointing," said the poet, Ocman. "I hate an anticlimax."

"You needn't worry about that," replied Chellac with a grin.

Yorka pressed the buttons, using his broad back to shield what he was doing from his inquisitive audience. When the beam shot from the other side, there were expressions of surprise, because Orbs of the Prophets did not usually behave like beamed weapons. When a blazing wall of green flame consumed the barren land, and the wind began to howl, while the sky darkened with furious clouds, the observers clustered together nervously. Within a few seconds, they had so much to watch that their heads swiveled back and forth like communication arrays gone mad.

Although he had seen it before, Chellac gaped along with the others as the desolate wasteland erupted with sprawling, teeming life. Monstrous plants and vines shot into the air and crawled along the burning ground like the tentacles of a terrible beast. The swirling air smelled like a mixture of sulfur, blooming flowers, and decomposing filth. Minister Gatryk bent over and vomited, and Chellac fought the impulse to gag. All of them retreated from the hellish green flames and twisting, writhing thickets.

"This is an abomination!" screamed the minister over the roar of the wind.

"No, no, it's *beautiful!*" insisted the poet, Ocman. "It's fantastic!"

"Magnificent!" yelled General Mira. "We must have it!"

The Vulcan calmly pulled out a padd and began to take notes.

With a satisfied grin on his face, Prylar Yorka walked back to join his guests. "Do you still think it's a parlor trick, Vedek Zain?"

She stared at him. "I'm not sure what it is . . . but it warrants more study."

"Is that *all* you can say?" cried Ocman in disbelief. "With this, we could feed billions of starving people! We could turn a barren planet into a paradise. With this Orb, we can create *life!*"

"Or destroy it," said Minister Gatryk.

The general stepped between her and Yorka. "What do you want for it?"

"Ah, that's where I come in!" said the Ferengi, jumping into the conversation. "Let's step into the shuttlecraft, where we can talk terms away from all this noise."

"No!" answered Ocman. "I want to keep watching it. I will write an epic poem immediately. By tomorrow, Yorka, all of Bajor will praise your name."

"As an Orb, it belongs to the religious establishment," insisted Vedek Zain.

"Not until I am returned to my rightful place in the Vedek Assembly," warned Yorka.

"We have immediate needs for cash," said Chellac, getting back to the subject.

"That, I can remedy."

Everyone turned to look at the Vulcan, as these were the first words he had spoken since refusing to introduce himself. He reached into the bag that never left his shoulder and pulled out a thick ingot of gold-pressed latinum, which he promptly handed to Chellac. "There is more where that came from."

The Ferengi smiled at the tall, noble Vulcan. "I think I like you best of all."

"A private word with you, Chellac," said Yorka, motioning the Ferengi to follow him. The two of them walked away from the others, who were still awed by the explosive growth which was turning thousands of square meters into a rampant, otherworldly jungle.

"So far, so good!" said the Ferengi, slipping the latinum ingot into the deepest pocket on his vest.

Yorka replied, "We must use the Orb to help others more unfortunate."

"There's no one more unfortunate than *us*," insisted Chellac. "If you'll remember, we lost everything we had."

"We can help people and further our own goals," said the Bajoran. "I didn't have a chance to tell you, but while you were collecting our guests, we inspected the Orb and found the power supply had weakened."

The Ferengi blinked in surprise. "Well then, how did you—"

"There was the replicate we used."

"Oooh," said Chellac, rubbing his hands together. "That *is* good news. But it's news we must keep to ourselves, until we decide how to handle it. We could probably chain the devices together and give life to a whole planet, but we don't want every household on Bajor to have an Orb of Life."

With a doubtful look on his face, the prylar glanced at the teeming forest sprouting miraculously from barren sand only a few meters away. Monstrous black trees now towered in the sky, and thick mossy vines gyrated in the rushing wind. "We've got to learn to program it. I just wish we knew more about that thing," said Yorka worriedly.

"Let's take the Vulcan with us," suggested the Ferengi. "He has money, he doesn't make any demands, and he seems smart. The others are good for publicity, but my instincts tell me that *he* ought to be a partner."

"But he's associated with a criminal element," said Yorka.

"Precisely," answered the Ferengi with a smile. "A Vulcan criminal—who could be more trustworthy than *that?*"

"Red alert!" shouted Captain Picard. "Warp drive . . . on my mark."

"Course?" asked the Deltan on the navigation console.

"Away from the rift!" answered Picard, giving his

helmsman the second he needed to aim in a direction. "Now!"

The *Enterprise* extended into a gleaming diamond of light just as the blackness reached out with grasping tentacles, absorbing everything into its gaping, destructive maw. Horrible, unspeakable creatures swirled outward from the massive rift, cavorting like the demons of Hades in the void of space.

"We have escaped in time," reported Data on the ops console.

"And the Romulan ships?" asked Picard.

"Unknown," answered Data. "Sensors are inoperative. Communications are impaired. Radiation is beyond measurable levels."

The captain glanced worried at the viewscreen, which showed nothing but streaks of static interference. "I hope they saw it in time," he said grimly.

"Deanna!" shouted Beverly Crusher, leaning over the prostrate form of her best friend, who had collapsed in her own office. She felt for a pulse and found one, but very weakened.

The doctor hit her combadge. "Crusher to sickbay. Emergency medical team to Counselor Troi's office. Hurry!"

The little girl gazed in wonder and joy at the tall figure standing in the doorway of her quarters. "Daddy!"

"Yes, Suzi," said the smiling, red-haired human, who was wearing a hospital gown. He bent down to hug the six-year-old. "Daddy's come home."

eleven

"But, Suzi, you mustn't tell anyone I've come home—not even Mama."

The six-year-old stared in puzzlement at her father, Andrew Powell. "But why, Daddy? Why can't I tell Mommy?"

"Because I'm on a secret mission, and I'm leaving again very soon," he answered with a comforting smile. "I don't want to get Mommy worried. I wasn't supposed to come see you, but I couldn't help myself." He rose to his feet and looked at the closed door to Ogawa's quarters, as if worried that she might come in any second.

"But, Daddy, I don't want you to leave!" cried the child, hugging him fiercely.

"Pumpkin, I'll just be gone for a little while," he said, returning her heartfelt hug. "Don't worry, I'll come and see you often, and we'll play and have fun just like we did before. It's better that we have a little time together rather than no time at all. But you've got to promise not to tell anyone, or they'll be mad at me and won't let me see you until I'm all done with my assignment."

"Okay," answered Suzi, nodding bravely through her tears. She was young, but she knew about a Starfleet officer's devotion to duty—it came before family and everything else. "Is this secret mission about the Genesis Wave? Are you fighting bad guys?"

"Oh, yes," he replied, "many bad guys. It will just be a little while longer, and then I can come home and be with you all the time. Do you promise not to tell anyone you saw me?"

The girl nodded again, and her father stepped to the door and pushed the panel to open it. After glancing both ways down the corridor, he tousled her wavy black hair and said, "I love you, Suzi."

"I love you too, Daddy," she answered hoarsely.

He smiled, then strode swiftly away. It took all of the girl's willpower not to follow her daddy down the corridor, but she was so happy just to see him that she couldn't disobey his request. Although it would be hard to keep his secret from Mommy, she resolved to do so, if that's what her daddy wanted. Her mama might keep worrying, but at least the little girl knew the truth.

"My daddy is safe," Suzi told herself with a tearful smile.

"Any idea what caused this?" asked Captain Picard, gazing at the unconscious figure of Deanna Troi, stretched out on an examination table in sickbay.

"No, not really," answered Beverly Crusher. "It seemed to occur at the same time that the anomaly expanded and forced us to go to warp, but I have no real proof that the two are related. Her condition has stabilized, and I think I could bring her out of it without any ill effects. But I prefer to let her sleep and come out of it on her own."

"What happened exactly?" asked the captain.

"We were having a counseling session," said Crusher, "and I was complaining to the universe about Wesley being gone so long. And she just collapsed in her chair."

"Hmmm," replied the captain with a troubled frown. "If her condition changes, let me know."

The door to sickbay opened, and the Antosian, Raynr Sleven, strolled into the examination area. Crusher fixed him with a doctor's gaze of disapproval. "And where have you been, Lieutenant?"

"Oh, just taking a walk," he answered, striding toward them. "What happened to the counselor?"

Beverly glanced from one patient to another. "She passed out. We're still trying to determine why."

"It's that *thing* out there," answered Raynr, pointing to no place in particular. "I felt kind of funny, too, so I decided to take a walk. Besides, everybody was so busy here that I didn't think they would mind, or even notice."

"You seem fully recovered," observed Picard.

The Antosian slapped his broad chest and grinned. "Never felt better, Captain. Your doctor and her staff are the best I've ever seen!"

"We like to think so," said Picard, managing a slight smile.

"In fact, I'd like to apply for permanent assignment to the *Enterprise*," continued the Antosian. "I'm ready to get back to work, and I have no ship to report to."

"That's up to your doctor," replied the captain with a glance at Crusher.

She shrugged. "Well, if I can't keep a patient in bed, maybe I should release him. Ideally, we should turn him over to Starfleet Medical for examination, because they've had more experience with this radiation poisoning."

"I don't know, Doctor," said Raynr Sleven. "From what I've seen in those bulletins you're issued, they haven't had the success you've had. Of course, they weren't courageous enough to try cellular metamorphosis, like you did."

" 'Desperate' is the word, not 'courageous.' " Crusher turned to the captain. "We'll miss him—he's been the most cheerful patient we've ever had."

"Thank you, Doctor," replied the Antosian with a fond grin, which Captain Picard seemed to notice.

"I'll have Commander Riker go over your file—see where we can best utilize you." As the captain started toward the door, his combadge chirped, and Will Riker's voice broke in,

"Bridge to Picard."

He tapped his badge. "Picard here. Go ahead, Number One."

"We've just received a message from Starfleet—a reply to our report," said the first officer. "Under no circumstances are we to go anywhere near that anomaly. The same thing happened all over the quadrant, wherever they were studying these strange events. Until we get an explanation, Starfleet is not going to risk any more ships or personnel."

The captain scowled. "And how are we supposed to find out what's going on if we can't investigate?"

"Probes have disappeared, and the scanners are hit

and miss," answered Riker. "We'll keep working on it."

"Any sign yet of the Romulan ships?"

"No, Sir. But they might have escaped to warp, like we did."

The captain heaved a frustrated sigh. "All right, I'm on my way to the bridge. Picard out." He turned to the doctor. "Keep me posted about Troi's condition."

"I will, Jean-Luc."

With that, the captain strode toward the door, which slid open at his approach.

"It's *him*, isn't it?" said Raynr Sleven with dawning realization.

"What's him?" asked Crusher, who was too tired for riddles.

The Antosian lowered his voice to reply, "Captain Picard is the member of the crew you've been seeing for a number of years. Why didn't I figure that out before?"

Crusher grimaced. "This conversation is getting entirely too personal."

"Please excuse me, Doctor. No, not 'Doctor.' Beverly. At least let me call you by your given name." The doctor nodded cautiously.

"Beverly," he began again in a quiet voice that almost seemed to caress the word as he said it. "You know how I feel."

"I know how you think you feel, Lieutenant. And believe me, it's perfectly normal. I've encountered other patients who thought . . ."

"No. This is real."

Once again she was about to object, but the determined look on his handsome face stopped her. He was right. This was not misplaced gratitude. The symptoms in this case added up to only one possible diagnosis: Raynr Sleven was in love with her.

Crusher glanced around at the other workers and patients in sickbay, none of whom seemed to be paying very much attention to them. Nevertheless, she motioned for the Antosian to follow her. "Let's continue this in my private office."

He smiled. "Thank you."

A moment later, they stood awkwardly facing each other in the confines of Beverly's office. "If you're already happy with your life," he said, "I don't want to do anything to upset that. But I don't think you're happy."

Bull's-eye again. This man's perception was unnerving, which was probably one of the reasons she found him attracting. So against her better judgement, she decided to speak freely. "The problem is . . . there's lot of gray area between being happy and unhappy. I haven't been deliriously happy since my family was whole and together. I miss my husband, Jack, and my son, Wes, but memories of us—as a handsome young family—are like snapshots now. This ship is my family, and it requires a lot of care . . . nowadays all my parenting instincts go into my work. Most of the time, I'm too busy with work to think about what I might be missing. Then there's Jean-Luc—"

"Yes?" asked Raynr expectantly.

She sighed. "Jack and Jean-Luc were best friends, and that's always clouded our relationship. Somewhere in the back of our minds there is guilt . . . a feeling we're dishonoring Jack. The three of us were once inseparable."

"Too much 'water under the bridge,' as you humans like to say." Raynr smiled sympathetically.

"Yes, I guess so. I think one of us would have to leave the *Enterprise*—we'd have to spend some serious time apart before the sparks could ever fly again."

"Then there's nothing to prevent you from loving me, Beverly," said the Antosian, taking her hands in his and gazing at her with intense black eyes.

"Except that I outrank you," she said, not realizing just how foolish the words sounded until they were out of her mouth. That sort of thing didn't matter to her and he knew it. Rayner smiled.

"Surely you can come up with a better excuse than that," he replied.

"Fair enough. All right then, here's a better reason. I'm not the kind who falls head-over-heels in love in a few days," she replied, gently pulling her hands away. "Especially with a patient."

"But I'm not going to be a patient much longer," he insisted. "If Starfleet approves my reassignment, I'll just be a regular member of the crew, no different than anyone else. We could start slowly—a dinner here, a concert there. I don't want to rush you."

"I have trouble believing you. Considering that's all you've done so far, rush me."

"Fair enough. But remember I thought I was dying," he said with a laugh. "I mean, I *was* dying, until you brought me back to life. Maybe that's what's giving me this sense of urgency . . . that I've got to seize the moment while I can. Before those things attacked us, I was like you—cruising through life, concentrating on my duty. Then they killed every friend I had."

"I'm sorry," she said. "Still there's Jean-Luc, who is very much alive."

"What if the captain were in love with somebody else?"

Crusher tried not to wince at that thought, although it was always a possibility. Jean-Luc was a dynamic man to whom women were often drawn—a bit too often for her tastes. Even now, she sensed there was an attraction between him and that Romulan commander, although a Romulan commander was certainly a poor candidate for any kind of long-term relationship. Even so, the fact that Jean-Luc was attracted to her was irksome.

"You're thinking about it, aren't you?" asked Raynr.

Beverly snapped out of her moment of self-pity. "Right now, you're still a patient under my care. And the fact that you feel an urgent tendency to fall in love, because life could end any minute, shows that you're still suffering trauma." There. Nice, neat, and professional. With any luck, he would buy it. "If our ship's counselor were well, I would send you to her for some therapy," she added.

"I will gladly go," he answered. Not her lucky day, she thought.

If only his smile were less appealing. Her anger fading, the doctor considered the grinning Antosian. Yes, she had to get him out of here and back to a more well-rounded life, with pursuits other than mooning over his doctor. And to be honest, at least with herself, she could use a break from him too. She headed for the door. "Right now, I have other patients to attend to. I'll grant you your wish and release you from sickbay, putting you on outpatient status. We'll assign you quarters, and you can start adjusting to life aboard the *Enterprise*."

"As long as I have an excuse to come see you,"

answered the Antosian with a broad smile. "I don't give up easily."

"And I don't give in easily," Crusher called out to his graceful retreating figure. She wasn't entirely sure he heard her.

"How do you feel?"

Deanna Troi sat up in her bed and glanced around at the familiar faces in sickbay, including Beverly Crusher, Alyssa Ogawa, and the Tellarite doctor, Pelagof. Her body felt weak and numb, and her mind felt as if she'd had a lobotomy. Looking around at people she knew well, she couldn't sense their emotions, except for the obvious realization that they felt concern for her.

"Lousy," she answered. "What happened to me?"

"We're hoping you can tell us," said Crusher. "Remember, you and I were in your office, talking—and the next thing I knew, you're out. There's nothing physically wrong with you."

Troi nodded, although her recollections were very fuzzy. "I remember being in my office, all right. And then a blackness came over me. It was like—" She hesitated, frowning.

"Like what?" Crusher gently prodded.

The Betazoid collected her thoughts while the medical staff looked on patiently. Taking a deep breath, she began, "It's like I've gotten a glimpse of somebody I know on the street. Someone I've met before. Do you remember when we were called to Gemworld a year or so ago . . . an interdimensional rift was destroying the planet. I get that same feeling—an overwhelming sense of dread, the idea that something evil is taking over my mind."

Deanna looked puzzledly at them and shook her head. "Only then, I sensed an intelligence on the other side. This time it's mindless . . . chaotic."

Crusher frowned at her patient. "How long have you been feeling like this?"

"These encounters aren't identical," said Troi. "I've been grumpy and out of sorts, not exactly myself, since we got here. But until I passed out, it didn't really hit me the same way. Did something change with the anomaly?"

"Without warning, it expanded again," answered Ogawa. "The *Enterprise* barely got away in time, and we don't know what happened to the Romulan ships."

"All this occurred at the same time you collapsed," added Crusher.

Troi nodded grimly. "It's too much of a coincidence not to be related. But strange creatures were not pouring out of that other rift, like we've seen them here."

"But we know there were plenty of unusual creatures in that other dimension," said Crusher. "The Lipuls on Gemworld stole many of those species to repopulate their own changing world."

Dr. Pelagrof cleared his throat importantly. "I'm unfamiliar with the Gemworld operation—it was before I arrived here. Since Gemworld still exists, I presume we found a way to make this interdimensional rift go away. What exactly did we do to combat it?"

Troi smiled wistfully. "I *asked* it to go away, after I found out it was getting revenge against the Lipuls. To be specific, the entity wanted forgiveness, and I granted it."

"Yes, but . . . there are differences this time," said Ogawa with a frown. "We saw some radiation from the

Gemworld rift, but not like this. Most of the damage there was caused by increased gravity and mind control, not monstrous creatures crawling out of the woodwork. Plus these recent anomalies have occurred all along the path of the Genesis Wave, while the other rift was localized."

"The Genesis Wave," replied Troi wearily. "That's the difference this time. We have to tell the captain." The counselor started to rise from her bed, but Crusher gently pushed her back down.

"I'm capable of reporting to the captain," replied the doctor, "and you have to rest. If this *is* the same thing, we're going to need you to be healthy and strong—to communicate with it."

Deanna nodded, unable to argue with that conclusion. At the moment, she felt anything but healthy and strong. With a parting smile, Beverly led her colleagues toward the door, but the Betazoid called out, "Wait!"

"Yes?" asked Crusher, stopping in her tracks.

"I may not be the only one who's mentally affected by this," warned Troi. "We'll have to be on the alert for symptoms in others."

"Yes," said Crusher gravely, "I'll keep my eye on everyone."

"I'm sorry, but Linda Feeney died last night," said the nurse on duty at the reception desk of the hospital ship *Harvey*.

In shock, Admiral Nechayev glanced at Teska, who registered no emotion except for a slight pursing of her lips. "What was the cause of death?" asked the Vulcan.

"We haven't done an autopsy yet," answered the

nurse, "and I'd have to pull her chart to even make a guess. One moment please." As the two visitors from the *Sequoia* looked on, the medical worker consulted her computer screen.

After a moment, she answered, "Preliminary indications are that it was choriomeningitis. She was also suffering from hepatomegaly, uremia, endocarditis, and a host of other serious ailments. These rescued slaves are the sickest patients any of us have ever seen, and it doesn't help that most of them have no will to live. They don't even know they're on a hospital ship. The slightest swelling or infection can cause systemic failure."

"But she was lucid just a day ago," said Nechayev.

"That made her different," agreed the nurse, "but it didn't make her any healthier than the others. Believe me, Lomar has been a very depressing place to work— we're beginning to think they should have sent a team of undertakers, rather than medical workers."

Lights flashed on her console, and an urgent alarm sounded overhead. "Excuse me," said the nurse with a sigh, "now we've got radiation victims coming in, and they're also hopeless." She charged down the corridor, where she was joined by two more haggard figures in white gowns.

Nechayev looked wearily at the Vulcan. "Undertakers . . . that's what she thinks. Morale is awfully low with this group."

"You said this mission would be unpleasant," replied Teska. "Those were prophetic words, but the unpleasantness does not end here. Unknown parties and a number of Romulans possess Genesis emitters. While we bury the dead of Lomar, thousands more are dying elsewhere."

"We may have made some small progress there," replied the admiral. "The *Enterprise* reported to Starfleet Command that they think they've identified the rift near them."

"Are they receiving enough resources to deal with it?"

"I don't know," admitted Nechayev, her shoulders slumping. She looked around at the efficient and orderly front office of the beleaguered hospital ship. "With everything else that's going on . . . probably not."

"We desperately need more information," said the Vulcan, "and we are unlikely to find it here. Still I must return to the complex." She squared her shoulders and looked for the turbolift.

"Starfleet is sending investigators to Torga IV."

Teska raised an eyebrow. "I hope they arrive in time."

The large storage room, which had been chilled for preservation purposes, was filled with rows and rows of male corpses, all of which carried certain racial characteristics. Their hair was straight and dark, their skin pale and greenish tinged, and their ears distinctively pointed. That's where the differences ended, because some were tall, others short; most were on the slim side, but an occasional specimen had excess body fat. Teska slowly approached the rows of bodies, her nostrils shooting steam in the chilly room.

His head bowed in sorrow, wearing a thick expedition jacket, a bald human shuffled toward her. "Here are the Vulcanoid bodies you asked for," said Franklin Oswald, gesturing around at the cold specimens. "A few we were able to identify as Romulan, Vulcan, or Rigelian based on forensic evidence. We've marked those. It's kind of hard to get accurate on age . . . especially for a human like me. So we have most of them."

"Thank you, Franklin," said Teska sincerely. "You can leave me alone now."

"Okay," he said with a forced smile, backing toward the door. "Just call if you need anything."

Teska ignored him as she steeled herself to start looking at their faces. Suffering a pang of dread so uncommon to her that she didn't know how to react, she gazed down at the nearest corpse. It was clearly not Hasmek, and she released her pent-up breath. Now there were only a hundred twenty-three more to inspect, and each one would elicit this awful but mercifully brief stab of fear. Only Hasmek could affect her like that.

In didn't help that these victims had all died in a deluded state, with no control over their mental facilities. It was the worst death a Vulcan could imagine. She didn't wish to find him here—like this—although she did long for a resolution. Finding his body would at least guarantee that the search was over.

Teska stepped to the nearest corner and began a systematic stroll down the first row of dead Vulcanoid males, her eyes peering intently at the lifeless faces.

twelve

On a blustery night, flying gravel and sand clattered like ancient ammunition against the corrugated metal of an ugly building on Torga IV. A Romulan stood outside the communal transporter platform in Celestial Square, watching two brawny humans and two stocky Deltans emerge from the open-air archway. They were dressed like cormaline miners, and they carried brand-new tool kits. But they weren't miners, decided the Romulan, who answered to the name of Jerit. The majority of miners on Torga IV were impoverished Bajorans, not clean-cut humans and Deltans who had Starfleet Security written all over them. He ducked behind the corner and put up his hood before the new arrivals could get a good look at him. Even though it was night, this transporter station was one of the few places in the drab city that was brightly lit.

Jerit almost reached for his communicator, but he realized that the new arrivals might be intercepting their signals. So they would have to maintain silence, which meant rounding up his two comrades by foot. After turning off his communicator to make sure he wouldn't use it, Jerit peered down the dusty street, where neon signs were shaking in the wind. The four newcomers were walking briskly with a purpose, and he realized he would have to run to follow them.

Best to let them go, he decided. *Orders or no orders, it's finally time to leave this filthy planet.*

For several days, they had searched in vain for the Bajoran monk who had run off with the portable device. At least they assumed Prylar Yorka had it, based on his disappearance and the events of that fateful night. Prylar Yorka had been a fixture on Torga IV since the colony first opened, but he was always considered harmless . . . until now. Jerit was still disgusted with himself for letting the device slip through his fingers during that contrived chaos. They should have been more cautious in the temple, or stationed someone in the rear, or done something! Now they would have to declare utter failure and slink away in retreat from Torga IV. As squad leader, he would be disgraced.

When Jerit looked up again, his pursuers had disappeared into the grimy byways of the mining town. *How had they known to come to Torga IV? Did the Federation already possess the missing emitter? Was Prylar Yorka working for them the whole time, and why did the moss creature decide to bring it to his temple?*

For answers, he had found nothing but hearsay and conjecture. None of their questions mattered now, because their mission was hopelessly compromised by the arrival of Starfleet. The Federation had much more influence in a place like this, and they would find the monk, if they didn't already have him. It was time to withdraw, without waiting for orders, without any anticipation of success. His career was finished, but he still had his squad to save.

Forsaking the transporter pad and the jittery pool of lights in Celestial Square, the Romulan slipped into the shadows.

From the pilot's seat, Cassie Jackson looked back at the cabin of the shuttlecraft, where there was one calm face amid several indignant ones.

"I still say this is a terrible idea," grumbled the Bajoran acolyte, whose name she had found out was Alon.

"As do I," muttered Prylar Yorka, setting the folds of his face into deep furrows. "But our colleague is right in one respect—we must find out more about the Orb of Life—how it works, how to program it. Right now, we can't use either the original or the copy, without recharging the fuel cells."

"This all makes sense in theory," muttered Chellac. The little Ferengi rose to his feet and paced the narrow aisle; he was the only one who could do so without ducking. "But how are we going to find a Romulan shuttlecraft and capture three hard-core operatives?"

"If they're even still on this planet," said Alon with a sniff.

"Begin by thinking calmly and logically," answered the Vulcan. "They know more about the Orb than we do, because they were chasing after it before we even knew it existed. They may have other devices, or know where they are stored. We have surprise on our side, and no other choices. No matter what you call this apparatus, we all know what it is. And we know that our leverage lies in keeping a monopoly on it."

Yorka shifted uncomfortably on his feet, then sunk back into his chair, while Chellac stopped pacing.

"These Romulans are your competition," added the Vulcan.

"You're right, let's grab them!" exclaimed the Ferengi, punching his fist outward. "I know we bought a lot of stuff on the black market, but I don't think *we're* the right crew for a disruptor battle in the streets."

"Nor do I," answered their mentor, "and we would want them unharmed in any case. They are looking for you, Prylar, and the last thing they expect is for *you* to come after *them*. I have a plan to capture them all without firing a beam or incurring danger."

"How?" asked Alon skeptically.

"Allow me to change my clothes," said the Vulcan, reaching for his bag. "If you would all face forward for a moment."

Cassie was already facing forward, scanning her instruments and glancing out the viewport. They would reach Torga IV in only half an hour, so she hoped he would explain it quickly. Although she considered the Vulcan's plan risky, they were at a crossroads with this thing. They had a secret bank account that was filling up nicely, but they would need more information before they could really control the Orb of Life.

"You may look now," said an unfamiliar voice. Everyone did so, and there were surprised gasps in the cabin. The noble Vulcan had turned himself into a sneering Romulan, complete with the padded shoulders, sashes, regalia, and arrogance of someone very exalted in the Star Empire. He was even wearing a disruptor, and strapped to his back was a small yellow box, like an armored backpack. His expression, his posture, his haughty smile—it was all different from his previous persona.

"Now that's impressive," said Chellac with a grin. "What are you, really?"

"What I am is a thief," answered the Romulan, "and a very good one. I have tricks that you haven't seen yet. I wouldn't suggest that we capture these three unless I thought the task would be trivial. Bakus sent me to see your object, learn about it, and protect it. That's what I intend to do."

"You're Rigelian, right?" asked the Ferengi, wagging his finger in triumph.

"Just listen," he said, kneeling down and leaning into the group. "There are a few details you must remember, and timing will be important. If we do this right, we'll end up with another shuttlecraft, too. During this operation, you can call me Regimol."

"Regimol!" shouted Cassie Jackson from the pilot's seat, tossing her pert sandy-colored hair. "There are a lot of big ships in orbit, more than I thought would be here. Prylar, didn't you say there are usually only three or four freighters, plus a handful of shuttlecraft on the surface?"

Within seconds, both the Romulan and the Bajoran pressed at her back, each taking a shoulder and peering over. The Bajoran glanced suspiciously at the stranger who had seized command of their gang in a matter of hours, by doing no more than changing his clothes. Cassie wondered what other tricks he had.

"I count ten starships," said Regimol.

Yorka considered the number. "That's more than normal but not unheard of. Some customers will send a fleet for pickup, and a lot of refugees from the wave have been dumped here—or dispersed, as Starfleet calls it."

"We'll proceed, but with caution." The Romulan squeezed closer to the pilot and gave her a charming smile. "I bet Cassie could identify those ships."

"If I had time to work the computer . . . maybe," she answered, not pulling away from him. In fact, she dug her shoulder deeper into his chest. "But right now I'm flying."

"Yes, please concentrate on that," he answered, making a slow retreat from her supple shoulder. "Most of the ships will be Federation, anyway. Listen, Torga IV has three shuttlecraft hangars where you can get repairs and service. Go to the one on the eastern outskirts of the city—it's called Dinky's Dry Dock."

"Dinky's Dry Dock?" she asked as if disbelieving him.

"It's a real place," added Yorka, his eyes narrowing suspiciously at the Romulan. "Out of the way and disreputable."

"Land outside in the desert and let us walk in," said Regimol. "You can always transport us back."

"But only one at a time," cautioned the Bajoran.

"We aren't going to confront them. We aren't going to confront *anyone*." The Romulan straightened his sashes for emphasis.

Yorka lowered his voice, but his eyes drilled into Regimol's. Above her head, Cassie could feel the heat generated by the confrontation. "You just remember one thing," whispered the prylar, "the Prophets gave the Orb of Life to *me*. Not you, not Bakus, not Chellac. Me. Only *I* know where the two devices are hidden, and I won't tell you."

Regimol gazed sympathetically at the monk as one might look at a child. "This craft isn't very large. I could steal your two devices any time I wanted, and you wouldn't know it. But I'm not a thief among thieves. In fact, I salute your intent to work this discovery to its fullest advantage for you."

"See what a great guy he is!" exclaimed Chellac, barging into the conversation.

"I have bigger designs than *that*," declared the monk huffily. He rose to his feet and plodded down the aisle to his seat.

After that, it was quiet in the cabin as everyone settled down to think about their upcoming offensive. Until now, this thing with the Orb had been fun and games—a combination of hide-and-seek and keep-away—but now they were talking about attacking trained Romulan thugs.

The silence only lasted until they came out of warp near Torga IV, when subspace crackles filled the communication bands, followed by voices.

"Hey, fellas," asked Cassie, "what do I tell flight control to get clearance to land?"

"Shuttlecraft repair," answered Regimol, looking over her shoulder and pointing at a map of the city. "And head straight for Dinky's—due east—so they see you're telling the truth. There's too much going on here for them to be worried about us. It might be different getting away from here, especially if we're in a hurry."

"Going into landing pattern," reported Cassie as she worked her instruments. "I need some elbow room, please."

"Sorry," said Regimol, backing away once more. "Your skill and confidence gives me great comfort, Miss Jackson."

"I wish I could say the same," she muttered.

They soared over a sprawling cormaline refinery, with glistening towers and sweeping searchlights warning them away from noisy pulverizers, huge vats, snaking conduits, and gigantic coils buzzing with energy. Then they sped over the drab city, which looked like a collection of huge Quonset huts, mired in a dust storm. The brightest lights seemed restricted to gaudy bar-lined streets running through the center of town. These tawdry thoroughfares pointed like arrows to an oasis of lights in the distance, perched on the outskirts of an opaque desert. Dinky's Dry Dock, presumed Cassie.

As they drew closer, she could make out well-lit landing pads, runways, a fenced yard with a dozen resting shuttlecraft, and a modern terminal in the center. Where the light melted into the darkness outside the fence, she could see more hulks which might be shuttlecraft. It was hard to tell if they were junks, partial hulls, or capable ships, but it might be a good place to hide their own craft.

"Do you want me to land near those shuttles littering the desert?" she asked the Romulan.

"No," he answered quickly. "Get an isolated position with some space around you, so you can see people coming. You don't want a vole or a scavenger to set off your sensors."

"I warn you," said Yorka darkly, "refugees are trying desperately to get off this planet. They'd be happy to hijack a lone, defenseless shuttlecraft in the middle of nowhere."

"They won't be defenseless," said Regimol calmly, "they'll have their shields up."

"I don't feel right about going out there and only having one person here," declared the monk. "I'm staying with the shuttlecraft and Cassie."

"I still need Alon," said Regimol just before the thin Bajoran also tried to weasel out. The acolyte put his finger down, waiting for his master to save him.

"Yes, he can go with you," grumbled Yorka, turning away from his underling. The crushed look on Alon's face was priceless, thought Cassie.

She turned back to business, ignoring their bickering. A minute later, she reported, "I've found a landing site. Return to your seats, please."

"Still the good manners of a professional tour guide," said Regimol, gazing down at her with a smile.

She tried to ignore him and concentrate on her landing, which was easy enough thanks to many similar landings in the wilderness of Meldrar IV's moon. After compensating for the increased gravity, she dropped the shuttlecraft into the fine yellow sand, adding more dust to the swirling night wind.

Regimol smiled as he gazed out the window at scrawny thorn bushes, buffeted by the gritty wind. "Ah, this is a good night for matters of stealth. Kill your running lights."

"We won't be able to see," protested Yorka.

"You're going to trust your eyes on a night like this?"

asked Regimol, scoffing. He looked appealingly at Cassie, expecting her to back him up, and she killed the running lights. There was still enough light from her instrument panel for her to see everything she needed to see, but the others were crouched in shadow like the gang of conspirators they were.

The Romulan smiled fondly at her. "Remember, if you have to take off without us, the rendezvous point is the Oasis of Tears on Bajor in two days."

"Yes, I remember," she answered. "It will have to be bad for me to do that."

"It's good that you'll be here to help her," said Regimol to the Prylar. "Those Romulans will be dead weight when they tumble off our transporter. She'll need help handling them."

"If you cause us to lose the Orb—" warned Yorka, letting his thunderous preacher's voice trail off.

"If only the Prophets had given you an instruction manual along with it," replied Regimol with a teasing smile. "Chellac, are you ready?"

"Yes," answered the Ferengi, hefting a Bajoran assault rifle and checking its settings.

"And you, Alon?"

The acolyte gulped and nodded hesitantly as he fingered the phaser on his hip. Cassie was worried that he might turn tail and run, but he was the only one of their assault team who really knew the town, who had lived there. Regimol knew about Dinky's, but that was all; and the Ferengi knew only a couple of spots. As a Bajoran, Alon was the one who was most likely to fit in.

"It's going to be a long walk," said Alon, peering out the dark window at the distant light of the terminal. It was separated by so much black that it looked like a far-off nebula, and the town beyond it wasn't even visible.

"I can transport you closer," replied Cassie.

"No," responded the Romulan, wrapping a cape around himself. "The walk won't hurt us. You can often learn things from a walk in the countryside. But there won't be any chitchat over the combadges. We won't contact you unless we're ready to evacuate, or we're going to abort the mission."

She nodded. "Only if there's trouble."

"Do you have your lamps?" he asked, glancing from Chellac to Alon. They hefted their miner's lamps, which were able to put out a lot of light thanks to a plasma element. They were also common as dirt around here, according to the Bajorans.

"I don't see as well as you do in the darkness," protested the slender Bajoran.

Regimol lifted a calming hand. "Fear not, Chellac sees the best of all, and he will go first. There's more starlight out there than we see from in here. Wear your goggles, because the sand will be harsh unless the wind dies down."

As the Ferengi and the Bajoran fumbled with their goggles, Regimol smiled confidently at Cassie. "Do a sensor sweep."

"I already have," she answered. "I don't need you to tell me my job. You just bring back that instruction manual you keep harping about. It's clear outside. The nearest life-forms are in the yard, a kilometer-and-a-half away. Shields are down, and I'm popping the hatch."

"Go for it!" exclaimed Chellac, gripping his weapon. With a whoosh that was like a pent-up sigh, the hatch sprang open, and the Ferengi jumped into the murky sandstorm.

Through a dust devil of leaves and plastic bits, a black-hooded figure strode from the entrance of Dormitory 16, a bustling sleeping station for male miners. He turned a corner and joined a crouching confederate, who rose to his feet at his approach.

"Is he there?" asked Jerit.

The younger Romulan shook his head. "I don't know where he could be. If he's on the move, we might be passing each other. I say we use communications."

"No!" snapped Jerit. "He knows his orders are to stay put. There's one more place—the water fountain—and that's on the way to the vessel. That would be his final fall-back position."

Something caught the Romulan's eye, and he pulled his confederate out of the way just as two humans and a Bajoran exited from the dormitory. They were holding tricorders, making no attempt to hide their scans of the area.

"Move out," he whispered urgently, slapping his cohort on the back. The youth dashed into a dark alley, with Jerit on his heels, because he heard voices right behind them. Then he heard unmistakable footsteps, and he lowered his night-vision goggles to cut through the dust and gloominess of the alley.

As they ran, Jerit removed a stun grenade from his belt and hefted it in his hand, ready to flip up the safety with his thumb and push the button underneath. "Keep going! To the next spot."

In fear, his comrade took off like a shot, while Jerit

slowed to get a good look at his pursuers. They obliged by stopping to fire a wild phaser beam at him, which streaked by his head and scorched the corrugated metal—he got a good estimate of their distance. Now he ran, pushing up the safety with his thumb, then hitting the trigger. Twisting his body athletically, Jerit bowled the grenade along the ground, not chancing a bounce. After that, he ran full out, yet he could feel himself being swept helplessly off his feet by the detonation of the concussion grenade. The pufflike sound followed a split-second later.

Sapped of energy, the Romulan's body was as limp as a beanbag, and he bounced across the pavement and crashed into a trash can, spilling a family of snapping voles into the alley. Mustering all his willpower, he managed to shield his face, but the rodents kept fighting among themselves with mad squeaks. Some scampered away, and they seemed confused and disoriented. He took some comfort in being able to hear, because the footsteps behind them had definitely stopped.

Jerit felt hands shaking him, and the touch seemed to bring back other sensory nerves. With effort, he rolled over and saw his young subordinate nodding reassuringly at him. "Well done, Sir."

The squad leader tried to speak, but only a grotesque mimicry of words came out of his mouth. His young apprentice reached into his boot for the handle of a dagger. "At ease, Sir. You'll be fully recovered in a minute or two. Do you want me to go back there and slice their throats?"

Jerit nodded weakly. He couldn't voice all the good reasons for that, but any action which cut the enemy's numbers and made them cautious was a good idea, especially when attempting to retreat.

The subordinate nodded with determination and drew his assassin's blade from his boot. He jogged into the dense shadows in the alley, where it was very quiet indeed, and where soon the voles would have an unexpected feast.

"I bet we can take these Romulans," bragged Chellac. "I bet they're nothing." He mimicked firing his gun as he ran between dusty old hulks of shuttlecraft and machinery, playing soldier. They were taking an eerie shortcut among the junks, because their noble leader would only approach the west gate, requiring this route. *Among these wrecks would be a good place for an ambush,* thought the Ferengi, and he began to dash from hulk to hulk.

"Lifesign readings are negative," said Alon with a sneer as he consulted his tricorder. "Nobody can see you."

"They could see us with binoculars from that wall," piped in Regimol, pointing toward the shimmering lights. "So let's walk normally. Holster your weapons, or sling them over your shoulder."

"Aw, you people are no fun," grumbled Chellac, fumbling with his assault weapon, which was nearly as big as he was.

Picking up the pace, Regimol marched right up to the gate, which was cut crudely from a high fence of the same corrugated metal they saw everywhere. Barbed wire, with sparkling force-field emitters, was at the top. It was impressive for a place called Dinky's; Chellac got the impression that security had just been upgraded. The

Ferengi and the skinny Bajoran rushed to catch up with Regimol, but they stood in silence and let the Romulan make conversation with two seedy Bajoran guards.

"That's close enough," said one of them, holding up his hand. His female companion held up a phaser rifle. "We've got no shuttlecraft to rent, buy, loan, or steal. We're not taking passengers. If you're on foot, go somewhere else."

"We are not refugees," answered Regimol as he pushed back his hood to reveal his full Romulan splendor. "My shuttlecraft needs a part—a plasma injection coil."

The two guards looked uncertainly at one another, as if this meant something; then they looked worriedly at the yard they protected and the foreboding desert beyond the wall. "You people should get out of here," warned the male guard. "Strangers have been asking about you all day."

"Thank you for the advice. We're going to pack up," answered Regimol with a wave. Casually he asked, "How many others are back?"

"Just one of them," said the female guard. "He's in the clubhouse, I think." She took a portable device from her vest and worked it for a moment. A small door in the larger door slid open just wide enough for the visitors to enter single-file. Chellac could feel the dry static of the force-fields just waiting to power back on.

"Did you bring more ale?" called the guard, leaning over the inner rail of the watchtower.

"No, next trip," answered Regimol.

As they entered the yard, they were almost blinded by all the light. Most of the wattage was focused on the ten or so docked shuttlecraft, representing half-a-dozen different worlds. *Customers*, figured Chellac. Landing pads were also ready for action, as were the force-field towers and repair buildings, where robot workers sent sparks shooting into the night air.

In the middle of all of this, the terminal stood like a blazing mountain of light, surrounded by armed guards. They were casual about their leisurely patrols around the yard; but they could afford to be, because there were a lot of them.

He sidled up to Regimol and whispered, "I don't think we'll be able to beam out of here with all those force-fields."

"That's true," agreed the Romulan. "So we'll fly out in our new shuttlecraft. Let's go take a look at it." He motioned for Alon to draw closer, and the three of them zig-zagged a bit as if they were lost. While his entourage bumped into each other, the Romulan was carefully studying the docked craft, even though he appeared to be window-shopping.

"There it is," he whispered to his confederates, veering in the direction of a large shuttle parked out in the corner of the yard. As they walked, the Romulan opened his tricorder and began to take readings. "Don't stop to look, just keep walking as if we're new here—tourists, gawking at everything."

They kept walking past a squat, twin-nacelled torpedo, which looked used and beaten. Oil was leaking from a gash in its side. Regimol looked up from his tricorder and whispered, "It's a *Danube*-class runabout, adapted for civilian use. There's no one onboard."

He closed up the tricorder and pointed elsewhere. "We used these ships in the Maquis, also modified for speed, like this one. It's probably the fastest ship in the yard, but it has no weapons in order to keep a low profile. It's either our quarry, or it's Starfleet—but they would have left someone on board. This is a break, because I'm sure I can fly this."

"Oh, you weren't sure you could fly the ship before?" muttered Chellac. "You know, for a mission with no danger, this is starting to feel awfully risky."

"Just relax—we'll find that part you're looking for," answered the Romulan loudly, slapping him on the back. "Let's go to that clubhouse we heard about." As he walked, he lowered his voice to add, "I'm sure people are watching this vessel. Anyone who attempts to get in— even the rightful owners—will find it hard getting out."

"Oh, great," grumbled Chellac.

"That might be good for us. Our quarry will be in a hurry—even careless—when they get back. It's not often you find a Romulan in a careless state."

"Who else is out there?" asked Alon, peering nervously at the well-lit shapes all around them. "You said Starfleet security?"

"At a minimum," answered Regimol. "That's enough speculation for now—let's see what's real."

Regimol led them to the terminal, past the parts department and reception desk, straight into the raucous tavern, where laughter mingled with the scent of Romulan ale, which seemed to be on special tonight. What a surprise that was, thought Chellac. While a loud clientele hoisted mugs of the blue libation, other patrons sat in communication booths or gambled at tables in the back. There was even an advertisement for a holodeck, for more private pursuits. Times were good on Torga IV, thought the Ferengi; the town was thriving in the teeth of disaster, like a good neighbor should. Despite the noise level and distractions, the crowd seemed to notice everyone who came and went. For good or ill, it was a see-and-be-seen kind of place.

Hood down, Regimol darted stealthily through the revelers. His destination seemed to be the bar in the rear, and Chellac wasn't sure what he was searching for until he saw another slender figure at the bar take notice and move toward him. It was all the little Ferengi could do to watch the action over the taller patrons, so he missed bits of it while he worked his way closer. The two Romulans seemed to connect very quickly, and when Chellac looked again, both of them were gone.

The Ferengi finally found a spot out of the way, under a banister, where he could keep an eye on things. Because Chellac didn't like Romulan ale, he took a swig of the water in his canteen and surveyed the crowd. They looked young—pilots and adventurers—plus the newly rich class of entrepreneurs. On a planet where transportation was scarce, a shuttlecraft yard had become the most exclusive place to be.

Like Regimol, the Ferengi was now glad of all those guards around the place. But he didn't have fond memories of Torga IV, and this little side trip was dredging up the pain of his ruin, his desperate escape, and his subsequent abandonment here. "I must be crazy to come back here," he muttered to himself.

"What did you say?" asked Alon. The thin Bajoran hovered over his head like a mother bird.

"Do you see Regimol?"

"No," snapped his accomplice, hefting his shoulder

bag. "Now what are we supposed to do? You know, these signal amplifiers are useless, and if we get caught with the—"

"Quiet!" snapped Chellac. "We're here now, doing this—let's tough it out. I think he found the other Romulan and is talking to him. So far, he's talked his way in everywhere, like he promised, so give him some credit."

"Will he talk his way onto their ship?" asked Alon, scoffing.

Chellac stood on his tiptoes and tried to point over heads. "They were at the left of the bar, in the back. Right where—"

The Bajoran was much taller, and he peered over the bobbing heads with considerable success. Grasping the Ferengi's shoulder, he cried, "I see him!"

Then the tall Bajoran frowned and sucked in his breath. "No . . . on second thought, it's the other Romulan. He seems very agitated . . . as if he's looking for something. Perhaps our Romulan has given him the slip."

The Ferengi's combadge beeped once, and his breath caught in his windpipe. "There's the signal," he whispered, gripping his cohort's hand and pushing it off his shoulder. "He needs us. Are you ready to do your part?"

"Right now?" asked Alon in amazement. "We just got here."

"Let's obey orders, shall we? Even your boss agreed to this caper." Chellac began to move toward that door they had entered, but he felt as if he were moving through mud. Neither his legs nor the crowd cooperated in helping him move.

"This is crazy," insisted his comrade. "I believe that's what you said before."

The Ferengi sighed. "You know, Alon, if you want to bail out, this would be a good time. Give me the stuff you're carrying, and I'll tell everyone we lost you in the commotion. You can rejoin Tornan society, such as it is."

"No," hissed the Bajoran, although he seemed to think about it for a moment.

As they reached the door, two brawny humans stepped in front of them, blocking their way out. "We'd like to buy you fellas a drink," said one of them jovially.

"We hear you're looking for parts," said the other. "We've got them."

"No!" snapped Chellac indignantly. "You huuu-mans get out of the way. We've wasted enough time in here." He bowled his way past them, hoping Alon had enough sense to do the same.

With a long arm, one of the humans grabbed Chellac's thick collar and yanked him back into the tavern. When he landed on his feet, the two of them tried to steer him toward the back; they laughed in his ear and slapped him on the back like great friends.

"You won't need this," said his big buddy, forcefully removing his weapon from his hands. "And you don't understand—there's a special room for Ferengi, and the owner is waiting for you."

He blinked up at the muscular human. "Dinky?"

"None other. Who did you think owned this place, a huuu-man?" The big man grinned, while Chellac glanced worriedly over his shoulder to see how Alon had fared. He was shocked to see him smiling, surrounded by other Bajorans who appeared to be *his* friends. Maybe it was just that kind of place where strangers were made to feel welcome—it was certainly crowded enough.

However, Regimol was trying to kidnap three Romulan spies without their help. It was hard to tell if that was a good or a bad deal for him. Chellac heard a shout, and he turned to see two big humans accosting Alon.

As he hoped, several Bajorans leaped to the defense of their species when they spotted Alon grappling with a much larger human. When he didn't let go, the fight escalated into a brawl, and Chellac tried to steer his abductor into the pile of swinging arms and legs. But the big human was strong and determined.

With a pang of guilt, the Ferengi kicked the man on the shin and bolted away from him. With the other thug chasing him, he got just far enough to bang on his combadge and shout, "Chellac to base! Get us out of here! *Help!*"

On the shuttlecraft over a kilometer away, Cassie and Yorka looked at one another as the Ferengi's frantic voice echoed in the cabin. When she turned away and reached for the instrument panel, the monk jumped up and cried, "Don't answer him!"

"I'm not," she replied, changing the sensor readouts to reflect conditions inside the gate. "There are a ton of lifesigns . . . and force-fields, too. We don't stand a chance of beaming anyone in or out of there. It's got better security than that prison where I used to work. So do you want to—?"

The young woman turned to look at the Prylar, and

she came eyeball to barrel with a Romulan disruptor. "Don't do anything," he warned her.

Cassie rasped a nervous laugh. "You don't need to pull that weapon on *me*. I know what you're thinking, Prylar. You want to take off and ditch the others. Hey, I understand you . . . I don't know if I can trust that pointy-eared impostor, or the Ferengi either. Sorry to lose Alon, but the fewer, the better, huh?"

He nodded, although he looked shaken by her blunt assessment.

The young human took a breath and turned serious. "You put that weapon down right now and tell me that half of the money in our account is *mine*, and so is half of everything that comes in, until I decide to bail. And I *do* know where you've hidden those things. You need me more than I need you."

Yorka blanched at that statement, and his face clouded with doubt.

"Swear by your Prophets that half of the proceeds are mine!" she insisted. "Or we can just sit here and let the Romulans, Starfleet, or whoever find us and take everything in the craft. I *know* where you've hidden the Orbs—maybe I'll throw *them* out along with you."

"All right," he said grimly, "I swear by the Prophets that half is yours. But we *must* do the will of the Prophets."

"Do what you want with your half," she muttered. "And stow that weapon before you hurt someone."

Grimacing painfully, the Bajoran looked as if he wanted to say more, but he was drowned out by a voice crackling over the comm channel: "Mayday! Request immediate transport for one!" shouted Chellac.

"After we pick up the money, we need a place to hide." Cassie worked her board, and the thrusters started a low whine. "Best of all, since the mission has been blown, we can always meet them at the rendezvous and act as if nothing happened. That is, if we ever miss those idiots and they aren't in jail."

"Yes," answered the monk, sounding unsure of himself again.

"Sit down, please," said the pilot. Cassie lifted the shuttlecraft off the desert floor so fast that the Bajoran was hurled back into his seat. The dust storm swirled around the tiny craft as it punched its way into space.

"Hey, we both get what we want out of this," Cassie mused aloud. "You're famous, and I'm rich. I say we find a graceful way to get out of the Orb business. One last act of good versus evil, as you always say, then we scoot. Maybe the Orb disappears again, so we don't have to spend our days being chased."

"Yes!" exclaimed Yorka, suddenly brightening. "Let's keep it simple—good versus evil. Then the Orb is retired."

"Then all of us retire," said Cassie with a dreamy sigh.

thirteen

"Let us in!" demanded Jerit. The Romulan shook his fist at the guards atop the watchtower at the west gate of Dinky's Dry Dock. "You know who we are."

"Sorry," said the Bajoran, craning his neck to look back at the center of the yard. "There's a big crowd at the clubhouse, and the guards have been tripled." He finally nodded to his partner. "Open it."

As the two Romulans passed through the pedestrian door, the guard leaned over the railing and whispered, "Like I told your buddies, I want you out of here."

They kept walking, feeling the urgency of their situation. "Our buddies?" asked the young Romulan.

Jerit glanced at the brightly lit landing pads, buildings, and shuttlecraft. Nothing seemed amiss, except for the number of slow-moving guards. He whispered, "We've got to assume that people will be watching us, so we get in and take off."

"We don't wait for Lanik?" asked the young Romulan with innocent shock.

"No."

"He might be in the clubhouse—"

"We're not chancing a roomful of strangers—I'm surprised we've gotten this far," Jerit said testily. "Maybe he's on board already." They took a walkway branching off from the main path and were finally able to see the runabout in the distance. It seemed like an oasis of calm, but Jerit knew that was an illusion. If somebody wanted to stop them from taking off, they had better do it right now.

As they approached, the youth got out his tricorder and did a scan of the vessel. His impassive face broke into a brief smile. "You were right. One Romulan on board."

"Finally . . . we find him in the last place to look," grumbled Jerit, although he felt considerable relief. Maybe Lanik didn't retreat according to the book, but returning to the vessel was an understandable reaction.

His subordinate entered a code on a handheld device, and the hatch whooshed open a second before they reached it. Almost skipping with joy, the two Romulans ducked into the small starship. At the copilot's seat sat their third member, who didn't rise to greet them; his back remained turned toward them.

"Good, you're already plotting a course," said Jerit, stripping off his body armor. "Save your explanations for now, because I don't want to know why you disobeyed orders. Just start the launch sequence and notify the tower."

The comrade nodded, and Jerit and the youth put on their flight suits. Suddenly the air in the cabin seemed stuffy, and he couldn't breathe without difficulty. Grasping his collar, the leader staggered a few steps before he forgot why he was concerned. He just wanted to lie down and take a nap . . . a good long nap. Jerit's legs finally turned to rags, and he collapsed face-first onto the deck, just centimeters away from the copilot's seat. His youthful associate lay at his feet, unconscious.

Lanik turned in his seat to look down at Jerit, only it wasn't Lanik, but a stranger. The squad leader blinked helplessly, trying to focus on the smiling face . . . trying to figure out why he didn't recognize him, when he should.

Well, for one thing, the intruder was wearing a gas mask, which muffled his voice slightly. "Just relax, Centurion. Your flight will depart soon."

The stranger got up and moved to the pilot's seat, where he continued to study the console. "Now why did you have to modify the navigation subroutines?"

Jerit gargled some angry words, but nothing recognizable came from his mouth except spittle. "Sorry, can't have you making noise." The intruder aimed a phaser at him, and he saw the flash and felt the jolt an instant before everything went black.

The humans dragged Chellac into a dimly lit room and tossed him unceremoniously into a very comfortable chair. He looked around and saw a proscenium stage, several tables surrounded by plush furniture, and a handful of Ferengi sitting on the overstuffed seats. The audience numbered about eight in all, and he was sure it was an audience because their attention was directed toward the empty stage. Pleasant Ferengi chamber music played in the background, and one of the humans placed an elegant glass of Saurian brandy in front of him, followed by a sparkling glass of water.

"Thank you," said Chellac, relaxing a bit. He looked at the audience again, but it was hard to make out faces in the dim light. Still he could see one wrinkled, sagging elder in the middle, who was obviously the star around which the satellites revolved. He lifted his glass and toasted Chellac, pointing to the stage with his other speckled hand.

Chellac toasted his glass in response, wondering if he should move closer to the potentate. But the music suddenly changed, getting heated and more sinuous, with rolling drum rhythms and dissonant chords. A naked Ferengi woman strolled onto the stage, which was not at all unusual or titillating, except that she was very attractive. What was unusual was the bright pink suitcase she carried with her.

She held the suitcase away from her body, and four legs sprang out of the bottom. The performer placed this instant table on the floor and very lovingly opened the case. Then she began to teasingly draw out filmy underwear and lingerie, followed by a skimpy human sundress. *She's not going to put those things on, is she?* thought Chellac with excitement.

The first thing she put on was a sock, which made Chellac's pulse beat so fast that he thought his head might explode. Then she slipped on a set of spotted underwear, which made the patrons in the back laugh nervously. When the female encased her bosom in another thing— Chellac didn't even know the name for it—you could have heard an eyelash drop to the floor. When she wriggled into the dress, the whole room erupted with applause.

At this point, Chellac had to rush back to his host, while the talented performer strutted around in her clothes. "Thank you for your hospitality," he gushed. "This is . . . the most decadent show I've ever seen!"

"You liked it, huh?" The wart-covered Ferengi wheezed a laugh. "There's nothing like an old-fashioned dresstease . . . it's a dying art. Wait, she's got some flannel pajamas to try on."

While the others hooted and hollered for the pajamas, Chellac was forced to bend closer to the seated potentate. "I'm afraid I can't stay. I wish I could."

"Dinky is the name," said the elder. The fruity scent of his wart cream almost made Chellac gag. "Did I mention that I have a business proposition for you?"

"You do?" The visitor leaned closer, despite the awful smell.

"Yes," he hissed happily. "One of your traveling companions is a wanted criminal with a high price on his head. Did you know that?"

Chellac was momentarily distracted as the girl on the stage tried on a ski jacket. "No, I didn't know that," he said hoarsely. "But I never trusted that Bajoran."

"It's the *Romulan*, as if you didn't know." Dinky scoffed at him and slurped down some more brandy. "So you help us capture him, and we'll split the reward, minus our expenses, of course."

"Expenses?" asked Chellac doubtfully. "Look, I don't know what you're talking about."

"Psssst!" hissed a voice from the darkness. Chellac whirled around and saw a figure motioning to him from a table in the corner. "Come here, Chellac!"

The fellow blurting his name got the Ferengi's attention. "Excuse me," he said to his host as he hustled over to the slender patron, who didn't have the ears to be a Ferengi. However, the ears he had were pointed.

"Regimol!" whispered the Ferengi. "What are you doing here?"

The Romulan shook his head in amazement. "You don't know this is a holodeck, do you? I've been looking all over for you." From a bag on his shoulder, Regimol took out a tubelike instrument and handed it to his comrade. "Here's a signal amplifier, in case I have to transport you."

"This is a holodeck?" asked the Ferengi, looking around with sad realization.

"Rented by the hour. That *mugato* skin she's wearing . . . it's not real."

Chellac pleaded, "Any chance you can steal me a copy of this program?"

With a glance past the Ferengi's shoulder, Regimol rose to his feet. "Not now, because your playmates have seen me. Get out as best you can."

Without warning, the exclusive café faded into a dingy industrial gray, and Chellac turned to see two brawny humans running straight toward them.

"How are *you* getting out?" asked the Ferengi, whirling around. But the Romulan was gone—disappeared, even though there was nothing behind them but two walls and the corner they formed. Chellac ran into the glowing holodeck grid, hoping the walls would give way, as they must have for Regimol. But all he got for his efforts were a stubbed toe and a bashed nose.

"Owww!" groaned Chellac. He reached into his pocket for a handkerchief, and the two humans skidded to a stop a few steps away, thinking he had a weapon. When he pulled out cloth instead, they crouched down and spread their arms, maneuvering to keep him pinned in the corner.

"Just answer a few questions, and we'll let you go," promised one of them with a smile. "We don't want *you*."

"I don't know that Romulan!" shouted Chellac, stepping one way and then the other. "You can't hold me. I haven't done anything wrong! I demand to see the Ferengi consul!"

Without waiting for them to reply, Chellac rolled into a ball and scooted between the nearest one's legs.

"Hey, come back here!" he shouted.

Both humans lunged for him, but Chellac kept crawling and rolling just out of their grasp. A combadge beeped, and one of them broke off the chase to answer the call. Chellac jumped to his feet and used the big, empty room to keep up his evasive maneuvers. When he tried to reach the door, his pursuer had to veer off to protect it.

"We don't have time for games," said the angry human, drawing his phaser.

"They're moving out, anyway," reported his cohort, hiding his combadge behind a turned-down collar. "Stun him."

Chellac hurled himself at the one with phaser, trying to get under his legs, so that they couldn't shoot him. Suddenly there was a blur in the room, and a disembodied arm appeared from nowhere, whipping a metal pipe into the shooter's head. By the time he hit the ground, his associate got the same metal pipe in his gut and then on the back of his head. Before Chellac even had time to breathe, the fight was over and his two abductors had been dispatched.

Gradually, a whole being sizzled into view, looming over Chellac. With a grin, he saw that it was Regimol, come back to rescue him once again.

"Okay, now you can get back to the runabout," insisted the Romulan. "You won't be able to follow me—I'll be invisible and passing through walls. Keep that signal amplifier activated in case I have to beam you out."

"Thanks!" blurted Chellac. "So how do you go through walls?"

"Take the phaser," muttered the Romulan, pointing to the weapon laying on the floor beside the fallen human.

Chellac bent down to pick it up, and when he looked back, the Romulan was fading from view, not as a transporter does but as a poor visual signal might die out. Chellac noted the yellow device he wore on his back; it blinked while he vanished and lasted a moment longer than the rest of him.

The Ferengi fumbled at the door before he finally found a control panel that would open it. He stepped into a corridor that was crowded with people trying to exit the building. Chellac couldn't tell the cause of the stampede, but it apparently came from the clubhouse. He got caught up in the surge and had to kick and punch to keep from getting trampled. At the front of the crowd, he spotted Alon, being escorted by fellow Bajorans. It was up to Regimol to decide whether to rescue the Bajoran or not. Chellac had his orders.

A moment later, the Ferengi stumbled into the street, along with a few dozen other patrons. While guards rushed back and forth with weapons, Chellac did exactly as he'd been told and made a straight dash for the runabout in the far corner of the yard. He heard shouts and yelling, and he never even turned to see if they were directed at him. To keep them from shooting at him, the Ferengi darted among the other shuttlecraft. He could spot his destination easily enough, because others were moving toward it, and the launch thrusters were firing.

He rushed past two Bajorans who were wrestling with a dark-suited Romulan, as more guards converged upon them. That wasn't *his* Romulan, Chellac noted with relief. It had to be the third spy, who was going to end up in custody. The Romulan aided the escaping Ferengi by drawing a weapon and squeezing off a beam, which caused most of the people in the vicinity to flop to the landing pad.

But not Chellac, who kept huffing and puffing as a sliver of light appeared under the hatch. "Halt!" someone shrieked as he plodded past. The hatch started to rise, and Chellac increased his speed as a phaser blast streaked past him. He dove the final few meters into the doorway, landing on a hard metal step. Strong hands dragged him into the cabin as the hatch snapped shut where his legs had been.

Stepping over two fallen Romulans, Regimol bounded into the pilot's seat and tapped the instrument panel. "There! Shields are back up. Take a seat, Chellac, we're not hanging around."

"What about the force-field?" asked the Ferengi

breathlessly. He didn't have enough energy to even move from the deck.

"I took care of it while I was out," answered Regimol with a smile. He worked his board, and the runabout began to lift off the landing pad. Outside the craft, small weapons fire shimmered against their shields, but it did no damage to the sturdy craft. Chellac covered his eyes, expecting to be blown up any second.

When he was still alive a moment later, the Ferengi pried his eyes open and peered out the rear viewport. He saw the bright lights of Torga IV rapidly receding into the distance, and he laughed joyfully at their daring escape. After a few more seconds, the black curtain of space fell all around their tiny craft, and they were anonymous once again.

"So how do you walk through walls?" asked Chellac conversationally as he filed his fingernails, while reclining in a soft passenger seat on the runabout.

When Regimol ignored his question, one of the bound Romulans lying on the deck piped up. "First you become a traitor, that's how," said the one named Jerit. "Then you steal an interphase generator and become a common criminal."

"I hate to correct you," said Regimol from the pilot's seat, "but I didn't steal it, I *invented* it. And I never wanted to become a criminal—just a dissenting voice who thought we should share technology with other races, especially Vulcans. It was our own Senate who turned me into a criminal."

"And a good job they did!" said Chellac cheerfully. "I take it, you all know each other?"

Flopping about on the deck, Jerit scowled and tried to twist away from the Ferengi's gaze. His younger associate just lay still, staring hatefully at his captors.

"They all know me in the Legion of Assassins," said Regimol matter-of-factly. "They've all been sent to kill me a time or two, with pathetic results, as you can see. Now we'll find out what *they* know, and what they were searching for on that planet."

"I'll never tell you a thing!" vowed Jerit angrily. "You'll have to kill me first."

"That's not my department," said Regimol with a shrug. "I captured you, and now I'll take you to someone who will extract what we need to know."

"Who?" asked Jerit defiantly.

"My master, Bakus."

That caused the Romulan to blanch a lighter shade of green, and Chellac found it amusing that even Romulan killers could fear a master criminal. He rose to his feet and sat in the copilot's seat beside Regimol.

"When do we rendezvous with Yorka and the shuttle-craft?" whispered the Ferengi.

"We don't," answered Regimol. "We can't trust them. They deserted us, Chellac . . . they ran out on us."

"No, no, they didn't," insisted the Ferengi, although in his heart he was beginning to wonder. "It was just a misunderstanding. They got scared and couldn't wait for us. It was *my* fault—I overreacted."

The Romulan smiled with amusement. "A trusting Ferengi! That is sweet. Yes, you gave them an excuse to leave, and they thought about it for a nanosecond." He sighed longingly. "I try to set a good example, but perhaps there is no honor among thieves. I thought Cassie would have more sense, but she must have surrendered to greed. I don't think they'll want to see us again."

"It's all over then, isn't it?" said Chellac, shaking his head miserably. "All that work I put in, and there won't be any profit. There won't be anything for us."

"I wouldn't say it's over," replied Regimol thoughtfully. "Also a fast runabout and two prisoners is not a bad day's work. But the big prize eluded both us and our friends."

He glanced back at their two sullen captives and added, "I will be curious to see what these fellows do next."

Captain Picard and Geordi La Forge stood outside sickbay on the *Enterprise*, discussing the engineer's latest idea. "I know, Captain, that nothing has worked so far, but that's because we're approaching this as a conventional body in space, which can be measured and analyzed. It can't—it doesn't make any sense, except when seen from another dimension. This experiment with Counselor Troi is a good start, from that angle, but we need to move physically into it. If beings can come out of the rift, then *we* can go into it."

The captain's lips thinned. "We're like a village nestled in the shadow of a live volcano, which is about to erupt any second. Justifiably, we're under orders to keep our distance from this thing."

The engineer was still thinking out loud. "If we could get them back, the Brahms prototype suits would be perfect to penetrate the rift."

"What about the subspace cracks that Data discovered?" asked the captain, moving to a different tact. "He seemed to think that was a viable source of information."

Geordi looked doubtful. "That's like studying the cracks in the sidewalk and ignoring the roots from the huge oak tree next to it. Data and I agree that the subspace cracks seem to link these various anomalies, which accounts for them behaving in unison. But if we try to block them or jam them, we don't know what that will do. Data's been trying to figure out how to use subspace to communicate with the rift, maybe send it a signal to contract instead of expand, but that could take a long time."

"Can we step up the search for biological beings?" asked Picard. "In particular, can we tell if a second Romulan vessel was lost?"

The engineer shook his head. "Not unless our sensors return to normal, or we get a good deal closer. Something alive may be out there in the debris, but it couldn't live long in all that radiation."

"I see," muttered Picard.

"I'd like to explore the possible link between the rift and those portable Genesis emitters," said La Forge, "but we don't have any of them to test the theory. Our best bet is to go into the rift."

The door to sickbay opened, and Beverly Crusher stuck her head out. "We're ready to induce the dream state," she said.

Picard nodded and glanced at La Forge. "I'll consider it."

With the engineer following him, the captain entered sickbay, where he smiled cordially at Dr. Crusher. She led them into a private room, where Deanna Troi lay in bed, with Nurse Ogawa in attendance.

Captain Picard approached Troi's bedside and gave the counselor an encouraging smile. "Are you sure you want to do this?"

She nodded thoughtfully. "Yes, but I can't guarantee anything. I haven't felt it again—that sense of recognition that I had when I passed out. I'm not even sure I was right about this being the same entity we encountered at Gemworld."

"This is just one avenue we're pursuing," replied Picard with a glance at La Forge. "I'm entertaining almost every idea these days."

Conversation paused as they watched Beverly Crusher prepare a hypospray. Nurse Ogawa checked Troi's vital signs on the overhead display, and Picard shifted uneasily on his feet. He had an overwhelming sensation that something was about to happen. Bad or good, he couldn't tell, but this untenable wait had to come to an end soon.

It didn't help that Troi appeared less than confident about her ability to contact the entity. The physical danger to her seemed minimal, since this was a mental excursion conducted under close supervision. The real danger lay in accomplishing nothing, as they had for days on end, just waiting for the next shoe to fall.

"You seem nervous," said Crusher, breaking him out of his reverie. Picard expected the doctor to be looking at him—instead she was gazing at the counselor's readouts.

"Not surprising," said Troi. "I can't help remembering what this thing did to me last time. It was like a bottomless pool, trying to suck me in."

"We'll be here to revive you," said the doctor. "You

only want to communicate and gather information—learn whether it's related to the Gemworld rift."

Picard's combadge chirped, and he backed away from the examination table to answer. "Picard here. I thought I left word not to be disturbed."

"Sorry, Sir," answered Riker apologetically. "I thought you would want to know—the Romulan ship has returned. The *Javlek* is just off our bow, and Commander Kaylena is hailing us."

"Kaylena," echoed Picard. He glanced up and saw Beverly Crusher looking thoughtfully at him. "I'll be right there. Picard out."

He held his palms out helplessly. "I'm sorry, but we're going to have to postpone this experiment. The Romulan ship has just returned—the one we thought was lost. Maybe they have news or have discovered something about the anomaly. At any rate, I have to confer with them."

"Of course, Jean-Luc," said Crusher magnanimously. "This was a long shot, anyway."

"Ask them about the Brahms prototype suits," insisted La Forge. "We need them back."

"I will," promised the captain as he rushed out the door.

Once in the corridor, he virtually ran for the turbolift. The feeling of loss and uncertainty had been overwhelming since the rift expanded a few days ago, forcing them to flee. Plagued by inaccurate sensor readings, they couldn't even tell if the Romulan ships had been destroyed or had merely escaped into warp. Now that the Romulans had returned, the relief was staggering, and the captain had to ask himself if he was feeling all right. He felt emotionally drained, and he couldn't attribute it solely to frustration and worry. Commander Kaylena, the blackness, the monsters—it was all related, all holding them in bondage to this place.

When he stepped off the turbolift, he paused in the corridor for a moment, realizing that he wasn't headed to the bridge. He pressed his combadge. "Picard to bridge. I'm beaming over to the *Javlek*. Patch me into Commander Kaylena."

"Making connection," replied Data. "Proceed, Captain."

"Commander Kaylena," he said with a pang of joy. "Welcome back."

"Thank you, Captain," she replied urgently. "We must . . . we have to talk."

"I'm on my way to our transporter room," answered Picard, on the run again.

"We will send coordinates," she promised.

Minutes later, the captain stepped off the platform in the Romulan transporter room and saw Commander Kaylena waiting for him, her back ramrod-stiff but her face revealing her pleasure at seeing him. "Leave us," she told the transporter operator.

A figure bowed and scurried through the shadows, slipping out the door with barely a footstep. She stared wild-eyed at him. "Why should I care so much what happens to you?"

"I don't know," he answered, stepping hesitantly closer. "I was distraught . . . thinking you had been killed. Now I find you still in command."

"I'm only in command of this ship . . . nothing else," she answered hoarsely. Kaylena twisted her hands, and the words came out in a jumble. "I escaped censure . . . over the loss of the *Petrask*, because disaster is everywhere. The third ship in our task force was reassigned, but I knew I had to come back here. Our fleet is in danger . . . whole worlds—"

"That's not what brought you back," he said.

"No," she admitted, "you've gotten inside me. I don't know how." The commander stepped forward and seized Picard by the shoulders, planting her lips upon his. Passion unexpectedly overwhelming him, Picard wrapped his arms around her body, grasping the rich fabric of her uniform. Swallowed by the moment, they clung to each other tightly.

fourteen

In the deepest reaches of the moss creatures' stronghold on Lomar, the dripping of green ooze from the vines overhead was constant. So was the stench of decomposing bodies and the sight of rotting corpses, hanging from the moss-covered rafters. These bodies were so disfigured that it was impossible to tell what species or what sex they were. No matter how many of these dank caverns she inspected, it was impossible for Teska to shake the sense that she had entered some hellish underworld dredged from a human psyche.

"We need refrigeration in here," said the Vulcan to her assistant. They were wearing lightweight environmental suits for their own protection, and her voice was amplifed in her headset.

"It's been ordered," answered Franklin Oswald, making a note on his padd. "The work crews are behind schedule, as usual."

"How could we not reach these bodies sooner?"

Oswald pointed to the scorch marks on the floor, as

well as the scattered bits of moss all over. "According to reports, the Romulans finished them off down here. This is the last room in this wing of the complex—it's the end of the line."

"It certainly was for them," said Teska, gazing at the oozing masses hanging from the rafters.

"The first crew down here was convinced this place was haunted," said Oswald. "Since there was no possibility of anyone being left alive, it was shoved to low priority. Unfortunately, at the rate we're going, it will take a long time for the autopsy crews to get down here."

"Approximately twenty-five months," replied Teska. "Can you imagine yourself being stationed here that long?"

Oswald laughed nervously. "That's a joke, right?"

"Somebody will have to be stationed here that long," said the Vulcan, "if we wish to identify these remains."

"I'm beginning to think that a decent burial would serve them better," answered Oswald quietly. "So often, I've just wanted to take a genesis torch to a room like this."

Teska nodded thoughtfully. "An understandable response, if overly emotional." Something caught her eye, and she peered upward into the gloomy shadows.

"I'll resign before I stay on Lomar twenty-five months," grumbled Franklin Oswald. "I didn't do anything to deserve duty like this."

"That is an illogical correlation," said Teska, drawing a phaser from her belt. "Stand back, please."

"What are you shooting at?" he asked nervously.

"Something that is active." The Vulcan fired two pinpoint beams into the rafters, and a large chunk of vine fell to the floor. At least it looked like a chunk of vine, until it began to spark and blink, while giving off a wisp of smoke.

Franklin Oswald stepped closer. "What . . . what is it?"

"At a guess, I would say a Romulan listening device," answered Teska, crouching to inspect the camouflaged device. "I don't know how they masked it from our sensors, but they are experts at cloaking. It must have malfunctioned due to the damp conditions in this chamber. A spark caught my attention."

"Do you think . . . that's the only one?"

The Vulcan shook her head. "If there is one, there are many."

Admiral Nechayev scowled angrily at the stripped, cleaned, and labeled apparatus resting on her desk. It was about the size and shape of a laboratory beaker, but full of intricate circuits. Standing at attention in her ready room were Specialist Teska and the *Sequoia*'s first officer, Commander Marbinz. The Benzite's anger matched her own, but the Vulcan gazed impassively at the Romulan device she had uncovered.

"It's inert, so you can speak freely," muttered Nechayev. "Not only did the Romulans take everything that wasn't nailed down, they left these souvenirs. We have to assume they know everything we've talked about, everything we've done since we arrived on Lomar. They know we've found out about them having portable Genesis emitters."

"There must be a subspace relay somewhere on the planet," observed Teska. "Until we find it, any removal process will be incomplete."

"Don't remove them," suggested Marbinz. "With this network, we can feed them false information."

"I thought of that," said Nechayev, "but we're not at war with them. We haven't got fleet movements or massive deployments to hide. The bottom line is, they have Genesis, and we don't. We know it, and so do they. I let Genesis slip through my fingers once before, and now again."

"It is pointless to dwell on the past," said Teska, picking up the Romulan apparatus. "I believe we should reverse-engineer this and leave the current network in place until we decide the correct action. All personnel can be instructed to discuss trivial matters while on duty on the planet—nothing related to the mission."

"They hardly ever discuss their work," said the Benzite. "It's too depressing."

"What more could they learn?" asked the admiral. "Except that we curse them every day for the way they left this place."

"Bridge to captain," interrupted a voice.

"Nechayev here," she responded.

"Sir, a decommissioned civilian runabout has just entered orbit," reported the duty officer, "and they're hailing us. They're asking for you specifically, Captain."

"Did they give a name?"

"Sehlat," answered the officer cryptically.

"Patch him through," responded the admiral with a sly smile. She motioned to Teska and Marbinz to stay and listen.

After a moment, another voice sounded over the comm system. "Is this really the admiral?"

"Yes, it is. You found me, Sehlat."

"It was easy, since you're staying put these days," answered the stranger. "I've got four witnesses to events which interest you. Two are Romulans from Torga IV, and one is Ferengi. He's a friend of mine."

"Who's the fourth witness?"

"Myself. I've seen it . . . a live demonstration."

That brought a silence which seemed to last for an hour. "But you don't have it?"

"No. Beam us over, and we'll talk," he answered. "I'll need security for the two Romulans, plus a nice warm brig. They're not here by choice."

"Good work," said Nechayev. "Send us your coordinates, and we'll beam them directly to the brig. We'll meet you in the transporter room. Nechayev out."

She turned to her first officer. "Make sure we get these two prisoners on board without a hitch. Teska and I will meet the other two witnesses in the transporter room."

"Yes, Sir," answered the Benzite, frowning with concern. "When he says he's seen 'it,' what does he mean?"

"Genesis in a suitcase," answered the admiral.

"Bakus," said the Romulan warmly as he stepped off the transporter platform to shake the admiral's hand.

"No, you can't call me that anymore," said Nechayev with amusement. "I've retired. *You* have to be Bakus."

"But I'm not convincing as an ex-Maquis leader," protested the charming Romulan. "You have to be a tough, embittered human to play that role."

He gave Teska a wry smile. "You don't qualify either, my dear."

Nechayev began introductions. "Regimol, this is

Teska, my mission specialist. Teska, this is Regimol, a dissident scientist formerly of the Romulan Star Empire."

"Now a common thief," he said with a shrug. "But I've been the admiral's 'mission specialist' on more than one occassion."

Regimol turned toward the transporter platform just as another figure materialized. This was a short, barrel-chested Ferengi wearing a flight suit and a bewildered expression.

"Don't tell me that Bakus is a starship captain," said the Ferengi, stepping off the platform and gazing around the transporter room.

"Bakus is still indisposed," said the Romulan, "but Admiral Nechayev here is the best one to deal with our two prisoners."

After Regimol completed the introductions, Chellac rubbed his hands together excitedly. "Let's get a bite to eat, Admiral, and then I'll tell you all about the Orb of Life. Although you know it by another religious name."

In a quiet corner of the lounge, Teska and Nechayev sat in stunned silence, listening to the Ferengi tell his story between chomping mouthfuls of food. After the second demonstration of the portable Genesis Device, Regimol took up the tale, detailing the capture of the Romulans and bringing them to the present.

Nechayev narrowed her eyes and lifted her finger. "Go back to that second demonstration. Are you saying that a replicate made on the fly worked just as well as the original?"

Chellac nodded. "Yes, the good monk could make as many Orbs of Life as he wanted."

In dismay, Nechayev pushed herself away from the table. "I've got a lot to do. It may be pointless, Chellac, but you *will* go to the rendezvous to try to meet Prylar Yorka. Get some rest first, and avail yourself of our facilities. Come with me, and I'll turn you over to passenger relations."

"That sounds delightful, Admiral," replied the Ferengi. He wiped his mouth daintily with his napkin, then rose to his feet. "Listen, if you want to find them, follow the money. It was starting to roll in."

"We will."

The Ferengi turned to Teska. "It was a pleasure to meet you, Priestess."

"Likewise," she answered with a nod.

"Teska," said Nechayev, "I think you and Regimol have something private to discuss. I'd like both of you to meet me in the brig in an hour. Regimol, you're welcome to stay here on the *Sequoia*."

"Thank you, Admiral, but I think I'll return to my ship. I haven't had one in a while, and I'm enjoying it. There are nice sleeping quarters for a vessel that size."

"Suit yourself." With a nod to the Ferengi, Nechayev led the way out of the lounge.

With a raised eyebrow, the Vulcan looked expectantly at the Romulan. "By the admiral's remarks, am I to believe that you know my husband? His name is Hasmek, and he was—"

Regimol held up his hand. "Yes, I knew him."

She noted his use of past tense. "Is he dead?"

"I didn't see him die," answered Regimol. "His offenses weren't as serious as mine, but he was also listed among the ranks of dissidents for wanting to normalize ties with Vulcans." He gazed at her. "I can see why."

"What happened to him?"

"I know they arrested him the same day they came for me, but I escaped." Regimol folded his hands and looked down. "His name was on the arrest record—I saw it. I know there was a secret trial and several executions after that, but I didn't see him killed. However, I included his name in a list I gave Nechayev of dissidents presumed dead, because it fit the facts. I'm sorry."

"So being married to me got him killed," observed Teska. "I detest Romulans."

"You're not supposed to detest anyone," said Regimol.

"I make an exception in their case. Exceptions occur in nature and physics and are logical. As humans say, they prove the rule." Teska rose from the table, looking a bit shaky but still impassive.

"I could try to find out for sure if he's dead," said Regimol. "It might take a while."

"It has already been a while," she answered, turning and striding away.

"Admiral, I really must protest!" declared Commander Marbinz, staring at the paddful of orders Nechayev had just handed him. "You want to abort our mission on Lomar, disregard orders, and head toward the *Enterprise*? Plus you want to send some of our crew off to Bajor . . . with a Romulan spy? What about our work here? Per your orders, I've got ninety percent of the crew down on the planet!"

"I understand that," said the captain, glad they were having this discussion in her ready room instead of on the bridge. She found that she was retreating to this office a bit too often, but it felt more comfortable than the bridge. "We have time to recall our crew and suspend operations. Shouldn't take more than a couple of hours."

"But . . . but!" he sputtered, "you've got to see that I have to report this. You're going to get in all kinds of trouble over this action."

Nechayev slapped him good-naturedly on the shoulder. "Go ahead, do what you want. After this, I'll either be back in the admiralty, or I'll be retired. I really don't care, because being ship's captain is not my forte. No matter what happens, the *Sequoia* will be your ship. But while I'm captain, God help me, I'm going to be the insane kind who is going to ignore orders, throw out the book, and run off to save the universe. So get accustomed to that, okay?"

"Okay." The Benzite nodded crisply, a smile creeping across his blue face.

"And Regimol would resent being called a spy," said the admiral. "He'd prefer to be called a thief, but just say he's one of my operatives. First, could you get me a crack team to go to Bajor with Regimol and Chellac—we need two pilots who can handle the runabout, and four of our best security officers. I want to meet with them before they go."

"Yes, Sir," answered Marbinz.

"By the way," said Nechayev, "I haven't been comfortable with my people working in a place that's bugged. It's depressing enough down there already, and now we have to watch what we say? But we do need to use Romulan Radio to feed them some misinformation. We could tell them that we have the missing device, or . . . maybe I'll know after I talk to the prisoners."

"I'll consider it, too," promised the first officer. He couldn't help but to smile as he backed toward the door. "I'll file my log later. There's plenty to do right now."

Admiral Nechayev nodded in appreciation.

In the austere brig of the *Sequoia*, the two Romulans stared sullenly from their cells at their visitors, Nechayev, Teska, and Regimol. Even if the prisoners seemingly stood in the same room with their captors, they were held at bay by invisible force-fields. They paced briefly in their recessed quarters, glaring at those who had come to interrogate them. Teska found their behavior fascinating.

"You can torture me if you wish," said the older Romulan, who called himself Jerit. "I'm not telling you anything. I don't *know* anything."

Nechayev scowled. "So you went to Torga IV on vacation, and to take a tour of the temples. You won't even admit you were searching for a portable Genesis emitter?"

"I don't know about such things," muttered Jerit, turning away.

Nechayev shrugged and turned to her colleagues, whispering, "Play along with me."

Both Teska and Regimol nodded, although the Vulcan hoped she wouldn't be asked to lie.

The admiral moved closer to Jerit's cell and took a friendlier tone. "Consider speaking of your own free will, and we'll protect you afterward. But if we have to use a mind-meld, we'll learn everything you know—and the answers to more questions than we care to ask. Then we'll return you to your superiors, telling them everything you told us."

Jerit lunged at the admiral and bounced off the forcefield, landing on his rear and skidding across the cell. He bared his teeth and glared at the gray-haired woman, while she merely strolled to the adjoining cell to confront his young associate.

"Regimol," she asked, "what is the League of Assassins likely to do to this one, when they find he has told us all their secrets?"

"Target practice," suggested the Romulan. "Perhaps medical experiments. Or they might harvest his organs—they do with most condemned prisoners."

"If you speak to us," insisted Nechayev, "you can still limit what you tell us. If we use the mind-meld, we'll find out *everything*."

"We're trained to resist a mind-meld!" shouted the young one.

"Shut up!" barked his superior.

"Teska is a priestess on Vulcan," said the admiral, "and she's been a master of the mind-meld since she was a child. Yours would be easy compared to the work she's been doing on Lomar. Isn't that so, Teska?"

The Vulcan nodded. "That is so."

Nechayev moved toward the door and motioned her associates to follow her. "So we're going to give you a few minutes to think about it. You can act independently, you know. If one of you wants to talk freely, we'll protect him, and we may be lenient to both of you. Or we can use the mind-meld. It's your choice."

Once outside the brig, Nechayev marched briskly

into an adjoining control room, where she told the guard, "Put them on screen."

"Yes, Sir." The guard did as ordered, and soon they could observe the two Romulans arguing with each other in hissed whispers. The young one seemed to want to talk and save himself.

"Shall I clarify the audio?" asked the guard.

"No, this is fine," she answered with a smile.

"Admiral, I will not force a mind-meld against someone's will," declared Teska.

"You won't need to," said Regimol with amusement. "Old Bakus here is a master of this fine art. She could *be* a Romulan."

The admiral pointed to the screen and frowned. "The leader has calmed the young one down. They'll probably resist another round, and we'll have to go to the next step."

She turned to the beefy guard in the red shirt. "Ensign, get a phaser, set it to heavy stun, and if I order you to fire, don't hesitate."

"Yes, Sir," he answered, jumping to his feet and drawing his weapon. Carefully, he checked the setting, while Nacheyev drew her own phaser and checked it.

"You'd better call sickbay and send for a medteam, just in case."

"Yes, Sir." He worked his board briefly, then the admiral motioned her entourage to follow her.

Once back in the brig, they again confronted the pair of Romulan prisoners. "All right, which one of you would like to talk to us first? We'll make sure to have dinner sent up while we're chatting." Nechayev smiled pleasantly.

The two prisoners looked at one another, then marched defiantly to their bunks and sat down. After they did nothing but stare at their hands for several seconds, Nechayev went on, "Ensign, turn off the force-field in cell one, on my mark. Regimol, cover me."

The guard went to the small wall panel which controlled Jerit's cell, while the admiral strode up to the defiant Romulan. Leveling her phaser, she took point-blank aim at him from two meters away. He looked like he wanted to dodge or somehow resist, but there was also fear etched in his face.

"Last chance to talk willingly," said the admiral. "After this, we just take whatever is in your brain— every murder, every sexual encounter, and every silly dream."

He spat at her, but the spittle sizzled brightly on the force-field. The admiral waved her hand at the ensign and took aim. As soon as the force-field dropped, she drilled Jerit in the chest, and he slumped to the deck. It was the most cold-blooded thing Teska had ever seen, although logically she knew the Romulan wasn't hurt. The Vulcan realized that getting on the wrong side of the diminutive admiral was a bad idea.

"Gentlemen, bring him along," said Nechayev calmly.

Regimol and the guard entered the cell, grabbed a leg apiece, and rudely dragged the Romulan across the deck toward the door. The young one tried to be stoic, but he ended up leaping to his feet and watching from the front of his cell. All he saw was the two males dragging his comrade out, while the females followed.

In the corridor, they were met by a puzzled medical team, who gathered around the unconscious Romulan.

"He's only phaser stunned," explained Nechayev, "but I want you to give him something that will keep him unconscious for an hour or so. And I want him to wake up confused."

"That's highly unethical and irregular," muttered one of the medical workers, looking indignant.

"Then I'll just keep shooting him with my phaser," said Nechayev. "Whatever you think is better for him."

That threat forced the medteam to confer and decide what to load into a hypospray. While they dealt with the prisoner, Teska moved closer to Nechayev and whispered, "I do not understand the point of this."

The admiral took her arm and walked her down the corridor, out of the prisoner's unconscious earshot. "When we drag him back to the brig in an hour, the young one will think that we know everything already. So his resistance will be weakened, and he'll talk. In fact, he'll go with us easily while the other one is still unconscious and can't see him."

"And if this ruse does not work?" asked Teska.

Nechayev looked evenly at the Vulcan. "Then I'll order you to perform the mind-meld on one of them."

"And if I refuse?" The Vulcan looked at Nechayev, expecting an answer.

"Weren't you the one who criticized me for sitting around and doing nothing? Do you want to be the one who fiddles while Rome burns?" The admiral walked a bit farther down the corridor, and the Vulcan dutifully followed. "Out of respect for you, Teska, I haven't forced you to do a mind-meld while we could try another method. But if we have no choice, I expect you to obey my orders, like anyone else on this crew."

"You are not obeying orders," pointed out Teska.

"And you're not winning this argument," answered the admiral. They turned back to see Regimol strolling in their direction.

"I hope I'm not interrupting anything," he said with a smile. "You've got the young one right where you want him. He's pacing furiously—you can see his mind working."

"Regimol, you and I have a crew to brief for your mission to Bajor," said the admiral. "I want them to understand that you're in charge. Teska, I would appreciate it if you could stay here and keep an eye on things. We'll be back in an hour."

She nodded, and the admiral and her thief walked toward the turbolift. Teska turned and looked at the unconscious Romulan lying in the corridor, surrounded by medical workers.

"He's out, and his condition is stable," said the doctor who had protested earlier. "What do you want us to do with him? Just leave him in the hallway?"

"Yes, give me a medical tricorder," said the Vulcan. "I can check his vital signs—I know what the norm is."

Still looking disgruntled, the doctor handed over a tricorder, then he rounded up his crew and left. Teska still had the security officer with her, and his phaser was set to heavy stun. She sat on her haunches and gazed at the prisoner, who appeared to be sleeping peacefully, despite everything.

The Vulcan fought the temptation to reach a hand to his face, meld with him, and steal the contents of his mind. In truth, the mind of a Romulan was just so ugly—so perverted in its values—that she dreaded going into one. For a Vulcan, it was like Jekyll meeting Hyde, the hero facing his evil twin. And she assumed this craven assassin's mind was worse than most.

Teska shivered as she stood up, deciding that she would perform the meld if so ordered. If he knew anything about her mate, she would find out then. It was really the only logical thing to do.

Captain Picard lay asleep, his arm draped over the Romulan commander, and she had to squirm slightly to avoid waking him as she rose. Kaylena swung her lean frame off the bed and put on a plush red robe before she scurried into the adjoining room. She paused briefly before a mirror to pull back her long black hair, which was hopelessly tangled, and she glimpsed her pointed ears. The woman still couldn't get used to them, and she would be happy when she could go back to her own ears and skin color.

Her door slid open with a hiss, and she gasped, startled. A stooped Romulan female with a streak of gray in her severe bangs stuck her head into the room. "Is he asleep?"

Kaylena nodded. "Yes."

"Get dressed and step into the corridor. I want a little briefing before he wakes up." The older woman vanished.

"Yes, Sir," answered the younger woman glumly.

A few moments later, Kaylena stood in a deserted corridor with a woman a head shorter than her. Even through they were dressed in identical uniforms, it was clear that the elder, wizened Romulan was in charge. They could talk freely, because this section had been closed off to regular personnel while Captain Picard was onboard.

"Have you talked about Genesis?" asked the elder.

"Yes," answered Kaylena, "and I don't believe he knows anything about it. He's been very forthcoming— I believe their interest lies in the anomaly which claimed the ships, not Genesis."

"Then why did he keep asking us about it?"

The younger one shrugged helplessly. "You know, humans are like Ferengi—they love to bargain. When we demanded the prototype suits, he demanded something in return—something he guessed we had. That gave him a chance to save face and buy time. I'm convinced he didn't really know we had it, and that he's focused on the anomaly. Or he was . . . until now. By the way, he wants the prototype suits back to enter the rift, and I think it's a good idea."

The elder laughed. "*You* think it's a good idea? You're just an actress hired to play a part, and shed some tears. Elasian tears—if we could somehow duplicate them."

"But you can't," said the Elasian snidely. "I think you've wasted me on someone who can't help you. He's hopelessly in love with me, would do anything for me, but he's just the captain of one starship. And he's not thinking about Genesis at the moment."

The stooped woman cleared her throat and considered the beautiful Elasian. "Just what *is* he thinking about?"

She sighed at looked at the closed door. "He'll be obsessed with me for some time. His crew will probably notice a change in him. So if there's something you want to get out of this liaison, you had better tell me about it fast. Or let me end it. He'll be heartbroken, but he'll live."

"Keep going with it," ordered the wizened commander, shuffling down the corridor. "We've invested this much trouble. When he awakens, tell him that we'll return the prototype suits and let them risk their lives in that blackness. We want to keep their good faith, don't we?"

"Thank you, Commander," said the Elasian with a nod of her head.

After her superior left, she reentered her quarters and paused in front of the mirror to arrange her hair in the severe Romulan style. The hair was a fraud, just like her, but it didn't matter because the captain was hers. Even if she told him the truth, he would still love her.

She padded softly to her bed, where her lover had not stirred. "I tried to protect you, Jean-Luc," she whispered to the sleeping human, while gazing at his slim, well-toned body. "I didn't pick you for this—they told me to do it. We made a mistake, and I'm sorry."

A tear trickled from her eye, and she angrily intercepted the drop with her fingers and wiped it on her tunic. "I hate myself," she muttered. "I've sold my love too cheaply. And I do love you, Jean-Luc. I didn't mean to, but I do."

fifteen

On the *Enterprise*'s main viewscreen, the blackness ebbed and flowed gradually, like some kind of opaque amoeba, blotting out the entire starscape behind it. In front of this monstrous apparition floated various shimmering clouds of radiation-soaked debris—detritus of two smashed starships and the unidentified flotsam from the rift. It looked like an ugly wound, thought Beverly Crusher, as she stepped off the turbolift and walked the center of the bridge.

Will Riker turned to look at her with some concern. "He's not back yet," said the first officer.

Beverly tried to treat this news cavalierly. "It's still time for you to be relieved, Will. How long has he been on the *Javlek*?"

"Six hours."

She nodded sagely, as if that meant something, when all the time she was afraid to admit what it meant. "The captain can take care of himself."

"They've sent word that he'll be back soon," said

Riker hopefully, "and that he'll be bringing the Brahms suits with him. So the trip has accomplished something."

"I'm sure it has," answered Crusher, trying to keep the sarcasm to a minimum. "We just seem to be mired in quicksand here, and we don't know which way to go. I don't want to experiment with Deanna, especially if the captain has other pursuits. I mean, other ideas—" She gave up stammering and looked down at her clenched fists, which she loosened immediately.

He gave a big sigh of relief. "Oh, good . . . that takes a load off my mind." The big man glanced up at the gaping, quivering maw hovering in space—it seemed to be breathing, like something alive. "We could deal with it, if we could deal with the radiation. But we haven't even identified it yet."

The doctor patted him on his beefy shoulder. "Go grab Deanna and get some dinner. She's in her office. I'll let you know as soon as he returns."

"Okay," said Riker, glancing back at the dark anomaly on the viewscreen. "Now we know that somebody will be taking a spacewalk into that thing, and we had better start planning for it. Computer, transfer control of the bridge to Commander Crusher."

The computer responded affirmatively, and Riker nodded to the bridge staff as he strode to the turbolift. A moment later, Crusher was in command of the *Enterprise*, which entailed waiting for the captain to return and the anomaly to change for the worse. It seemed no wonder that they were all on the verge of going crazy.

*   *   *

"Daddy! No! No!" cried Suzi as she ran around the couch in Ogawa's quarters. Then the six-year-old cut loose with a wild giggle and kept charging as her bungling father plodded after her, waving his hands like an inept gorilla.

"I'm gonna get you!" he roared, moving even slower. In exasperation, he suddenly turned and ran in the other direction, and Suzi had to reverse course, screaming with laughter. Still he managed to catch the little girl, tickling her for a few seconds until she squirmed away. Collapsed on the floor, he panted and grinned happily, until he glanced at the chronometer on the desk.

"Suzi, I've got to go," said Daddy.

"No, no!" insisted the little girl, jumping into his lap. He hugged her longingly for a moment, then reluctantly held her away as he scrambled to his feet.

"Mommy will be here soon," she informed him.

"Like I said, Pumpkin, I can't see your mommy yet," answered her father, stepping hesitantly toward the door.

"Why not?" she shouted with a child's determination to hear the logic behind parental edicts. "Why can't you?"

He was out of excuses. "Do you want me to keep coming or not?"

Suzi frowned at him, trying unsuccessfully not to break into tears. When she began to blubber, he couldn't help but to bend down and give the girl another hug. "I know it doesn't make sense," he explained, "but you'll understand someday."

"No, no," she said, struggling to get out of his arms. "Mommy is unhappy, too. I'm going to tell her!"

His face grew dark, and his eyes narrowed. "Don't do that."

Suzi pulled away from her father, crossing her arms and staring at him with a disapproving frown. "It makes no sense for only you and me to be happy."

"All right, all right," he said with another glance at the time. "We'll tell her next time I come, okay? But don't tell her beforehand—this will be our little surprise."

"Okay," said the dark-haired child, judging that to be a fair bargain. "Next time, Daddy."

"Next time," he echoed as he hurried toward the door. When it opened, he peered cautiously into the corridor, then dashed out.

"Good-bye, Daddy," said Suzi with a sniffle.

Jean-Luc Picard felt drugged, sated, and blissfully happy as he blinked awake, until he realized that he was in a strange bed on a strange ship. And Kaylena was no longer in his arms, although this was her bed. "Oh, my word," muttered Picard as he sat up and rubbed his head. "What the hell am I doing?" It had been years since he'd had a hangover, but that's how he felt—drunk on love.

Covering himself in shame, although there was no one else in the luxurious quarters, he sprang out of bed and searched for his uniform. He never dressed quicker in his life, and he wondered how he was going to get back to the *Enterprise* with the least amount of embarrassment.

On her vanity was a companel he had seen her use before, and he walked up to the device and pressed it.

"Yes, Captain Picard," said an officious voice.

"I wish . . . to return to my ship," he said simply. Wild horses wouldn't drag any more information out of him.

"But of course, Captain," answered the voice. "Commander Kaylena is occupied at the moment, and she sends her regrets. She hopes to meet with you again at the earliest opportunity."

Picard felt a stirring in his heart and elsewhere, but he kept his mouth shut. Meeting with Kaylena again was his fondest desire, and he already felt pangs of loss at her absence. But he was glad that she wasn't here, or else he would be making a fool of himself all over again.

The voice on the companel continued, "An escort will arrive there soon to take you to the transporter room. We will transport the prototype phase suits at the same time."

"Oh, good," said Picard, breathing a sigh of relief. "Thank you."

"At your service," responded the voice.

Well, thought Picard as he slumped into a chair, *I can't complain about being made to feel unwelcome here*. But he also felt used in some odd way, although he had been a willing participant. He couldn't shake the feeling that this was more important to him than it was to Kaylena. In fact, he couldn't shake the feeling that to him this romance was more important than anything.

When Captain Picard walked onto the bridge ten minutes later, he was a bit dismayed to find Beverly Crusher in charge. He had been mentally prepared to face Riker, but not her. He tried to keep his demeanor businesslike as he approached her, although it was difficult to meet her eyes.

"Hello, Beverly," he said softly, taking her arm and leading her toward an unoccupied auxiliary console to starboard. She smelled good, too, and he found himself drawn to her, thinking back to some very fond memories.

Picard cleared his throat, and tried to clear his mind. At least they were out of earshot of the crew. "I have a feeling I might need a trip to sickbay. But for the moment, I'd like to be on the bridge."

She peered at him with a professional eye. "You don't feel well?"

"I'm not myself," he replied, having never said anything more truthful in his life. "I fell asleep over there."

She withdrew a step, lifting a suspicious eyebrow. "I think you'd better come to sickbay right now."

He nodded and lowered his voice to say, "If you'll let me sit here on the bridge and get my bearings for a minute, I'd appreciate it. Then I'll go to sickbay. But you finish your shift—I'll talk to Ogawa or Pelagof . . . or somebody else."

"Anybody else." Beverly gave him a feisty look, and her green eyes blazed. He found her very desirable.

"What's our status?" he asked, taking a step away and forcing himself to look at meaningless readouts on the empty console.

"The same. We were waiting for you, and now I presume we're going to put those suits to use and go in there. That wouldn't be my first choice, but we haven't got many good options. I don't want to induce a dream state in Deanna either, and I canceled that."

"First we're going to look for biological beings just outside the rift," promised the captain.

Now she stepped away from him. "I promised Riker I would let him know when you got back. Excuse me."

Picard nodded and walked to his command chair. He

sat down and studied the image on the viewscreen. After he heard Crusher tell Riker that he was going to sickbay, he knew he was, although he felt awfully silly doing so. He was a mature man—a Starfleet captain—laid low by lovesickness.

Picard suddenly realized that he would have to stop moping around, or it would be difficult to see Kaylena again. And it would be difficult to do his work. He rose to his feet and stretched his arms vigorously.

"You know, I feel better now. It must have been something I drank or ate over there. But I'll still have Ogawa check me out." He gave her a hearty smile and started toward the door. "The bridge is yours, Doctor."

"Go straight to sickbay," she ordered.

"Yes, Sir," answered Picard good-naturedly on his way out. As soon as the turbolift doors closed, he fought the temptation to tell the computer to take him back to the transporter room. *Too much of a good thing*, he concluded. *You've got to pace yourself—you can't let her take over your life.*

Too late, another voice in his head answered.

"Destination?" asked the computer.

"Sickbay," he answered glumly.

Admiral Nechayev stood in the corridor outside the brig, gazing at the drugged Romulan, who was lying in a stupor and muttering to himself. She looked with satisfaction at Teska, then at the security officers who had accompanied her back to the brig.

"He's in perfect condition to return to his cell," declared the admiral. "Has he said anything coherent or useful?"

"No," answered Teska. "And where is Regimol?"

"He's gone back to the runabout, taking a Starfleet crew with him, plus the Ferengi. They've left Lomar, and we have about another hour before we can leave." Nechayev motioned to her beefy security team. "Pick him up and drag him in."

"Do you want me to go with you?" asked the Vulcan.

"But of course. And I know you'll keep your poker face," said Nechayev with a smile.

The door opened, and the security officers dragged the unconscious prisoner into the brig and tossed him into his cell, reapplying the force-field. That seemed unnecessary, as he was not going anywhere.

Teska glanced at the other prisoner, who was taking this all in. The emotions in his youthful face went from fear to hatred, then down to melancholy. "If you've hurt him—"

"We haven't hurt him," snapped Nechayev. "We take no pleasure in this, believe me. We would just as soon have you cooperate and give you asylum." She stepped closer to the young Romulan's cell and lowered her voice to say, "You can go to live in the Rigel System, be a Rigelian. We have a special colony, where former Romulans are quite happy."

"Defector Farm?" he asked with a laugh. "I've heard about the place. You expect that to get me to defect?"

Nechayev glanced at Teska, who tried to look a bit more heartless than usual. "You are going to tell us, one way or another. We'll reward you for sparing us all another mind-meld. Be aware, the longevity in your chosen career is short, and we're offering you a way to get out alive."

Her eyes and voice grew steely. "Force us to do a

mind-meld, and we'll return you to your masters, with a note pinned to your chest outlining everything you told us. They won't be so kind."

"And Jerit?" asked the youth.

"That's also up to you," answered Nechayev. "If you cooperate, we'll return him, but we won't say we learned anything. If you want, we'll return you both, with no comment. We'll even offer *him* asylum . . . however you want to structure it. We're getting our information, anyway. Your decision now is to determine what happens to both of you after this."

The young Romulan bowed his head and whispered, "I'll go with you."

"Thank you," said Nechayev sincerely. She motioned to the guards to turn off his force-field and conduct him from his cell.

A minute later, the spy and the admiral were ensconced in an interrogation room, seated across from each other at a table, while Teska and the security officers were watching them from the control room.

After the prisoner supplied his name and rank, Nechayev consulted her padd. "All right, what are the names of the Romulan vessels which took portable Genesis devices from Lomar?"

The young Romulan narrowed his eyes. "If you read Jerit's mind, then you know that already."

"We have to have a cross-check to see how truthful you are," answered Nechayev evenly. "Plus your memories may be better than his. We probably know the answers to all the questions I'm going to ask, which is another reason you needn't feel guilty."

"I heard she was good," said one of the security guards,

"but to get a Romulan assassin to spill his guts, she's amazing." The others in the control room with Teska grunted their admiration for the admiral.

"Now," said Nechayev forcefully, "the names of your ships which have portable Genesis emitters, taken from Lomar—"

The young prisoner licked his lips, then finally replied, "There are four of them—the *Terix*, *Baltrun*, *Javlek*, and *Petrask*. One was given to each ship."

"Those four devices were the only ones you found on Lomar?"

"Yes."

"Your team was on Lomar as part of the operation?" asked the admiral.

"That's right. We killed a lot of moss creatures."

She nodded. "Searching the place, you found out about the fifth device on Torga IV, and your team was sent there to retrieve it?"

"Yes," he answered. "How did you know we were on Torga IV?"

"I'll ask the questions, if you don't mind." Nechayev glanced at her padd as if she were studying information, when Teska knew she had nothing but educated guesses. "Those four ships that each took a Genesis emitter— where did they go?"

"Two were recalled to Romulus, as I recall, and the other two were sent—" He frowned in hard recollection.

"Sent where?" prodded Nechayev.

"Sent to see if the *Enterprise* had a Genesis device," the Romulan finally answered.

The admiral nodded appreciatively. "You're doing a fine job, Son. Let's send out for some food."

*   *   *

"Physically, the captain is fine," said Alyssa Ogawa over the communications panel on the bridge. "His blood counts and hormone levels have improved since his last exam, and he seems well rested, really energized. He said he was a bit confused when he saw you, but he doesn't exhibit any of that now."

Frowning with concern, Beverly Crusher walked toward the edge of the viewscreen. "And you're keeping him there for observation?" she asked. Only it wasn't a question.

There was a long pause and finally, "Noooo. He wanted to go to engineering, so we released him. There's nothing wrong with him, Beverly."

The turbolift door opened, and Commander Riker strode onto the bridge. Beverly took a deep breath and said, "I have a feeling I'll see you soon. Crusher out."

"Status?" he asked cheerfully.

"Unchanged," she answered. "The captain reported to sickbay, but he's been released."

"Yes, I just talked to him," replied the first officer. "He sounded in good spirits, and he's down in engineering, working with Geordi. I guess his long visit to the *Javlek* didn't do any harm."

"And he wants to go back, right?" asked Crusher.

Riker squinted at her, then looked away. "As a matter of fact, he did mention that. They're going to help us test the Brahms suits, and if we have any problems, they'll help us fix them."

"Am I relieved of bridge duty?" asked Crusher, fearing what would come to light if she said anything else.

"Yes, I feel rested after dinner," said Riker, forcing a smile. "Thank you, Doctor."

Beverly transferred control of the bridge to him, then strode briskly to the turbolift. When confronted with her choice of destination, she had about four places she wanted to go, but she figured she should change from her duty uniform into her medical togs. So she gave the level of her quarters.

Stepping off the turbolift not far from her door, Beverly was confronted by another complex man in her life, with whom she didn't want to deal at the moment—Lieutenant Raynr Sleven. The broad-shouldered Antosian seemed to hear her coming, and he turned and looked joyfully at her.

"Beverly!"

With a sigh, she tried to look uninterested as she brushed past him. "If you've come courting," she said, "this isn't exactly the best time."

"No, no! You misunderstand," he insisted, following her to her quarters. "You said I should see you . . . if I had any problems."

Her door slid open, and she looked at Raynr curiously. "What kind of problems?"

Two people were walking toward them in the corridor, and the Antosian looked at her beseechingly. "May I come in? Please."

With a pained expression, Beverly nodded and motioned him inside. "Are we talking about psychological problems, or physical problems?" she asked as the door slid shut behind them. "Are you having trouble adjusting?"

"No, I like it on the *Enterprise* just fine," he answered. For a moment, he searched around her quarters in confusion, until he found a chair in which to sit. He sat in the same seat he had sat before, near the shelf where she kept her family portraits, mostly of Wesley and Jack.

Hesitantly, twisting his big hands, Raynr Sleven went on, "It's in the nature of one of those side effects you warned me about."

"Really?" she asked, growing concerned for the first time.

"And I've done something bad, too. Not terrible . . . but bad. I was only trying to help, but it's gotten out of hand." The Antosian gazed at a holographic portrait of Jack Crusher and said, "You must miss him very much."

"Can we get back to *you?*" she insisted.

He rubbed his throat and said, "I'm dry. Can I have please something to drink? Just some water would be fine."

Beverly nodded and went to the replicator to get two beverages—water for Raynr and iced tea for herself. With the glasses in her hands, she turned to walk back toward him. She got only a few steps before she gasped aloud and dropped the glasses, which clattered on the deck of her cabin.

Before her stood Jack Crusher, looking about thirty years old in the prime of life. Rationally, she knew it wasn't her husband, but she was unable to be rational when he stepped toward her and put his arms around her. "Beverly," he said, nuzzling her neck, and she trembled.

She touched his face and gaped in awe. "You look just like him . . . it's incredible." Then the joy was replaced by a grimace of horror. "But it's not *you!* You're not really here."

Caressing her shoulders, the young, beautiful Jack Crusher answered, "If this is the way you want me, I can be this way. I can be anyone you want—even Captain Picard. I can be a different man every night."

Beverly stared at him, then jerked away with a surge of willpower. She pointed accusingly at him and shouted, "If you come near me again, I'll call security!"

He held up his hands and looked at her helplessly. It made her ache for when she had been young and innocent, like him. Only it wasn't Jack, she told herself. "I came to you for help and understanding," he pleaded. "I want you to see what a temptation this has been. You warned me it could happen with cellular metamorphosis, and I thought I was mentally prepared. But I wasn't. Listen, I'm not evil, Beverly—I just want some help."

The doctor slowly relaxed, her professional responsibilities taking the place of her personal reaction—a strange mixture of revulsion and attraction. "I would appreciate it if you could change back to yourself," she said hoarsely.

"I need to concentrate," he responded, sounding as shaken as she felt. He turned away from her and covered his face, then he staggered toward her couch, twitching uncontrollably. Finally he slumped onto her couch and remained bent over, as if he had stomach cramps. When he looked up, sweat drenched his face, but he was again Raynr Sleven, recently assigned to the *Barcelona*. That face that had just hours ago looked so strong and handsome now just looked pathetic.

She breathed a sigh of relief, but that didn't last long

when she thought about everything he had said. "All right, who else did you do this to?"

He caught his breath and couldn't look her in the eyes. "Alyssa Ogawa's daughter, Suzi," he rasped. "She thinks her father has come home."

Now Beverly gasped in true horror. How could she ever, ever have even entertained the thought of a romance with this man? "Sleven, how could you? That's trifling with the emotions of a little girl."

"I thought I was trying to help her . . . I don't know what I was thinking, except that I made her happy." The Antosian stared at her, tears welling in his eyes and his crown of sleek black hair looking disheveled. "It was such a thrill to see her face when she saw her daddy."

Crusher rubbed her eyes wearily. "What am I going to do with you?"

He nodded glumly. "I don't feel crazy. In my joy at being saved, I thought that her father would soon be rescued! I didn't realize that it might be a long time . . . or never."

"I take it that Alyssa doesn't know," said the doctor.

"Not so far, because Suzi has kept our secret," answered Raynr, looking down at his hands. "I mean, we just play, talk a little bit—I don't stay long."

Crusher crossed her arms and glared at him. "All right, you did this to Suzi Ogawa and me. Who else?"

"No one else," he answered, pleading with his tearful eyes. "I had to show *you!* You are my doctor . . . if nothing else."

She looked away, dropping her angry pose. His shoulders heaved as he broke into tears. "And with Suzi," his voice croaked, "I realize I made a terrible mistake.

Maybe I am a little crazy, but I've come to you for help."

"You're not the only one on this ship who's acting funny," said Crusher. She grabbed the tablecloth from the dining table and used it to wipe up the spilled beverages.

"Yes, I heard about the captain."

Crusher's back stiffened, and she stood up. "I'm not talking about the captain," she snapped. Who did she think she was fooling? Of course this was about Jean-Luc, like so many of her thoughts over the past few days. But she wasn't about to share confidences with Raynr Steven on this matter. "You know, I probably should have you put under protective custody—restraints, the whole works."

"I promise not to do it again," said Raynr, begging with his hands and eyes. "I really feel that by telling you, I've cured myself. Maybe the temptation will always be there, but maybe I can channel it . . . somehow."

"All right," said Crusher, coming to a decision. "I'm going to do you two big favors. First, I'm going to tell Alyssa Ogawa about this myself. You are not to have any more contact with either her or Suzi. Do you promise?"

"Yes," he answered softly.

"Second favor, I'm going to keep all this quiet for now and let you keep working your shift."

"Oh, thank you!" he exclaimed, jumping to his feet. "Thank you, Beverly."

"But when you're not working, you're restricted to quarters. I want to be able to find you at all times. If there's a special occasion when you need to be out, I want you to clear it with me first."

"Absolutely," he nodded, dabbing a big knuckle to his eye.

"And fight those temptations next time," she warned. "You've got a dangerous psychological weapon in your hands."

"I promise," said the big Antosian. "And thank you, Beverly. I'm going home right now."

He slipped carefully out the door, and Crusher found her eyes drifting to the shelf where the family photos rested. Her gaze fell upon Jack.

"For a moment, I held you in my arms again," she told the image. "It brought back a flood of wonderful memories. Of a time I should be grateful for . . . even if it was too short. I just worry that I'm getting bitter without you . . . without anyone. It's so hard to let go, while I still want to hold on."

She put a finger to her lips, then touched it to the picture of the handsome Starfleet officer.

sixteen

"Captain, we're ready to leave orbit," reported Marbinz, the first officer of the *Sequoia*. The slate-gray lump called Lomar floated like a blight in their main viewscreen.

"Just one thing," answered Nechayev from the command chair. "Did our Drama Club get to the surface to send our message over Romulan radio?"

"Yes," answered Marbinz, looking at his panel. "At nineteen-thirty hours, they had a conversation which made it clear that we have the missing Genesis emitter, and they described it in as much detail as we know. Caretaker staff on Lomar will relay more information as needed. Otherwise, they are taking extreme precautions."

"Good," said Nechayev with a brief smile. "Let's hope this will keep them from trying so hard to have a monopoly. They don't have one, anyway, so maybe they will back off. Conn, take us out of orbit, into a standard warp approach."

"Yes, Sir," responded the Bynar on the conn, as he worked his instruments.

"Course laid in for the last reported position of the *Enterprise*," said the Bynar on ops.

"ETA is ten hours, twenty minutes," said the first Bynar.

To everyone's relief, they blasted away from the depressing corpse of a planet littered with dead; and they made quickly for deep space. After she felt the rush of going to warp, Nechayev rose from her seat and headed for her ready room.

"I have to send the *Enterprise* a message, and I'm not sure what to say," she told Marbinz as she walked past him.

The Benzite nodded sympathetically. "Nor would I. A Genesis Device aboard a ship would be more devastating than a bomb."

"And it would erase the evidence after it, leaving something unrecognizable as a starship." The admiral nodded sagely as she walked into her ready room. "I know." She vanished into her office, and the door slid shut behind her.

Teska walked into the brig and studied the older Romulan, Jerit, who now sat alone in the row of recessed cells. His younger, more cooperative comrade had been whisked away for his own protection, leaving just Jerit as possible exchange bait, if it came down to that.

She knelt down to face him, because he was sitting on his bunk. He looked up sullenly at her curious face. "Care to look at the zoo animal? I thought I was supposed to be returned to my people with a note pinned to my chest?"

"I fear I do not have any control over your fate," she answered. "But I would like to request a favor. Would you allow our minds to meld?"

He laughed with amazement, then looked angry. "I thought we already did that?"

"Yes, but . . ." Teska cocked her head as she composed an answer that wasn't a lie. "A willing, freely given mind-meld is a different experience than one performed on a drugged, unwilling subject."

"Is it?" he said with a smile. "So it wasn't good for you. I'm sorry to hear that. Say, you have a lot of gall to come here and demand something which you took by force. This is like being asked, 'Was that rape fun? Would you care for another one?' "

She rose to her feet. "I meant no disrespect. I regretted we even had to think about it. I merely asked if you would meld freely with me. Yes or no would be a sufficient answer." The Vulcan turned and walked away slowly.

"Wait!" he called, and she stopped. He peered at her through the sparkling force-field. "What would I get out of this?"

"I have no idea," replied the Vulcan. "I have not discussed this with my superior."

He laughed. "That tough eel-bird—she doesn't know you've come to me with this?"

"No," answered Teska, moving a step closer to him.

Jerit stared at her. A male of about her own age, he could be called handsome by Terran definition of the word. "Would I know everything that's in your mind, too?" he asked softly.

"Yes," she answered. "This mind-meld would be open and freely given on both sides."

"You'd better ask your superior about that. And find out what she's offering."

"I will," replied Teska with satisfaction. She walked out the door and exited into the corridor.

A few minutes later, the Vulcan stood in a corner of the bridge, activating the chime on the ready room door. Nechayev called, "Come."

The Vulcan entered to find the admiral seated at her desk, working her terminal. "Hello, Teska," she said curtly, not looking up. "I'm trying to finish a subspace message, and I've got more to write after that. What is it?"

"I believe I have convinced the prisoner, Jerit, to meld with me."

Nechayev stopped working and looked up. "You mean, he'll do it of his own free will?"

"I would not do it otherwise," replied Teska. "If he gives his consent, I will perform the meld, but you must sweeten the deal."

She sighed. "It could be a trick. He may try to use you as a shield or something."

"It was my idea," said Teska. "However, you should know that it will be open—he will know my mind."

"Do you have to do it that way?" asked Nechayev.

The Vulcan raised an eyebrow. "No, but I prefer it that way. So much of what I have done lately has been selfish, trying to find information without sharing myself. A meld is supposed to be just that—equal, a pooling of minds. I am skilled in all the variations, including priestly functions, where I am often a conduit between two others; but this meld needs to be fair."

Nechayev went back to her screen. "In that case, we'll have to keep him prisoner a little longer. You know, I hate to turn a cold-blooded killer loose on the quadrant. I almost prefer to hand him back to his own people, sadder but no wiser."

"Please," asked Teska, "allow me to do this."

"Of course," answered the admiral with a smile. "Tell him that after we return to Federation space, he can choose any of the options we gave his friend. Don't schedule this for at least an hour, so I can be there with plenty of security. I have to finish this correspondence now."

"Thank you, Admiral," said Teska, backing toward the door.

"Wait until I get my hands on him!" shouted Alyssa Ogawa, leaping to her feet in the half-crowded Saucer Lounge and clenching her fists.

"Sit down," snapped Crusher, trying to pull her irate coworker back into her seat. "Sit down, and that's an order."

"No, you're not . . . you're not going to stop me!" she sputtered.

Crusher grabbed her faithful assistant and tossed her back into her chair. "If you get anywhere near him, I'll call security on you. You'll be in the brig—am I understood?"

The chastised woman stared wild-eyed at her superior. "You're a mother—what would you do if somebody did this to your son?"

"Somebody has taken my son, and I haven't seen him

for years," muttered Beverly, returning to her own seat. "You're a mother of a young child, and what you should be learning right now is that you can't protect her from bad things, no matter how hard you try. No matter how little she is. You couldn't protect her from her father disappearing, and you couldn't protect her from this. In fact, you had a hand in Raynr Sleven's condition, and we all knew it could happen."

"But I didn't think . . . I didn't think it would be Suzi—" Ogawa buried her face in her hands.

"No, we all think it will be somebody else's child who is in danger," said Crusher. "But the danger is past now—we only have the aftermath to deal with. He has confessed what he did, and he's trying to deal with it."

"He's not running around loose, is he?" asked Ogawa in horror. "Tell me he's confined somewhere?"

Crusher frowned. "He's confined to his quarters, except when he's on duty. Nobody knows about this, except for the three of us, and I'd like to keep it that way. Of course, Suzi will have to be told."

Ogawa balled her fists together and nearly started crying again, but somehow she gained control of her emotions. "Normally, Beverly, I would agree with you," she whispered, "but this time I think you're wrong. He's clearly dangerous and should be watched. Are you sure you're not giving him a break because you like him?"

"I don't like him so much at the moment," muttered Beverly. "But I approved the procedure that left him like this, and you assisted me. We're the first people on the ship he got to know, so it's not that strange that he glommed onto us."

Ogawa wiped her eyes with her napkin. "And here I

thought Suzi was so happy lately because I was wasn't talking about Andrew as much. I suddenly feel the need to hug her tight. Should I make her tell me, or what should I do?"

"Maybe we should bring Deanna in on this," mused Crusher. "For now, just let her know that she's surrounded by love."

Ogawa's eyes flashed with anger. "All right, but if I see him anywhere near—" The angry mother was cut off by Beverly's combadge chirping.

"Riker to Crusher," came a familiar voice.

"Crusher here," she replied, while Ogawa jumped to her feet and hurried off.

"Hello, Doctor, I need to talk to you. Where are you?" asked the first officer.

"I'm in the Saucer Lounge," answered Beverly, "and I happen to be alone."

"I'm nearby," he answered. "I'll be right there."

The commander was as good as his word, and his broad shoulders filled the doorway a moment later. He strode right to her table and sat down, waving off the server who started toward him.

From his expression, Beverly knew it was bad news, but she couldn't figure out from which direction it was coming. Riker leaned forward and grimaced as he said, "It's about the captain."

She almost smiled with relief. Any news that didn't involve Raynr Sleven was welcome. "He's gone back to the *Javlek?*"

"Yes, for no particular reason."

"Did you try to stop him?"

"On what grounds?" asked Riker. "He is captain of the

ship. If she invites him, and he accepts, there's not much I can do to stop him from beaming over. We're so buddy-buddy with the Romulans now, it's sickening. We've got the Brahms suits back, and we're ready to try them, but it still feels like we're treading water. I get the feeling that something terrible is about to happen."

He looked around for the suddenly vanished server. "Maybe I should get a drink."

"Who's going out in the Brahms suits?" asked Crusher.

Riker shrugged. "Undecided. Data is the logical one, but he can't leave the bridge. I need him on that conn every moment, because we might have to get out of here fast again. I've moved Data over to the conn right now because Perim is in sickbay. What about the captain?"

"I could put him on medical disability, but what would be my justification?" Beverly stirred the melting ice in her tea. "That he has the hots for a Romulan commander?"

"That's just a rumor," muttered Riker unconvincingly.

"Last time, he got off the transporter and came straight to the bridge," said Crusher. "He still reeked of her."

"I see." With a troubled expression, Riker rubbed his chin. The silence was mercifully broken by his combadge.

"Bridge to Riker," came Data's voice.

"Yes, Data, what is it?"

"We have just received an urgent message from Admiral Nechayev," answered the android. "We are to be advised that the Romulan warbird *Javlek* is in possession of a portable Genesis emitter. We are to limit contact with the Romulans and treat them with the precautions reserved for hostiles. We are not to exchange information, technology, or personnel with them, and we are not to allow any cargo or personnel from the *Javlek* to come aboard the *Enterprise*. At the same time, we are ordered not to let them out of our sight. We are authorized to use deadly force to keep them from escaping."

After a brief pause, Data continued, "There is some intelligence information in the message, but those are our immediate orders."

"We've broken every one of those orders already," muttered Riker, gazing with concern at Crusher.

"We are breaking them as we speak," added Data.

"I'll be right there. Riker out." The big man rose to his feet and looked at Beverly. "Do you want to come?"

"Yes," she answered gravely. "Maybe he'll listen to me."

Jean-Luc Picard clasped her body to his as soon as they reached Kaylena's plush quarters on the *Javlek*. He thought he would never get through the endless greetings and formalities, plus discussions on topics he couldn't even remember now—because all he could think about was getting her alone.

With a laugh and surprising strength, Kaylena pushed him off and strode quickly to her replicator. "Jean-Luc, you must have some patience," she said breathlessly. "We have to slow down."

"Why?" he asked with distress. "I'm here and we're together—that's all that matters!" He rushed up behind her and began nuzzling her neck.

"I wish," she said wistfully, pushing him away again and moving pointedly toward the gleaming gold replicator. "We heard about your secret."

"My secret?" he asked in confusion. "My only secret is that I'm in love with you, and I don't think that's much of a secret anymore. Do you want me to resign my commission? I'll do it. Do you want to keep me as a pet on a leash? Why not? As long as I'm with you, I can stand any indignity. But I can't stand being away from you." He followed her to the replicator, begging with his helpless eyes.

Kaylena laughed softly and tossed her well-coifed hair. "You're so quaint, Jean-Luc. All I want is honesty from you. You told me that the Federation didn't have a portable Genesis device, but now I learn that you do have one."

"That's news to me." He grabbed the beverage from her hand and put it back into the replicator. Then he brought her hand to his lips and began kissing it fervently, even as he tried to pull her closer with his other arm. "What does it matter, who has what? As long as we have each other?"

This time she let herself be kissed and caressed, although he could sense that she was holding back, not giving herself completely, the way she had before. His fevered body didn't care, but his mind was resentful and jealous.

Picard grabbed her by the shoulders and held her at arms' length. "Is there someone else? Are you in love with someone else?"

"A Romulan commander has many consorts," she said with a sneer. "You would be just one of them. Of course, I am truly mated to my ship."

The captain gave her a queasy smile. "There are Captains who say that all the time. To women . . . to themselves. You feel it, but I don't . . . especially not when I'm with you." He tried to embrace her again, but she slipped out of his grasp, and he watched her saunter across the room.

"To prove your love to me," she said, "I want you to get me the Genesis device from Starfleet."

"I don't know anything about this," he protested. "I haven't any idea where it is!"

She kept walking right out the front door into the corridor. "Don't come back to me until you have it."

"Kaylena!" Distraught, Picard charged after her, but the door shut in his face. When he banged on the elegant, quilted metal, it slid open, but when he got into the corridor, a phalanx of helmeted guards blocked his way. He could see Kaylena, striding away from him, and she turned the corner and was gone.

A brawny centurion pointed in the other direction. "We will escort you to the transporter room, Captain."

Irrationally, he thought about bursting through the guards to chase after her, but what semblance of logic he had left warned him it was pointless. She had told him what it would take to win her love—the Genesis emitter.

He nodded pathetically and tried to hold his chin high, but Picard could tell that these smirking Romulans already regarded him for what he was—the commander's consort. With a grim expression, knowing what he had to do, the captain led the cadre of Romulans toward the transporter room.

* * *

"Commander Riker," said the Deltan on the ops console. "Transporter room two reports that the captain has returned. He says he is going to his quarters and would like updates sent to him there."

The first officer glanced with relief at Dr. Crusher. "He wasn't there even an hour."

"Maybe the crisis is over," she whispered with a smile.

"Ops, send Captain Picard the recent message from Admiral Nechayev," ordered Riker, "and tell him that the admiral is due to arrive here on the *Sequoia* in about eight hours."

"Yes, Sir," answered the ops officer.

"If you don't mind," said Crusher, "I've got to catch up with some work."

"Understood," said the first officer. "Thanks for holding my hand."

Crusher nodded and headed for the door. *Maybe Jean-Luc's infatuation is over,* she thought hopefully, *and what am I going to do about it, if it is?*

Steeling herself for what was about to come, Teska entered the brig alone. Just outside the door and in the control room, armed guards waited to come to her rescue, should that be needed. The Vulcan doubted there would be any need, because she could see a broken man crouched on the bunk in his cell. That which he never thought would happen—failure, capture, and capitulation—had occurred at once, and he was thoroughly shamed and discredited in his own eyes.

She knelt down in front of Jerit, the Romulan assassin, not wishing to be standing over him. They had to be equals. "Are you ready to meld with me?"

After a few seconds, he looked up and shrugged. "Why not?"

"You know that Vulcans are stronger than Romulans as a rule," she said, "due to the greater gravity on our homeworld."

"Are you saying that you would best me in a fight?" he asked, his sagging face sparking with amusement.

"I am saying that if you volunteer to meld with me, you had better not be doing it as a ruse to escape." Teska peered at him with dark, attentive eyes. "I am opening myself freely to you. In a few minutes, you will know me better than any living creature, even my mate or family. You will be entirely up to date with my existence, as I will be with yours."

The Romulan shook his head puzzledly. "I don't understand—you were in my mind once before. What is it you didn't get then?"

"We did not meld before," she said with the whisper of a smile. "Do not be angry, my superior is very good at her job."

Jerit sat back on his haunches and laughed out loud. "This is too much! You never did the mind-meld on me? I'll say your superior is good. And all you did was stand there."

"I wish to do more now," said the priestess. "But meld with me because you want to. Your status will change if you do, and we will expedite your case—but I wish this to be completely voluntary on your part. I am a priestess, and I hold the mind-meld in a different regard than many, including Vulcans. So if you use the meld as a ruse to escape, I will send you to a stasis chamber in sickbay."

The smile vanished from Jerit's lips. "I believe you would."

"Shall I lower the force-field?" she asked, rising to her feet.

"You know, I was going to try to escape," muttered the Romulan. "But honesty like yours is not something I've seen much in my life. You'll have to forgive me . . . if I don't know how to react. I've been dealing with the fact that my life is over . . . after this."

He swallowed hard, then perked up. "So come on in, Vulcan priestess. But I warn you that my mind is not a pretty place."

"I have not anticipated that it would be pretty," she answered, walking to the wall panel and turning off the force-field. "However, I trust you. Now that you have committed to this act, you will follow through."

"You know me already," said the Romulan, sitting back on his bunk. He looked nervous.

Teska alighted on the bunk beside him and began to massage his neck until he began to relax. "Do not be afraid," she assured him. "I am giving, not just taking."

When he was as relaxed as he was going to get, she used her fingers to close his eyes. That got him accustomed to the feeling of her fingers on his face. As gently as she could, Teska spread her delicate digits across his left cheekbone, forming a pattern of contacts. Almost immediately, the bloody images and raw sensations rushed into her mind.

seventeen

Teska immediately slowed things down with her mind, showing Jerit that they had an infinite amount of time, and that they didn't have to hurry the meld. It was like a person holding a conversation in his head with himself, both sides having the same data at their combined fingertips.

For a Romulan, Jerit had not lived a life of privilege . . . he was born to poverty and low caste—the child of a comfort worker, as they were called. His first memory was of watching soldiers rape his mother, who disappeared shortly thereafter. Then Jerit was raised in a brutal orphanage, where he was schooled in violence and taught to suppress his feelings . . . but those two were mutually exclusive. He was smart enough to know that, and he had spent more time suppressing his emotions than a hundred Vulcans put together.

So much pain . . . so much passion . . . all left to wither. But he showed a penchant for inflicting violence, and he was taken to a special school. All of that flew by Teska like the leaves in a storm. She could catch bits and pieces to inspect, but it was all of a depressing piece, gladdened only by his swift rise in his craven profession. Inflicting pain and death was Jerit's art, as was hunting and survival. He took great pride in his skill and the fear he inspired—it gave him worth. But there was never much pleasure . . . the violence had ceased being pleasurable, and the women all seemed cloying. They were all sick in some way, like him.

A bleak life it was, but Teska saw the satisfaction in murder. There was no ambiguity, no doubt, no compromise. *Is he dead?* If he's dead, the job is over, and the next job begins. In some respects, Jerit's life flowed peacefully, like a river, with a predictable outcome based on his growing experience and determined sense of duty. Then a shred of jetsam flew past, which Teska had to pluck from the stream. In her hand, the bit became an ugly pool of memory, which she found to be deep and frigid. Yet Teska dove in and swam to the center.

Yes, the timing was right . . . four years after her uncle started to make overtures to a Romulan underground that was sick of autocracy and militarism. The Star Empire overreacted to the perceived threat; arrests were made; murderers were summoned. Jerit's mind responded to her questions, drawing her through the brutal but efficient chain of killings, until Teska saw it all—the one death she could not bear to watch. Hasmek . . . standing tall and defiant, professing his innocence while professing his love for his Vulcan mate.

It was an unjust fate, but he had ignored both her

and Spock—he had refused their help . . . their warnings. Arrogant to a fault like most of his countrymen, Hasmek had dared the Fates and lost. At that point, Jerit wrapped a shroud over Teska's eyes and spirited her past the actual scene of Hasmek's death. *He died bravely*, said the Romulan. *He frightened them more than I did.*

The two of them merged and melded their thoughts, dreams, and desires, becoming intimate in a way even lovers dared not. Jerit's mind was ugly because it was deprived of beauty, and Teska's mind was beautiful but deprived of wildness. Something had been lost to her—that almost-human child she had been a long time ago—but the Romulan found that child and made her face her unpredictable tendencies, which seemed mostly directed at his race. *Hate Romulans, love Romulans—both urges are valid*, his voice seemed to say. Jerit delighted in the fact that his species got under her skin.

With complete impartiality, they exchanged information on the current mission to the point where they were in complete agreement. At that moment they awoke, staring at each other.

Tears well in the hardened Romulan's eyes, and he gripped her forearm and wept upon her shoulder. "I killed your husband . . . I *killed* him! I'm so sorry—" He sobbed like the child who had watched his mother brutalized.

Teska patted him tenderly on the back. "It was my good fortune that it was you, Jerit, because now I know—" Her voice experienced interference, and she was unable to continue. There was no point in speaking, because they knew each other's secrets better than they knew their own.

"You will be all right here," she told him, rising to her feet and swaying on wobbly legs.

The murderer looked up at her with tear-filled eyes. Choking back sobs, he said, "Thank you, Teska. Just remember . . . what I told you."

"Yes." She nodded, and a smile flitted across her face.

Admiral Nechayev met the Vulcan in the corridor, and she was immediately surrounded by underlings with padds. "What else did you learn? Anything about Genesis?"

"Nothing new," answered Teska, mastering her composure. "Jerit is not prone to question his orders or demand to know more than he needs to know."

"I didn't think so. Anything personal?"

"To me, yes," said Teska. "Hasmek is indeed dead."

Nechayev winced with sympathy. "I'm sorry. Do you need to take some time off?"

Teska cocked a quizzical eyebrow as if such a thought were completely alien to her. "No, Sir. I have a ceremony to perform, but it has been delayed five years already. It can wait until I am home. The one who killed Hasmek is in that room beyond. If I could include him for the ceremony, it would bode well for a meaningful conclusion."

"Won't he try to escape?" asked Nechayev with a scowl.

"No," Teska answered with certainty. "He has committed himself to helping me."

The admiral nodded as if she didn't know what else to say, so Teska took her leave. The Vulcan walked slowly down the corridor. Although her mind was at peace, her legs were still as weak as a newborn *sehlat*'s, and her heart seemed to weigh twice as much as it thudded emptily in her torso.

"They're going to be there, Regimol, you'll see!" claimed Chellac as he lounged in the copilot's seat on the runabout, buttoning his vest and adjusting his cummerbund.

The elegant Romulan paced behind him, his head nearly brushing the ceiling in the small craft. "We're not staying long," he warned. "An hour, and if they're not there, we leave. Depending on what we find in our other queries—and if we have time—we might come back. But it's been two days, so they ought to be there."

The Ferengi leaped to his feet and snapped his suspenders. "You worry too much. I've been with Yorka since the beginning, and he won't desert me. Plus Cindy really liked me."

"Cassie," muttered the Romulan. "Her name was Cassie."

"Don't worry. If they're not there, nothing lost."

"Except time." Regimol scowled and began to pace again. Three security officers looked on from the passenger seats, while the lone Bajoran among them put on his civilian clothes, which consisted of a robe with a hood to hide his face. He carefully hid a phaser in his boot.

"Attention, Sir, we're entering synchronous orbit around Bajor," said the Coridan pilot. "We're in transporter range of the Oasis of Tears."

"Let's go," said Chellac confidently. He and the Bajoran, whose name was Potriq, stepped into the two-person transporter, while Regimol sat down at the controls.

"I'm beaming you down outside of the oasis, and you'll walk in," said the Romulan. "It's midday."

"Don't put us too far away," replied Chellac. "You don't want to waste time."

With a scowl, Regimol hit the membrane keyboard, and Chellac and his escort dematerialized with the usual tingle and flash. They rematerialized in a desert, standing among sharp, prickly succulents.

"Ow! Eeek!" shouted the Ferengi, jumping away from one thorny bush into another. "I'll get that Regimol!"

"Quiet," warned the Bajoran. "We're right outside the wall. He did as you asked."

In the bright sunlight, Chellac could see quaint earthen walls of an ochre color, surrounding a lush garden where gigantic trees and tall reeds sprouted seemingly from nowhere. He couldn't see any water, but there was a small gate with a creaking wooden door beckoning him to enter. Stepping gingerly through the thickets, the Ferengi managed to find a path. As he walked, he drew his dagger and pried prickly appendages off his trousers. "What a delightful place," he muttered.

"Do you know why they call it the Oasis of Tears?" asked Potriq.

"No," answered Chellac, making it clear that he didn't care.

Still the Bajoran went on, "It was always an oasis, but it had just one small artesian well, where the locals used to bathe and feed their herds. When the Cardassians took over, they brought in slave labor and excavated a big lake—all to build a resort, so their officers could have a special retreat. I don't need to tell you the unspeakable things that went on here."

"So nothing unspeakable goes on here now?" asked Chellac sadly.

"No, the buildings were torn down. We kept the lake but returned everything to a natural state, as much as we could," said the Bajoran proudly. "It's just a place for quiet reflection now, and you can water your herd again."

"I wish I had a herd, but all I have are puncture wounds from these damn prickles," muttered Chellac, mincing gently toward the gate.

Finally he pushed open the old wooden plank and entered a dreamy paradise. He could see why they had kept the lake, because it was absolutely gorgeous. Ringed by towering trees and gently swaying reeds, the body of water was an unexpected vision of loveliness in the thorn-infested desert. In the middle of the lake floated a small island, and a picturesque footbridge connected it to the shore. Chellac could imagine a gazebo, theater, or similar structure gracing the island in its heyday.

An overgrown creek connected the lake to an old stand of trees in a grassy meadow. Chellac assumed that was the site of the original artesian well. Now the only amenities were the occasional picnic table, drinking fountain, or comfort station, and no one seemed to be using them. Still the birds twittered, and the insects buzzed, inviting them to enter the oasis as surely as a band playing in a nightclub.

Potriq followed behind him, studying a tricorder. "Hold up," whispered the Bajoran. "Hold up, I said!"

The Ferengi stopped and glared at his confederate with indignation. "Why are you ordering me about? I've got people I need to meet in here!"

"There are a lot of lifesigns in here," said the Bajoran. "Too many, and we can't see any of them. They're hiding."

"What? It's a trap?" Chellac leaped toward the gate.

"Try to act naturally and keep your voice down," said the Bajoran, keeping his eyes on his tricorder. Then he lifted his eyes and gazed upward into the trees spreading their leafy boughs above them. Without warning, a large nut came hurtling down, and Chellac had to dive out of the way to avoid being hit. A chortle of whooping laughter greeted his escapades.

"Hey, you think that's funny?" screamed the Ferengi from his back, shaking his fist at the sky. "Come down here and show yourself!"

"Oh, they're not people," Potriq said with relief. "They're fleecy Kerood monkeys—a kind of primate. I had forgotten they were introduced here, because the Cardassians destroyed their habitat."

"Perhaps they had good reason," muttered the Ferengi. He staggered to his feet, brushed off his clothes, and peered dubiously into the leafy broughs spread above them.

As he walked deeper into the oasis, Chellac gazed at the lake, so peaceful and calm, with that quaint wooden bridge. The island beckoned like a second oasis within the first, and Chellac decided that the Bajoran slaves had not labored in vain. A fish jumped out of the water, and a moment later all the birds took off from the trees, squawking. He took a few more steps and heard rustling behind him; the Ferengi turned to tell the Bajoran not to dawdle.

However, the security officer was lying in the leaves and grass, his eyes staring lifelessly, his tricorder blinking under his twitching hand. He looked dead. Dropping into a crouch, the Ferengi dashed for cover, just as a tiny dart came hissing past his earlobe. "Whoa!" he shouted as he dove under a large fern.

A dark figure emerged from the creek, dripping wet and carrying a long, tubular weapon. This assassin stole across the meadow until he spotted his prey, then he dropped into a crouch and aimed his weapon. The Ferengi barely had time to leap and roll before another dart flashed his way, barely missing him. When he looked back at his pursuer, the ominous figure was already moving closer.

Suddenly, there was a shadow behind the murderer, and a disembodied arm holding a metal pipe came into view. Chellac caught his breath with excitement, because he knew what would happen next. Sure enough, the pipe flashed downward, striking the unsuspecting assassin on the head and dropping him into the gentle grass of the meadow.

Slowly, like an image under a microscope coming into focus, Regimol's entire body shimmered into view, leaning over the would-be killer.

Chellac ran up to him, pointing down the path. "The Bajoran—he's been injured!"

"Actually, Potriq is dead," said Regimol, not taking his eyes off his prisoner, who was also Bajoran. "I'm sorry about that, but it was worth it to catch this fellow. I was afraid they would try to kill us."

Realization dawned on the Ferengi. "Hey, wait a minute—you *used* me! You *knew* this was a trap . . . that's why you were so nervous!"

"I knew our former associates were not going to be here." The thief bent over the body and began to rifle through his pockets. "It was either going to be a trap or a waste of time. They grabbed an opportunity to get rid of us for good, although this smacks more of the girl than Yorka. She must be a rich woman by now."

"Why didn't you tell me?" complained Chellac. "I walked right into danger, totally oblivious!"

"That's how we had to play it. When he killed Potriq, he must have thought it was *me*." The Romulan's probing hand hit something. "Hello! What's this?"

He drew out a richly embossed piece of parchment, the kind used for fancy invitations. In fact, it was similar to the ones they had sent to Bakus, Ocman, and the other dignitaries for the last demonstration of the Orb of Life. Scrawled on the back were the words "Oasis of Tears" and the day's date according to the Bajoran calendar—Fifth Day of Circles.

As the breeze rustled through the trees of the oasis, Regimol opened the invitation and read aloud: "Devoted Servant of the Prophets, rejoice that our Masters will grant proof of their Benevolence on the Seventh Day of Circles. On that date, the Light will conquer the Dark, Good will triumph over Evil, and the graveyard of our allies will blossom with life once again. Watch the heavens, for you will experience the wonder of the Orb of Life. Signed with humility, Vedek Yorka, protector of the Orb of Life."

The Romulan folded up the announcement and

tucked it into his breast pocket. "His Vedekship didn't waste much time getting his old job back."

"With humility," echoed Chellac with a laugh, then he grew thoughtful. "Two days from now. What do you suppose that crazy monk is going to do?"

"I don't know. What's this 'graveyard of our allies?'"

The Ferengi shrugged. "I couldn't guess. But the big evil is probably Cardassians."

"And we lost our only Bajoran," said Regimol with a glance at their comrade. "We'd better send this information to Admiral Nechayev."

The Romulan picked up the unconscious Bajoran and dumped him beside the dead Bajoran, then he took the combadge from Potriq's body and stuck it on the unknown assassin.

"I wish we didn't have to take a prisoner," said Regimol, "but there's more to find out from him. Just to confuse his friends, we'll leave a Bajoran behind." He tapped his combadge and announced, "Away team to runabout. Three to beam back, one is a casualty. Lock onto our combadges."

"Yes, Sir," came the response.

The Romulan scowled and lowered his jet eyebrows. "Look around, Chellac, and say good-bye to our partnership with Yorka and Cassie. They're now the enemy."

"I guess so," said the gloomy Ferengi as the lush oasis disappeared all around him.

"Two days," said Alynna Nechayev, rising from her desk and pacing the short length of her ready room. Commander Marbinz and Teska stood at attention, waiting to hear what they would be doing next.

"We've got to stop Yorka from deploying Genesis on a large scale," continued the admiral. "That means solving the riddle of Yorka's announcement. At the same time, we've got to get our hands on a Genesis emitter—to test it and see if it really affects the anomalies. We know the *Javlek* has an emitter, but how do we get it from them without destroying the warbird and the device? And without losing the *Sequoia* and the *Enterprise* in the process?"

The Benzite gritted his teeth, and the tendrils on his mouth curled downward. "The only Bajoran on our crew is now dead, but we have researchers and subspace links to Bajor."

"We should bring Regimol back," said Teska. "To steal an object from a Romulan warbird, we need him."

"Yes," answered the admiral, gazing thoughtfully at the floor. "There are witnesses on Bajor we wanted to question, but this takes precedence. Plus he has another prisoner for us to question."

Nechayev looked up, her decision made. "Commander, inform the runabout to meet us at the *Enterprise*'s position. I'll bring Captain Picard up to date. Teska, you research the clues in this message. Use as many of the ship's resources as you need."

"Yes, Sir," replied the first officer, hurrying out. The Vulcan strode silently behind him.

Captain Picard pounded his fist on the conference table and glared at the senior officers gathered in the Observation Lounge. Crusher couldn't remember the last time she had seen Jean-Luc quite so haggard or short-tempered.

"Let's recap, shall we," he began. "The Romulans think we have a portable Genesis emitter, and we don't. We think *they* have one, but maybe they don't either. And the only person who has Genesis for certain is this Bajoran monk, Yorka. Only he calls it the Orb of Life, and he's going to replicate it, daisy-chain a number of them, and presumably terraform a place called 'the graveyard of our allies.' Two days from now."

Riker cleared his throat. "Sir, Admiral Nechayev seems convinced that both the *Javlek* and the *Petrask* had Genesis Devices, which they took from Lomar."

"The Romulans are convinced that we have one, too," snapped Picard. "We'd better think carefully before we go to war with the Romulans over assumptions. Starfleet is in a weakened state, but the Romulans aren't. Furthermore, the admiral says they have two more Genesis boxes hidden safely away on Romulus. So it's hard to see why they need us." The captain seemed troubled by that conclusion, and he stroked his chin tensely.

"Except that they believe they are close to having them all," reasoned Deanna Troi.

La Forge lifted his dark eyebrows over his pale implants. "If they find out about this mass detonation, they'll probably head right there."

"Yes," murmured the captain thoughtfully, a slight smile playing across his face. "Presuming they can figure out where it is."

"The admiral is right about one thing," said La Forge. "We need a Genesis emitter to see whether its energy really affects the rifts and the radiation levels."

Riker sat forward, rapping his knuckles on the table.

"Perhaps we should schedule the EVA in the Brahms suits before the *Sequoia* gets here. After that, we might be in action."

Picard rubbed his forehead, as if troubled by so many thoughts hitting him at once. "There won't be an attack on the *Javlek*," he declared, rising to his feet. "There's no need for that. I can . . . I can talk to Kaylena, the commander."

He tapped his combadge. "Picard to bridge. Hail the *Javlek* for me—tell them it's Captain Picard and it's urgent."

"Yes, Sir." Everyone in the lounge waited expectantly, while they gazed out the window at the ominous green warbird, glimmering in the starlight just off the port bow. They seemed close enough to touch the hull of the immense vessel, thought Crusher, if only she didn't have her shields up.

"Sorry, Captain," came the Andorian's voice from the bridge, "the *Javlek* continues to ignore our hails."

Picard slammed his fist into his palm with frustration. "I'm not going to play this ridiculous game! Number One, go ahead and schedule the EVA, just as soon as you can. And I want a small crew assembled for the captain's yacht."

"The captain's yacht?" asked Riker with surprise. "For what purpose, Captain?"

"Somewhere out there is a Genesis device," answered Picard, pointing out the window into the unfathomable recesses of space. "And I'm going to find it." With that, he marched out of the observation lounge, without dismissing anyone else.

All eyes gravitated toward Crusher, giving her quizzical looks, as if she would know exactly what was wrong with the captain.

The doctor shrugged. "He's had a complete physical, and he's perfectly healthy. I've been watching everyone on the ship for signs of diminished capacity, due to the rift, but I'm not ready to restrict anyone to quarters yet."

Riker sighed and slapped the tabletop with both hands. "Well, let's get busy on that EVA. La Forge, who do you see making the spacewalk? How many?"

"I think we only need two people," answered the engineer. "Since time is short, I'd prefer to have people who have already logged time in a Brahms suit. That would be myself, Data, Counselor Troi, and yourself, Commander."

"Since we need Data on the bridge," said Riker, "along with—"

"Along with you," replied Deanna Troi, smiling at her beloved. "That leaves Geordi and me. That's fine . . . he'll see things I wouldn't see, and vice versa. Plus I may be able to sense living creatures, and I presume our tricorders won't work very well."

Dr. Crusher scowled and looked at her old friend. "Can't someone else go instead of you?"

Troi shook her head. "I feel fine. And believe me, I trust those suits." The counselor rose to her feet and looked at the chief engineer. "So when do we leave?"

"The suits are recharged and checked out," answered La Forge. "We've got coordinates picked, and a jet sled to get us around. We could leave in half an hour from transporter room one." He glanced at Riker for confirmation, and the first officer nodded solemnly.

Crusher could see Will and Deanna studiously avoiding each others' eyes. "See you there," said the counselor, moving toward the door.

The Brahms prototype radiation suit looked like a giant white golem, thought Troi. It housed life-support systems, communications, and enough Romulan phase-inversion technology to keep the wearer slightly out of phase. The field oscillated, allowing the wearer to interact with his surroundings, while being protected from them. With the addition of advanced shielding and shock resistance, the prototype suit could survive a core meltdown, or even the Genesis Wave.

Once inside the bulky suit, Deanna Troi couldn't help but to remember the last time she had worn a Brahms suit—during the awesome destruction of the planet Persephone V. The only reason she had beamed down to the doomed city of Carefree during the height of the wave was to rescue Will and Data. This suit had done the job then, and it would do it again. She wiggled her fingers in the stiff gloves and glanced at the glittering readouts just above her eyes. Despite its bulk and sense deprivation, the Brahms suit felt safe, even comfortable. She wondered if it was the same prototype which had saved her life on Persephone V.

Geordi La Forge gave her a thumbs-up from his own white armor, and the two of them stepped awkwardly onto the transporter platform. Deanna used the emitters in the ceiling to guide herself into place on the pad, because seeing her feet was just too difficult. All of this awkwardness would change when they were weightless, which was just a few seconds away.

They turned to look at Rhofistan, the transporter chief, who was double-checking his settings. Troi was glad that Will was on the bridge, and not down here seeing her off. He would be worried, while she saw this as a grand opportunity to continue Leah Brahms's impressive work.

Will was on the bridge, because Captain Picard was still missing in action. The Betazoid couldn't sense anything different about the captain, but then she had lost much of her empathetic skills since her blackout. For once, that didn't bother her, because it was such a relief not to be the unwilling conduit of the entity inside the rift—if indeed that same being existed in this massive blackness.

La Forge waved a hand in front of her faceplate, breaking her out of her reverie. Troi checked her readouts and found them normal, so she gave him a thumbs-up. They could hear each other's voices over the sophisticated communications system, but there seemed no reason to talk yet. These moments of solitude were meant to savor.

"Energize when ready," said La Forge.

"Yes, Sir," answered the lofty Andorian. "Remember, you can initiate a transport by yourselves, directly from the suit. Just press the left pinky button."

Troi nodded gratefully, because that button was very difficult to push accidentally. It required jamming the left pinky finger into the right palm. Safely ensconsed inside the armor, she barely felt the transporter beam rearranging her molecules and shunting them into space.

But she instantly felt the relief of weightlessness when

she materialized in the low gravity. A few meters away floated a jet sled—a two-person conveyance with short-range thrusters. It had been stripped down for use here, because all of the electronics were useless. Yet its skeletal frame still afforded some protection, in addition to numerous handholds and footholds. La Forge shot a small grappling hook at the sled, got a secure fix, and began to pull himself along the rope to their vehicle.

From a vantage point that even an experienced space traveler seldom saw, Troi had a chance to study the wonders arrayed all around her. In the distance, but looking surprisingly close at hand, were the two massive starships, one silver and multilayered like a three-dimensional chess set, and the other hunched and sly, like a vulture. In the other direction was a glittering ocean of confetti—the ruins of two starships—and these sparkling bits of metal and insulation were framed by a massive black curtain. Although she was floating, the immense rift made it seem as if she was falling into the blackest, deepest pit in the universe.

With a couple of tiny thruster burns, La Forge got the sled headed in her direction, cruising on its own momentum. Troi casually grabbed a handle as the craft slid past, and they journeyed deeper into the debris field. She tried not to look at her readouts, because the radiation was off the scale. It was ridiculous to think that something could be alive out here.

As they cruised deeper into the debris, it was like riding a real sled through a golden snowstorm, and they sliced a tunnel through the glittering dust. The suits protected them, and so did La Forge's deft steering, but the visibility grew worse with every centimeter.

La Forge's amplified voice finally echoed in her ears. "So what do you think?"

"I think the chances of us seeing something in here are pretty remote." Troi looked around and couldn't even spot the rift or the *Enterprise*, thanks to the swirling cloud of debris. Out of nowhere, a shape shot toward them like a torpedo, and Troi ducked as a horribly disfigured humanoid cruised past, his mouth agape and his eyes bulging. It was impossible to say what species he was, or what propelled him past the rest of the space junk. But he was certainly dead.

"Wow," said the engineer. "Should we try to recover the body?"

"No," answered Troi with a shiver. "Well, maybe on our way out. Can't we get at the edges of this cloud, where we can see what's coming? I don't want to stumble into that rift, it may have some gravitational pull."

"Okay," agreed La Forge. After he shot a few bursts, they were headed in what felt like an upward direction, although no such bearing was possible out here.

"Geordi, my readouts are off the scale. Do you think we could even transport out of here?"

He didn't answer—he just continued to ride on the other side of the sled, one thickly gloved hand stuck in the handle.

"Geordi!" she yelled. "Geordi!" She pounded him on his shoulder, and he lost his grip and floated away, obviously unconscious. Troi yelled a useless warning when she saw a purple starfish-like creature latched onto his faceplate, writhing and twitching. Then she realized that similar creatures littered the debris, grasping desperately with their tentacles.

One of them struck a thruster on the sled, and Troi applied fuel and toasted it, while others came swirling through the golden drizzle. Ducking behind the sled, she avoided the onslought and hit her communications button. "Away team to transporter room one. Beam up La Forge immediately! Medical emergency."

Nothing happened. There was no response, except that a blackness surged over Troi's mind, puncturing her sinuses with pain. Could it be coming from the starfish creatures, or the rift, or the blasted corpses which floated past her fading consciousness? Or everything at once?

Not now! begged Troi. *Don't take me now!* But it was already too late.

eighteen

Help me! cried a voice. Or voices . . . a billion voices.
Once again, Deanna Troi felt a mixture of recognition
and repulsion, as one might experience when meeting
an old friend and finding she is sick and dying. That was
the feeling Troi had as she floated in a darkness alit with
glittering shreds of debris, unable to move or do anything other than hold tenuously onto to her consciousness, and the sled. There was no longer *one* entity in the
rift, but billions and billions—all of them in a mindless
stampede—trampling over each other to escape from
the burning fires.

The Betazoid clung to these images, unsure if they
were real or the last fevered stages of her death hallu-
cinations. At Gemworld, the overlying motives of the
entity were control and revenge—now it was just a
mad yearning for survival, a mindless dash over the
cliff. With a start, Deanna realized that the ruling entity
of the other dimension was dead, and chaos ruled in
its stead.

This conclusion brought Troi to full consciousness, and she realized that she was still had control of the sled, which was drifting farther and farther away from La Forge. Firing thrusters, she carefully reversed direction and followed her own tunnel through the glittering space dust, until she had thoroughly retraced her route. Now she followed La Forge's trail through the debris until she saw the white Golem floating like an artificial asteroid. The starship creatures were still floating about, but they now seemed dead—as inert as the metal shavings and silvery bits of insulation.

As soon as Troi reached La Forge, she jammed the pinky of his left hand into her own palm. Then she backed off and watched him dematerialize in a shimmering transporter beam. Although she didn't know his condition, she had done everything she could for him, and she had learned more than she needed to know. The rifts were like cracks in a dam, and when they exploded, there would be a flood of alien life and deadly radiation from one dimension into another. The flimsy membrane between this reality and the next could be ruptured permanently.

Figuring they must have their hands full in the transporter room at the moment, Troi piloted the sled out of the shimmering cloud and back into view of the *Enterprise* and *Javlek*. At once, the communications channel erupted to life.

"*Enterprise* to Troi," said Riker's concerned voice. "Come in! *Enterprise* to Troi."

"I'm here, Will, I'm okay," she answered. "How is Geordi?"

"He seems all right," answered Riker, "and he has no

idea why he lost consciousness. We thought his suit might have malfunctioned, but it seems okay, too. Are you ready to come back?"

"In a minute," answered Deanna, gazing over her shoulder at the gaping maw behind her. It was oddly inviting, as well as repelling—and she wondered if the Brahms suit would survive a trip inside the crack.

"There was a dead animal clinging to his helmet," said Riker with distaste. "At least it was dead after it got through the biofilter. Are these things dangerous?"

"Only that they're afraid and dying," answered the counselor with realization. "And they have kind of a psychic death scream. If you have a large flock of them, it can be overwhelming. I think that's what caused him to black out."

"I'd like you to come back, Deanna," insisted the first officer, sounding more like a significant other. "We finally have a biological specimen, which is what the captain has wanted."

"All right," agreed Troi, knowing she probably shouldn't be out here—on the edge of the dimension—alone. "I'll leave the sled here, for when I return. One to beam back."

In the engineering section of the *Sequoia*, Teska walked past a bank of workstations all devoted to parsing Bajoran history, language, and mythology, trying to find the planet mentioned cryptically in Vedek Yorka's announcement. It had to be a planet, in her opinion, because nothing else could provide a suitable showcase for the Orb of Life. Nothing else could justify the lofty claims and Yorka's promotion.

A "graveyard" connoted a place that was dead, or devoted to death and corpses. That fit the needs of a Genesis experiment, thought the Vulcan, because it should be performed on a lifeless planet without a functional biosphere to supplant. To use Genesis indiscriminately on inhabited worlds—that had been the evil of the moss creatures. If only they had created one homeworld instead of trying to create thousands.

In Yorka's announcement, the graveyard belonged to "our allies." This clue seemed to go hand-in-hand with the idea of good versus evil, and the truest evil in the Bajoran experience was the Cardassian occupation. Who were the Bajorans' allies in the struggle to win their freedom? There weren't very many—a few weapons sellers, starship salvagers, and the mutual enemies of the Cardassians. Who were most prominent among them?

The Cardassians had many enemies, especially during the Dominion War, when they had allied themselves with the invaders. But that war was not as personal to the Bajorans, and they would have been thinking of an earlier time—when friends had been scarce and even the Federation had been viewed with suspicion.

She strolled behind the backs of her researchers, who were lined up in the bowels of engineering on every available workstation, taxing the ship's computer. She glanced over their shoulders and saw one word occurring with considerable frequency: Maquis.

Fading into the memory of younger Starfleet officers, the Maquis had been a rebellious group of Federation colonists who faced removal from their homes in the Demilitarized Zone—due to an ill-fated treaty with the Cardassians. Battling both the Cardassians and the Federation, they fit the definition of allies to the Bajorans. Besides, their homes and bases had been mostly in the Demilitarized Zone, and one would presume their graveyards were there, too.

The DMZ would be an ideal place for Yorka's showcase, thought Teska, because the decimated Cardassians couldn't monitor it very well, and Starfleet was supposed to stay out entirely. The DMZ was littered with sites of battles, massacres, and destruction, and she had her researchers correlating that data with significant events which included the Maquis—with a cross-check on dead planets. After that step, another name began to show up with some frequency on their screens: Solosos III.

The worker seated in front of Teska stiffened her back and glanced nervously at the entrance. The Vulcan could see the cause for her concern when Admiral Nechayev strode purposefully into engineering. The captain of the *Sequoia* made straight toward her mission specialist and asked, "What have you turned up?"

"Nothing definite," answered the Vulcan, "but a few possibilities."

"Is a planet called Solosos III one of them?"

"Yes."

Nechayev nodded sagely. "Regimol just sent word that he's wracked his brain, and he thinks that could be it. As you must know, there was a Maquis colony there, led by a Starfleet officer named Michael Eddington. A Starfleet effort to capture him made the planet unlivable. It wasn't perhaps the best way to handle the situation, but it worked."

Teska nodded. "Yes, firing quantum torpedoes with

trilithium resin into the atmosphere was effective in making the planet unlivable."

"I meant that Eddington surrendered," said the admiral with a scowl. "Regimol says that both the Bajorans and the Maquis revere Solosos III as the site of the Maquis's most noble defeat, because *we* had to destroy the planet to save it. When you root for the underdog, that's the kind of battle you appreciate, I guess. I wasn't involved, but it was a turning point. Eddington was a charismatic leader."

"Logically, what can we do about an experiment on a dead planet in the Demilitarized Zone?" asked the Vulcan.

"Logically, not very much," answered Nechayev. "Illogically and unofficially, we'll do everything we can. Now I'm tempted to divert the runabout to Solosos III. On the other hand, they've got a prisoner, and perhaps he can verify our guess, or tell us where the detonation will really be."

The admiral looked pointedly at the Vulcan. "With only a day and a half left, we can't afford to be too subtle in our interrogation."

"Understood," said Teska, bowing her head. "In my opinion, we should keep Regimol on course to rendezvous with us. Confirmation is more efficient than rash action, and Solosos III is only an educated guess."

"You're right," said the admiral with a decisive nod. "But I want to tell the *Enterprise*. Then I'll get some sleep until we meet up with them."

"In the meantime, we will keep searching," promised Teska.

*   *   *

"Captain," said Commander Riker, trying to block Picard's way in the corridor. "Can't I talk to you for just a moment before you do this?"

"No," answered Picard, slipping past the big man. "Out of my way, or I'll have you thrown into the brig. You don't need me—the situation is under control. I'm not going to sit here and play games when I know what she wants." His eyes darted away from Riker's, and he strode down the corridor to the hatchway of the yacht, which was stowed under the saucer section.

The fastest shuttlecraft in the fleet, they called it, and that's exactly what he needed. He was taking three other crew members, a pilot and two veteran security officers. If Kaylena demanded a quest—some proof of his love— he could fulfill it. All he needed was a destination— Solosos III—and his passion for her would furnish the energy.

"Well, then, good luck, Captain," said Riker unenthusiastically. "We expect to get a report soon on that biological specimen. Do you want us to keep in touch with you?"

Picard paused before entering the hatch, and his thoughtful expression made him appear almost like his old self. "Yes, keep sending me updates. But after I enter the DMZ, I won't be able to respond."

"Yes, Sir," said Riker with a worried frown. "Should we tell her what you're doing?"

"Tell *her*?" he asked suspiciously, dreading the idea of the handsome first officer contacting his Kaylena.

"Yes, tell Admiral Nechayev," repeated Riker. "Should we let her know now, or wait until she gets here."

"Wait until she gets here," said Picard, entering the yacht.

A few moments later, a small, oblong craft took off from the underbelly of the saucer section, streaking away from the two gigantic starships and bursting into warp.

"What?" barked Nechayev. "Picard just took off?"

"That's right," answered Commander Riker, offering a hand to the admiral as she stepped off the transporter pad onto the deck of the *Enterprise*. "As soon as he got your message about Solosos III, Captain Picard boarded his yacht and was gone. But he had planned beforehand to go after the missing device—he had a crew waiting."

"Hmmm," replied Nechayev with annoyance. "I salute his initiative, but he's not the one I would have risked on that mission."

But Riker had already turned his attention to the stunning Vulcan who accompanied her. "Welcome to the *Enterprise*."

"Mission Specialist Teska," said the admiral. "She's been invaluable so far. This is the first officer of the *Enterprise*, Commander Riker."

"Commander," said the Vulcan with a slight bow of her head.

"A pleasure," answered Riker with a smile.

Nechayev inserted herself between them. "Commander, there's a civilian runabout just a few hours behind us. When they get here, I want them to dock immediately in your shuttlebay—before the Romulans can get hold of them."

"Yes, Sir," answered Riker, leading them out of the transporter room into the corridor. "I've arranged to have a briefing with our senior staff in the Observation Lounge—to bring you up to date. Using the Brahms radiation suits, we've done a spacewalk near the rift and have gotten a biological sample. We think we're ready to go even deeper into the rift."

"That sounds very dangerous," said Teska, lifting an eyebrow.

Nechayev scowled as they neared the turbolift. "Really, all I want to know is how are we going to get that Genesis box off the *Javlek*."

The turbolift door opened, and the trio entered. "Observation Lounge," said Riker. "You know, Admiral, the captain had two lengthy visits to the *Javlek*, and some personal dealings with Commander Kaylena, and he was convinced that they didn't have a Genesis emitter. And they were convinced that *we* have one."

"Teska, you were inside our prisoner's mind. Did the *Javlek* have a Genesis box?"

"They had one when they left Lomar to intercept the *Enterprise*," answered the Vulcan.

The turbolift door opened, and Riker led the way into the Observation Lounge, which now offered a partial view of the *Sequoia* as well as the *Javlek*. Seated at the table among several empty chairs were Commander La Forge, Dr. Crusher, and Counselor Troi.

After a few curt greetings and introductions, the admiral sat at the head of the table and folded her hands. "I'm sure you have many interesting findings to report to me," she began, "but I've seen all the radiation readings and chemical analyses I need to see. I know that any creature from that rift is unlike anything in we've seen in this quadrant, except maybe on Gemworld. I'm inclined to agree with Counselor Troi that this rift is related to the Gemworld rift. I wish that knowledge helped us more."

Nechayev took a breath and went on, "Of greater concern is the possibility that these expanding rifts, deadly radiation, and the development of these weird creatures have been exacerbated by the Genesis Wave. They've gotten worse with every demonstration of the so-called Orb of Life, so we're assuming that Vedek Yorka's newest stunt will cause massive problems. But the relationship between Genesis, the Orb of Life, and these rifts must be proven one way or another before we risk everything to stop Yorka in the Demilitarized Zone."

Nechayev scowled as she gazed at the senior officers of the *Enterprise*. "Of course, your captain has taken matters into his own hands and has flown off to Solosos III," she grumbled. "So he isn't here to help us get the Genesis emitter away from the Romulans, one way or another. If we had it, we could test it, and we could verify with our witnesses that the Orb of Life really is a Genesis Device.

"Fortunately, I've also had some dealings with Commander Kaylena," said Nechayev. "How is her health?"

"Her health?" asked Riker puzzledly. He glanced at his fellow officers, and all of them seemed a bit confused.

"Yes," answered Nechayev. "Kaylena is older than me, somewhat frail, overweight, walks with a limp from an old war wound she refuses to get fixed."

Now the senior staff really looked confused. "That's not the Commander Kaylena *we've* seen," said Riker, "or the one the captain has visited. She's young, statuesque, beautiful." Deanna shot him a fishy look at his description, and Will sunk deeper into his chair.

"Well, that's interesting," said Nechayev, stroking her chin thoughtfully. "That explains why she didn't answer my hail. But I'd like to see her."

"They haven't answered our hails lately either," answered Riker, "but I can show you a video log of an earlier conversation the captain had with her."

Nechayev crossed her arms, swiveled in her chair, and looked at the overheard viewscreen. "Proceed."

After a quick call to Data on the bridge, they all watched Commander Kaylena's first conversation with Captain Picard, where she demanded the return of the Brahms suits and he demanded the Genesis technology. Admiral Nechayev had a big grin on her face as she watched the exchange of almost a week ago.

"Picard made an excellent guess about the Genesis Device, and it must have spooked them," said the admiral, "because that is *not* Commander Kaylena of the *Javlek*. It's someone impersonating her. Those Romulans—they never cease to amaze me."

Now the *Enterprise* officers looked at one another with true consternation. "Why would they do that?" asked La Forge.

The women seemed to figure it out, and both Crusher and Troi gazed knowingly at the admiral. "The captain was over there for six hours on one visit," said Beverly.

"Are you saying that Captain Picard was infatuated with this impostor?" asked the admiral bluntly. "I know he's not here to defend himself, but this is a serious matter. Give me your honest answer, and it won't go any farther than this room. Was he involved with this woman you knew as Commander Kaylena?"

Riker nodded slowly, followed by Crusher and Troi.

"Now it's beginning to make sense," said the admiral, putting her fingertips together and making a steeple of her hands. "The Romulans have several means to accomplish what they did—they've even been know to use an Elasian's tears, which would be my guess here. In any case, we can assume that Captain Picard told them everything he knows. Did he contact her after he found out about Solosos III?"

"No," answered Riker, "they weren't answering our hails."

The admiral nodded. "And it appears that they believed some misinformation I fed them. What we don't know is if Picard is being heroic or is still under her control."

Nechayev rose slowly to her feet and began to pace, thinking out loud as she did. "Since we've figured this out—and they don't know we have—we could turn it to our advantage. Maybe we could even work a con to get Genesis from them. But to do this right, we would need someone to impersonate Picard—someone who wasn't infatuated with our beautiful commander."

Riker rapped his knuckles on the table. "We don't have anyone on board with that much skill at disguise."

"Uh . . . hmmm," said Crusher, frowning indecisively. After a moment, she seemed to overcome whatever doubts she had, and she sat up in her chair to say, "I know someone on board who could impersonate Captain Picard so well that *we* wouldn't know the difference."

Now the doctor had everyone's attention. "He's a

patient," she said. "Raynr Sleven, the only survivor of the *Barcelona*."

"We'll see him in a moment," answered Nechayev. Crusher nodded, and the energetic admiral went on, "We're going to get that box from them—by hook or by crook. Do you hear me, people?"

"Yes, Sir!" came a chorus.

"Commander Riker, you are acting captain," said Nechayev. "Even after Picard gets back, until he sees me, you are acting captain. When the runabout gets here, I want you to hustle them into the shuttlebay as quickly as you can; after you do, let it slip on an open channel that Regimol is with them."

"All right," answered Riker, not questioning why.

"Come on, Doctor," said Nechayev, headed for the door.

"Admiral," called Teska. "May I go back to the *Sequoia?*"

The admiral stopped for a moment and looked at the regal Vulcan. "Yes, but there's a good chance that we'll have to keep our shields up, so we can't transport. So, pack a bag and be prepared to stay on the *Enterprise.*" With that, Nechayev led Dr. Crusher out the door.

Alyssa Ogawa looked up from filing her reports to see a large figure come striding into sickbay. From his distinctive hair style, she knew exactly who it was—the Antosian—and she wanted to escape from sickbay before she confronted him. But Raynr Sleven was headed straight toward her.

"Is Dr. Crusher here?" he asked softly.

"No." She glared at him but lowered her voice to add,

"And don't you know you're not supposed to come here when I'm here? It's for your own protection, believe me. Now go away."

Raynr turned toward the door but stopped. "I can't. Dr. Crusher just contacted me and told me to meet her here. I was nearby . . . I'll wait outside."

"No, no," said Ogawa, reaching out a hand to stop him but quickly withdrawing it. "I've never kicked anybody out of sickbay before—I'm sorry."

"Understandable," he said apologetically. "I just wanted so badly for Suzi's father . . . your Andrew . . . to come home. When I was saved miraculously, it made me an optimist. Maybe too much. I keep thinking that Beverly will fall in love with me . . . that I can entertain Suzi for a few days until her real dad gets back. I always think everything will work out."

Ogawa lowered her head and tried to get back to work, but she realized that she had been punishing a patient who was still going through trauma . . . all because of *her* loss.

She looked up, tears streaking her face. "Okay," she said, "you and I have got to tell Suzi. You can even do your little parlor trick for her—"

"But—" Raynr protested, holding up his hands.

"But after we tell her that," Ogawa continued, despite the lumps in her throat, "we have to tell her that her father is probably dead. This much you can do with me . . . since it's something we all have to admit to ourselves."

"Okay," he answered, has face drooping with sorrow. "But I've got to get Dr. Crusher's permission before I . . . change again."

The sickbay door opened, and a whirlwind blew through in the person of Admiral Nechayev. In her wake came Dr. Crusher, who pointed to both Alyssa Ogawa and Raynr Sleven. "In my office, please."

A few seconds later, they were gathered around the diminutive admiral in Crusher's private consultation office, but all eyes were on the big Antosian, especially the admiral's. "Lieutenant Sleven," she began, "I know you've had a rough time of it lately, and I'm sorry. I can't imagine what it must be like to be the sole survivor of an entire starship. On top of that, you went through radical medical treatment. The doctor tells me that you've experienced a known side effect of cellular metamorphosis."

The Antosian looked mortified. "I'm sorry, I never meant to hurt the child . . . just make her feel better."

"This isn't about Nurse Ogawa's daughter," said the admiral. "I'm going to be blunt. If you can make yourself look like other people—for even a short time—we need that ability. It's a life-or-death matter involving the anomaly that claimed your ship . . . and the Romulans."

A shy smile came over his face. "You want me to do it again?"

"If your medical advisors agree," said the admiral.

Ogawa looked doubtful. "I'm not sure this is good for his recovery. . . ."

"He has to learn to control it, anyway," said Crusher. "Perhaps it would be easier if he had an outlet."

"Before I put much faith in this, I've got to see it in action," declared Nechayev, crossing her arms and staring expectantly at Raynr.

Crusher reached into her desk drawer and pulled out

a photo of Captain Picard, which she handed to the Antosian. He looked at the photo and smiled. "I would probably be able to do this without a reminder. Has something happened to the captain?"

"He's on a mission," said Nechayev. "But we need him to make an appearance for our Romulan friends."

"Uh, can you turn away for a moment?" asked the Antosian.

"All right," muttered Nechayev, motioning to the other two women to turn around. Ogawa felt singularly uncomfortable about compelling this sick patient to perform an act that might become addictive, even leading to insanity; but she wasn't surprised that Nechayev would make use of such a skill. Like everyone else, she had heard the Captain Picard rumors, followed by his abrupt departure.

"You may turn back," he said, showing a remarkable vocal adaptation, too. The three women turned around, mute with surprise. Before them stood Captain Picard in an oversized uniform with the wrong rank, but Captain Picard, nevertheless. Ogawa was now in awe and fear of this disturbing talent, so reminiscent of what the Changelings, moss creatures, and other dangerous beings were able to accomplish. If his ability could be harnessed, it could have great benefits, but at what cost?

"Excellent," proclaimed Nechayev, studying him closely. "And you can maintain this façade for how long?"

"Indefinitely, as far as I know," answered Raynr Sleven. "To be truthful, I've never done it for more a few minutes at a time, and I've never tried to sleep like this."

"Dr. Crusher, you will coach him to behave like

Captain Picard," ordered Nechayev, "and he is to keep this appearance for as long as he can."

"All right," said Crusher, "but can Ogawa monitor his vital signs and brain patterns? If he's going to do this, we need to gather information and watch for stress. You don't want him snapping out of it at a bad moment."

"Agreed," said Nechayev with a forceful nod. "There are other things I'd like to know, too. Such as, can he change from this into another identity? And how often?"

She touched the fake Picard, as if to make sure he was real. "But don't bother yourself with that now, Lieutenant. For now, just get this one impression down, and we'll see about the others. Practice hard with the doctor, and we'll meet again later." With that, the admiral marched out the door.

"Yes, Sir," answered Crusher belatedly. She turned to face a Jean-Luc Picard who was grinning like a fool. "Save that smile for something special, like a rare wine for your birthday. Captain Picard is more reserved than that."

"Yes, Doctor," he answered, coming to reserved attention.

Crusher gazed into his eyes. "You know, Sleven, I don't know what the admiral is planning, but I'm sure it's going to be dangerous."

"That's all right. I feel lucky," said the bogus Picard with too much of a smile.

Teska walked quietly into the brig on the *Sequoia.* Before she even got halfway across the floor, the Romulan looked up from his cell and gave her a welcoming smile. As was her custom, she knelt down in front of him, so that their heads would be on an even level.

"Hello," he said softly. "This is a good surprise."

"Are they treating you well?" she asked.

"Well, they could let me out for more exercise," answered Jerit. "The area outside the cell—where you are—is the only area I'm allowed. I can't really run, like I'm used to."

He chuckled and shook his head. "Of course, I'm not accustomed to spending much time on a starship. I might suffer from claustrophobia even if I could go anywhere on the *Sequoia*."

"I wish I could grant you free rein," replied Teska sincerely. "I am troubled for two reasons and need your advice."

"You're troubled. Must be serious." Jerit got off his bunk and knelt in front of her, their eyes locking with unspoken communication.

"Because of the urgency of our mission," she began, "I may soon be forced to perform a mind-meld on an unwilling subject. I fear I must do this, because time is so short. There will be another Genesis detonation in a day-and-a-half."

The murderer grimaced and looked down. "You know what you have to do, Teska. Genesis is an affront to the natural order. It cannot be used at all, even against a rock or a lifeless cloud. You might think you can control it, but you can't. Nobody has been able to control Genesis yet. So if your mind-meld contributes to shutting down Genesis, then do it. The needs of the many outweigh the needs of the few."

Teska cocked her head, as if considering his every word. "I have one more question. Due to thoughts you shared with me, I have a good idea where on the Romulan ship they might be storing the Genesis device. Do you mind if I use that information?"

Jerit smiled wistfully. "I'm beyond worrying about being called a traitor. The Romulan Star Empire has gotten good value from its investment in me—far more than I got out of it. If you promise to bury Genesis in the deepest hole you can find, use my mind. Use anyone's mind."

"Your ruthlessness," said Teska, "I could use some of that, too."

"You'll pay to use it . . . eventually."

With reluctance, she rose to her feet. "I may not be back for some time, or I may need to talk to you again soon."

Jerit stood, too, and he motioned around his stark cell. "Although my body is here, my mind and soul are with you. Even if I should die this minute, I continue with you. It gives me much comfort knowing that."

The Vulcan extended her hand then brought her fist back to her chest in the Romulan salute, perfectly executed. Then she turned on her heel and marched toward the door.

nineteen

"Hmmmm, a *D'deridex*-class warbird," said Regimol admiringly from the copilot's seat of the runabout. The Romulan studied the short-range scans of the rendezvous point, where they would be coming out of warp in a few seconds. There were three starships in close proximity, but only one really captivated him. "Now *that* is a warship," enthused Regimol, "and it has a cloaking module I helped design. It's hard to cloak a ship that big—it's much easier to cloak one *this* size."

"I wish you *could* cloak this runabout," muttered the Coridan in the pilot's seat.

Regimol felt a certain Ferengi gazing over his shoulder at the warbird. "Come on," said Chellac, "if you build a ship that big, you don't want it cloaked. You want people to look at it and be afraid."

"You sound just like a Romulan general I know," observed Regimol. " 'You don't hide a warbird,' he used to say. 'You terrify your prey with it.' The Federation doesn't have anything that quite matches her."

"We still outnumber them," said the pilot, "two to one."

"I still don't like those odds," replied the Ferengi worriedly. "We've got to lower shields to dock inside the *Enterprise*, and so do they. Then we've got to get some great piloting. No offense, Ensign, but I don't know how well you fly under fire. That warbird could blow us away with a sneeze."

Regimol glanced back at Chellac, then past the Ferengi's big ears at their Bajoran prisoner. He was a defiant hard case who had not said two words since falling into their hands. Even Bakus might have trouble breaking him.

The Romulan said, "It might be a good idea to transport our crew off the runabout as we come in, as long as the shields are down."

"Now we're talking!" said Chellac. "I volunteer to transport off just as soon as we get close!"

"I appreciate the offer," replied Regimol, "and you'll be taking our Bajoran friend with you." He patted the Coridan pilot on the shoulder. "I'm sorry, but you can't leave until we're in the shuttlebay."

"That's all right—I prefer to fly in." The pilot checked his instruments and made a few adjustments. "We're coming out of warp in less that a minute. Anybody else have any strategy they want to talk about? What do we do if the Romulans hail us?"

"Ignore them," replied Regimol. "Use an encrypted channel to talk to the *Enterprise*. Chellac, you and our friend get on the transporter platform."

The Ferengi jumped at the chance to get off the little ship early, and he drew a phaser and pointed it at the

Bajoran, who was shackled to one of the passenger seats. Two brawny security officers unlocked the prisoner, dragged him to his feet, and shackled his wrists behind his back. Then they deposited him on the transporter platform beside Chellac.

The little Ferengi waved his phaser and snarled at the sullen assassin. "Don't try anything funny, I warn you. You got caught, so take your punishment like a Bajoran. Unless . . . is there anybody willing to pay a ransom for you?"

The Bajoran growled loudly at Chellac, and the Ferengi jumped back. "Just asking."

"Coming out of warp," announced the pilot. Regimol moved to the transporter console and sat down. "The Romulans are hailing us—telling us to go away."

"Keep shields up until we enter transporter range," ordered Regimol. "Go in at one-half impulse until you have to slow down."

"Yes, Sir. I'm sending encrypted requests to the *Enterprise* transporter room as well as the shuttlebay." The Coridan glanced at his readouts and squirmed in his seat. "The *Sequoia* is taking matters into their own hands. They're powering up phasers."

Now the three starships loomed ahead of the runabout, looking like fantastic works of art hanging from a child's mobile—the massive green knife blade, the three-dimensional chess set, and the silver snowflake. What made the sight even more disturbing was the sparkling debris field and the jagged black rip outlined against the starscape.

"Are you sure it's not too late to turn back?" asked Chellac with a gulp.

"We'll be fine once we get to the *Enterprise*," answered Regimol. "You two are going to be the first ones aboard. Hold on for another second while I—"

Suddenly the small vessel was jolted, and Regimol nearly fell out of his chair. Chellac did fall off the transporter platform, and the prisoner leaped off and kicked a security guard. It was suddenly chaos inside the cramped cabin, with guards tussling with the Bajoran and the ship shaking like a leaf in a storm. Twisting, straining her thrusters, the runabout began to slip toward the massive warbird.

"There's a tractor beam on us!" barked the pilot.

An expanding blue beam, barely detectable to the eye, shot from the *Sequoia* and swept over the *Javlek*, dealing the Romulan vessel a severe blow. The runabout broke free and careened toward the *Enterprise*. But the Romulans retaliated with a brace of quantum torpedoes, which struck the *Enterprise* and *Sequoia* with impressive fireworks but did little damage against their shields. As the battle raged, the runabout was like a fly caught between two charging bulls. Still the pilot soared bravely onward, oblivious to the danger.

"When do I get off?" whined Chellac, bounding back onto the transporter platform. The security officers were still struggling to subdue the shackled prisoner, but they were getting the upper hand. All of them were bloodied.

"We can't beam anyone anywhere yet," answered Regimol, studying his instruments. "Nobody but the Romulans have dared to lower their shields. And their shields are back up."

"That was a pretty good phaser blast they took," said the pilot.

"Yes, magnificent ship," observed Regimol.

The *Sequoia* maneuvered to insert itself between the warbird and the *Enterprise*. As soon as the *Sequoia* was in place, she lashed out with an array of multiple phaser beams, which raked the *Javlek*'s shields and kept the Romulan ship at bay.

"Sit down, Chellac," said Regimol, "they're not going to make it easy on us. So we're all going in together. Ensign, you keep flying, and I'll drop the shields . . . as soon as the *Enterprise* drops her shields. You just land this bird."

"Is that all?" asked the Coridan dryly.

While the *Sequoia* continued to pummel the *Javlek* with phasers, doing little harm but forcing them to keep power diverted to their shields, the runabout swooped around the battling ships. The small craft leveled off and slowed to take an approach to the aft of the *Enterprise*'s dorsal section, where the shuttlebay doors waited. So far, they were still closed. Under bombardment, the warbird tried to reposition itself, but the *Sequoia* moved quickly to intercept, all while pounding the *Javlek*.

"If they keep up those phasers," said the pilot, "they're not going to have any warp core left."

"*Enterprise* shields are down!" announced Regimol. "And now ours are down, and the doors are opening. Brace yourselves!"

The Romulans unleashed a phaser attack of their own, thinking the broader firepower would circumvent the *Sequoia*'s shields, but the smaller starship bravely took the brunt of it. Still the runabout bounced like a runaway wagon careening down a hill, and sparks flew

everywhere in the suddenly smoky cabin. Even the
Bajoran and the security officers paused in their scuffle
to see what would happen next.

"Impulse engines out!" shouted the pilot. "We're on
landing thrusters."

Somehow the quivering, quaking runabout held
together long enough to spin through the open shuttlebay doors. As it skidded across the deck, foam shot from
emitters, and nets stretched between the deck and ceiling, catching the runabout and preventing any serious
damage to the craft, its inhabitants, or the shuttlebay.

Chellac was still screaming when the craft finally
came to a complete stop, and he touched his chest,
amazed that he was alive. He rushed to the pilot and
kissed him on his partially bald head. "Great job!
Beautiful flying! Pop that hatch."

The Coridan tried popping the hatch, but it remained
steadfastly closed. "I guess the hull is pretty badly damaged," he muttered. "Just before we came in, Regimol, I
heard them say your name over an open channel."

"Is that so?" asked the Romulan with curiosity.
"Normally the admiral doesn't announce my presence."

"Maybe she wanted to rub it in," said Chellac. "So
how are we going to get out of here?"

Suddenly, sparks flew all around the recalcitrant
hatch, while technicians outside cut through it. A few
minutes later, the hatch was pulled off the damaged vessel, and they were met by a dark-skinned human with
opaque devices over his eyes.

"Welcome to the *Enterprise*," he said cheerfully. "I'm
Chief Engineer Geordi La Forge. The security detail
can take your prisoner to our brig, and the admiral

would like to see Regimol and Chellac on the bridge."

"Well, of course she would," declared the Ferengi importantly as he brushed past La Forge.

Regimol stepped outside the craft and looked forlornly at his banged-up runabout. "Ah, it was nice while it lasted."

"We'll fix it up good as new," the engineer assured him. "Come with me, please." He led the way toward double doors marked with exit symbols.

"Are they still fighting out there?" asked the Ferengi.

The human shook his head. "No, they stopped just as soon as you were safely inside. We're back to a stalemate, although they are demanding that we turn Regimol over to them."

"I'm always so popular with my own people," replied the thief dryly.

On the crowded bridge of the *Enterprise*, a tight-lipped, bald-headed human stood before the viewscreen, addressing his attractive counterpart on the *Javlek*. When La Forge, Regimol, and Chellac stepped off the turbolift, they caught the eye of Admiral Nechayev in the corner, who motioned them to her side. The gray-haired human put her finger to her lips in the universal sign for quiet, and the Romulan and Ferengi did as they were told. The stunning Vulcan, Teska, stood at the admiral's other side.

"I'm sorry to have displeased you, Commander Kaylena," said the human captain apologetically. "On the other hand, there wasn't any reason for you to fire at the runabout, which was only attempting to dock in our shuttlebay."

"That vessel belongs to a peaceful trade commission from Romulus," declared Kaylena, "and it was stolen by an infamous criminal, named Regimol. We demand that you hand him over to us immediately."

The captain looked shocked. "He is here under the personal invitation of Admiral Nechayev, on the *Sequoia*." His voice took on a pleading, personal tone. "Please, Kaylena, if you and I could get together and talk about this *privately*—"

A slight smile graced the beautiful commander's face. "You may come over, Captain Picard, if you bring Regimol with you."

The captain could barely contain his joy at this point. "We also have a prisoner . . . from your trade delegation. We could return both at the same time, although the admiral won't be happy about it."

"Half an hour, that's all you have," declared the statuesque Romulan. "Just yourself and the two prisoners."

The captain glanced off to the side, and Regimol saw the admiral give him a nod of approval. "Yes, uh . . . Picard out." The viewscreen shifted to a study of the hunched warbird, looking like a green vulture. The captain heaved his shoulders in relief and smiled shyly.

Regimol frowned at the engineer, La Forge. "I'm not sure I like being handed over so cavalierly to people who want to kill me."

"That's not really Commander Kaylena," said La Forge. "But it's okay, because that's not Captain Picard either."

The Romulan raised an eyebrow. "All right, I'm liking this assignment better." He watched as the captain, the admiral, and a beautiful red-haired woman conferred. They were joined by a tall dark-haired man, who seemed to be in charge of the bridge.

The crowd began to move toward a passageway in the corner, and La Forge gently pushed him and Chellac in that direction. "To the Observation Lounge."

"What are you devious huuumans planning?" asked Chellac in admiration.

"There's only one of us planning. The rest are along for the ride," answered the engineer.

"As it should be," said the Ferengi. "After this, I'm through with partnerships and gangs. From now on, I will devote myself to *me* and making *me* rich."

"To serve a strip of latinum is the same as serving Starfleet or the Romulan Star Empire," answered Regimol. "They're all tyrants."

"You work for yourself," said Chellac.

"That's how I know."

Conversation ended there, and they soon found themselves seated around a large conference table, flanked by a stunning view of the warbird, *Javlek*, through the viewport. Admiral Nechayev hovered around Captain Picard, as if he were a valuable work of art which might be stolen any second.

"So far, so good," said the admiral. She turned to Regimol and gave him a wry smile. "Welcome, old friend. We have to get a suitcase-sized box off that vessel. Teska has a good idea where it might be—where do you think they would store something so valuable?"

"The commander's quarters," he answered. "That's traditional. On that vessel, the commander has an impressive vault, with dampening fields, so you can't transport anything out."

Teska nodded knowingly, as if she agreed with him. Nechayev leaned forward, her palms resting on the table. "They've given us a window to get a team aboard. Three people." She looked from Regimol to Teska and then at the fake Captain Picard.

The door opened, and an ensign came in with a stack of richly embroidered clothing—Romulan clothing. There were also two disruptors in the pile.

"I have my own, thanks," said Regimol with a smile.

As soon as the three visitors from the *Enterprise* materialized in the transporter room of the *Javlek*, Captain Picard dropped into a crouch and waved a phase shifted detonator in the faces of numerous helmeted security officers. Beside him stood the two Romulans, shackled wrist to ankle, their heads drooping and eyelids heavy, as if they had been drugged.

On the chest of each groggy prisoner was a blinking red device, and Picard pointed ominously at them. "Those are shaped explosive charges," he warned, "and this is the detonator. Take one step closer, and I'll *kill* them! Do what I say, or I will destroy us all, I swear!"

Picard craned his neck, looking in vain for a face in the stunned crowd. "I don't see Kaylena here, and I was promised *Kaylena!* Bring her to this transporter room alone, or I will kill them!" His finger hovered over his handheld device. "Now get out of here! Go! Go!" he shouted insanely.

This episode was especially galling for the real Commander Kaylena, who stood in the shadows at the back of the transporter room. *No, my attractive stand-in is not here*, she mused, *and the problem with using Elasian tears is that the subjects eventually became unpredictable when deprived of the object of their desire.*

She barked an order and was the first one out the door, with the others dutifully following her. Once in the corridor, the commander stationed a number of centurions to keep watch on the transporter room, although she didn't know that Regimol had already slipped through the bulkhead and was listening to every word—from a vantage point about five meters away.

"Summon the Elasian!" ordered the squat, limping Romulan. "Quickly!"

There was a lively discussion among her officers, but the elder Kaylena made it clear that this was only a short delay. "He is the commander's consort," she reminded her underlings, "only it's the wrong commander. When this is all over, I will take Picard as my own."

Those words brought a round of nervous but appreciative laughter, and the diminutive officer pointed at two more helmeted centurions. "Go double the guard on my quarters."

That clinches that, thought Regimol, and he quickly eased through the bulkhead and back into the transporter room.

"Reporting back," he said to his comrades, who couldn't see him either. Raynr Sleven was seated on the transporter platform, conserving his energy as he was supposed to, and Teska was waiting by the door.

"Have you disconnected the sensors and video logs in this room?" asked Teska.

"On my way through the bulkhead," whispered the disembodied voice. "And I have good news for you. The goods are definitely in her quarters—no need for a mind-meld. That was good emoting, Picard. A bit over the top, but then Elasian tears will do that to a man."

Picard grinned. "You naturally want to go big when you're playing insane. But I'll tone it down."

The door suddenly slid open, and the only one who had to move was Picard, who rose to his feet, his finger nervously hovering over the detonator. The young, willowy Commander Kaylena stepped into the transporter room, and the door swiftly shut behind her. She took a few steps toward the distraught figure of Picard, waving his detonator.

"Darling, calm yourself—" Before Kaylena could finish, a hand descended from behind, and elegant fingers alit on the base of her neck, applying pressure to certain nerves. With a surprised blink, the Elasian fell to the deck.

After having rendered her unconscious, Teska quickly turned the actress over so that Raynr could get a good look at her. He was already stripping down to change into a Romulan commander's uniform. Thankfully for the embarrassed Antosian, male and female Romulan uniforms differed little. The Vulcan turned to the door and activated the manual locks.

A disembodied voice said, "Teska, you would make a great thief. When this is all over, if you would like—"

"No."

"And you, too, Raynr," said the invisible Romulan, undeterred. "I definitely have good-paying work for *you*."

"Can we survive this first?" asked the nervous Antosian. "Now I've got to play an Elasian female, playing a Romulan female, whom I've never met."

They looked down at the unconscious Elasian, who

now looked so young and innocent, stripped of her arrogant façade and femme fatale personality.

"Turn away, please," said the Antosian. "Regimol, I won't know if you've turned away—"

"I'm leaving," said the Romulan. "See you at the loot."

After Regimol was presumably gone, taking a pedestrian but direct route to the commander's quarters, Teska dragged the unconscious Elasian to the transporter platform. When she turned around, she saw a duplicate of the beautiful commander right where Captain Picard had been standing.

"How do I look?" asked this new Kaylena, her voice sounding feminine although not exact, since they hadn't had much time to study and practice the Elasian's voice patterns. Still, the Antosian had done an impressive job of altering his vocal cords as well to create a feminine pitch.

"You look fine," said the Vulcan. Suddenly there came loud voices and banging on the outer door, which Teska had locked. "Hurry! Get on the transporter platform."

The conscious Kaylena took her place beside the unconscious Kaylena, while Teska dashed to the transporter controls. Although shields were up, making it impossible to beam on or off the *Javlek*, there was nothing preventing them from beaming anywhere inside the ship, and they had to vacate the transporter room.

"All right, coordinates entered," said Teska.

She dashed back to the platform just in time for her molecules to be seized by the transporter beam, along with those of the two young Kaylenas. With frantic pounding and blazing disruptors, the Romulans forced the transporter room door open just as the intruders disappeared, leaving the place mysteriously empty.

All three of them arrived in a storage room on level four, traditional deck for the officer's quarters. Fortunately, thought Teska, the Romulan transporters didn't store used coordinates, due to security concerns.

Alarms started sounding immediately—intruder alarms—and Teska gave the Elasian another nerve pinch, making sure she wouldn't wake up any time soon. Then she and Raynr, who was still a duplicate of the fake Kaylena, strode from the storage room into the corridor. They were perhaps taller and more striking than the Romulan females who rushed past them, but their studied determination fit in with the mood of the officers of the *Javlek*.

It was easy to spot the commander's quarters because of the extra guards standing about—four in all. Because of the alert, they looked edgy, and they scrutinized everyone who walked past them. So the two fake Romulans slowed in their movements. They were supposed to receive a signal from Regimol if he had gotten the Genesis emitter, but so far it only looked like chaos in the corridor. Failing to hear from him, they were to take matters in their own hands.

"Stop here," said a voice urgently, and Teska grabbed the disguised Antosian and pulled him to a stop. "The vault," whispered the thief, "it's got a double vault inside of it, which is too small for me to enter. We've got to blast it."

The two of them started back in the other direction,

away from Kaylena's quarters. "That will bring everyone in the ship down on us," said Teska.

"Maybe not," answered Raynr Sleven, slipping into a masculine voice. "Are there pictures of the real Commander Kaylena in her quarters?"

"Yes," answered the voice.

"Bring them to me—in the storage room."

The conversation ended, and the two Romulans made their way back down the corridor. A gray-haired officer stopped them at one point, as if to demand they take their stations; but when he recognized the Elasian imposter, he scowled and let them wander on their way. A minute later, the two of them were back in the storage room, and Teska made sure the real Elasian would stay unconscious a while longer.

The tiny room, which was crammed with emergency food rations and medical kits, seemed to fill with an unseen presence, and slowly the dapper figure of Regimol materialized. He handed the duplicate Kaylena a collection of holographic photos stolen from the real Kaylena's boudoir.

"If you can dismiss the guards and get in there," said Regimol, "we might be able to crack the inner vault without anyone knowing."

"Nechayev said she was short and limped," added Teska.

The Antosian nodded, his deep frown looking incongruous on such a lovely face. He paced quietly as he studied the photos of the venerable commander, taken in the company of various dignitaries. Teska looked away, because she knew that Raynr didn't like to be watched while he made his transformation, especially when it was one for which he hadn't prepared. She respected his privacy, and she looked pointedly at Regimol. The Romulan scowled and looked away, too. While voices and footsteps echoed outside in the corridor, the Antosian exploited his side effect.

"Okay," he said in a nondescript female voice. They turned to face a rather dumpy, older Romulan female, who looked authentic enough to them, although none of them had ever met Commander Kaylena.

"Let's move," said Regimol, pointing to the door. "We'll be your officers—just tell them to go to the bridge . . . or engineering."

Before Teska had been trying to blend into the bulkheads, but now she donned a Romulan's typical stiff-necked disdain. They shoved their way through the pedestrian traffic in the corridor, and many in the crew stopped to salute Kaylena, which was a good sign. Teska kicked Raynr in the shin to remind the commander to limp; he grumbled and started limping convincingly. Fortunately, the lighting in the corridor was a bit dim, due to the alert.

They strode up to the guards at the commander's quarters, and they also snapped to attention. "Open the door," ordered the fraudulent Kaylena.

Moments seemed to pass like hours, but one of the guards finally responded and opened the door. "We have to defend engineering," said the commander as she brushed past them. "All of you, report to engineering."

"But, Commander—"

"Do it!" snapped Regimol in his most arrogant tone. "We'll guard the commander. You protect engineering."

The door slid shut behind them, and the Romulan

sunk against the bulkhead and drew his disruptor, in case they hadn't followed orders. When they hadn't stormed the quarters a few seconds later, he breathed a sigh of relief.

"My, this is nice," said the Antosian, looking around at the plush, yet oddly gaudy surroundings. He wandered toward the magnificent bed and prodded the mattress admiringly. "Did they . . . did they entertain Picard in here?"

"No time to be salacious now," answered Regimol, rushing toward a nondescript curtain near the door to the lavatory. "Raynr, you'd better stay by that door, in case they try to get in."

"Yes, Sir," answered a male voice, still struggling to find a suitable pitch.

"It's in here, Teska," said Regimol, yanking aside the curtain and revealing a large rectangular panel, which looked innocuous, until one realized that it was several centimeters thick, and the only lock worked by thumbprint. "It's all electronic—nothing I can force," he explained. "I can squeeze inside, but the inner vault makes it impossible for me to include the box in my phase-inverted field. In other words, I can get in, but I can't get the case out."

"So we must detonate the charge," Teska replied coolly. "Do we put it outside on this door, or inside on the inner vault?"

"Oh, out here." Regimol took off the bomb he had been wearing as a ruse, only now it was to be used for real. With a pained expression, the thief placed the charge in the Vulcan's hand. "It's shaped—to direct the force inward. I hate to resort to blowing things up, because it seems so unprofessional. And I'm afraid we'll damage the prize."

"Better we do that than leave it in their hands," answered the Vulcan.

"You really don't like Romulans, do you?" said Regimol with amusement.

"This negates our main escape plan," she continued, ignoring him. "In the backup plan, we must lower the *Javlek*'s shields. You could take care of that, Regimol, while we secure the device. If the *Enterprise* is alert, they will beam us back the moment they see the *Javlek*'s shields go down."

"And before the fireworks start," muttered the Romulan. "But how will I know when you've got the booty?"

"You will feel the effects of the detonation," she answered, "and the crew will also notice them. You might want to give us another minute after the detonation before lowering the shields. If you are having difficulties, it should provide a useful distraction for you. At any rate, we are dependent upon you to handle the shields."

"Right," he said with a smile. "See you back at the Big E." A second later, Regimol was gone, and Teska began to rig the charge on the outer wall of the vault.

"Do not move," said a voice, and Teska turned to see a Romulan disruptor leveled at her head. Holding it was an elder Commander Kaylena, and she was surrounded by twinkling transporter beams, with armored centurions materializing in every square meter of the elegant sleeping quarters.

twenty

In her opulent quarters, Commander Kaylena waved her disruptor at Teska's head, then she limped back and motioned to her guards. "Seize her!" she ordered. "But don't kill her."

The Romulans closed in, using their hands to capture her, and Teska fought hard against them . . . until they started to howl and collapse all around her. The Vulcan looked up to see Commander Kaylena mowing them down with the disruptor in one hand and a phaser in the other. Shooting them in the back, she decimated the security detail before they even knew what hit them.

Reaching over the carnage, she helped Teska to her feet. "I'm sorry," explained the commander, who the Vulcan realized was her comrade, Raynr Sleven. "When they started beaming in, I figured I'd better pretend like I was on their side."

"Let's finish this," muttered Teska, troubled at the loss of life. "Hand me the detonator."

"Of course," replied Raynr, handing the small remote over to her.

Working with a measure of urgency, Teska finished attaching the bomb to the vault door, then she made sure it was set to discharge via the detonator. Motioning to her colleague to follow her, the Vulcan overturned the sumptuous bed and used it to form a protective barrier, along with every other stick of furniture in the room. When they had put as much distance and obstacles between them and the vault as they could find, they hunkered down, and Teska pushed the recessed button.

Ka-boom! went the explosion, showering metal, debris, and smoke throughout the suddenly devastated quarters. The entire warbird seemed to reverberate with the blast, but Teska didn't wait for the dust to settle. She leaped over the smoldering barrier and bodies and ignored a flaming curtain to reach the immense hole they had made in the bulkhead. Feverishly, she dug in the rubble, trying to find the gleaming metal box buried somewhere within.

"Help me dig!" she urged her partner. "We have only a minute!"

By the time Raynr joined her in the blast hole, he had reverted to his normal appearance. "I feel stronger this way," he explained. Both of them applied their impressive strength to rip away the twisted metal and crumbling rubble, but they finally encountered a scorched and slightly dented box underneath. Teska lunged through the wreckage to grab the box, and Raynr pulled her out.

Bam! An explosion shook the door, adding smoke and dust to the upheaval, but the door remained in place. Romulan cursing quickly followed, and several boots began to kick the shattered remains of the door. Raynr drew his disruptor to fire, but Teska dragged both him and the Genesis device into the 'fresher.

She checked her chronometer and whispered, "I want them to think we're gone."

"If they see us, we *are* gone," answered Raynr.

With much shouting and blasting, the Romulans stormed the commander's quarters, and Teska gripped her own phaser, although she didn't want to use it. She felt the blessed tingle of the transporter just as a red disruptor beam streaked over their heads. Ducking as low as possible, the Vulcan clutched the dented box as the 'fresher door was blown away.

When Teska arrived on the *Enterprise*, still in a fetal position and clutching the box, the entire transporter room shook, and debris rained from the ceiling. The Antosian rolled off the transporter platform and covered his head. "Are we under attack?"

"What do you think?" muttered Chief Rhofistan. Another blow struck the ship, and sparks shot from his console. Waving his long arms at the smoke and flying embers, the Andorian backed away from his useless equipment. He pointed to a pile of assorted uniforms and jumpsuits on the deck.

"They might beam over to board us," said Rhofistan, grabbing a fire extinguisher. "Best to get out of those enemy uniforms."

Teska looked in vain for Regimol, but the Romulan was nowhere to be seen. Suddenly a disembodied hand tapped her on the shoulder, making her jump. "It's okay," he said. "I'm here."

"We got it," she said, holding up the prize. Teska allowed herself a fleeting smile of triumph.

Regimol's wavering likeness solidified into view, and he was also grinning. "The booty!"

Raynr Sleven was already stripping down and putting on a Starfleet uniform. "They're going to need me on my repair crew. I'll see you later." He dashed toward the door.

"Nice working with you!" called Regimol, gazing fondly after the departing Antosian. "To me, that shifter is more valuable than a Genesis box. How much do you think Starfleet would take for him?"

More enemy fire hit the *Enterprise*, but the effect seemed to be muted. "Good, it seems we got shields back up," said Rhofistan as he put out the last of the fire. "You two change clothes—the admiral wants to see you on the bridge."

"Let's bring the prize with us," said Regimol, grinning as he stripped off his ornate Romulan finery.

Five minutes later, the Romulan thief was not smiling as he stood on the bridge of the *Enterprise*; he was glum as he watched the magnificent Romulan warbird, *Javlek*, careening out of control. One of its nacelles was aflame, and the other sputtered helplessly. Tiny fires burned all over her glistening green hull, and it looked like acid eating away at the corpse of some fantastic bird.

"Did . . . did you have to do this?" asked Regimol in a hoarse voice.

"I'm sorry," said Admiral Nechayev, bowing her head. "We asked them repeatedly to surrender, but they kept firing. You did a job taking out their shields, didn't you? They were so angry about the theft, they never stopped firing at us. The *Sequoia* got two direct hits on them. We only fired one phaser, even though we took quite a bit of damage, too. But we were able to get our shields back up. She wasn't."

"Conn," said Commander Riker. "Get ready to go to warp at the first sign of a self-destruct sequence. Keep checking for escape pods."

"Yes, Sir," answered Data on the conn.

"I see you got the box," said Nechayev with a smile of relief. "Well done."

"They're sure to have a self-destruct sequence," the Romulan said gravely, running his fingers through his jet hair. "You'd better pull back."

"No need. The *Javlek* is going into the rift," reported Data.

Regimol stepped closer to the viewscreen as the great warbird banked into the glittering swirl of debris, where it looked like a flying fish in a sea of stardust. With half the hull in ruins, the *Javlek* was a spectacular sight, cutting through the shimmering waves; but the rift loomed ahead of it like a storm cloud. In a final surge, the sputtering starship soared from the debris field into the emptiness of the anomaly, and it was snuffed like a candle wick. After a brief crackle of energy, all was dark and still again.

On the cabin of a much smaller spacecraft, Jean-Luc Picard suddenly dropped to his knees, gasping for breath. He felt as if a knife had been plunged into his chest, and he was certain he was going to die. When the captain still drew ragged breaths a few seconds later, he knew someone else had died . . . someone very close to him . . . the person on his mind every waking second.

"No!" whispered Picard, slumping forward. "She's dead."

He wept even as two crewmembers of the yacht gathered at his side to help him up. "Captain, do you need medical attention?"

"No!" he shouted, pushing them away. "What I need . . . I can't have." He wept anew, not bothering to hide his sorrow from his inexperienced crew of three ensigns.

The tears were oddly cathartic. As he shed them, Picard felt better, as if a great responsibility had been lifted from his shoulders. He still loved Kaylena fiercely—in death as well as life—but he no longer felt beholden to prove his devotion to her. He had loved and now lost, and the burning had been replaced by sodden embers of grief.

With a cough, Captain Picard picked himself up off the deck, and he looked around at his young crew, who quickly turned back to their instruments.

One of them cleared his throat. "Captain, there's a message from the *Enterprise*."

He nodded gravely. "I know . . . the *Javlek* has been destroyed."

The young Ardanan stared at him, mouth agape. "Sir, how did you—"

"Do they have Genesis?" he asked.

"They don't say, but we are to continue with our mission." The young ensign looked wild-eyed at his captain.

"Relax, Ensign," said Picard, tugging on the bottom of his tunic. "I had a special attachment to someone on that ship. So what is our ETA to Solosos III?"

"Three hours, twenty-five minutes," answered the Ardanan.

"Start looking out for Cardassian patrols," ordered Captain Picard as he headed aft. "Alert me when we get close. I'll be in the sleeping compartment. I think I can sleep now."

"What planet is Vedek Yorka using for the detonation of the Orb of Life?" demanded Admiral Nechayev, staring at the Bajoran assassin. He was barely a slip of a man, thought Commander Riker, almost a boy. But his wary eyes bespoke experiences that no boy should have.

"I will never betray my Prophets," he said defiantly.

"But you would kill for them?" muttered Nechayev. She looked with exasperation at Teska. "Will you use it?"

"Let me ask first," said the Vulcan. "I would like to perform a mind-meld with you. Do you agree?"

"No!" shouted the prisoner, glaring at her with indignation.

Teska raised an eyebrow and said, "Then I apologize for this assault and can only justify it because billions of lives are in danger if he detonates Genesis. Hold his head."

Riker nodded, and the big human got a tight grip on the lad's head, keeping his struggles to a minimum. Without hesitation, Teska extended her long fingers and made contact with his cheekbone. At once, the Bajoran relaxed, and the Vulcan's head rolled back.

"I am sorry," she muttered. "Do not fight me . . . do you understand why you must cooperate?" After what seemed like an unpleasant, even painful experience, Teska twitched and broke free. She almost slumped to the deck, but Riker grabbed her and steadied her.

"Thank you," said Teska gratefully. "It is Solosos III, and they have elements of the Bajoran militia protecting them."

"Damn!" Nechayev winced and began pacing the brig. "Let's continue this conversation outside. Ensign, return the prisoner to his cell."

"Yes, Sir," answered the brig officer, taking charge of the dazed Bajoran.

A moment later, Nechayev, Riker, and Teska stood in the corridor outside the brig, and the admiral was still pacing in agitation. "We have a little over a day left," she grumbled, "and it would take a day to send another ship to Solosos III."

"The *Enterprise* is too damaged," said the first officer. "We can't manage a sustained flight at warp speed, but I agree—we should send someone to back the captain up." Riker didn't add, "in his condition," but it was implied in his tone of voice.

"Yes, that's clear," the admiral agreed. "And you have experiments to perform, in addition to watching the rift. Regimol's runabout is also out of commission, so that leaves the *Sequoia*. But if I take a Starfleet ship into the DMZ, we risk a war with the Cardassians, and we won't make the Bajorans very happy either."

"We could speed up repairs on the runabout," said Riker, "make them a priority. But we haven't got anybody who can legally travel in the DMZ."

"Incorrect," answered Teska. "You have a Ferengi on board."

"Ah, yes," said Riker with a smile. "I forgot about Chellac, and we've got an Antosian who can look like a Ferengi. I'll get busy on that runabout." He started down the corridor.

"Teska and I will check on La Forge," said Nechayev. "We need that test as soon as possible—to see if there's a connection between the rift and Genesis."

In a laboratory off engineering, Geordi La Forge and Data presided over a busy team of scientists and engineers, taking a crash course on Genesis technology and its specific use in a portable device. Because they had been told they could replicate the device, they had, and there were workbenches all over the room with emitters spread out in various stages of disassembly.

After conducting a brief tour, La Forge escorted the admiral and the mission specialist to Data's workbench, where the android was measuring tolerances on the outer hull of the dented chrome box.

"This is the original," said the chief engineer. "It doesn't appear to be damaged too badly, but we've only opened up the replicates. We understand the power system and the relationship of all the components, but we hesitate to touch the protomatter injector or the programming module. With those gizmos, we're operating in unknown territory, and the wrong adjustment could make it useless or extremely dangerous."

"How will we test it safely?" asked the Vulcan.

La Forge deferred to Data, and the android put down his tools. "Time is too short to reverse-engineer or alter the programming, but we can achieve a crude measure of control by regulating the power output. The power comes from a pair of traditional fuel cells and is relatively uncomplicated, being a single-use device. I believe that we can perform a mild detonation in a controlled environment by installing nanocapacitors to limit the field dispersion and mutagenic flux. We might also be able to reverse the polarity and create other complementary effects."

Nechayev nodded. "So you supply enough power to trip the emitter, but you lower the output."

"Yes," answered the android. "However, the result of this experiment is still unpredictable, requiring a large amount of isolated, expendable land."

"I feel we're no better than they are, setting off one of these things," muttered Nechayev. "But we've got to see if it's related to the rift. If we can limit the damage—"

"We will," promised La Forge.

"All right," said the admiral, "the two of you get over to the *Sequoia*, and I'll give them orders to take you to an approprite test site. Test it, but do it within the hour."

Even the android looked somewhat flustered by the accelerated pace. "Sir, we have not done our preliminary—"

"No time for that," snapped Nechayev. "Do the best you can to muffle it, but set off one of those boxes. I'll notify Starfleet to have everyone pull back from the anomalies. I wouldn't ask this, but we've got to know how important it is to stop Yorka. Can you do it in an hour?"

"Yes, Sir," answered both La Forge and Data.

He found her in transporter room one, where Deanna Troi looked rather incongruous hunched over one of the Brahms prototype suits, cleaning a filter. Will Riker heaved a sigh and walked over to his beloved. "*Imzadi,*" he said softly, "what are you doing?"

"Just making sure the suits are in good repair," answered the ship's counselor. "Call it a hobby—or a necessity—but I've taken a real interest in these radiation suits. I've got a feeling we're going to need to use them again. Soon."

"Well, Data and La Forge didn't take them when they went to test Genesis," said Riker. "I wish they had."

"They won't need them for that," answered Troi, screwing a clean filter into the condenser intake valve. "But we'll need them when we go into the rift."

"We're not going inside there," claimed Riker. "Specifically *you* are not going inside there."

The beautiful Betazoid raised an eyebrow at him. "I'm the ideal one to go inside, because I've faced it several times now and have overcome the mind control. La Forge wasn't able to stand it, and neither can anyone else."

"No," said Riker adamantly. "It's bad enough that the captain, Data, and La Forge are gone—we're not risking anyone else on some foolhardy stunt."

"Just in case, I'll keep these suits in repair," insisted Troi, closing the compartment where she had been working.

"What do you say to dinner?" asked Will hopefully. "That's why I came to find you, not to argue. It might be the last quiet moment before all hell breaks loose."

She smiled fondly at him and took his arm. "Then we'd better make the most of it."

Teska found Regimol in a repair facility near the shuttlebay where he and the runabout had landed a day earlier. He was standing by himself, thoughtfully watching a six-member repair team working briskly on his ship. Since the runabout now had the highest priority, crack *Enterprise* crews were working around the clock on her, while their own damaged systems waited.

The Romulan seemed to sense her arrival, and he turned to look at her. But the smile Regimol manufactured seemed forced and melancholy. Watching the warbird go down to destruction had sapped the spirit from him, and he seemed to be questioning his choice of profession, or perhaps his allegiance. Possibly guilt was involved, too, because his actions in cutting the shields had resulted in the *Javlek*'s demise. Teska would be more inclined to blame the Romulans, who were by nature stubborn, untrustworthy, and prone to violence.

The Vulcan said nothing as she strode to Regimol's side. She knew what it was like to be an outcast, although she had never been as outcast from her own people as Regimol was from his. They had used his very notoriety as bait to work their devious plot; his hands had doomed the *Javlek*, along with the crews' arrogance. Had he been Vulcan, she might know what to say to him, but even then it would be difficult.

"How are repairs progressing?" she asked finally.

"Oh, fine," he answered. "They're good, and it's going to be first-class after this, with a new warp reactor and four micro torpedoes. They've disguised the torpedoes as probe launchers. This craft will be very valuable—I hope they let me keep it. I know what I will name it."

"The *Javlek*?"

He nodded, gulping down a lump in his throat. "I forget that when you work for Nechayev, there are no insignificant jobs. Everything is life and death, on a grand scale."

"You sound like a person who is tired of his job," observed the Vulcan.

Regimol shook his head in frustration. "How do we get like this? How do we dig ourselves into these trenches? I never chose this path for myself, yet here I am. Oh, I know, at some point I grew to love the game, especially the moments when I defied the odds to grab the prize. But what do I pay for this thrill? I risk my neck constantly, live in a stolen shuttlecraft, and work with a devil like Nechayev."

"She speaks highly of you," said Teska.

"You know, I call her a devil in the fondest sense," Regimol replied with the ghost of a smile.

"You could have been a conformist," said Teska, "but you have taken risks to make your life interesting. We have both been cursed to live in interesting times."

"I heard about your husband," said Regimol gently. "You've been on the front, too, in your own way. Don't you ever want to get a quiet farm someplace, grow hydroponic vegetables?"

"I believe in something bigger than myself," she

answered. "We were destined for a higher calling than most humanoids realize."

He laughed hollowly. "Oh, this is where I get the sales pitch for your Vulcan mumbo-jumbo. Are you going to tell me to try a mind-meld? I heard you converted that killer in the brig, and now he's as gentle as a *sehlat*. But I doubt it—I think he would still slit your throat as soon as look at you. So save your speech for someone else."

"I was going to deliver no speech," the Vulcan answered. "I was replying to your question about how I accept the vagaries of life. As for Jerit—I do not want him to go on any more missions like this. In terms of outgrowing his job, he is far beyond you. Perhaps you could help him adjust to life without the Romulan Star Empire. Without allegiance to the Empire to sustain them, many Romulan expatriates feel lost."

"I don't feel lost," protested Regimol. "I know right where I am. But I choose to question my own actions— that's how I became a criminal in the first place. So don't preach to me."

"Then do not complain about being on the wrong path," observed Teska.

Suddenly, the hatch of the runabout opened, and a squat Ferengi came bounding out, almost knocking over a technician's cart. "Hey, what do you think of my ship?" asked Chellac smugly. "Beautiful, isn't it?"

"*Your* ship?" muttered Regimol.

"Yes, I'm to be captain when we enter the DMZ," answered Chellac, studying his fingernails importantly. "Only Ferengi allowed, you know. You'll have to hide in the pantry."

"We'll see about that," snapped Regimol, moving toward the merchant.

Teska inserted herself between them. "A truce, please," she requested. "In truth, we will all do whatever Admiral Nechayev tells us to do. I would think that both of you would welcome a chance to meet Vedek Yorka again."

Chellac snorted. "He was lucky to be a *prylar* when I met him. That fraud. That *cheat!* We are allowed to cut his tongue out, aren't we?"

"I would ask the admiral for permission," suggested Teska.

"She'll probably say no," muttered the Ferengi. "But at least I have this fine ship for my voyage to the DMZ! Are you going along, Teska?"

"I have not received word."

"I wish you could go instead of me," complained Regimol. With hunched shoulders, the thief shuffled away from his shipmates, leaving them in the repair bay.

"I worry about him," said Chellac. "The fire has gone out of his eyes."

"He killed over fifteen hundred of his own people," answered Teska, "or so he believes."

Chellac gave a low whistle. "That is a heavy burden, but he's got a job to do."

"You may have to take the initiative," observed Teska. "After all, it is your ship now."

Geordi La Forge and Data trudged across the fine, gray sand of a nameless asteroid in the Rixx System. La Forge wore an environmental suit, but Data functioned well in the thin atmosphere without a suit; he easily carried the portable Genesis device under one arm. Their small shuttlecraft was parked behind them, and the *Sequoia* was monitoring them from a safe distance.

"I hope the *Sequoia* can ascertain fluctuations in the subspace cracks," said Data.

"You and your subspace cracks," muttered the engineer. "We're about to be turned into gelatinous goo, and you're worried about subspace cracks!"

"This looks like an appropriate spot," said the android, setting the metal box in the fine gray sand. He carefully aimed the device into countless hectares of lifeless nothingness. The stars glittered all around them in the sky, like an audience waiting to see them create life.

La Forge shivered, although it was a perfect temperature inside his suit. "We're going to have moss creatures hanging from the trees."

"There was no report of moss creatures in the two instances where these small emitters were used before," replied the android as he knelt down to open the door of the device. Its lights and panels blinked reassuringly, and it did look like a Bajoran orb, thought La Forge.

"I believe these devices were designed to create temporary habitat," said Data. "We will not be turned into gelatinous mass either. The lens is fixed, pointing in a specific direction. The beam cannot bend around and threaten us. However, earthquakes, heat, wind, toxic gases, acid rain, and other effects of Genesis—"

La Forge waved his hand helplessly. "I've seen it all, and don't want to see it again! Just turn the damn thing on, and I'll try not to look." The suited figure crouched down behind Data, then tapped him on the shoulder to indicate he was ready.

"Your tricorder," said the android, pulling his instrument off his belt, turning it on, and leaving it in the sand.

Geordi fumbled but got his tricorder out, and he waited nervously while Data finished the final preparations on the doctored Genesis emitter. They had a backup box in the shuttlecraft, a replicate with an unaltered power system.

"All right," said the android, pushing the combination of colored buttons which Chellac had given them—the same combination which had worked in the laboratory on a defused device.

Geordi flinched when the beam spread out, although it only went about fifty meters before becoming invisible to his ocular implants. The fearful green fire burned and roared, shooting licks of flame about waist-high, but it was like a campfire trying to burn in a rainstorm. The right combination of elements did not seem to be present. Feeble plants twisted from the dead soil, and noxious clouds swirled fitfully over the sputtering Genesis effect—but this ugly new life wasn't destined to last long. A moment later, the beam stopped, and the plants instantly withered in an atmosphere that was wispy and unstable.

It was kind of sad, thought Geordi—like an old-fashioned firecracker much anticipated by a gang of children until it turns into a fizzling dud. He patted Data on the back. "Well done. I like this Genesis Light."

"I did not mention it," said Data, "but we could use the nanocapacitors to sabotage virtually every one of these devices in existence."

"I know," said Geordi with a sly smile. "Now that

we've made it safe to play with, we can try all kinds of things. Reversing the charge is a good idea, but I can go it one better. What if we amplified the power into a burst and overloaded the boxes? Then we might get a reverse Genesis Wave, in which the device would try to Genesize itself. It could end up pulling Genesis energy back through your subspace cracks."

"An interesting theory," conceded Data. "First, let us see how this experiment turned out." He tapped his combadge. "Data to *Sequoia*. Come in, *Sequoia*."

There was no answer, and the android cocked his head. "That is not a good sign."

"Are you sure they're in range?" asked La Forge.

"Our signal is being boosted by the shuttlecraft," answered Data. "We should return." He picked up the spent Genesis emitter and his tricorder and dashed back to the shuttlecraft.

The engineer had to jog through the thick dust in order to arrive two minutes behind him, panting heavily. He found the android in the pilot's seat, going over screen after screen of readouts.

"The rift has grown so large that it swallowed the debris field," reported Data.

"What?" La Forge dropped into the seat beside him and brought up the readouts at a speed he could comprehend. The scans were incomplete, but there was no denying that the rift nearest them had increased exponentially as a result of their little experiment. Setting off a whole chain of portable Genesis emitters would no doubt merge their dimension with the radiation-filled blackness which threatened to drown them.

"Let's get out of here," muttered La Forge.

"No, we have another experiment to perform." Data glanced back at the unused Genesis device in the rear of the craft.

Geordi gulped. "What I suggested was only hypothetical. I really don't want to overload a Genesis box and send it into reverse."

Data popped the hatch on the shuttlecraft and gathered up his tools to head back into the barren wilderness.

The engineer groaned. "Me and my big mouth."

twenty-one

The tether stretched two kilometers, and it had been rigged together from at least a hundred shorter lengths. At the far end was a shuttlecraft manned by Data, and at the leading end was Deanna Troi, wearing a Brahms radiation suit. She gripped the handles of her jet sled and cruised slowly toward the immense blackness. Seen from such a close angle, the rift looked like space—only without stars, nebulas, or any stellar bodies. The void was without even the glittering debris which had characterized it for days. All of that had been consumed by the expanding darkness, as the counselor soon would be.

Troi had fought hard to be allowed to perform this mission, and it had taken Admiral Nechayev overruling Riker to grant permission. Before they attempted to heal the rifts with a reverse Genesis Wave, they had agreed that someone had to explore the other side. Their solution had to help both sides and cause no peripheral damage, taking the chance the cure might be worse than the disease. Then they had to answer the question once and for all—had an accident brought the two dimensions into such perilous contact, or had the incursion from the other side been an attack, as first suspected?

The counselor had been chosen over Data to perform the EVA, because of her empathetic link with the entity which had once ruled the other dimension. She was convinced that that entity was dead, or at least withdrawn. All she sensed was fear—overwhelming fear—and it wasn't coming from her. Still she was relieved to know that Data was monitoring her vital signs through the tether and would reel her back to the shuttlecraft at the slightest sign of trouble. Of course, if something happened to the lifeline—

"Shuttlecraft to Troi," said Data's voice, coming over the tether instead of a comlink, due to the interference.

"I'm all right, Data," she reported.

"By my calculations, you will enter the event horizon in another thirty-eight seconds."

"I'm ready," she answered. "You just be my guardian angel and keep watch over me. Troi out."

In the final few meters, she could see strange, ungodly shapes writhing in the darkness like eels in a fish barrel. It was as if they were scared to come across, yet scared to remain where they were. And Troi couldn't blame them. That side was permeated by horrendous radiation; on this side, there was only cold, unfriendly space. Their panic was bad enough when they had come across into inhabitable places, such as the *Barcelona*, but when they ventured into the vacuum of space, they died in absolute agony.

Troi realized that many of these creatures communicated telepathically, so they must have sensed what happened to those who escaped into her dimension. But to remain behind was certain death. They were dying by the billions and billions, all because humankind had once been foolish enough to play God.

With a blink, she was among them in a startling landscape of billowing blue clouds and a pale pink sky. Four black planets and a gleaming purple sun were aligned in the distance like some kind of solar system seen in a negative image. This dimension teemed with bizarre life, all of it in some kind of frenzied activity, flitting between the black barrier of her dimension and a grim mass of corpses which littered the clouds. Troi had to remind herself that hundreds of these rifts existed along the path of the Genesis Wave, and this was only one place where their dimensions crossed.

With a burst of activity, panicked creatures rammed her jet sled and fouled the thrusters, and they oozed around her like sharks in a feeding frenzy. Still she was unafraid, because they weren't attacking. She sensed curiosity and a desperate need for help. Like herself, they had ventured to the other side, only with disastrous results. They wanted to know how this creature encased in white could survive in such a monstrous place as the darkness beyond.

Even as she huddled against the sled to keep from getting pelted, Deanna closed her eyes and tried to communicate telepathically. To her surprise, an answer came:

We know you.

"Yes, you do," she assured the entity, who seemed weak and distracted. "An accident happened . . . a terrible accident."

You killed us.

"No!" she protested. "We can stop it, we can reverse it!"

We are dead.

Overcome by feelings of grief and remorse, Deanna Troi began to cry. "It's not too late!" she told herself, or anyone else who was listening.

There was no further answer. Sniffing back tears, the Betazoid composed herself enough to say, "Troi to shuttle-craft."

"Data here," came the reply.

"Bring me back," she ordered.

"Are you injured?"

"No, but the sled is damaged. I need to return, and you need to close this rift. By any means available."

"We will not create any peripheral damage?"

"No," she answered grimly. "We can't make matters worse than they already are."

With relief and sadness, Troi felt herself being pulled back into the darkness, and the creatures squirming around her withdrew in fear. A moment later, she floated in space on the edge of the abyss, and she began to cry again for all those who had perished on both sides of the rift—killed by a machine that was supposed to create life.

Jean-Luc Picard stepped gingerly out of the captain's yacht onto a foggy planet with crystallized dirt and swirling yellow clouds, through which he could see maybe six meters in front of him. Thunder rumbled ominously from every direction at once, and an acid-filled sleet bombarded him and the crusty soil. He supposed he should be glad he was wearing an environmental suit and couldn't smell the air, such as it was. Looking around, he found it hard to believe that Solosos III had once been a thriving Class-M planet with a happy colony of Federation citizens. All of that had been destroyed by the Federation itself, and now Solosos III was mired in a trilithium winter.

This entire planet was strewn with hastily abandoned structures and equipment, so there was no use looking at sensor readings. There were enough old power lines, wells, sewers, data lines, and other remnants of infrastructure to disguise a mammoth network of Genesis devices. So they had looked for lifesigns, which were normally nonexistent in this place. It had taken them hours of searching from orbit in the tiny craft, but finally they had spotted lifesigns—about twenty of them, to be exact. As long as the conspirators were still on the planet, he figured, they weren't quite ready to detonate Genesis yet.

Now time was running out, and Picard wasn't even sure what he was looking for. His previous orders to continue with his mission made little sense. His superiors didn't even know what his mission was, although everyone assumed he had run off to secure the Genesis Device in Yorka's possession. But Yorka might have a million of those boxes by now, and Picard's true mission had died with Kaylena. To bring back one, a million, or none of the boxes—it hardly made any difference now. At least the cryptic missive from Nechayev had made it clear that they were on the right track—this forsaken place was the next planet in the deadly sights of Genesis.

Footsteps crunched behind him, and he whirled

around to see a vague outline in the pea soup fog. He almost fired his phaser, because no one was supposed to be following him. Instead he ducked down and waited, until he saw the suited figure wave to him. It was one of his young comrades, whose names were still a bit vague to him. They dared not use combadges to talk to one another, so he walked stiffly toward his companion.

When they were helmet to helmet, Picard demanded in a muffled voice, "What are you doing? I left word for you to stay put."

"New orders," replied the ensign, holding up a padd with text on it.

The captain took the hand-held device and read it. With surprise, he noted that it was from Data. In the android's usual comprehensive style, there were detailed instructions on exactly what he was supposed to do with the network of Genesis Devices when he found them. There were even diagrams. In essence, he was to patch into the network, reverse the current, and overload it with as much power as he could muster.

It sounded somewhat desperate, but that fit his mood.

"Return to the ship," he told his underling. "Keep monitoring lifesigns. If you see our quarry leave, let me know immediately."

"Over the comlink?"

"Yes, if they're gone, it won't matter. When I contact you, be ready to move."

"Yes, Sir." With an awkward salute in his environmental suit, the ensign stole away into the dense yellow fog.

The captain slipped the padd containing his instructions into his pocket and closed it. Then he took out his tricorder and attempted to locate the lifesigns they had spotted from orbit. Their quarry were less than five hundred meters away, toward the southwest.

He took another step and nearly tripped over it—a fat electrical cable which looked undamaged by the catastrophe that had befallen Solosos III. In fact, it looked new, and it led in the direction where the lifesigns were congregated. Picard put away his tricorder and drew his phaser, then he slowly stalked his prey.

After following the cable for about a hundred meters, he found one of the Genesis emitters. It was propped up in the dirt like a fancy trashcan, and the door was open, with the instrument panel blinking ominously. He considered patching into the device right here, but that would no doubt alert Yorka and his party. He would either have to find some way to neutralize Yorka's crew, or he would have to wait until they were gone. If he waited that long, it might be too late.

Stalking in a crouch, Picard followed the cable until he spotted a shadow in the fog. He instantly threw himself to the ground to create the lowest possible profile. Inching forward on his stomach, Picard reached a spot where he could clearly see his adversary—an armed guard in an environmental suit festooned with insignia of the Bajoran militia. Still lying on his stomach, Picard checked his tricorder to make sure the guard was alone. There was another guard about thirty meters away, but he might as well have been thirty kilometers away in this deadly fog.

Picard drew his phaser, took aim, and fired. The suit dropped to the crusty dirt as though empty. The captain crawled forward on his stomach, grabbed the stunned

Bajoran, and dragged him back to a safe position. Then he threw his prisoner over his shoulder and carried him back to the yacht, retracing his tracks in the dirt.

Half an hour later, Captain Picard was wearing the Bajoran environmental suit as he again followed the electrical cable to its source. Behind him walked one of his ensigns, wearing a Starfleet suit so that he could communicate with the yacht. Picard stationed his man in the spot where he had subdued the Bajoran, then he continued on his own. Dressed in a disguise that covered him head to toe, he saw no point in being subtle.

Ghostly buildings loomed ahead of him in the fog. As he drew closer to the deserted village, Picard noticed that one of the buildings had a protective tent stretched over it. A figure suddenly emerged from the mist, startling the captain, but when he saw the Bajoran suit, he waved in a friendly fashion. Picard waved back and continued on his way, but he never took his hand off the phaser in his pocket. In his other pocket was the padd which contained his instructions from Data.

In the middle of the street loomed another recognizable shape—a Bajoran troop transport. There were probably people inside, but his destination was the tented building, which he assumed was the headquarters of this misguided mission. A portable airlock had been constructed over one door, and a guard stood outside it. The guard waved as he approached, and Picard drew his phaser and drilled him with a stun beam.

The captain quickly dragged the unconscious Bajoran into a foggy sidestreet, then he took his place at the door. When no one seemed to have noticed the switch, Picard slipped inside the airlock.

He found himself in a house of worship—it was hard to tell what denomination, but there were pews, an altar, and a small stage. There was also breathable air, because several unsuited Bajorans were hovering over a portable generator. Electrical cables snaked from the machine out every door and window, and a Genesis Device blinked ominously in the corner.

A heavyset Bajoran paced in front of the altar, glancing frequently at his work crew. A young blond woman lounged in a pew in the front row, calmly filing her nails. They had to be Vedek Yorka and Cassie Jackson, respectively, thought Picard. It was hard to believe that these blundering fools were about to shred the fragile curtain between dimensions, but possessing Genesis made them the most dangerous force in the galaxy.

"What's taking so long?" complained Vedek Yorka. "We're behind schedule. We've promised people— they're waiting for this moment!"

"Excuse me, Your Holiness," said one of the technicians. "The stress tolerances have to be exact if we wish to activate all the emitters in unison. We're almost there—just one final diagnostic check."

"All right, but hurry up!" He began to pace anew.

"Will you relax?" said the blond woman. "Why don't you pray to the Prophets for some patience?"

The rotund vedek waggled his finger at her. "Don't you take the name of the Prophets in vain. You're only doing this for profit, I'm doing it for the greater good of all Bajor."

She rolled her eyes. "Right. I'll just be glad when it's over."

"So will I." Yorka wrung his hands nervously as he

paced. "I think we're doing the right thing. Really, I mean, the Orb fell into my hands for a reason, didn't it? It was meant to do some good for people."

"It's done some good for me," claimed Cassie.

As they talked and the technicians worked, Picard maneuvered along the back wall, hoping to make it down the side aisle and get closer to the generator. As he moved, he drew his phaser out of his pocket and put in on a destructive setting. His intent was to take out the generator and worry later about Data's instructions.

Yorka suddenly spotted him. "You there! Get back outside—get back on guard duty!"

The suited figure waved and turned to leave, but Picard stumbled as he walked, trying to stall for time. At the same moment, another suited figure charged through the airlock, and he was holding a Starfleet environmental suit in his hands.

The new arrival pulled his helmet off and yelled, "Vedek Yorka! There are intruders on the planet! We caught one, and we spotted a shuttlecraft."

"What?" bellowed Yorka.

Suddenly all eyes turned to look at Picard, and the guard at the door rushed him, grabbing his phaser hand and forcing the weapon upward. The captain didn't mean to shoot, but he blasted a thick blue beam at the ceiling. With a monstrous explosion, a chunk of the ceiling disintegrated, and plaster and debris rained down on them. Worse than that, the deadly yellow fog rushed into the room like a pale ghost, and the Bajoran gagged and went limp in Picard's arms. Gasping for breath, he dropped to his knees and then to the floor.

In a panic, his comrades rushed toward a pile of environmental suits, but none of them made it. Within a few seconds, everyone in the room but Picard had collapsed. They lay on the floor, choking, writhing in agony—victims of the trilithium-tinged air.

Unable to help them, the captain instantly drew the padd from his pocket and rushed to the generator. He studied Data's notes, then looked at the generator and the cables snaking away from it. Movement at the back of the building caught his eye, and he looked up to see an armed guard dash through the airlock. Picard took aim with his phaser and drilled him, and his body exploded as the ceiling had.

Suddenly, three transporter beams glowed like shimmering columns in the center of the building, and Picard almost shot them, too. It was fortunate that he waited a microsecond until he identified their environmental suits, which were Starfleet.

They aimed their weapons at him, and he held up his hands. "It's me! Picard! It's *me!*" he shouted, trying to be heard through his helmet.

One of them strode toward him. "Could you use a little help?"

"Yes, guard the door!" His order came just in time, as the Bajoran militia began their assault in earnest, and his rescuers were forced to return fire.

Dying Bajorans were gasping for breath all around him, but it was too late to help any of them. Picard tried to clear his mind and concentrate on his task. Fortunately, he had everything at hand he needed to execute Data's instructions, including tools and power. He wouldn't have to patch into the network, because the hub was right in front of him. Still it seemed ludicrous to set off the string of Genesis Devices when they had tried so hard to prevent them from being used. But Data's instructions were explicit, and there was no one in the universe he trusted more than that unique being.

As a phaser battle raged and technicians vomited in the last throes of death, the captain carefully reversed the charge and set the system to overload. Suddenly there was an explosion, and the front wall of the building was nothing but smoke and rubble. His unknown comrades fell back, firing intently at the advancing militia, and Picard knew he didn't have another moment to lose.

He pushed the button.

The Genesis box in the room with them began to hum like a bad transformer, and smoke wafted from its glowing circuitry. Picard held his breath, thinking they would all be blown to bits or mutated into primordial sludge. Instead, he began to feel enormously happy and relieved.

The firing stopped, and both sides dropped their weapons and stood perfectly still, gazing in awe at each other. Even the dying Bajorans, who had been writhing in agony a second before, smiled blissfully at one another. Throughout the galaxy—in the depths of the oceans, in grimy caves, in palaces and prisons, in starships and starbases—every form of life from Melkotians to amebas experienced one shining moment of peace. All living things felt connected, part of a single wonderful creation.

"What has happened?" croaked a voice.

Picard turned to see Vedek Yorka crawling toward him, his eyes begging for understanding. Also in his eyes was imminent death, and Picard dashed toward the Bajoran, knelt down, and put a hand to his feverish brow.

"You have done this," he said. "With the Orb of Life, you have brought peace to the universe."

The joyous smile which graced the monk's face brought a round of tears to Picard's eyes. Yorka gripped his hand and nodded with exultation, then the strength in his fingers began to wane. A second later, Vedek Yorka was dead.

Picard looked up to see the girl, Cassie Jackson, staring at him. Then she smiled as innocently as a child. The captain rushed to her and held her, until the life ebbed from her body.

Without saying anything, the Bajorans began to collect their dead. One of the Starfleet officers approached Picard and offered him a hand. When he stood up, the captain got a good look at his rescuer for the first time, and he was surprised to see it was a Ferengi.

"Good thing you started blowing things up," said the grinning humanoid, "or we never would have found you. Ready to go home? I'll take you in my nice new runabout."

"*Whose* runabout?" asked another suited savior. This one appeared to be a Romulan.

"I don't know who you people are," admitted Picard, "but I'm glad you're here. I am ready to go home."

twenty-two

As she stood in the transporter room of the *Sequoia*, Admiral Nechayev extended her hand to her former first officer, Commander Marbinz. "I speeded up the paperwork for you," she said with a smile. "Get yourself another pip for your collar—this is now your ship. But if you mess up, I'll be on your case faster than rust on a bucket. Ask any captain of mine."

"Thank you, Admiral," said the Benzite with a broad smile which caused his blue tendrils to lift upward. "Please give my regards to Starfleet Command. I understand that you're getting some pips back."

She shrugged. "They're just metal. The important thing is that you surround yourself with good people. May you be as fortunate with your first officer as I was." With that, the admiral stepped upon the transporter platform.

"Coordinates laid in for the *Javlek*," said the operator at the console.

She shook her head. "I'll never get used to that name,

but that's okay. It's not my ship. I'm perfectly content *not* to have a ship. Have a good journey to Vulcan, Captain."

Marbinz frowned for a moment. "Are you sure that's a wise idea, releasing that Romulan assassin to Teska's custody?"

"I promised her," answered Nechayev. "Besides, haven't you heard? Prisoners have been released all over the place. It's a new dawn of peace and understanding. Even the Romulans have volunteered to destroy their Genesis emitters, after what's happened. We're going to make sure they do."

The Benzite nodded. "I hope so. It's been a pleasure serving with you, Admiral."

"You, too," replied Nechayev sincerely. "Energize when ready."

A moment later, she stood on the much smaller bridge of the runabout *Javlek*, facing the Romulan, Regimol; the Antosian, Raynr Sleven; and the feisty Ferengi, Chellac.

"Our crew is complete," said Regimol with a broad smile. He sat down at the controls and brought up a navigational chart. "Where to, Admiral?"

"Our first stop is Ferenginar," she replied, sitting in the copilot's seat. "We need to get our friend Chellac home."

"Wait a minute," said the Ferengi angrily, "is that it? I risk my life I don't know how many times, and you just drop me off! Is this the kind of thanks I get for saving the universe?"

"We save the universe all the time and don't expect a reward," replied Regimol. "Isn't that right, Raynr?"

"Um," said the big Antosian doubtfully, "I guess so. Although I'm not sure what I'm doing here. I may save a food replicator or a pylon grid every now and then, but I usually don't save the universe."

"That's going to change," said Nechayev. "Your talents make you too valuable to be a technician. I think you'll find the new assignment I have for you to be a bit more exciting. As for you, Chellac, you like this runabout so much that I've arranged for one to be delivered to you. It should be orbiting Ferenginar by the time we get there. You'll also get the exclusive holodeck concession on our revamped starbase, 411, which I understand is a very lucrative contract."

"Oh, Admiral, thank you! Thank you!" The Ferengi fell to his knees and began kissing her hand. "Are you single?"

"That's enough of that," she replied, quickly withdrawing her appendage.

"There's a certain holodeck program I want to be sure to get," said Chellac, tugging on his earlobe.

Nechayev turned to her pilot. "Captain Regimol, I think we can be going now."

"Admiral," said Raynr Sleven with concern, "I never got a chance to say good-bye to the Ogawas."

"That's all right," Nechayev answered with a smile. "I have a feeling they won't mind."

"Daddy!" screamed the little girl, charging into her father's arms.

Andrew Powell lifted Suzi high over his head and swung her around joyfully. Then he gave her a great big hug, and Alyssa Ogawa joined them to make it a group hug. Tearfully, the reunited family clung to each other for several moments, unable to speak or do anything else.

Standing in a corner of the *Enterprise*'s transporter room, Beverly Crusher dabbed a handkerchief to her eye as Captain Picard put his arm around her.

"I don't understand," she said. "Why were the Satarrans holding him prisoner?"

"They misunderstood the Genesis Wave and thought it was something *we* had done to their colony," answered the captain. "I think they automatically blame us for everything that goes wrong. But after the wave of harmony swept over everyone, they forgave their prisoners and released them. If not, we might never have known what happened to him and three other officers."

"And you?" she asked warily as she put the remaining antidote away. "How do *you* feel?"

Picard scowled. "I'm never touching anything on a Romulan vessel again. Truthfully, the pain of Kaylena's death still hurts. No matter how or why I was in love with her, I really loved her. I would have killed for her, betrayed Starfleet—whatever you can think of, I would have done it. In one way, I'm grateful, because I never knew I could love like that."

"I was more shocked before," said Crusher, "but now I'm really jealous."

He gave Beverly a tender squeeze and a sly smile. "I'm still in a romantic mood." The captain began to steer her toward the door.

"But Alyssa . . . we were going to have dinner with her and her family."

"I don't think they need us," said Picard with a glance at the jubilant family. The door slid open, and the doctor and the captain slipped away.

*   *   *

Deanna Troi sat in the Saucer Lounge of the *Enterprise* with Will Riker, gazing out the observation window at space. Just space. There was no blackness, no rift, no sea of sparkling debris—nothing but blessed, beautiful space. Although Troi was relieved that the threat was over, in a way she was sad that the mysterious entity had again vanished into its own dimension. Twice now she had encountered the being while convinced it was the enemy, only to find out it was actually the victim. Someday she would like to renew their acquaintance under less adversarial conditions.

"A penny for your thoughts," said Will.

"I have many thoughts," she answered. "One of them is that I'm very happy to be here with you."

"Even though I fought you over making those EVAs?"

"Well, you're not always right, are you?" She gave him a playful smile. "I'm glad I was right this time, and that so were Data and Geordi."

"It's ironic," said Riker thoughtfully, "that after all the trouble Genesis has caused us, it was finally used for good. And those subspace cracks that Data discovered—they have a lot of potential for faster communications, power transmission between worlds, and maybe even a new form of space travel that is almost instantaneous. It's all hypothetical of course, but we never would have known about subspace cracks without Genesis and its aftereffects."

"Yes," mused Deanna, "but will we finally ever leave it alone? Will we ever stop playing God?"

Will gave her a shrug and shook his head. "I don't know. It seems to be a natural tendency of our species to want to play God. We always want to improve things, make them faster, better, more efficient. Or maybe we just want to understand life and how it works."

"For all our meddling," said the counselor, "we still don't know much. The problem is that we tend to learn through trial and error, but playing God isn't one of those places where error is easily forgiven. We were lucky this time."

"I can't argue with that."

Deanna took a sip of her hot chocolate while she gazed out the window, and another thought occurred to her. "What is to become of the Brahms suit? Can we keep using them?"

"We're in negotiations," answered Riker. "They'd like get Leah Brahms in custody and put her on trial for espionage, but we're not going to let that happen. No matter how much peace there is in the universe, some things never change."

The first officer sat up stiffly. "While we're talking business, we're going to need you when we get to Bajor. We have a lot of ruffled feathers to smooth over, and a lot of explaining to do. For example, they think Captain Picard killed one of their vedeks. We may be there for weeks sorting this out, but you and I might be able to slip away for a little side trip to Deep Space Nine."

"I'd like that," answered Deanna Troi, holding her beloved's hand.

Two solitary figures stood on a foreboding mountain-top overlooking an arid, copper-colored plain, which was bubbling with lava pools. One of them was dressed in the regal scarlet and beige robes of a priestess, and the other wore a simple monk's garment. It had taken the better part of a day to climb to this isolated place, but Teska felt she had to make the trek. It was a place where she and Hasmek had come often to meditate. The priestess took the Romulan's hand and motioned across the breadth of the rugged plain.

"Do you like it?" she asked. "It is called the Valley of Everlasting."

Jerit smiled. "Yes, I like it. I'd always heard that Vulcan was an ugly planet . . . a barren wasteland. But this is beautiful."

"This valley is old, eroded, beaten down," she replied. "Yet the lava replenishes, creates, and makes it new again. This is a place I came often with my mate."

Jerit hung his head and averted his eyes. He tried to pull his hand away, but Teska grasped it all the tighter.

"In our beliefs," said the priestess, "the *katra* is our soul . . . the essence of our being. Just before death, a Vulcan uses the mind-meld to entrust his katra to a loyal friend, so that he can share it with the departed's loved ones. I know that neither you nor Hasmek is a Vulcan, and you have no training in this, yet when we melded I sensed that Hasmek's death made a deep impression on you. It was not just a memory, but an event which represented much of what was wrong in your life. As the last person he saw, you undoubtedly made a strong impression on him. Because of this, I feel that Hasmek lives on in you."

The Romulan looked pained. "But I killed him. He's dead because of me."

"No," she insisted, shaking her head. "That is like blaming the knife. Better you should blame me, or my uncle, who arranged our marriage. Or we could blame our feuding ancestors, who tore the Vulcans and Romulans apart millennia ago. The past is like a pool of water—put your hand in anywhere, and the ripples spread across the entire pool. It is all joined—there is no way to separate one event from another."

Now Jerit gripped her hand and looked plaintively into her eyes. "I want to make it up to you, Teska. I want to make it up to everyone I've harmed."

She nodded with understanding. "Like this valley, we constantly reinvent ourselves. You are not the same person who killed Hasmek, and I am not the same person who married him. We spent a great deal of time apart, which both of us saw as normal. In hindsight, I am uncertain of the wisdom of that. Being apart made both of us weaker. It doomed Hasmek."

"If you were mine, I would never leave you," he said solemnly.

"You speak with the learned wisdom of all three of us," Teska concluded. "Now take my hand and look into my eyes, and I will speak the ancient ritual of grief and loss. Only Hasmek is not lost. He has been found."

Look for STAR TREK fiction from Pocket Books

Star Trek®

Avenger

Star Trek: Odyssey (contains *The Ashes of Eden*, *The Return*, and *Avenger*)

Spectre

Dark Victory

Preserver

The Captain's Peril

A Hard Rain • Dean Wesley Smith

The Battle of Betazed • Charlotte Douglas & Susan Kearney

Novelizations

Encounter at Farpoint • David Gerrold

Unification • Jeri Taylor

Relics • Michael Jan Friedman

Descent • Diane Carey

All Good Things . . . • Michael Jan Friedman

Star Trek: Klingon • Dean Wesley Smith & Kristine Kathryn Rusch

Star Trek Generations • J.M. Dillard

Star Trek: First Contact • J.M. Dillard

Star Trek: Insurrection • J.M. Dillard

Star Trek Nemesis • J.M. Dillard

Star Trek: Deep Space Nine®

Enterprise®

Star Trek®: New Frontier

Star Trek®: Invasion!

Star Trek®: Day of Honor

Star Trek®: The Captain's Table

Star Trek®: Dark Passions

    #1 • Susan Wright
    #2 • Susan Wright
Star Trek®: The Brave and the Bold

    #1 • Keith R.A. DeCandido
    #2 • Keith R.A. DeCandido

Star Trek® Omnibus Editions

    Invasion! Omnibus • various
    Day of Honor Omnibus • various
    The Captain's Table Omnibus • various
    Double Helix Omnibus • various
    Star Trek: Odyssey • William Shatner with Judith and Garfield
      Reeves-Stevens
    Millennium Omnibus • Judith and Garfield Reeves-Stevens
    Starfleet: Year One • Michael Jan Friedman

Other Star Trek® Fiction

    Legends of the Ferengi • Ira Steven Behr & Robert Hewitt
      Wolfe
    Strange New Worlds, vol. I, II, III, IV, and V • Dean Wesley
      Smith, ed.
    Adventures in Time and Space • Mary P. Taylor, ed.
    Captain Proton: Defender of the Earth • D.W. "Prof" Smith
    New Worlds, New Civilizations • Michael Jan Friedman
    The Lives of Dax • Marco Palmieri, ed.
    The Klingon Hamlet • Wil'yam Shex'pir
    Enterprise Logs • Carol Greenburg, ed.
    Amazing Stories • various